RAIN
MUSIC

Di MORRISSEY

RAIN MUSIC

MACMILLAN

Pan Macmillan Australia

First published 2015 in Macmillan by Pan Macmillan Australia Pty Ltd
1 Market Street, Sydney, New South Wales, Australia, 2000

Cataloguing-in-Publication entry is available
from the National Library of Australia
http://catalogue.nla.gov.au

Internal images:
Chapter 1: Guenter Guni/iStock; Chapter 2: Dirk Ercken/Shutterstock; Chapter 3: Courtesy of Cooktown Historical Society; Chapter 4: Holger Mette/iStock; Chapter 5: Lee Yiu Tung/iStock; Chapter 6: iofoto/Shutterstock; Chapter 7: Courtesy of John Oxley Library, State Library of Queensland; Chapter 8: worldswildlifewonders/Shutterstock; Chapter 9: Courtesy of John Oxley Library, State Library of Queensland; Chapter 10: Courtesy of Cooktown Historical Society; Chapter 11: Hayley Anderson; Chapter 12: Wendy Townrow/Shutterstock.
Endpapers by Zhanna Smolyar/Shutterstock.

Typeset in 12.5/15 pt Sabon by Post Pre-press Group
Printed by McPherson's Printing Group

For my wonderful Boris (Janjic)

With my love

Acknowledgements

Thanking my children, Gabrielle and Nick, for their continued love and support, and hoping they will continue to explore Australia.

For my four precious grandchildren, Sonoma, Everton, Bodhi and Ulani. I hope the Australia you inherit survives the ravages of climate change and greed. Do your best to fight for what is right and meaningful.

Hearty thanks as always to my formidable editor and good friend, Liz Adams.

Huge thanks to my Pan Macmillan family: Ross Gibb, Tracey Cheetham, Katie Crawford, Samantha Sainsbury, Maria Fassoulas and Praveen Naidoo. And welcome to Team Di to Kirsty Noffke and Emma Rafferty!

Special thanks to the late Dorothea Mackellar, who told a young girl to 'write down the stories you make up in your head and put them into a book so that other people may enjoy them one day'. Quotation from Dorothea Mackellar's 'My Country' reproduced by arrangement with the Licensor, The Dorothea Mackellar Estate, c/- Curtis Brown (Aust) Pty Ltd.

Many thanks to Brianne Collins for her meticulous copy editing.

And special hugs to Wayne Brookes, Macmillan UK.

A big thanks to Ian Robertson and congratulations on your achievements.

Special thanks to Andrew and Karen Stewart of Palmer River Roadhouse for sharing your knowledge and advice.

Hugs and thanks for Irene Barrett for your help and shared memories of GMA days.

Fond memories of Len and Honey Barnes, coconut pioneers of 'Utopia' FNQ.

And in memory of photographer Stuart Owen Fox.

I

FOR A MAN WHO surrounded himself with music, Ned Chisholm found the silence strangely comforting. His vehicle was old and tough, made for these outback conditions, but it lacked accessories like Bluetooth or a CD player and as there was no radio reception he had no music to break the silence and monotony of the landscape. As always, the guitar case sheltering his worn, loyal friend rested on the back seat, but it was no good to him while driving. He was unused to such silence. For him music was a barrier against unwanted intrusions.

The vista before him could have been from the dawn of time he thought, as he drove along the sealed road with its rough, red-gravelled edges. This vast part of Far North Queensland seemed untouched, as though no one before him had passed this way. But he knew that people had penetrated this arid woodland interior, with its eucalypts and dried grasses. The delicate barefoot tread of forty thousand years of hunters and gatherers had touched this country lightly. Colonial adventurers had plundered it; later, there were the thwarted dreams of pioneers, and even now, the tracts of grazing land and the presence of mines encroached on the wilderness. Out here, the baking dry seasons were replaced by surging wet seasons, when the land turned green and wildlife was replenished. This was not country for the faint-hearted.

Ned had been working on the coast, making forays into the hinterland behind Cairns, performing as a singer and guitarist. He was well known and his album successful enough that he was frequently offered gigs and steady work. But always at the back of his mind was the idea of giving up performing for a while and following his dream of composing something substantial. He'd always thought that if he could find a place where he could retreat he would be able to search for the trigger, the spark, the new idea that could form the basis of a long simmering goal of writing a dramatic musical. And now, finally, he'd found his chance.

He'd left the lushness of Cairns to drive up to Cooktown. He'd heard a bit about the small and isolated coastal township, so when a friend of a friend had mentioned that a musician mate had a place going for free for a couple of months while he was doing a tour down south, Ned had decided to check it out. With some trepidation, he'd rejected offers of steady employment in various bars and hotels in favour of a vague refuge where he could try to capture the music and songs that spun in his head like children waiting to be born.

An hour passed without his seeing another vehicle. Ned knew there were few people within the boundaries of the hills, gullies and far-glimpsed granite peaks around him.

It was that pearly cool hour before the sun seared through the soft sky; the moments when the leaves were erect and shadows lightly pencilled, not charcoal dark. Ned well knew how the midday heat in this part of the world sent leaves limp, scorched rocks and sedated animals.

Thoughts flickered through his head as the landscape rolled on. He frowned as he recalled an email he'd received from his mother the day before asking him to return home to Victoria. His frown deepened. The message from his mother had reminded him that his father had been dead almost a year. He could not believe that his father had been gone so long. It hardly seemed possible. *I can't deal with this right now*, he had thought when he'd read the email. Before he'd set off that Tuesday morning he'd replied to his mother's email saying he couldn't make it home anytime soon.

The predawn was still. Soporific. But he knew danger always lurked. He kept his speed down to take into account the possibility of swinging around a corner to find a stolid Brahman bull standing in the centre of the road, or meeting a kangaroo leaping across the bitumen to greener grass. A glance at the wilderness around him made him smile. This was so far from his home in Victoria. He had no idea why remote Cooktown drew him or what he might find there, but he hoped that it would be the place where he could hunker down, focus and see what inspiration came to him. *It's now or never*, a small voice inside him nagged.

Suddenly, as he drove around the lazy curve of the road, everything seemed to lapse into slow motion. A scene unfolded in front of him, as it would do again and again later in his head; the dead cow, the massed birds unfolding giant wings, the curled talons, the evil beaks, all suddenly startled, rising up. But their bellies, heavy with meat, slowed them. The last bird, too ungainly, struggled to rise above the car. In a flash Ned saw what was about to happen. The windscreen would be filled with a solid chest of creamy bronzed-edged feathers as the bird and car collided. Ned swerved to avoid this, pushing his foot hard on the brake. He missed the raptor, but as he hit the red gravel on the side of the road he felt the car spin out of control and careen down a slope into the undergrowth, scraping past trees and bushes until it jolted to a halt. Then there was only silence.

Ned blinked, but before he could focus properly his body filled with throbbing pain and he passed out.

When he finally opened his eyes once more, the bright light made him squeeze them shut. He tried to move and a sharp pain shot through his arm and his head pounded. He wondered how badly injured he was. Everything seemed to hurt and his breath came in short, painful stabs. Slowly he forced his eyes open and looked around.

He was jammed behind the steering wheel, the car on its side, its windscreen shattered. His arm was throbbing and he could see that it was covered in blood. When he tried to move, he realised his foot was pinned down by one of the pedals. Instinct told him he shouldn't shake the car, for although he could see a tangle of branches beside him, he had no idea if the car was in a dangerously precarious position.

The day now felt burning hot and Ned realised he must have been unconscious for some time. Because of the angle of the car, he could see full sunlight filtering though the leaves of the tree above. Fumbling beside him, the fingers of his good arm found a bottle half filled with water. He gulped several mouthfuls of the warm liquid, fighting the desire to drink more as he knew he might need the water to last for . . . how long? He had no idea how far off the road the car had stopped. Would anyone be able to see him as they drove past? He could well be out of sight of the road, as he remembered the car crashing downhill for what had seemed like forever. *Besides*, he thought, *how many cars use this road? It's pretty remote out here.*

He groped around in the restricted space until he found his mobile phone. He suspected that there would be no coverage, but a quick glance at the splintered screen told him that it hardly mattered as the phone was useless anyway. He dropped it in despair. He suddenly felt tired and he rested his head against the door and dozed off again, oblivious to his awkward position and the slow seepage of blood from the gash on his arm.

When he next stirred, his body felt stiff and he ached with pain, but his mind felt clearer. Ned saw that the sun was now low in the sky, and he knew night was creeping in. He drained the rest of his water and touched his injured arm. The blood had started to congeal. *That's good*, he thought. *The bleeding has stopped.* Slowly he tried to move his body to assess how he was caught. The car was tilted onto the driver's side and jammed against a tree trunk, pinning him between the door and the steering wheel.

Suddenly a frantic desire to free himself, to live, to survive, came over him. No one was coming for him. He would have to save himself.

Mustering what energy he had, Ned made an effort to free his trapped foot. He cried out as he twisted it, but suddenly it was free. Ignoring the pain, Ned dragged himself across the gearstick and onto the passenger seat. The car shuddered alarmingly with all this movement, but did not budge. The window was open on this side as the air conditioning hadn't worked for several months, so he was able to drag himself through the gap, another cry of pain escaping him in the process. He slid down to the ground and lay there, dazed. Looking at his car on its side, he realised how lucky he was to be alive.

He saw that the car had come to rest in a small gully, well beneath the shoulder of the road. No passing traffic would ever see him or the car in this well-concealed hollow. The incline up to the road was steep, but probably no more than a hundred metres.

The sun was setting behind him and already the road was in deepening shadow. He shivered in a sudden burst of evening breeze. Night came quickly this far north. There would be very little twilight. He tried to get to his feet, but the hurt foot was difficult to stand on. He dragged himself away from the car, grasping plants and the small trunks of saplings, avoiding the sharp razor grass until, after what seemed an endless and painful journey, he reached the edge of the shoulder of the road. He pulled himself onto the loose gravel and lay there for a moment to catch his breath. He was dripping with perspiration and he felt the warm gush of fresh blood course down his arm.

It was almost dark. He rested for a few more moments, then, using a dead tree branch he'd found nearby for support, he dragged himself to his feet. Ned had no idea how long it might be before a vehicle came past. This was not a busy road at the best of times, but now, in the evening, most tourists and even the locals would have arrived at their destination. He hoped that there might be a passing truckie who would come to his aid.

The air was cooling and he was parched. How little water had been in that bottle, he thought ruefully. His legs began to shake, but he realised that if he sat down he might never manage to attract a passing car. He lost track of time, leaning on the stick, shivering and perspiring, feeling the night air wash over his feverish, bloodied body.

Then he heard the sound of an engine. He edged closer to the side of the road so he would be seen in the glare of headlights. A car approached and he leaned out, waving his arm frantically. But to his horror, the car swerved slightly to the other side of the road and sped on past. The driver had obviously seen him but had no intention of stopping.

Ned was stunned. This was the bush, the outback, where people looked out for each other. Surely whoever was in that car had seen he was injured and needed help. He could not believe the car had not stopped for him. He sank to the side of the road, unable to stand any longer, feeling weak and deflated and very scared. Then he realised that he must look a terrible sight, covered in blood and dust, his clothes ripped by his climb to the top of the gully. And people passing couldn't see his car, so it wouldn't be obvious to them that there had been an accident. He thought of the well-publicised stories of recent years, where innocent backpackers had picked up hitchhikers, only to be assaulted, robbed and even murdered. Horror movies covering the same themes would not aid his case, either.

Geez, Ned, he thought. *No wonder those people didn't stop.* Maybe he'd have to wait till daylight, so that drivers could see clearly that he really needed help. He was suddenly gripped with fear. What if he didn't last through the night? He felt overwhelmed by the situation.

He wasn't sure if he had nodded off as he slumped by the road, but the next thing he was aware of was the sound of a car braking. He tried to focus his eyes when he heard a door slam. Suddenly he felt a firm grip under his armpits, lifting him to a sitting position.

'What happened to you, mate? You fall off the back of a truck or what? Anything broken? Don't move till I get my torch.' The female voice was concerned and yet quietly assured.

Ned took a breath. 'Got any water?'

'Yeah, yeah.'

7

Seconds later, as Ned gulped the welcome water, his rescuer shone a light swiftly over him, pausing for a closer look at his damaged arm.

'Can you stand?' she asked.

'I'll be okay, with a bit of help. I've crashed my car.' Ned winced as he was helped to his feet. He leaned heavily against his rescuer.

'That arm looks as though it could use a few stitches. Are you injured anywhere else?'

'My right foot is pretty painful,' replied Ned. 'And I had a bump on the head, too.'

'And your car? Where's that?' she asked.

Ned indicated where his vehicle had run off the road.

'Here, let's get you into my car. Do you want to lie down in the back, or will you be all right in the passenger seat?'

'I'll be okay in the front,' said Ned. The woman, who seemed about his own age, helped him into the front seat of her modest four-wheel drive. Ned winced, but managed to settle into the seat.

'I'll take you into Cooktown. You might not think it, but this is your lucky day. My name is Toni and I'm a physio at the local hospital. I'll get you straight there and we'll arrange for a tow truck tomorrow. Anything important in your car?'

'My guitar is in the back seat. It's pretty special. Do you reckon . . . ?'

'You a muso?' She sounded amused.

'You guessed right.'

Toni went to the edge of the road and swept her torch into the gully. She gave a low whistle. 'You were lucky. How'd you get out? Or were you thrown?'

'I crawled out.'

'Okay, I'll give it a go. Nothing else of value? Not that anyone is going to spot your vehicle down there. I think everything else will be safe till morning.'

Toni hurried out of sight and Ned leaned back, closing his eyes, his head pounding. A few minutes later, the back door of her car opened and, with a grunt, she placed Ned's guitar case on the back seat and got behind the wheel.

'It's less than an hour to town. You hanging in there?' Ned felt light-headed as he struggled to answer her.

Toni touched his face. 'You look pale . . .'

He tried to focus on her but Toni's face swam before his eyes. The pounding in his head grew intense and a buzzing filled his ears. His head lolled forwards against his chest and he felt his body go limp.

'Hey!' He could hear Toni's voice sharpen in alarm. As she gunned the engine, it seemed to drift away as the blackness closed in and Ned passed out.

2

BELLA STRAIGHTENED HER PAPERS, tidied her *In* and *Out* trays, turned off her computer (noticing as she did so that there was yet another email from the HR department telling her that she needed to take some of her holiday leave), put her diary in the top right desk drawer, checked the water in the vase which held a single rose, pushed her chair in, picked up her handbag and phone and closed her office door. She was the last person to leave the office that Monday evening, so she flicked the lights off as she passed through the main lobby and out into the carpark.

Bella liked order around her. She was methodical, organised and efficient. When crises occurred at work, Bella was swift to deal with them in a calm and effective manner. She knew she was a lateral thinker, and while she hoped to solve whatever dramas occurred in the simplest possible way, part of her was already thinking of alternative solutions just in case. She worked for the Tourism Office for Tennyson, the large provincial city in Victoria where she lived. She'd initially worked for a few years in Melbourne, which had been a useful experience, but it had also confirmed that living in such a large and impersonal metropolis wasn't for her. She earned a good salary, her co-workers were nice people and she loved living in the place where she'd grown up. But sometimes she thought she'd really like to run her own business, although she wasn't driven enough to take the plunge. Occasionally she trawled through job websites looking at other opportunities but the longer she stayed in local government and the more benefits she accrued, the harder it became for her to consider moving on, despite a gnawing feeling that her job wasn't always fulfilling.

Between her old schoolfriends and her workmates, she had a busy social life. She sang with an *a cappella* group, went to pilates classes and loved doing courses like pottery or cooking. She enjoyed being out and about, involving herself with various events and functions in the local community. Bella's outgoing, vivacious nature made her the well-known face of tourism for the area, and the local media loved her. She'd had no shortage of boyfriends, but her relationships rarely became serious. Brendan, her current boyfriend, had suggested several times that they move in together, but something was holding Bella back from agreeing. Nevertheless, she cared about Brendan a great deal and they spent most of their weekends together either at her place or his.

She nosed her car into her mother's driveway and made her way into the house. Bella and Josie Chisholm tried to have dinner together once a week. They got on very well, never running out of things to talk about, be it mutual friends, the current news, books or movies. Sometimes on weekends Bella and Brendan took Josie out

11

with them when they went exploring or picnicking. Josie protested that they didn't have to include her, as she had a wide circle of her own friends and a busy social life. But Bella insisted, saying quite truthfully that both she and Brendan enjoyed her company.

'Hi, Mum. Sorry I'm a bit late. Something smells good. What gourmet delight have you concocted tonight?' Bella asked as she walked into the kitchen.

'Nothing too special,' replied her mother, kissing her daughter's cheek. Although Josie was in her mid-sixties, it would be impossible not to notice how alike mother and daughter were, with their petite figures, untamed curly hair and huge, attractive brown eyes. 'A nice fresh mushroom and cream risotto and a pomegranate, mint and apple salad. Heather gave me a bag of fresh mushrooms this morning at tennis. She has some secret source but refuses to tell me where.'

'I suppose she knows which ones are mushrooms and which are toadstools.'

'Of course, you know what a gourmand and food snob she is,' Josie said with a laugh. 'How's work? Pour us a glass of vino, please, sweetie.'

'Work is the usual,' Bella said, opening a cabinet and taking out two wineglasses. 'I'm late because I was working on that big project for the council, you know the one. It's on track, just awaiting the funding. It'll be even more work when that comes through, though,' she said with a grimace. She unscrewed the lid on a bottle of wine. 'Not much else to report, except I think Margie might be leaving. Her boyfriend has a job promotion interstate. She'll be tricky to replace, she's good at PR. Personally, I think she's nuts to follow him to New South Wales.'

'Maybe she wants a permanent relationship.' Josie looked as though she was about to say something further but then changed her mind.

Bella avoided her mother's eye and studied the wine as she filled their glasses. 'Hmmm, well, I don't think Margie will have any trouble getting another job.' She replaced the cap on the wine bottle and put it on the bench. 'So, what's new with you, Mum? What have you been up to this week?'

'There is news,' Josie said accepting a glass of wine from Bella. 'You'll never guess. I've been hanging out for you to get here. I knew you were coming for dinner, so I wanted to tell you in person. Just read that letter on the bench. I think it's very exciting.'

Bella picked up the letter and saw that it was from the Tennyson Hospital, where her late father had spent most of his working life. A smile spread across Bella's face when she realised what it contained. Her father had been a brilliant surgeon and a fine administrator and was very well liked and respected amongst his colleagues as well as by the general community. It seemed the hospital wanted to dedicate one of the lecture rooms in the new hospital wing to him and they were hoping Josie would unveil the commemorative plaque. The letter explained that the health minister was coming from Melbourne just for the occasion and the mayor and other important dignitaries would also be in attendance. Bella looked at her mother in delight. 'Wow! This is a seriously big deal! And they want you to do the unveiling. Will you?'

'Of course. I'm so proud that the hospital board wants to recognise Alex's work. It's a really great honour. He's the only doctor in Tennyson to be recognised in this way, you know. I had no idea they were doing this.'

'I think that is no more than Dad deserved. What about Ned? I suppose he'll want to be there, too.'

Josie paused. 'I emailed Ned earlier today, but, you know him, there's been no reply.'

'Yes, I do know my brother.' Bella frowned. It was so typical of Ned not to check his emails and to ignore the family and it rankled her. 'Do you think he'll come? I think he should be here for the dedication. It's not every day that your father gets such a huge honour.'

'It would be nice, of course,' said Josie, her smile tight. 'But goodness knows where he is. I assume he's fine, or we would hear something.'

'But Mum, it's so selfish of him not to reply,' said Bella.

'Maybe he hasn't checked his email today.' Josie shrugged. 'We all walk to the sound of our own music.'

'I think Ned only hears what he wants to, and ignores anything inconvenient.'

Josie looked at her daughter. 'It's just how he is . . .'

'Mum! Let's not get started on "Ned is just Ned". I just think that he is not always very considerate towards you.'

Josie peered intently into the risotto pot. 'Ned just needs to find himself.'

Bella held her breath for a moment to control her anger. She didn't want the argument about her brother to continue. Privately she thought that now that Ned was pushing forty, he should have found himself already.

'Don't be harsh on him, Bella,' Josie said, sprinkling some seasoning into the risotto. 'He may not call as regularly as I would like, especially lately, but he rings when he has something to tell me. He's not like the two of us, who love to chit-chat regularly about anything and everything.'

'That's for sure.'

'But that doesn't mean he loves us any less, honey.'

'Well, I think it's ridiculous that we can't reach him when we want to. What if there was an emergency?'

'Well, there's not. He'll get back to me,' said Josie. 'Just the same, I agree with you about his attending the dedication. It would be nice for your brother to be here, so that all of Alex's family can acknowledge what a

14

wonderful man he was. He wasn't just a loving father and husband, he was admired by so many people in the community.'

Bella glanced at a photo of her handsome father pinned to the fridge. 'He was a pillar of Tennyson, wasn't he? It's hard to believe he's been gone for nearly a year. I know you still miss him terribly.'

Josie's eyes misted over. 'Of course I do. He was everything I could have dreamed of in a husband. Funny, clever, wise, and so loving. Life with him was never dull because he was such exciting company. You know something, Bella, when I first looked at the invitation, the first thing I noticed was that the date of the ceremony is the same date as his death.'

'Oh, Mum,' Bella glanced at the invitation again. 'I didn't see that. Why would they do that?'

'I'm sure it wasn't on purpose. They just wouldn't have realised. But it did rather bring home to me again just what I lost when your father died . . .' Josie's voice trailed off and she put down her wooden spoon as she tried to collect herself.

Bella patted her mother's hand. 'Look, Mum, when you speak to Ned, I really think that you should put your foot down with him. You should tell him exactly how you feel and that you want him to come home for this dedication.'

Josie sniffed and straightened up. 'I can only tell Ned that it's happening in a few weeks and hope that he decides for himself that he wants to come. It's up to him to make the decision.'

When Bella looked at her mother in complete exasperation, Josie looked away from her and changed the subject.

'You've been working so hard lately,' Josie said, tasting a spoonful of risotto. 'Have you got plans for some time off soon?'

'I've certainly got a lot of accumulated leave, and I'm being pushed to use it. They don't like you storing up too many holidays, but I don't want to go on leave while this project is on. It'll be a while till I've got some free time again.'

'Why don't you and Brendan take a trip?'

Bella wrinkled her nose.

'I thought you both got on very well. Brendan Miller is a very thoughtful and kind man,' said Josie.

'He is, he's nice and he's smart, but the relationship just isn't . . .' Bella chewed her lip. 'Well, it's just not all that exciting. I think that going on holidays with a dentist would be just too dull.'

'That's a shame, because as far as I'm concerned I think that you could do a lot worse than Brendan,' said Josie firmly.

'Anyway, enough about Brendan. Come on, let's eat dinner. I'm starving.'

Bella had dropped the subject of her big brother but still felt annoyed by his cavalier attitude to their mother. If he refused to attend the dedication, and she was pretty sure that's what his response was going to be, she would certainly be calling to tell him in no uncertain terms that he had to be present at the dedication of the 'The Dr Alex Chisholm Lecture Room'. It was the right thing to do. Their mother needed him and it was time he showed up.

*

The next day, Tuesday, Bella slammed down her phone in frustration, tears forming in her eyes. *I can't believe it. After all that work.* Her phone rang again and she recognised Josie's number. She gingerly picked up the receiver.

'Hi, Mum,' she said quietly.

'Hi, darling,' came Josie's bright voice. 'How's your day going?'

'Horrible!' said Bella, closing her office door and plonking herself back in her chair. 'I've just heard that my big project is off!'

'Oh dear,' said Josie sympathetically. 'And after all the work you've put into it.'

Bella sighed and rubbed her eyes with one hand. 'The funding got pulled. I can't believe it. And yet, somehow it seems typical!' She gave a bitter laugh.

'Well, I'm sorry to hear that, darling,' Josie said. 'I've heard from Ned though. He replied to my email this morning.'

'Oh yes,' said Bella. 'How is he? Where is he?'

'He said he'd been singing at a few festivals and some nightclubs but that he was going to stop in one place for a bit and try to do some serious composing.'

'So? Is he coming to the dedication?'

Bella heard Josie pause. 'He said he was a long way away, right up in the tropics in Far North Queensland. Said it's really interesting and beautiful.'

'Well, at least he's in the country. Are you going to insist that he comes back for the dedication?' Bella pressed.

'To tell you the truth, he wasn't very enthusiastic in his email. He said it was a long way to come just for one afternoon, and that it would go ahead whether he was there or not. He sent his love.'

'So you're going to let him off the hook,' said Bella in frustration. 'I really think that he should make the effort. For heaven's sake, it's not that hard to fly from one part of the country to another, and not all that expensive, either.'

Josie made a noncommittal sound. 'The hospital has asked if there is anyone in particular we'd like to invite. I think we should add your cousin Sue, don't you?'

'Whatever you think best, Mum.' But Bella was mentally fuming.

*

17

As they walked his dog through the park the following Monday evening, Brendan tried to be supportive.

'Sounds like you've had a rough week, Bell,' he said gently. 'Don't be so hard on Ned, though. He probably figures there'll be so many people at the dedication ceremony that he won't be missed. And he's right, it is a long trip back here for one event, even such an important one.'

Bella bristled. 'Well, the dedication should mean a lot. It's a huge honour for our father, and if Dad can't be there to appreciate it, then I think the least we can do is to have all our family there. And it's on the anniversary of Dad's death. Mum wants Ned to come, but she won't say that to him. You know, sometimes I think that Ned could be a bit nicer to Mum all round. He needs to spend some time with her.'

'But he knows that you keep a close eye on her.'

'Spoken like a bloke,' said Bella giving Brendan a playful swat. But then her tone hardened again. 'I just want to find Ned and shake him and *demand* that he comes back home for the dedication. I just don't understand why he's not coming. He admired Dad greatly, just like we all did. I'm sure he misses him. I do.' She gazed out across the lengthening shadows of the park, a gentle breeze tossing her curls.

Brendan squeezed her hand and then threw a ball for the dog. 'I know you do, Bell. You loved him so much. But I remember you telling me how disappointed your father was when Ned said that he had decided to become a musician? Things weren't always so good with Ned and your dad, right?'

'Yes, that's true,' replied Bella. 'There was quite a bit of tension in the house when Ned made that announcement. It was no secret that Dad wanted him to become a doctor. But Brendan, that difference of opinion was years ago. After that was resolved, they made their peace and moved on.' She was quiet a moment. 'The last twelve months have been so hard. Ned seems so distant. I really wonder if he's okay after what happened with Ashleigh.' A silence fell between them. Brendan cleared his throat.

'He hasn't responded to you at all? Have you tried calling his friends to see if they know where he is?'

'No, I texted and left him a message this week but he hasn't gotten back to me. And I've rung around but no one really seems to know exactly where he is. I looked at his website and his Facebook page but they're not up to date.' Bella smiled as she watched Brendan's dog chase a duck by a pond but then her brow furrowed. 'I'm beginning to think that if I want to speak to him, I'm going to have to go and find him.' She paused thoughtfully for a moment.

They walked on for a while, chatting amiably. Bella talked about her work situation and Brendan tried consoling her but she found herself not really listening. Another idea was forming in her mind.

At the crest of a hill, Brendan stopped walking and looked at her intently. 'Bell, I know I've asked you before, but seriously, we've been together for nine months now and I really want us to move in together. Why won't you agree?' He put his arm around her.

Bella stiffened and then wriggled out from under his arm. They walked on in silence. She did care a lot about Brendan but for some reason she just couldn't bring herself to commit to living with him. She felt that gnawing feeling inside her again. It was the same feeling she had about her job. Something just wasn't quite right and she couldn't put her finger on what it was. She sighed and then she realised that Brendan was still waiting for her to answer.

'I tell you what,' she said slowly. 'I need a break from work. Now that this project has fallen through, it's the perfect time for me to take a holiday. I need some time and space to figure things out. And I really want to see Ned.

So I think I'll go on a holiday up to Queensland. Just me.' She could see the hurt forming on Brendan's face. 'But while I'm away I'll think about us moving in and maybe I'll be able to give you an answer when I get back.' She smiled encouragingly at him and, while he didn't look happy, he let the matter drop.

*

Just over a week later, Josie stood at her gate, arms folded across her chest as she said goodbye to her daughter.

'I hope you have fun and relax. I'm glad you're taking some time off, but keep safe, won't you?'

'I'll be fine, Mum,' Bella replied.

'I wish Brendan was going with you.'

'He just can't afford to take the time off right now. Too many patients to reorganise,' Bella said quickly. 'I'm excited about being on my own and not having to think about anyone but me. I need a breather.'

'I can understand that, I guess. I just hope that Brendan can, too. Bella, he is the loveliest man. Don't lose him.'

Bella groaned. 'He's not a stray puppy! Brendan understands why I need to take this holiday, and he's fine about it.'

'Yes, you work hard, so make sure this time is for you and get a real break. Take a leaf out of Ned's book. Too bad we don't know where he is, you could have spent some time together.'

'I'll call you when I can, but remember, I could be in places where there is no phone reception, so don't worry.'

'I won't, and enjoy yourself, sweetie. Send me photos so I can see where you are.'

'Of course.' Bella stepped forward and hugged her mother, but she couldn't help thinking to herself, *You don't lay these sorts of conditions on Ned.*

Bella climbed into her car and tapped the horn in a cheerful toot as she waved goodbye. She didn't feel dishonest not telling her mother the whole truth about the impetus behind this break. Bella told herself that if she did manage to find Ned and drag him home, then her mother would be happy, but if she failed, then her mother would be none the wiser and no harm would be done.

During the previous ten days, she'd planned her trip, wrapped up a few loose ends at work and tried to track down Ned. She'd emailed him, telling him of her plans for a trip, and had tried to call him a couple of times, but to no avail. From her Facebook contacts and ringing around some of their mutual friends Bella had discovered that Ned had been singing at festivals in Queensland, but then had appeared fairly recently in a club in Cairns, and this certainly tied in with what he'd told Josie. So, Bella had booked herself into a small coastal resort town that sounded nice and quiet and was only a few kilometres north of Cairns.

As she turned out of her mother's street and headed towards the airport, she felt a sense of relief wash over her. This break was long overdue. She was planning a few relaxing days first before starting her search for Ned. She hoped that when she arrived she'd hear from him and they could make a plan to meet. But it seemed more than likely that she'd have to track him down. That morning before her departure, more in hope than with any real expectations, she'd sent him a simple text: *Just touching base, get back to me.*

*

It was a modest sign pointing to Hidden Cove, but within minutes of turning her rental car off the busy Captain Cook Highway, Bella felt she'd travelled into a tropical paradise. Lush and colourful gardens sheltered hideaway homes.

She turned right and meandered slowly along the beach-front, past a row of leaning coconut palms and beyond them a strip of golden sand and the expanse of blue Coral Sea. On the other side of the road were a few busy outdoor restaurants, their colourful umbrellas fluttering in the gentle sea breeze. Rising behind them were a few tidy apartment blocks, complete with green lawns and azure pools.

She drove slowly, as people seemed to use this one-way street as an extended footpath, strolling along it in their resort fashions, walking their dogs, while children carried water toys and sunhats. Couples held hands as well as surfboards. The pace was leisurely, with an ambience of well-to-do relaxation.

Bella followed the road as it turned away from the beach towards streets of expensive-looking open-plan houses and the odd discreet sign advertising simpler accommodation. Hidden Cove was a tiny haven that had a cosmopolitan air reminiscent of a European coastal town until one looked at the blinding blue sea and the distant foam of white breakers.

Turning back towards the beach, she found Aloha House, an apartment block with large, sea-facing balconies. A small café and a newsagent sat either side of the main entrance. She pulled into the driveway and punched in her code and a metal gate slid open. She parked in the underground carpark and reached for her bag. Before getting into the lift Bella noticed another door, and she took a quick peek through it. A lush hideaway oasis at the rear of the building looked inviting, with its long lap pool surrounded by lawns dotted with lounges, umbrellas and shady trees and covered in its carpet of frangipani flowers.

As soon as she opened her apartment door, she was charmed. The rooms were decorated with large shells and bright paintings of tropical flowers, and a fat wooden seagull was perched by the door opening onto a balcony. The balcony faced the ocean and was furnished with a small barbecue and table setting as well as a comfortable lounge chair placed strategically under an overhead fan. She immediately dropped her things and headed downstairs to the pool. The humidity of Far North Queensland was draining, and she needed to cool down straight away.

After a quiet evening with a takeaway salad and her book, she woke before the sun and walked along the beach to the old jetty. As the sun rose, making the water sparkle, she watched the seabirds diving and a huge tame fish that swam tantalisingly around the piers of the wharf. On the wharf, early morning fishermen, young and old, optimistically cast their rods.

She walked barefoot along the sandy path under the trees where locals jogged and walked their dogs. The café near the entrance to her apartment block was open, so she bought a latte, then stopped at the small store which sold the morning papers and took both her coffee and paper home to enjoy on her sunny balcony. She sent Ned another text message, telling him where she was, in the increasingly forlorn hope that he would finally get back to her. She spent the rest of the day lazing by the pool, but there was no reply from Ned.

When it cooled down late in the afternoon, Bella decided to explore the southern end of the beach, so she set off along the shell-dotted strand, splashing through the tepid water. People were out walking and several frisky dogs chased each other over the sand, but no one was in the ocean. Everyone seemed to be heeding the large, prominent warning signs that ominously read: *Swim at your own risk*. Bella assumed they referred to box jellyfish which, the rental agent had told her, had stings so poisonous that they could put you in hospital and had even been known to cause death.

She reached the rocky headland at the end of the beach and turned and walked back above the high water mark, avoiding the leaning coconut palms, though their coconuts appeared to have been picked.

When she came to a creek of crystal water sluggishly making its way across the sand to the sea, she headed towards it in order to admire the water lilies and floating islands of grass that lay in the shadows beneath the overhanging trees. Here the creek looked darker and rather sinister, and it was then she saw a yellow sign reading, *Achtung! Warning!*, and sporting an illustration of a snapping crocodile.

Surely crocs didn't come onto the beach? she wondered. Bella shivered, turning away, and hastily walked back to one of the benches conveniently placed on the edge of the beach. She sat and watched the placid sea for a while. The view was so beautiful and in that moment she wished Brendan was there to share it with her. As the waves rolled gently in to shore, she thought about their relationship. What was wrong with her? They laughed at the same things, enjoyed the same movies and she agreed with his politics and quietly admired his ethical behaviour. And yet Bella couldn't help but feel that their relationship was dull. He always asked her what she would like to do. He never fought with her over anything. And while she liked his impeccable manners and quiet ways, she wished he would be more spontaneous, be willing to engage with her even if it meant the occasional quarrel, and sometimes surprise her. She knew Brendan had been hurt when she wanted to go away by herself but, as always, he'd been considerate of her wishes. He was just so *nice* all the time. Was he really what she wanted?

Suddenly, Bella became aware of a young woman several metres away, who was sitting in a yoga position, arms raised above her head, eyes closed as she meditated.

Bella thought of the crocodile warning. She'd heard how smart the reptiles were, spending time watching the habits and routine of their selected prey before striking, carrying their victim into a convenient creek and stuffing them in a watery trap beneath a tangle of tree roots. Very few victims had survived to describe this horror. Did the yoga girl know crocs were in the vicinity?

Bella got up and walked over to her.

'I'm sorry to interrupt you when you are meditating, but you do know that there are crocodiles in this area, don't you? You're by yourself here and with your eyes closed . . .'

The girl looked up and smiled. 'They're everywhere in this part of the world. Live and let live. They used to be hunted to near extinction and now they're protected. How the world works,' she added enigmatically.

'Doesn't that worry you?' said Bella, a little concerned at the girl's insouciance.

'I'm far enough from the creek to be safe, although a large croc was taken from the lagoon about a week ago.'

'You're kidding,' said Bella in amazement. This place looked so serene, and yet a killer croc had lurked beneath those beautiful water lilies.

'You've just arrived, have you?' asked the girl.

'Is it obvious?' laughed Bella. 'Ironic to think some- where so placid and beautiful could be so treacherous.'

'Still waters, as they say. Sit a moment and enjoy the remains of the day.' She gestured beside her, so Bella sat on the sand.

'It would be a nice way to start the day, too,' agreed Bella. 'Instead of rushing out the door to my office. Do you live here or are you on holiday?'

'I live here for now. I travelled a lot, then I found out about my great-grandfather. Funny how you never think much about the lives of your grandparents and their parents and what they did when they were our age.'

'That's true,' agreed Bella. 'So what did you find out? If you don't mind me asking.'

'No worries. Great-grandad was a prisoner of war in Changi in Singapore and apparently something of a character. He couldn't settle back into suburban life in Sydney after the war, so when he won some money in the lottery he married, came up to Queensland and opened a fish and chip shop near the beach. It did really well, so he sold it and moved further north and bought a rundown old coconut plantation. The trees were sixty years old. He started a nursery and exported them all over Australia.'

'So, he really made good after a hard time in the war?'

'He did. He sold the coconut plantation and he and my great-grandmother moved to Micronesia and started helping the villagers. Built a school for the kids. Then he came back to Australia and set up a kids' camp on an island on the Barrier Reef where Indigenous and outback kids could go and holiday for free.'

'What a great thing to do!' said Bella. 'And what happened to the old plantation?'

'You're sitting in it. Well, all that land there behind us.'

'No way! Hidden Cove belonged to your great-grandfather?' exclaimed Bella. 'What became of him?'

'He retired back to Sydney and lived quietly. When I discovered the story through my aunt, I just had to come and have a look. I work in the hotel over there. Just saving up to go to the islands.'

'Are you going to visit the school he started?' asked Bella, quite intrigued by this story.

'I thought I'd just go and see. You have to follow your intuition, right?'

'Yes,' said Bella slowly. 'I guess you do.'

The girl smiled and resumed her pose, closing her eyes again.

Bella stayed a while but then got up and walked back towards her apartment, thinking the girl was right. Sometimes you did have to follow your intuition.

*

By the end of the weekend, Bella could feel her head clearing. The break was doing her good. She decided she should probably start looking for Ned more earnestly and stop just checking social media and calling his friends hoping to find him.

She decided to head to Cairns. Bella saw why the girl at the reception desk of her apartment building had called Cairns a jumping place – there seemed to be people everywhere. After she had parked her car in the downtown area and begun to explore, she initially wondered why the CBD seemed to be filled with a small army of retirees in colourful shorts and shirts, loose frocks or snug slacks, until she saw them all wearing tags around their necks and realised that they were passengers from a cruise ship, having their day ashore in the capital of Far North Queensland.

Cairns had a lively atmosphere. There was a plethora of places to eat, drink, dance, listen to music and watch tourist shows. There were art galleries and tourist shops selling Aboriginal art and artefacts. The theme of Cairns appeared to be crocodiles, both alive and stuffed. Almost every gift shop featured crocodile leather handbags, belts, shoes and hat bands, crocodile teeth jewellery as well as ornamental crocodiles carved from wood. A photographer's studio featured close-ups of large crocodiles, their jaws wide open, displaying their awesome teeth, which made Bella shudder.

She had no trouble finding the club where a mutual friend had told her Ned had recently appeared. It looked an unprepossessing place in the daylight, but she went in and asked for the manager. As Bella's eyes adjusted to the gloomy surrounds of an empty music club, a woman around her own age came to meet her.

'I'm Sarah. I book the artists here and plan events. Can I ask you why you're looking for Ned Chisholm?'

'Ned's my brother. He's been on the road and the family's trying to find him – he's a bit slack at keeping in touch.' She gave Sarah her most charming smile.

'Yeah, musos are an itinerant lot,' Sarah said, shaking her head. 'Ned was here a while back . . . He was very popular.' She pulled out a chair at an empty table and signalled Bella to join her.

Bella sat down. 'That's nice to hear. When you grow up with someone who is always singing and playing music you tend to take it a bit for granted. So how come he played here?'

Sarah smiled. 'He walked in the door and asked for a gig. I knew who he was. He is seriously good-looking.' She fanned herself with mock passion as Bella laughed and rolled her eyes. 'You look quite like him. Are you musical, too?'

'Not really, not like Ned. So do you know where he is now?' said Bella. 'Have you any clue where he might have headed?'

'I have no idea. A local band backed him; they might know. I can give you their number, if you like. I've also got an address for them, somewhere up in the Atherton Tablelands. I know they liked working with him. Your brother is very professional, but easy to get on with. He'd have a sound check and then run through a couple of numbers with them, and that was all. But he was really good. He connects with an audience, y'know?'

Bella nodded and felt a warm glow hearing her brother praised. 'Yes, I know he's good. A phone number and address would be great.'

After Sarah gave them to her, Bella nodded. 'Here's my number in case you hear anything about him from someone else. I appreciate your help. Brothers can be such a pain at times.' She gave Sarah a grateful smile. 'Thanks for seeing me.'

'No worries.'

As Bella turned and headed towards the exit of the dark club, Sarah called after her, 'You might stop by the community radio station. Miz Irene interviewed him for her programme, *I Got the Blues*. I didn't hear it but he might have told her something about his plans.'

'Great. I'll do that. Thanks again, Sarah.'

Bella mulled Sarah's suggestion over for a moment, googling Miz Irene and the radio station's address. The station was only ten minutes away, so she decided to check it out first before she contacted the backing group.

A petite blonde in her fifties, her age disguised by her boyishly slim body, youthful clothes and beautifully cared for skin, greeted Bella in the lobby with a warm smile.

'I'm Irene. How can I help you?' she said.

'I wanted to ask you about an interview you did with Ned Chisholm. I'm his sister.' Bella glanced at the walls covered in framed photos of Irene with some very famous musicians. 'These photos are amazing. Have you been doing this long?'

Irene chuckled. 'I've always been a country and western and blues fan, so I kind of fell into this. Mind you, I've spent a lot of time in the US. I go to the jazz and blues festivals there, Nashville of course, and I've had the privilege of interviewing a lot of big names for my little ole show back here.'

'There's a big audience here in the north for the blues?' asked Bella curiously.

'Yes, but my show also streams on the net. I have fans all over the world, especially in the US. You'd be surprised how many people in the States know about Cairns. Of course, I think they knew about this place right back to Lee Marvin.'

'You mean the old-time American movie actor?'

'That's him. He was a keen deep-sea fisherman, and once the first thousand-pound black marlin was caught off Cairns he used to visit the place regularly. Brought his Hollywood mates with him. That was in the sixties and seventies, when marlin fishing was all the go. Still is. Cairns was apparently a pretty wild old town back then. You could fall over any number of big-time celebrities in the local pubs in the fishing season. Anyway, tell me again, what did you want to know about Ned?'

'I'm trying to track him down. Sarah at the jazz club told me you'd interviewed him when he was playing there?'

'Sure did!' Irene beamed. 'Lovely man. Big talent. His show was great, could have run for weeks. So you've lost touch?'

'He's not one for calling home unless he has to, and we have a family event happening and I need to pin him down,' said Bella.

Irene cocked her head. 'Um, I remember he said something about heading further north. I don't think he mentioned anywhere specific; maybe up to the Daintree?'

'Apparently it's beautiful up there. A bit away from everything. Maybe he's looking for inspiration,' said Bella.

Irene shrugged. 'Could be. These artists do their own thing, I've discovered. You don't hear from them for ages, then they just turn up. It drives me nuts when I'm trying to arrange interviews.'

'I can imagine. Musicians live on another planet, if Ned's anything to go by. Well, thanks for your time. Oh, is it possible to listen to the interview my brother did with you?'

'Sure thing. It's up on my website. I don't put everything up there, but Ned speaks from the heart. I'll give you the date we ran it so you can find it online.'

'I suppose my best bet now would be to drive up to the Daintree, if you think he's gone north.'

As she handed Bella a slip of paper with the date of the interview on it, Irene said, 'You'll enjoy the Daintree. There's a wonderful lodge up there, built in the area before it was all proclaimed a national park and no more development was allowed. It's all very eco-friendly. I try to escape up there when I can. A friend of mine works as a local guide, and knows the Daintree really well. Look her up if you want to see the area properly. She's very cool and will show you the real heart of the place. I'll give you her number if you like.'

'That would be great,' said Bella, and Irene added the details to the piece of paper.

'If you're back in town and get the chance, get in touch and I'll take you to a gig.'

'Terrific! And thanks for your help. You've been very kind.'

As she walked back to her car, Bella tried to ring the backing band to see if they could give her a lead on Ned's whereabouts. Her call went straight through to message bank, so she left a brief message. Hearing Irene speak so admiringly of Ned had softened some of Bella's feelings towards him. *I just hope I can see him soon*, she thought.

*

As she set off back to Hidden Cove, early evening was settling on Cairns. The sun was low and the boats at the marina were reflected in the calm sea. There was a pink tinge to the clouds and a fresh breeze brought down the oppressive humidity. People were walking about looking for a place to have dinner, and the visiting jet set had begun to emerge and settle themselves in for some serious partying.

She loved driving along the twisting coastal highway that threaded its way between the sea on one side and the high rugged hills on the other on the way from Cairns to Hidden Cove. In places there were small stretches of sandy inlets squeezed between bulky rocks where the waves flung themselves onto the shore, but all were deserted this late in the day.

Along the shorefront of Hidden Cove, fairy lights and flame torches glowed in the balmy air, and music and laughter rolled gently into the night. She parked the car in the apartment block and hurried upstairs to freshen up. Although she wanted to listen to Ned's interview on her phone, she decided to save it for later.

As Bella walked along the seafront, tantalising aromas made the choice of food difficult and she could see that most of the cafés and restaurants were nearly full. Eventually she chose an Asian-fusion restaurant that had a small empty table in the front. She ordered Thai fish cakes and a crunchy Asian salad. When her glass of white wine came, she picked up her phone and rang her mother. She told her mother about Hidden Cove and her quick trip to Cairns.

'I'm so glad you're relaxing,' said Josie. 'It sounds so tropical. We had a change in the weather through yesterday and it's freezing here at the moment.'

'Yes, it's certainly warmer here,' Bella said, a soft breeze lifting her curls. 'I'm thinking of going into the rainforest area, up to the Daintree.'

'I didn't expect you'd go so far. And you liked Cairns?'

'It was fun for a day. Are you okay? How're things there?'

'Apart from this cold spell, all good. I'll go over to your place tomorrow and water your plants and check your mail.'

'Thanks, Mum. Don't go out of your way, the plants will be fine and the letters will be bills. Ooh, my meal is here, looks fabulous. Talk soon. Love you.'

The waiter, Bella guessed, was a backpacker from Italy, and he lingered longer than was really necessary as he refilled her wineglass and gently probed into her plans. She was used to deflecting such overtures and charmingly let him know that she wasn't going to be spending much time in Hidden Cove and definitely was not available for a holiday fling.

Somewhat chastened, he asked, 'So where are you going after here?'

'I thought I'd go up to the Daintree. Have you been there?'

'I went to Cape Tribulation once but it is too dangerous, I think. Too much wildlife.'

'You don't like the wildlife?'

He shook his head. 'No, too many crocodiles and very poisonous snakes. Some of the people are a bit crazy wild, too. I like cities. I am here for, you know . . .' He rubbed his fingers together.

'To make money? I'm sure you get a lot of tips,' said Bella, smiling at the handsome man.

'*Si*. But,' he lowered his voice and leaned closer, 'not from the young girls. The ladies, the mamas on their own. They like some talk, some company. How come you take holiday by yourself?'

Bella also lowered her voice. 'I'm on a secret mission. I'm just pretending to be on a holiday.' She tapped the side of her nose.

He looked puzzled for a moment, then burst out laughing. 'Ah, *bravo*. A secret. I keep it to myself.'

Bella lifted her glass in a mock toast as he moved away. In his tight white T-shirt, his tanned, muscular arms were shown to full advantage. She had a slight twinge of guilt thinking of Brendan but then she laughed as the waiter winked at her. It was all in good fun.

Over her meal she googled information about the Daintree on her phone. *If Ned was headed that way, was it for pleasure or performance?* she wondered. The whole area looked beautiful and interesting, so she decided she'd go. *Sometimes you just had to trust your intuition*, thought Bella, and if she didn't find Ned there, then she would enjoy a different part of the world.

After dinner she returned to her apartment and listened to the programme that Ned had done with Irene. Although she learned nothing further about his plans, she enjoyed listening to Ned speak. Ned was so passionate about his music. Moreover, the respect and enthusiasm that Irene had shown him in the interview indicated that the DJ also regarded him as a very serious and talented musician. Bella felt a swell of pride.

After listening to the interview, Bella phoned Irene's friend Roberta. The introduction was fortuitous, and they spoke at length having immediately struck up a rapport. Bella didn't tell her the actual purpose of her trip to north Queensland, but simply said that she wanted to explore a part of the country she'd never seen.

'Being a World Heritage area, the Daintree Rainforest is a very, very special and rare environment,' Roberta said. 'As my family is connected to the area, I work with preservation, research and conservation bodies, so I can offer a more eco and cultural understanding by inviting people to join small working groups. I can take you if you're up for that. I think you'll find it deeply rewarding. I'm not into white-water rafting, skydiving, rock climbing or zipline jungle surfing through the canopy . . . I don't offer anything like that.'

'Good, I'm not into those sorts of extreme sports,' Bella told her.

Bella was intrigued, not just because she wanted to see the Daintree but also because she wanted to see how tourism was managed in such a special and sensitive area. She decided straight away to accept Roberta's invitation.

'I'll organise a tent and a sleeping bag for you, and of course the food. Just bring along a towel and basic necessities, including good walking shoes. No shampoo, I'm afraid. It pollutes the water system, but you'll only be without it for three days. How about I pick you up when I have to go into Port Douglas?' suggested Roberta.

Hanging up the phone, Bella found she was a bit surprised at herself. This kind of trip wasn't the sort of thing she usually did.

'You hate camping!' Josie exclaimed when Bella told her of her plan.

But this was exactly the reason for my trip, Bella thought. *I've got to try new things else I'm never going to know what's out there.*

Bella was glad she could spend the rest of the day doing very little at Hidden Cove. She walked along the beach, she read on her balcony, swam in the pool in the complex, read and dozed in the afternoon and, although usually gregarious, she happily ate another solitary dinner before going to bed with her book. She didn't turn on the TV and she ignored phone calls from friends curious about what she was up to. She exchanged a few texts with Brendan but kept the content casual. Occasionally her mind would turn to work but she pushed those thoughts away. She needed some peace for now.

Bella arranged to meet Roberta in the resort town of Port Douglas, just south of the Daintree, where she could leave her car for a few days. She waited in the lobby of a small hotel, watching the groups of tourists come and go and hoping that she would have no trouble identifying Roberta.

She spotted Roberta the moment the guide strode briskly into the reception area dressed in khaki shorts and shirt and sturdy boots. She was brown skinned and seemed slightly older than Bella. Her dark, curly hair sprang from the confines of an elaborate hairclip and the large brown eyes in her attractive, strong-featured face were friendly. The women greeted each other with big smiles and Bella followed Roberta into the bright sunlight of the hot tropical morning.

'You all set?' Roberta said as she swung Bella's gear into the rear of her Jeep. 'We're meeting the others down at the river crossing.'

As they drove north towards the cane town of Mossman, Bella gazed out over the lush green fields of mature sugar cane that lay on either side of the highway towards the forest-clad hills that rose behind them. Roberta came to a halt beside the narrow-gauge rail line to let a long cane train laden with wagons of cut cane chug past them.

'These trains are so cute, like toy trains,' said Bella.

'It's a very efficient way of getting the cane to the mills quickly. The cane needs to be crushed as soon as it's cut to get the maximum value from it.' Roberta paused as they watched the train rattle away. 'It was the sugar cane industry that brought my ancestors to Australia. Not that they all exactly came by choice.'

'Where did your ancestors come from?' Bella asked.

'My family originally comes from Melanesia, the South Sea Islands,' answered Roberta. 'The first member of my family came here in the 1870s when he was more or less shanghaied. You must have heard of blackbirding?'

'Only vaguely,' said Bella, suddenly feeling awkward. There was a fleeting expression on Roberta's face that made Bella realise she wasn't the first person to admit to such ignorance.

Calmly Roberta explained, 'In the late part of the nineteenth century, sugar cane began to be grown in tropical Queensland, but for the cane farmers to be able to compete with cheap world sugar prices, they needed cheap labour. So ships sailed to the Pacific Islands and induced young men, usually with a bribe of cheap shoddy goods, to become indentured labour. In some cases, strong-looking boys were just grabbed off the beach. They were brought to the cane fields and worked extremely hard cutting cane for very little money.' Roberta's face was composed but Bella could see her emotions shifting below the surface. 'Of course it was argued that these men came to Australia voluntarily, but that's rubbish. Those boys had no idea what was happening to them and if they did sign anything, they had no idea what they were signing because they were illiterate. This trade was called blackbirding.'

Bella was startled. 'That's appalling. Do you know how many Islanders were involved?'

'No one is really sure, but it was possibly up to sixty thousand. Our own quiet slave trade.'

'That's outrageous. I had no idea,' Bella exclaimed angrily. Suddenly the green of the cane fields either side of her seemed sinister. Not at all the tropical paradise that she had been admiring.

Roberta glanced at her and smiled. 'You're not alone there. Many Australians don't know much about it either.' The train rattled off into the distance and Roberta restarted the car and they resumed their journey.

'Did any of these Islanders return home?' Bella asked.

'That's the really bad part,' Roberta said with a sigh. 'Some of them returned home after their contracts expired, but many of them would sign up again after their initial indenture period, especially as their pay rates improved because they were considered to be experienced. Sadly, for some of them, contracts weren't honoured and they never got paid. Then, over the years they lost contact with their homes and formed new relationships in Queensland. Many learned to read and write and most became Christians and developed an attachment to their church. The ambitious ones who had been here long enough saved to buy their own land and grew cane or fruit and vegetables.'

Bella glanced at Roberta and asked gently, 'Is that what your family did?'

Roberta paused, but then said, 'Yes, in the beginning.' Her mouth quirked. 'But at the turn of the twentieth century, when Australia became one country, there was a push by the national government for racial purity. All races that weren't white, like Chinese, Japanese, Filipinos and Pacific Islanders, were no longer wanted, and most were forced to return to their country of origin.'

Bella rolled her eyes. 'How ironic. First your ancestors were brought here to help build the country and then, when they had contributed, they were sent back home. Hardly makes sense!'

'It wasn't just the government. Trade unions thought these other races would be willing to work for less and so would undercut white men's wages.'

'So what happened to your ancestor?' Bella could feel the heat from the sun beating through the windows, so she turned up the air conditioning. She was intrigued by Roberta's story and goosebumps rose on her skin.

'There was a protest movement amongst the Pacific Islanders and the Queensland government, objecting to this repatriation,' said Roberta. 'In the end most Islanders were sent back, although not always to their original islands. But a few hundred were allowed to stay. Others went into hiding. It was very sad. Families were torn apart and those who stayed were too fearful to visit their homeland in case they wouldn't be allowed back into Australia. My great-great-grandfather had been in Australia for twenty years by then and had married a Scottish woman who he'd met at the local church, and so he was able to stay. But he never went back to what's now Vanuatu to reunite with his Island family.'

Bella and Roberta were both quiet a moment. A flock of birds wheeled overhead and flew off above the cane fields.

'It was tough on my family for a long time because there was a lot of discrimination against the South Sea Islanders,' Roberta continued. 'When other migrants like the Italians came to north Queensland, they could get bank loans to purchase land, but it was much harder for my family to get financial help, and while the newcomers were quickly accepted, the Islanders were always viewed with prejudice.'

'That is so unjust,' exclaimed Bella indignantly.

Roberta shrugged. 'My family learned to survive and over time managed pretty well, but it took more than a hundred years for the Queensland government to formally recognise the South Sea Islanders as a distinct ethnic and cultural group, and acknowledge their contribution to the state's development.'

'Better late than never, I suppose,' said Bella sarcastically. 'Have you ever thought of going back to the Islands and finding your family's descendants?'

Roberta cocked her head. 'I once thought about it, but I have my roots here. I love this country. And that's why I like to share it with other people.'

'I'm looking forward to that,' said Bella quietly.

About twenty minutes after they left Mossman, Roberta turned the Jeep down a grassy track, following it until it petered out and then parked beside several other vehicles. The two women shouldered their bags and picked their way down a steep hillside.

It was a descent from heat and light into cool green gloom.

Bella craned her neck upwards to the sixty-metre canopy above her head, where the trees fought for sunlight. These trees hosted a myriad of plants, their trunks glowing emerald with lichen, mosses, ferns and orchids, while far above looped the tails of fat liana vines, strangler figs and epiphytes, all of which helped bind the tree canopy into a thick blanket. Occasionally, the canopy had been rent by a falling tree, so that scrubs and small saplings had sprouted, taking advantage of the spotlight of sun on this patch of earth.

The two walked softly over the carpet of leaf litter. This world was still, humid and seemingly silent. Suddenly, Roberta put her hand to her ear and tilted her head. Bella listened. Then she heard the whispering, rustling, scratching noises of the hidden wildlife of the rainforest.

'When we head down to the river you'll see lots of birds,' said Roberta. 'We're hiking to a section of traditional Aboriginal land which is now mainly used for research purposes and occasionally for ceremonies. There's no camping in the park proper, so we're going to camp just on its edge.'

After a fifteen-minute walk they came to some open country where the trees and foliage were sparse and where, in a sunlit clearing, a long table and old chairs were set up under a galvanised iron shelter. There was also an enclosed gas barbecue, and nearby was a well-used campfire made from a ring of stones. The table was covered in tins and plastic food containers, and several large eskies were stacked nearby. Half a dozen tents were set up and a billy was sitting beside a large metal teapot. A group of five people were standing around, drinking tea from enamel mugs.

'Cuppa char?' called out a plump, cheerful Englishman as Bella and Roberta walked into camp.

Two tanned women in their forties introduced themselves as Annabelle and Deidre. 'We're just heading out. We're photographing wildlife, mainly birds, in the Daintree. We do it every year,' they explained.

Roberta gestured to two men; one short with red hair, the other bald with glasses. 'Graham and Phil are geologists visiting from the UK.' Bella shook their hands. 'And this is Antony, who's brushing up his bush skills and local knowledge,' continued Roberta as a man in his early thirties with bleached blond hair wandered up from the creek. He grinned and extended his hand towards Bella. 'Ant works at the Lodge.'

'Oh, is that the eco-resort I've been told about? The flash place?' asked Bella as she shook hands.

Antony gave her an appraising look and a broad smile. 'Certainly is. You should spend a day or so there after roughing it down here. It's lovely, very luxurious. I'll make sure you are looked after.'

'I'm happy here, I think,' said Bella, glancing around at the dappled sunlight. 'A sylvan glade, no less.'

'Ah yes, we all disrobe and dance naked in the moonlight. You'll love it,' he said with a mischievous twinkle in his eye. Bella smiled. Antony seemed to be rather a fun person. When he smiled, Bella noticed that two charming dimples appeared on his cheeks, making him look very cute.

'Cup of tea and a sandwich and we'll head out towards the upper valley, shall we?' said Roberta. 'It's a fair walk but interesting, and we end up at the base of a stream coming down from the falls. Very refreshing and quite crocodile-proof, so bring your swimsuit. Tomorrow we'll start in the lowland rainforest and climb towards another peak in the upland forest. Bit of a hike, but you look pretty fit, Bella.'

'There's a great view from the top of the peak,' said Antony. 'I'll help you if you need it.'

It was late afternoon when they returned to the base camp. Bella and the three men had followed Roberta up along a crystal-clear stream as it bounced past them over glossy rocks, forming deep pools before gurgling down-stream to join a branch of a larger creek. Bella felt as though she'd entered another world; the forest was simply breathtaking.

A couple of hours earlier, they'd reached the rock pool Roberta had promised them. Bella had braced herself as she slipped into it, feeling the crisply cold water on her hot body.

'This is so good,' she'd said. 'Shame we'll get all hot and bothered again on the walk back.'

'At least it's downhill,' said Antony with a laugh.

The next morning, the two bird photographers headed out straight after breakfast, leaving just Bella and the three men with Roberta. As promised, she took them into the lowland forest and then up to one of the peaks. Peering out to the sparkling sea and reef, Bella acknowl-edged that Antony had been right. The view from the top was spectacular. Bella had never felt so energised, but after so long in a desk-bound job her muscles were starting to feel the workout, and by the end of the day they were very sore. The following morning, when Roberta told her where she planned to go hiking with the geologists, Bella begged off.

'Roberta, I'm not as fit as the rest of you and I would only slow you down. I'm happy enough to stay here. It's peaceful and I can easily amuse myself.'

Antony came over and touched her on the shoulder. 'Bella, you haven't seen half of what the Daintree has to offer. I've done the walk Roberta's taking Graham and Phil on a couple of times, so I'm happy to give it a miss. What say I show you other parts of the area? Take you to all kinds of magic places that we can access in my four-wheel drive?'

'He's persuasive, isn't he?' said Roberta chuckling. 'But you should see a bit more of the Daintree. It's so beautiful and so fragile and it would be a pity to miss it.'

'Come on, Bella . . . it's a once in a lifetime opportunity,' cajoled Antony. 'Isn't this what you wanted to do when you came up north?'

Bella grinned. 'I suppose so. Thanks, Antony, if you're sure I'm not putting you out. It'd be great.'

*

There had been a shower of rain in the night and the vegetation around them dripped and shone. Bella and Antony drove back along the rough road until they reached the broad expanse of the Daintree River, where the flat-bottomed car punt ferried their car to the other side. When they drove off the car ferry, Antony headed north, pointing out things of interest. After a while he pulled over to the edge of the rough dirt road.

'Come and walk. I know this area quite well.'

The place where Antony stopped seemed exotic and everything dripped with water, while each tree was home to an endless variety of ferns, lichens and orchids. He pointed at a tree with large leaves.

'That's a stinging tree and those leaves are covered in minuscule spears that prick you and make you itch painfully for hours. Awful thing. Beautiful . . . but dangerous. Like some women,' said Antony, his eyes twinkling.

Bella rolled her eyes, laughing. 'Give me a break.'

As they walked under the dense canopy of rainforest Bella began to feel perspiration running down her back and between her breasts in the dank humidity.

Antony glanced at her. 'We'll be out of these quandongs soon.' He bent down and picked up a bright blue pod. 'You can eat the fruit, but it's sour. The cassowaries love them. They spread its seeds all over the place.'

He moved towards Bella and leaned close before turning her head slightly. 'Look, over there to the left, up high.'

Bella didn't see what he was pointing at as his pepperminty breath on her neck was distracting. But then she saw it: a shimmering, fluttering cloud.

'Butterflies! How gorgeous.'

They watched for a few more moments, Antony still leaning close, his breath warm on her skin.

Bella stepped away. 'It's so humid. I thought you said we were near the coast.'

'We are. But you don't hear it because there's no surf. The beach is protected by the big outer reef.'

As they moved off, the path they were following became sandy and there was a fresh tangy smell in the air.

'The sea. At last. Wow.'

They walked from the rainforest trees onto the beach, and there before them was the huge amphitheatre of silver white sand and calm blue water. In the distance, a low white line marked the outer reef and the low tide exposed the flat fringing reefs close to shore.

'Captain Cook had trouble getting through those reefs and called them "this insane labyrinth", which is why he named this place Cape Tribulation,' said Antony. 'Want to go and look in the rock pools?'

Bella glanced around, spying a couple of other people picking their way across the rocks. The beach seemed pristine and unspoilt. Bella stretched out her arms and took a deep breath.

'It's so peaceful,' she said.

'Trust me, it wasn't always like that. In the eighties, the state government decided to put in a road to link Cape Tribulation to Bloomfield further to the north, in order to develop the growing tourist trade in the area as well as open up the place to more logging.'

Bella dropped her arms to her side. 'That's terrible. Any development would destroy such beautiful wilderness. What were they thinking?'

Antony shrugged. 'They had big plans but no thought for the environment, so a few locals started to protest peacefully against the venture and the protest grew.' He gestured to the forest. 'People climbed up those huge trees and stayed there, chained themselves to the machinery, buried themselves in the path of the bulldozers, in an effort to stop the road, but the government pushed it through. However in the next wet the hastily built road fell apart.'

Bella burst out laughing. 'Serves the government right. So what happened next?'

'They had another go at building it, but the federal government had the area listed as a World Heritage site and that put an end to further development. The road is still here but it's a mess, and only traversable by four-wheel drive in the dry season.'

They spent an hour looking at the miniature world trapped in the warm rock pools, then walked back to the shore. Bella looked at the solid wall of deep green rainforest sweeping down from the peaks and ending in a fringe of palms. The large, dense bush at the edge of the beach looked like great crinoline skirts brushing the sand.

'Duck under the branches and I'll take your picture,' said Antony, showing Bella some low, flat branches where she could sit under a seven-metre umbrella of foliage. She perched in the hidden room of the green roof and white sand floor as Antony snapped her photo. He handed her back her phone and their hands brushed.

'You're very beautiful. But you know that.' He smiled.

Bella hopped down from the low branch. 'And you're a flirt. But you know that,' she said playfully.

They bought some sandwiches and stopped at a small roadside ice-cream shop where the owner made luscious ice-cream from fresh fruit, and then drove back over the Alexandra Range. They stopped at the popular lookout at the peak and Bella admired the bird's-eye view of the coast.

'I'm ready to escape back to our private hideaway and our tents and campfire now,' sighed Bella. 'Thank you. It's been a glorious day.'

'One last stop,' said Antony. He pulled into a service station and topped up with petrol and then motioned Bella to follow him past the toilet block and into a small thicket well away from the road. As Bella looked puzzled, Antony put his finger to his lips and they walked quietly into the trees. He paused and then pointed.

Bella caught her breath as she saw under the trees a pair of magnificent long-necked birds, about two metres tall, their feathers a glossy black. Their upper necks were bright blue and red at the back of the nape. A loose red wattle dangled from the base of their throats. Each had a bony comb on the top of its head.

'Cassowary. Wow,' whispered Bella, and quietly reached for her phone to take a photo.

They watched the pair for a little while and Bella took some photos, then they left quietly.

'That was special,' said Bella.

'Talk to the girls tonight, they'll tell you everything you do – and don't! – want to know about endangered cassowaries. I do know that it's the male who sits on the eggs and protects the chicks when they hatch. We're not all playboys,' he added.

Bella's mouth twitched into a grin. She climbed into the car as he held open the door with a courtly flourish.

On the way home, as they re-crossed the Daintree River on the car ferry, Bella decided that she should raise the subject of her brother with Antony. After all, he lived and worked in this area, so he may have heard something.

'No, I can't say I've heard of a Ned Chisholm staying around here. He could be holed up in one of the more remote guesthouses, but this is a small community and I think if he were staying around here, I would have seen him about. Tell you what, give me your phone number and if I hear anything, I'll let you know straight away.' He winked at her and she smiled despite herself.

*

The night air of Bella's last evening in the Daintree was soft and warm. The atmosphere in the rainforest was very different at night, for the canopy completely blotted out the sky and it was very dark.

'I thought we might head out for a night walk, see what we can spot,' said Roberta.

Roberta strode into the forest as if it was broad daylight. The others were strung behind her, following the beams of light from their torches, which were partially covered in cloth to diffuse their intensity. No one spoke, and at a signal from Roberta they stopped, switched off the torches and stood listening. There was a slight rustling movement close to them but they remained still. Antony was standing close beside Bella. She could feel his body warmth and smell the now familiar tang of the pepper-mints he chewed.

Roberta switched her torch back on, shining the beam into the lower branches of a nearby tree. A startled black and white striped face with a sharp little nose stopped chewing the fruit which it held in its long claws.

'Striped possum,' whispered Roberta.

'He's cute,' said Bella.

'There's a tree snake,' whispered Annabelle, clicking on her torch and turning its beam onto what appeared to be a yellow and green vine, which began to weave slowly between tree leaves the size of dinner plates.

They watched the snake lazily stretch towards another branch and then they quietly moved on. Bella jumped as she heard a noise like a baby crying.

'Good heavens,' cried Bella in alarm. 'What on earth was that?'

'It's a bird called the spotted catbird, and it's a type of bower bird. Can't mistake its call,' said Annabelle, laughing.

Walking further along the ill-formed path, Roberta showed them strange, faintly luminous plants that opened to catch unwary insects. She told them about medicinal uses of some of the plants.

'Do you think it's true that there could be cures for other diseases, still waiting to be discovered?' asked Bella.

'We'll never know if we don't protect the forest,' said Deidre.

'My family also used grasses and vines to build weatherproof huts. My great-grandfather built a long-house on stilts which was rainproof, and the extended family used it in the wet,' said Roberta.

'Did they live around here?' asked Phil.

'No, further south. They worked in the cane fields until they started their own gardens and began to grow fruit and vegetables.'

'What's north of the Daintree?' asked Graham. 'I can't imagine that the population further north would be very big.'

'You're right, it's not. Years ago there was a major gold rush on the Palmer River and Cooktown was a very wild and busy port, but that's well and truly over, and these days Cooktown is no more than a sleepy little town. Not much goes on there now, although a lot of tourists visit it in the dry season. Maybe you should go there, Bella,' Roberta suggested.

Bella shrugged. 'I can't say it's a place that's ever been on my radar.'

*

Earlier that day, Antony had put a bottle of wine and some beer in a small rock pool, and by the time they returned from the night walk, the drinks were gloriously cool.

'How much longer are you going to continue your work here?' Bella asked Deidre and Annabelle.

'Another three days. Antony is coming with us this time,' replied Deidre.

'Lucky me. These two let me go out with them and showed me where the birds and their nests are, so now I can show off my knowledge to the guests at the Lodge. Let them think that I've stumbled across a nest, when in fact the girls have spied it out for me already,' said Antony cheerfully.

'What about you, Roberta? Will you go out with them?' asked Bella.

'No need. Deidre and Annabelle know what they're doing. I'll take you back to Port Douglas and then go out again with Phil and Graham.'

Later, sitting in the rock pool, her feet propped up on a mossy boulder, Bella lifted her glass in a toast.

'Roberta, thank you for sharing all this. It's been magic. I'll remember it when I'm stuck back in my air-conditioned office.' While she'd meant the comment as a joke, her tone was flat.

'Why go back?' said Antony. 'I left a mundane job in a finance company to come up here and work as a tour guide. A lot more fun. You're in the tourism business, Bella. Why don't you move up here? You'd easily get a job.'

Bella was startled by the suggestion. 'Well . . . it's not quite as simple as you make out. I have responsibilities.

49

I can't just *move*. But I might well come back; it's a truly remarkable place,' she added with a smile.

By nine o'clock, everyone had headed for their tents, except Antony and Bella.

'Feel like a nightcap? There's some wine left,' Antony suggested.

'Why not? Thanks. Wow, what a special treat this has been. Roberta is amazing. I never expected to see all this.'

'She's a great guide. I've learned a lot from her.' He handed Bella a glass of wine.

'Do you do tours like this?' she asked.

'Not quite. The Lodge, where I work, tends to have up-market guests who want to see and experience the Daintree in a degree of comfort. I think you have to grow up with the knowledge that Roberta has. I didn't know much at all when I first came up here, but I know a lot more now. People really like eco-tourism, and this area is unique in the world. It has so many opportunities.'

'I'll have to look into it,' said Bella thoughtfully.

'I know a great guide.' He leaned close to her.

Bella knew he wanted to kiss her, but she straightened up. 'Thanks for the wine. See you in the morning.'

'You should come to the Lodge. Be a shame to miss it.' He gave her his winning smile.

'I'll sleep on it and then see what my boyfriend thinks! G'night, Ant.'

He chuckled quietly. 'You do that, beautiful Bella.'

3

NED WOKE IN THE brightness of a small white room. He felt a hand on his wrist and opened his eyes. Turning his head, he saw a nurse standing by his bed looking at a hospital chart.

'How do you feel?'

'I've felt better. Where am I?' Ned asked.

'Cooktown hospital. You're a bit banged up, but not too bad under the circumstances. You're very lucky on two counts – getting out of a wreck and having Toni find you,' the nurse smiled kindly. 'We found your name in your wallet. Is there anyone we can call, Ned, to let them know where you are?'

'No. Thanks,' Ned muttered. 'Don't want to worry anyone. How long have I been here?'

'Only today. We'll be keeping you under observation

tomorrow as well, so just rest. Do you want to sip some water?'

Ned managed a small nod and the nurse's strong arm lifted his head and put a plastic straw to his lips. He swallowed two mouthfuls and lay back.

'Toni told us you're a musician,' the nurse said, nodding at Ned's guitar case sitting propped up in the corner of the room. Ned smiled to see his old mate safe. 'You might not be able to play for a few days because we've had to put a few stitches in your arm,' the nurse continued, 'but nothing that won't mend. And Toni sorted your car for you. The police have it down at the station, along with the rest of your personal effects. Someone will bring your gear over later and ask you a few questions about what happened. I'll be checking in on you during the day.'

The nurse bustled out of the room and Ned lay in the silence of the white oasis. He had no idea what was outside his door. There was a murmur of voices and the clatter of a trolley. Further away was the noise of passing traffic and what sounded like the throb of a boat engine.

He suddenly felt anxious. He had to find the fellow about the place to stay and get out of here. Gingerly he began stretching his limbs, but found one of his arms tethered to a drip. He shut his eyes in resignation, hoping that when he woke up it would all be over and he could walk away.

Instead, he woke an hour later to find Toni standing by his bed. He smiled to see her.

'Hello there,' she said. 'How do you feel?'

'Hungry.'

'That's a good sign.'

'Thank you for rescuing me. I guess you saved my life and I hear you arranged a tow truck.'

Toni waved a hand. 'No worries. Besides, someone else would have come along and picked you up.'

'Do you know how my ankle is? Will you have to perform professional services on it?' asked Ned, smiling weakly.

Toni looked at the hospital notes.

''Fraid not. It's only sprained, and not very badly at that. If it's well strapped and you don't try to run a marathon too soon, you'll be up and about on it in no time.'

'So I won't be here long?'

'Seems not.'

Ned nodded. 'I need to get sorted. Find this guy who was going to get me settled in his place. Replace my phone and get the car fixed.' He closed his eyes. 'What a bloody mess.'

'I take it that you're going to stay somewhere around here, then? Where'd you come from?' Toni sat down in the chair next to the bed.

'I was in Cairns, did a few gigs along the coast and up on the Atherton Plateau, too. I had an invitation to see a bloke up here about moving into a place he shares while he's away.'

'How long are you planning on staying?'

'Couple of months, maybe.'

'Up to the wet season? That's when sensible people leave town,' said Toni.

'Do you?'

She smiled. 'I have a job. I love it here. Been here a while now.'

He stared at her, really seeing her for the first time. She had an open, friendly face and sun-streaked hair, and she radiated health and fitness. He liked her voice. It was like warm honey.

'Where's home?' he asked.

'Mudgee, in New South Wales. I'm a country gal. You?'

'Snap! I'm from the country, too. Tennyson in Victoria. But I'm mostly playing gigs on the road these days,' he grinned.

'Yes, I know.' She looked a little embarrassed. 'I googled you. Your music is great. How come you've only made one album?'

'I like being independent, going my own way. But that costs money: finding the musicians, the back-up group, paying for studio time, trying to get a distribution deal . . .' He shrugged. 'Damned hard. Really, I just want to make the music. So, with me it's been mostly live gigs, one-man shows, though occasionally I do festivals with a group.'

'I guess that's life on the road.' Toni smoothed her hair. 'So why do you want to hang around up here so long? This is a small, out-of-the-way place, far from anything much. Not a big audience here; you might say that this is the town of last resort for many.'

'So why are you here?' he countered.

She paused only for a split second before breaking into laughter. 'Touché. Locals might feel a bit insulted by my comments, but the north gets to you. I like the sense of freedom, the feeling that the real world is somewhere down south. Besides, I like my job.' Toni laid a hand on Ned's arm. 'Ned, rest some more, and I'll be back this afternoon to check on you.'

At lunchtime, a lanky young policeman entered Ned's room. He dropped Ned's things into one corner and then approached the bed, looking down at Ned with some concern.

'You've given yourself a bit of a battering,' he said sympathetically. 'Bit of luck that Toni found you and brought you in.'

'Yes,' replied Ned. 'One car had already passed me by. I thought I was stuck there for the night.'

'Too bad. People are a bit wary about picking up strangers these days, even when they need help, but if it's any comfort to you, the driver did report in at the station to tell us that they'd seen you.'

That did make Ned feel better. It was good to know that if Toni hadn't found him, the police would have done so, eventually.

'Got the results of your blood test back, too. No alcohol or drugs. Saw the swerving tyre marks at the accident scene – you were trying to avoid the dead cow?'

'And some birds. I wasn't travelling fast, but I hit the gravel on the edge of the road and lost control.'

The policeman nodded. 'Can happen like that. Anyway, I'll make out a report, but it all seems straightforward. I'll have your car moved to the wreckers and they can see if it's salvageable. Good luck, and I hope you're better quickly. They tell me you should be out of here soon.' The policeman smiled and before Ned had a chance to thank him, he was gone.

Later that afternoon, Toni looked in on him again and they chatted easily for a while until Ned felt tired. He slept deeply that night and woke feeling better. Later in the morning Toni took him for a walk along the hospital corridor to test his ankle.

'I still feel a bit wrecked. But it's a relief to be able to move,' said Ned, leaning on her. 'It's good to be unhooked from the drip, too. How soon before I can leave?'

'I should think you'll be discharged tomorrow morning. All that's wrong with you is pretty superficial.'

Ned lifted his bandaged arm. 'How long is this going to be out of action? It won't affect my playing, will it?'

Toni smiled reassuringly. 'Judging from the hospital notes, the wound was quite shallow. It looks far worse than it is. So no, it won't affect your playing the guitar. Do you play any other instruments?' she asked.

'Double bass, violin, piano, and I can play a mean ukulele.'

'Very impressive. And you'll be fine tackling them all quite soon, Ned.'

'Thanks.' He looked at her as she manoeuvred a chair out of his way. She was so capable and kind. 'I feel like I can't thank you enough for rescuing me. I know it's your job and all, but you seem to have gone above and beyond.' He gave a slight smile.

'Well, having brought you in here I do have something of a proprietary interest in you. And, as I've said, you'll be fine. Don't worry. You'll be performing before you know it.'

'Actually, I came here more to do a little composing than perform.'

'Oh. More songs? That sounds terrific.'

'I'm thinking of attempting something a bit more ambitious.'

'Really? Like what?' She raised her eyebrows. He took a step on his ankle and winced. She put her arm around his waist to steady him and their eyes met.

Ned drew a breath. 'Something in-depth, not a song and dance show, but something with a serious sort of theme. Sorry, I'm not articulating it very well. I haven't even thought it all through properly myself. I just know it's what I want to do. I've actually never told anyone this before. I'm not quite sure why I'm telling you. I think it has to do with your proprietary interest in me.'

Toni studied him for a moment. 'That sounds really great. The thing that struck me about your work is that it's not just the music, but the lyrics. They make you think. The music is beguiling, but the story you tell gets inside you.'

They stared at each other, both sensing they had stepped over some previously accepted boundary. This was treading into new territory – the personal.

Ned was the first to look away. 'Ah, everyone in show business dreams of doing something special. Might never happen, or never get performed, even if I do actually write it.' He gave an awkward smile. 'Gotta give it a go, right?'

They continued walking down the corridor, Toni's hand supporting his bandaged arm. 'Yes, you do. You know what they say: you won't know if you don't try. Yes, I think you should really stretch yourself. And this is the place to do it. I found that when you step outside the safe and the familiar, well, things happen. Besides, there's not a lot up here to distract you.' She gave a slightly embarrassed shrug and withdrew her hand. 'Nothing ventured, nothing gained, eh?'

Ned nodded. 'Cliché it may be, I have a nagging idea inside me. Which is why I figured I'd take some time out,' he said. 'I got the offer of a place, and I've got a bit of money saved, so I don't have to worry for a while as long as I don't live the high life, and I can see if I can make my idea work.'

'Well, you won't be doing much else around here,' said Toni with a chuckle. Then she added softly, 'Good luck. Go for it.'

*

The following day, as he stepped out of the air-conditioned hospital into the fresh warm air, moist breeze and brilliant sunshine, Ned felt as though he'd entered another world. He took a deep breath as he eased into a taxi, which drove him to the auto-repair shop to enquire about his bruised and battered car.

'Thought you'd given her up, mate. I was thinking of flogging it,' said the mechanic with a grin.

'Been in hospital. We both got a bit of a hammering.'

'So the police told me. Hit something, did ya?'

'Birds. I swerved to miss them.'

'Cripes, must have been bloody big ones to make you take such evasive action.'

'There were a bunch of them picking at a dead cow. They were humungous. I thought if one came through the windscreen with a seven-foot wingspan and massive talons, I'd be worse off than the car.'

The mechanic stared at him. 'Really? Wedgies?'

'There were wedge-tails, but I think there were other raptors as well.'

The mechanic scratched his chin. 'Could be. I've heard that Brahminy kites and ospreys are hunting in-shore these days. Learned about roadkill. Reckon you were bloody lucky.' The mechanic led Ned to the back of the shop to the crippled remains of his car. 'I've got bad news about your vehicle. It's a complete write-off.'

Ned stared in dismay at the wreck. He shook his head then reached through the window to the glove box and found all his relevant papers. Perhaps not the safest of places to keep them, but being on the road wasn't conducive to order in his life.

'Where're ya headed?' asked the mechanic.

'Thought I'd chill in town for a bit while I sort out this mess.'

'Good place to spend time, Cooktown, but get out before the wet, that's when the place quietens down. You can't travel far then – not even the locals can. You're not looking for work?' Seeing Ned shake his head, the mechanic continued, 'Just as well. Not much around, though we do get the odd backpacker who'll work for less than the locals.'

'What will I do about a replacement for this?' Ned asked, looking sadly at his damaged four-wheel drive.

'You won't get much for this, but I know of a couple of vehicles that might suit you. You'll probably have to pay a bit more than what you get from the insurance. Get back to me in a day or two and I'll let you know. If I can't arrange something from around here, I might have to bring something up from Cairns or from Mareeba.'

The mechanic looked at Ned's crestfallen face.

'Don't worry, mate. We'll have you fixed up in no time. Say, why don't you go and see Yolanda up at the Toppie? She knows what's going on. I can give you a lift up there. Besides, you look as though you need a beer.'

The mechanic pulled over in Charlotte Street and Ned thanked him for his help and climbed out. The mechanic waved as he drove away.

Ned decided he should first sort out his phone. There wasn't much to be done with his old one, so with some reluctance he got a replacement from the post office. The post office worker let him plug it into a wall socket and fifteen minutes later he transferred his SIM card in to it and switched it on. It pinged with missed calls and messages from his mother and sister. He went to reply to one of the messages, but then stopped as he read the contents more carefully. Both Bella and Josie had sent him texts haranguing him about the dedication. He felt annoyance rising in his chest. He'd explained to Josie that he couldn't make it. What did they want from him? His father's face flashed in his mind and he closed his eyes. No, he wasn't dealing with this right now. He deleted the messages without reading them.

Next he called the number of the house he'd been told about, but it rang out with no voicemail. It seemed luck wasn't on his side, so he decided to check out the pub.

Ned crossed the street and stepped into the weatherboard hotel with its broad upstairs verandah. The year 1885 was displayed over the door. *It probably hasn't changed much since then*, he thought. Inside, however, it looked as though it was now a very popular watering hole with tourists. He wandered over to the long bar and put down his guitar case and backpack, then leaned on the counter, propping his sore foot on the brass rail which ran below the bar. The woman behind the bar, who was swishing a beer-stained cloth along the counter, came over to him, and without looking up asked, 'What'llitbe?'

'What have you got?' asked Ned in a reasonable tone.

The woman jerked her head at the question. 'What planet you from, mate?' She gave him a long hard stare, taking in his streaked blond hair and beard stubble, his tanned face, bright blue eyes and lopsided smile. A broad grin broke across her face. 'Hey, I know you! You're that singer I saw in Cairns. Ned . . . ?'

'That's me. Are you Yolanda?'

'Sure am. Are you in town for a show?'

Ned shook his head.

'Didn't think so, or I'd have heard about it. What kinda beer you drink?'

'Better have a XXXX Gold.'

Yolanda began to pour the beer. 'So, if you're not doing a show, what brings you up to this godforsaken place?'

'Chilling out for a while. Recovering from writing off my car.'

'Ah, too bad. A prang, eh? How long you gonna be around?' She pushed a schooner of beer in front of him.

Ned took a sip, and the beer went down very well after the tepid tea and sweet juices in the hospital. 'Not sure. I just want a quiet space where I can work for a while.'

'You write your own songs, don'tcha? That's cool. Doing a new album?'

'Not sure,' said Ned, noncommittally. 'I'm supposed to move into a place my mate's friend's going to lend me.'

'Good time to stay, now. Before the wet. Some people go stir crazy at the rain, storms and not being able to drive 'cause the roads get flooded. So who's this bloke?'

'Normie Brown. Everyone calls him Hashie. As in hash browns, I guess. Works in the music business.'

Yolanda nodded. 'Hashie? Yeah, I know him. Bit of a pothead. I thought that was how he got his name.' Yolanda looked thoughtful as she yanked out the cloth she'd tucked into her apron pocket and wiped it along the damp counter again. 'Heard he was moving on for a couple of months. But geez, I don't know that you'd want to move into his joint. A flophouse, if you ask me. Still, you musos are all into sex and drugs and rock and roll, aren't you?'

'Some are,' Ned replied. 'Well, my friend painted an interesting picture of this area and I thought I'd like to spend a bit of time here. I tried calling, but the phone rang out.'

'Well, let me give you the directions to Hashie's place. Come back to me if it doesn't work out. The house is on the hill, you can't miss it.' She scribbled out some directions on a coaster and handed it to him. 'It's an old Queenslander with a lurid pink verandah.'

'Yes, Hashie said it was very pink.'

'Someone's not-very-smart idea, as far as I'm concerned,' said Yolanda wryly. 'But if you like, I might be able to put you on to another place. It's low-key, peaceful like. Pretty remote, but it might suit. See how you go.' She moved down the counter to serve some of the other customers. Ned finished his beer before heading out into the glaring light.

It took only a short time for a taxi to get him to the house on the hill, which was exactly as Yolanda had described. He looked at it in dismay. It was very run-down, and there was an old lounge chair sitting in the middle of the overgrown garden.

'You going in here?' asked the driver dubiously.

'I'm supposed to be staying here. I'll go and see if someone's around, but I think you'd better wait for a couple of minutes, if you don't mind.'

Leaving his guitar and backpack in the taxi, Ned knocked on the front door of the house. He could hear music playing very loudly in the background. He knocked again and eventually the door was opened by a man who looked to be in his twenties and very spaced out.

'Yeah?' he mumbled.

'I'm Ned. Hashie said I could stay here while he was away.'

'You want his room? It's out the back. You'll like it here, man. Lotsa music and anything you want, if you know what I mean.'

Ned knew straight away what he meant. This was not what he had envisioned. There was no way he could stay in this place and be productive.

'Thanks, but I think I've made a mistake,' he told the man, and walked back to the taxi as fast as his sprained foot would let him. The taxi driver nodded sympathetically.

'That place has a pretty unsavoury reputation. Can I take you somewhere else?'

Ned decided that the best thing to do was to book into a motel, at least for a couple of nights, while he waited for a replacement car and for his stitches to heal. The taxi driver took him to a clean and attractive place in the middle of town. When Ned found out how much it was a night, he knew it was not at all suitable for a long-term stay, especially as he was going to have to put money into another car. Quickly he googled the pub and called its number, thinking he could ask Yolanda about the alternative accommodation she'd mentioned, but he got an answering machine. He left a message asking her to call him back. Having no other option right then, he booked in for the night and was shown to his room. He tooled around on the internet for twenty minutes looking at various accommodation websites but the prices all seemed about the same. Feeling despondent, he decided to go for a walk to clear his head and try to figure out what to do next.

He set off to walk up Grassy Hill, which overlooked the township. He hadn't gone very far when he realised his mistake. His foot was not ready for even moderate exercise. He tripped and stumbled, losing his balance. He swore as he felt a stab of pain in his ankle. Just then an enormous four-wheel drive pulled up beside him.

'You okay there, mate?' The driver was a large man who looked to be in his late-seventies, wearing a faded Hawaiian shirt. Beside him sat a bird-like woman, tiny and wearing a bright, loose-fitting dress, who peered at Ned with concern.

Ned clambered back to his feet and dusted himself off. 'I'm all right. I did my ankle the other day and it's still healing.'

'Want a lift to the top, then?' asked the man with a friendly grin. 'I'm Ron and this is Mavis, the wife.'

'Thanks,' said Ned, climbing into the car. 'I think I was being a bit ambitious trying to get up even this small hill.'

'No worries,' said Ron. 'How long have you been in Cooktown? We've only been here a couple of days. On the way to Bamaga, but we thought we'd like to do a detour to Cooktown first.'

'Bamaga's on the tip of Cape York, isn't it?' said Ned. 'Long way to go yet.'

'Only about nine hundred kays, but you have to do it before the wet, otherwise you can get caught by flooded roads. Still, we have plenty of time to get there and back before then.'

'We weren't sure about Cooktown, because it's not on the way to anywhere. Quite isolated, sitting out here on the coast, but I think we made the right decision to take a look. It seems a quaint place. Different from the glitzy towns further south,' Mavis piped up.

Reaching the top of the hill, Ron slowed the car to a halt. He and Mavis got out and snapped a few photos. Ned stayed in the car rubbing his ankle. He gazed at the view spread below – the scattered houses, short streets and old buildings along the seafront, none of which testified to recent development or progress. Further along the waterfront, fishing trawlers huddled at a wharf beyond them, past the mouth of the Endeavour River with its tidal flats. Further out, luxury cruisers lay at anchor, while lone sailors, tourist fishing craft and diving boats plied the clear reef waters and small tenders made their way up the river to the main Cooktown wharf.

'We're going on to the museum,' said Ron as he drove the behemoth of a four-wheel drive back down the hill. 'Can we drop you there?'

With nothing to do but kill time until he heard from Yolanda, Ned thanked the couple and it was only a matter of minutes before they pulled up at the corner of Helen Street, where an imposing, solid, colonial brick building rose amidst old trees and tangled gardens. A sign announced it as the James Cook Museum. Several other cars and a tourist minibus were parked out the front, and some of the tourists were posing for photos on the steps that led to its main entrance beneath a wide verandah.

With help from Ron, he gingerly climbed the front steps into the museum. Opposite the front doors was a grand staircase leading to the upper floor. Near the staircase was a gift shop and information desk, while to his right was a display room. Ned could see a sign indicating the way to the James Cook Discovery Room.

In the cool high-ceilinged interior it appeared that little had changed since the building's original construction, and Ned was suddenly enveloped in a strangely nostalgic embrace. The contemporary fixtures seemed irrelevant, and he felt that if he closed his eyes he'd see the place as it had been in 1887, the year it opened. The atmosphere was redolent of other lives, friendly ghosts, stories and the music of the past, and he felt drawn to explore the place.

He paid the entrance fee and farewelled Ron and Mavis, who seemed more interested in the gift shop than the museum, and Ned made his way to the display dedicated to James Cook.

Printed placards explained to visitors that in June 1770, as Captain Cook was exploring the east coast of Australia, his barque *Endeavour* had run aground on a nearby reef. The vessel had limped into the river, which Cook had named the Endeavour River, and he and his crew stayed beside it for several weeks while the damaged ship was repaired. This enforced stay in the area gave Cook the honour of leading the first European settlement on the Australian east coast, albeit a brief one. In pride of place in the centre of the museum sat a cannon and a massive anchor. These artefacts had been rediscovered in the mud off the Cooktown coast more than two hundred years after they had been left behind when the *Endeavour* had been refloated.

Ned thought the exhibition was interesting, but he decided not to stay long. He hadn't heard back from Yolanda and he wanted to try to sort out his accommodation as soon as he could. He headed back to the pub via taxi.

Yolanda pulled him a schooner as soon as she saw him walk into the bar. 'I was just about to return your call. You didn't like Hashie's house?' She pushed the beer towards him as he eased himself onto a stool.

Ned grimaced. 'I took one look and declined the offer. I could never work in the chaos that seems to pervade the place.'

'I'm not surprised.'

Ned sipped the icy beer. 'You mentioned something about another place. Peaceful, you said.'

Yolanda nodded. 'Let me serve those blokes and I'll be right back.'

She returned a few minutes later and leaned on the counter, tucking a damp strand of hair behind her ear. 'So, you reckon you want to stick it out here for a while?'

Ned nodded. 'Yes. I do.'

'This place isn't for everyone.'

'Cooktown, or the house you have in mind?'

She gave a bit of a smile. 'The house, though I guess you might not call it a house; it's more of an interesting dwelling. It's perfectly comfortable, just a bit unusual.'

Ned was intrigued. 'Whose place is it?'

'Belongs to a mate of mine, Carlo,' Yolanda explained. 'He built it about fifteen years ago. His parents came out from Italy and helped him with it. They liked Australia so much that they decided to stay, so they bought a place in Cairns, but they go back to Italy every year or so. Around this time every year, Carlo goes to Austria, but there's some family reunion happening in Italy so he's joining his parents and leaving earlier than usual this year.'

'Carlo goes to Austria every year?' said Ned in an incredulous voice. 'That's a bit of a change from Cooktown.'

'Yeah, his girlfriend is a ski instructor and that's where she makes her money.'

'So he visits his girlfriend each year in Austria?'

'Oh no, Lena lives here with Carlo for most of the year. They go back to Austria together. Do you want me to ask him if you can stay at his place for a few weeks?'

'Sure. Is his place in town?'

Yolanda laughed. 'Hell, no! It's outta town. Him and Lena are gold prospectors – well, fossickers really, if you get my drift. You'd never find the place. It's really hidden. His folks have a caravan on the site for when they visit, but God knows how they got it in there. Have you got somewhere you can stay tonight?'

'I've booked into a motel, but it's a bit pricey.'

'Okay, well, when you're ready, I'd say the best thing for you to do is to go out to the Golden Mile Roadhouse. They have accommodation, basic but clean, and you can wait there till Carlo comes in from the bush. He calls in to the roadhouse before he comes to town. It'll be cheaper if you stay there than in town, and the owners, Frederick and Theresa, are great people. At a pinch they can guide you to Carlo's place. It's very isolated.'

'When I'm into my music, isolation and time don't seem to matter. It sounds just what I want, but will Carlo want me out there?'

'You'll be fine. Carlo can check you out, but I reckon he'll be pleased he can do you a favour, and you him, by keeping an eye on things. Carlo's place is pretty special, and if you don't mind being seriously remote, it might be just the ticket.'

'A fossicker's campsite sounds pretty basic.'

Yolanda smiled. 'Wait and see. It's a bit better than that. You got a four-wheel drive? It's rugged country.'

'I will have in a day or two, I hope.'

'Haven't seen Carlo for a bit, so he must be due to pop up soon. Can't ring him, of course. No reception out in the backblocks where he lives.'

'It all sounds a bit unusual. Tell me, would you live out there in such a remote place?'

Yolanda flung up her arms. 'Not on my own! I'd go stir-crazy after a week. But it suits Carlo and it might suit you. You should know, though, that if you stay out there through the wet you'll be stuck because the roads become impassable and the river comes up. Do you know much about machinery? Are you good with running things like generators?'

'Um. Sort of,' Ned said dubiously. 'I'd need to stock up on supplies, might need some guidance there.'

'Ah, if this idea works out, Carlo will help you with that stuff. I haven't been out there for a couple of years, but it's a pretty interesting set-up.'

'So what does Carlo do apart from fossick a bit, or is he retired?'

'Lord no, he's not even fifty. But I reckon he gets enough gold out there to give him a good lifestyle, though he doesn't advertise it. Likes to fly under the radar. Never talks about what he does and never about what he finds. He plays his cards close to his chest.'

'You make it sound pretty intriguing. If he doesn't mind me out there for a few weeks, I'll give it a go.'

'Yeah. Well, as I said, my advice is to go out to the roadhouse and wait there for Carlo to turn up. Tell Theresa and Frederick I sent ya.'

'Thanks, Yolanda. I have to stay in town until I've got wheels and my stitches out, then I'll do just that.'

She shrugged. 'Then you'd better give me your phone number, in case Carlo turns up here while you're still about. I'll give you a call.'

*

Ned had to wait in Cooktown for another vehicle before he could make his way to the Golden Mile Roadhouse. By the next day, his ankle had improved rapidly, so he was able to get out and about. After walking along the water-front, he treated himself to a seafood lunch, fresh from a trawler that was tied up out the front of the restaurant. He walked slowly through Bicentennial Park and chatted to a couple of Aboriginal boys kicking a football, and over the headland he found the grounds of the Botanical

Gardens, a cool and quiet oasis, if a little neglected. There he found a building called Nature's Powerhouse, where he was able to buy a cup of coffee. The building also had a small gallery dedicated to the delicate watercolours of Vera Scarth-Johnson. Here Ned learned she was an English naturalist and conservationist and an extraordinary botanical illustrator. She had dedicated the latter part of her life to painting the plants of the Endeavour River valley, and her illustrations, which were recognised for their national significance, were given to the people of Cooktown in 1990, some years before her death.

Ned studied the beautiful representations of the region's extraordinary flowers and plants and imagined this intrepid artist exploring the untamed wilderness in search of specimens. He was not surprised to learn, in the caption below a photograph of her that was mounted on the wall, that she had been inspired by the work of Joseph Banks and Daniel Solander, the two scientists who had been travelling with Captain Cook. While the repairs to the *Endeavour* had been taking place, Banks and Solander had explored the area and taken many samples of flora and fauna back to England. Ned bought a series of small prints, thinking he'd give them to his mother when he had a chance, as he knew she would appreciate them.

Late in the afternoon, he sat on the upper balcony of his motel with an apple and a bottle of water. He'd stopped in again at the museum on his way back to the hotel and was now enjoying the view of the town and the sea, and thinking about the variety of artefacts this unusually fine regional museum had on display. The exhibits were impressive, from Indigenous bark canoes to a fine bone china English Minton dinner service, as well as family mementos, clothes, photos, letters, sailing equipment, maps, various Aboriginal artefacts, some geological specimens and a lot of dusty and rusty implements and tools that had been used on the goldfields. He was amazed by the vast collection of Chinese porcelain and cookware the museum housed, and there was also a reconstructed opium den, complete with smoking accoutrements, as well as a joss house.

He had climbed the beautiful staircase, and as he'd stood in the shadows of the landing and the rooms beyond, cluttered with memorabilia and displays, Ned had been drawn to the end of the hallway. In a corner was an ancient piano. A small framed printed notice had told him its story, which had piqued his interest.

The piano had been made in Paris in 1878, and its connection with Cooktown began a few years later when a ship was wrecked off the coast. Amongst the jetsam was the piano, which was salvaged by a bullock driver. The bullocky left it in a freshwater stream to clean it of salt and there it sat for several years, until he heard that Mrs Boyd, the wife of the butcher in Coen, some four hundred kilometres to the north, might be interested in buying it. So the bullocky took the piano north and offered it for sale for twenty-five pounds. The offer was accepted and Mrs Boyd had it restored, having new strings, ivory keys and felt sent up from Sydney. Within three months it was in perfect working order and was used for the first dance to be held in Coen.

Eventually the Boyds sold up and the piano was purchased by a family from Laura, some two hundred and fifty kilometres south and closer to Cooktown. Later it had been bought by two nurses, who took the piano to Cooktown. After they both left the town, the piano once again returned to the Boyd household, and later the family donated it to the museum.

What a charming story, Ned had thought. How much pleasure that instrument must have given the pioneers of the far north. *And how long since those yellowed keys had been touched?* he wondered. Maybe the young pupils at the convent school had practised playing on the faithful old instrument. Maybe the strings had rotted and the old piano had been silenced, but in that moment, Ned could hear music: hymns, children's songs, and a haunting tune that needed the accompaniment of cymbals and bells and old Chinese instruments. He had stood, transfixed, as he imagined the music of another era dancing through the ether and into his head.

Finishing his apple, Ned decided that he needed to do more than daydream. It was time to thank Toni properly for rescuing him, so he made his way back to the hospital and asked at Admissions if it would be possible to see her. About five minutes later, Toni came down the corridor with a smile on her face.

'Hi, Ned, what can I do for you? It doesn't look as though your ankle is giving you much trouble.'

'No, it's not. Actually, it's mended very quickly. The reason I'm here is to ask if I can take you to dinner tonight to thank you for rescuing me. I really haven't had the chance to do that properly.'

Toni smiled broadly. 'You don't have to do that, Ned, but I'm delighted to accept. Where did you have in mind?'

*

That evening they met at the seafood restaurant that had earlier impressed Ned.

'It's nice here. I love that the seafood is literally straight off the boat,' he commented, glancing around the bustling restaurant.

'Yes, I always enjoy this place. Most locals do,' replied Toni as they settled themselves at a table overlooking the river. 'So what have you been up to?'

Ned filled her in on the past few days he'd spent in

71

Cooktown. Toni laughed easily and Ned found himself relaxing in her company.

'Seems you've met a fair few of the locals!' she said when he told her about Carlo's house. 'I can't say that I know Carlo well, but I do know Yolanda and Frederick and Theresa at the roadhouse and they're good people, so I'd trust their judgement. If they think it's all right for you to stay there, then it is. How's the car situation?'

'Not the best. The car's a write-off but the mechanic at the local wreckers assures me that he can lay his hands on another four-wheel drive in reasonable shape. I'm just waiting for his call. That, and having my stitches out, are the reasons I'm still in town, but it's all for the best because it gives me the chance to thank you properly.' He smiled at her and she grinned back.

'I feel very thanked,' she said, holding his gaze.

They both enjoyed their meal of fresh prawns, oysters and mangos as they chatted about their careers and impressions of Cooktown.

Toni lifted her glass of verdelho to toast Ned. 'Here's to your interesting move. I hope it works out for you. I'm sure you'll be back in town soon enough. For supplies, I mean.'

'I certainly will let you know when I am.' He touched his glass against hers. 'Thank you again for everything.'

As Ned paid the restaurant bill, Toni said, 'Why don't you let me drive you back to your motel? I've got wheels and it's on my way.'

When they arrived, Toni turned off the engine and unbuckled her seatbelt. She turned and smiled softly at Ned. He leaned over and kissed her gently.

'Do you want to come in for a coffee?' Ned asked, tucking a strand of her hair behind her ear.

'Sounds good,' said Toni. They kissed again, got out of the car and went inside.

*

Toni left early the next morning, as she had to go back to her own place to get ready for her shift. She said goodbye to Ned with a lingering kiss. As Ned finished his first coffee for the day, he kept thinking about her and the lovely night they had spent together. He would make sure he found a chance to see her again. Just as he was draining his coffee, he got a call from the mechanic saying he had a four-wheel drive for Ned, if he wanted to come and have a look. Ned made his way over to the repair shop and met the mechanic outside.

'Here she is,' he announced. 'What do you think?'

The vehicle looked in better condition than the one he had wrecked, and when he took it for a drive, he was quite pleased by how it handled.

'How much does your mate want for this?' he asked the mechanic.

Ned tried not to smile too much when he was told the figure, and quickly made arrangements for the transfer of ownership.

'Thanks for all you've done,' he said to the mechanic.

'No worries, my mate will be pleased. You leaving town?'

'Only for a while. I'll be back sometime and I'll shout you a drink at the Toppie.'

'Thanks, you're on. And be careful of those big birds,' replied the mechanic with a smile.

Ned felt relieved to have wheels again. He drove back to his hotel, gathered his gear and checked out. Then he headed to the hospital and had his stitches out. It took a little time but the doctor was satisfied that he'd healed well. Back on the road, Ned drove south, following the directions the receptionist at the hospital Admissions desk had given him to the Golden Mile Roadhouse. He drove cautiously, the memory of his accident still very fresh.

He was pleased when he saw the sign for the road-house. As he pulled into the large parking lot he spotted several trucks and a road train refuelling. Tables and benches were set up outside the rustic log cabin building, which bore a sign, *The Golden Mile*, and a painting of a gold nugget over the door.

Inside the roadhouse it was cool and spacious, although dimly lit and filled with long wooden tables. There was a pool table where a couple of truckies were enjoying a game while they ate their hamburgers. In a corner was a display showing a variety of objects, which included some old bottles, broken ceramics, a few battered hats and several very worn boots. Faded, fly-spotted photos and old news-paper cuttings revealed a potted history of some historical events, as well as stories about local characters and fortunes made and lost. Ned went to the counter and looked at the menu before ordering a steak sandwich and a coffee. He checked his phone and saw he only had one bar of reception which quickly petered out to none. Phone coverage was worse than he'd expected around these parts but then, he reminded himself, that was the whole point of coming out here: to find some quiet. The friendly dark-haired woman who took his order asked him which way he was headed.

'I don't know. I'm Ned. Are you Theresa?'

'I sure am!' She reached over and shook his hand. 'We hear you had a bit of a prang. How're you doing?'

'Getting there, thanks. I'm a lot better than I was a few days ago.'

'Sit down, and when I have a break I'll come and chat. Frederick is out the back in the machinery shed. He'll be here shortly. Sure you don't want a cold beer?'

'No, thanks. A coffee will be great.' He eyed the Italian espresso machine. 'That looks very civilised.'

'Some things in life are non-negotiable, and that includes good coffee,' she said with a grin.

Ned had just taken his coffee over to one of the tables when a tall, solid man with a ruddy face and friendly smile came over. He pulled off his hat and held out a hand. 'Frederick. I take it that Yolanda suggested you might like a break from civilisation for a while.'

Ned rose and held out his hand. 'Good to meet you. Yes, she suggested that I come out here to meet Carlo and see if I might be a suitable resident for his place for a few weeks. I know very little about Carlo's place . . . other than it sounds like a peaceful location where I could chill out and do some work without interruption. Yolanda said I could meet Carlo here,' Ned said.

'Yeah, well, the thing is, Carlo and Lena have already left. I've been going over to their place every few days to check on things. So if you want to stay out there for a bit, it would suit us. Do us a favour, in fact, save us the extra trips.'

'Are you sure that Carlo won't mind a stranger just turning up and making himself at home?'

'No, Carlo won't mind. He's pretty easygoing, just so long as you keep an eye on things, he'll be sweet. Anyway, Yolanda seems to think you'll be okay. And you don't need to worry about the supplies you'll need for your stay. We'll work things out.'

'What sort of amenities does Carlo have out there? Does the generator run things?'

'Yes, but only at night. Rest of the time it's all solar. Only problem is that there is no phone reception for your mobile. Carlo uses a satellite phone, but it's been sent down south for repairs. Don't know when it will get back, so when I say it's all quiet out there, that's exactly right.'

'Well, that does sound like what I'm after,' said Ned with a smile.

'Ah, you'll have a neighbour a couple of miles away, but he keeps to himself. Carlo is on a mining lease and the joint is surrounded by mining and grazing leases, and of course there's Maytown, that's on a heritage reserve section.'

'Maytown?'

'The original town out there. More than a hundred years ago it was a bloody big place. Not much left now.' Frederick scratched his chin. 'Still, it's a bit of a tourist attraction for those keen enough to push out to see it. Shit road, and not much to see except bits of rusty mining equipment surrounded by the bush, really. Hard to believe the tons of gold that came out of the place.'

'All of it gone now?'

'For sure. But there's gold around if you know where to look,' he added with a grin. 'Just ask Carlo.'

Theresa hurried over to join them. 'Sorry, had a big group come in all at once. So, do you want to stay here the night or head on over to Carlo's?'

Frederick looked at his watch. 'The day is getting on and it'll be dark before I can get back here. Don't fancy driving that track at night unless I have to. Tell you what, I could take you out there now and spend the night. In the morning, I could show you the ropes.'

'I hate to put you to any trouble,' said Ned.

'Carlo is a mate, and like I said, you'll be doing us all a favour,' said Frederick with a big grin.

'I'll put together some basic supplies to hold you for a week or so, then you can decide what you want,' offered Theresa. 'I can help you put a list together and what I don't have, well, you'll have to go to Cooktown for that, or go without. By the way, Frederick, have you been watering Lena's garden?'

'Yeah. Her herbs and stuff seem okay.'

'You like to cook? Well, that's a silly question. There won't be anyone else to do it!' Theresa said, laughing, before Ned could muster a reply. 'Well, I'll go and pack up some groceries for you. Frederick will drive you over, show you what's what. You can barbecue a couple of steaks for dinner tonight. Sound okay?' She stood, not expecting any argument.

Frederick gave a small shrug. 'The boss has spoken. Okay with you?'

Ned had found all these swift arrangements very confusing, but he suspected that it was just the way things were done out here. Besides, one could hardly sniff at a few weeks' free accommodation in a tranquil setting. It was just what he wanted in order to explore his musical ideas without any interruptions.

'I really appreciate this, but I don't want to be any trouble,' said Ned. 'I'm very grateful to you both and to Carlo, even though he has no idea that I'm about to move into his place.'

'I'll send him an email saying we gave you a big tick,' said Theresa.

Later that afternoon, Ned had no trouble following the dust cloud kicked up by Frederick's old truck as he drove along a dusty road surrounded by dry, lightly forested savannah country.

This had been gold country, a place where fortunes had been found and probably lost, but it was hardly hospitable. Men had traversed these hills and gullies in terrible conditions, according the information at the museum, many pushing all they owned in a wheelbarrow from one goldfield to another. Gold fever, Ned supposed, that potent mix of excitement and greed that drove men to dig into the earth, hoping to make their fortunes. But the days of these goldfields, smothered in a patchwork of leases where men worked cheek by jowl, were long, long gone. Now, Ned knew, this scrubby country was good for cattle but not much else. Damned hot most of the year, and awash with surging creeks and rivers in the wet.

He saw that Frederick had pulled over and he drew up behind him. They were stopped on a rise and Ned was glad to stretch his legs. Frederick was checking under the bonnet of his truck. He walked over to him.

'A problem?'

'Bit of an unwanted rattle. Thought I'd better check it. These rough roads play havoc with vehicles.'

'Road? More of a track,' said Ned.

'Ah, this will seem as smooth as silk once we cut cross country to Carlo's. I won't be long.'

Ned stretched as the sun warmed him and a hint of feathered wind brushed against his cheek. The sweet tang of a eucalypt in blossom hung in the air. A bird call rang out. A line from Dorothea Mackellar's famous poem came to him:

An opal-hearted country,
A wilful, lavish land –
All you who have not loved her,
You will not understand –

Looking around him, Ned sensed freedom, an honest, friendly, safe silence, a blank canvas for one to write their future on and a quietude that calmed the spirit. Lonely, rugged, tough, yes, but somehow embracing. He felt reassured he was doing the right thing.

Frederick straightened up and called over to Ned, 'Let's push on. A beer is going to be good come sunset.'

Shortly afterwards, Frederick veered to the left, seemingly into the underbrush, but as Ned slowed behind him he saw the wheel ruts in the grass and realised they were following a track. He wondered how he'd ever find the turn-off again in daylight, let alone in darkness. With no phone reception out this way, he hoped he wouldn't get into any trouble.

The track wound up a rise, and at the top, where there were no trees, Ned caught his breath. The hillside sloped down to a lake surrounded by palms and dotted with water lilies. Hundreds of birds were gliding over its surface. *What a wonderful place*, he thought, gazing at the grassy verge surrounding the lake.

The vehicles bumped through the grass and over some scattered rocks, passing a tree which had the bleached skull of a cow tacked to its trunk. As he passed, Ned thought he saw a separate track branching downhill from the tree with its skeletal marker, and wondered where it led. He was disoriented, having lost all sense of direction and not sure if he'd ever find his way out again.

The trees were now smaller and spindly and grew closer together. Large boulders erupted like volcanic hiccups between them. Suddenly Ned caught a glint of water glistening in the sunlight and realised they were heading towards a river, but he couldn't get a better look because he had to focus on his driving as they zigzagged downhill. Then, ahead of him, there was an explosion of colour that made him catch his breath. Huge trees he'd expect to see in a street or park or old-fashioned garden were thriving – the lush green foliage of mango trees, laden with their exotic fruit, tropical wattle and, in full bloom, the rich red and orange sprays of poinciana trees. In the middle of them were two massive boulders, each the size of a shed, and between them hung a huge wooden gate.

They'd arrived.

4

NED STOOD STARING AROUND him at this unexpected oasis in the sparse, hot Australian bush. The tropical trees and the unusual carved wooden gate marked the entrance to a private world. Frederick picked up his small backpack and called to him.

'Come on, I've got the key and I'll let us in, then I'll run through the way this place works: the generator, if you need it, and the solar control panel, water system, and all the other fandangles Carlo and his dad have set up.'

Ned stopped in amazement as he stepped through the gate. 'What is this place?' he asked.

Frederick paused and looked over his shoulder at Ned. 'Ah, I guess it's a bit of a surprise when you come in the first time,' he said with a grin.

Once inside the gate, Ned was immediately struck by the maze of narrow canals set out in a geometric design and flowing down the garden in cascading steps. All were covered with a smattering of water lilies and papyrus. There were wooden paths surrounded by clusters of palm trees, and large urns planted with bougainvillea stood between the canals and the main building, which was made of corrugated iron and painted in a muted lavender colour. The overhang of its roof sheltered and shaded the walls and formed a verandah which was propped up by rough-hewn wooden poles covered in a climbing shrub. There was no verandah floor, just pounded earth dusted in smooth sand, with large river stones clustered in deliberate piles along its length for decoration. Orchids in pots dangled from the roof.

'This is unreal,' exclaimed Ned.

'The water feature? It's actually Carlo's flood mitigation plan.'

'So it doesn't flood up here?'

'Well, the bottom of the garden does, but the water's never made it into the house. Anyway, as they say, you ain't seen nothin' yet. Have a gander at the rest of the joint.'

As Ned walked around, he realised that it was the most unusual place he had ever seen. It really wasn't even a house, just a huge space. The rooms were all open plan and airy, as the windows had no glass but simply drop-down shutters. There was a complete absence of doors. The pounded-dirt floor was covered in loose woven grass mats. The walls were lined with wooden slabs or narrow bands of weathered bamboo, stacked on top of each other like bricks, although in some places they were made of unlined iron. Hanging throughout were paintings of local scenes, Aboriginal art, and several Italian religious pieces which had been painted directly onto the wooden walls. There were also framed prints and posters, mainly of Italy and Austria, and hung high up near the ceiling was a collection of tools, old bottles, broken Chinese ceramics and other objects Ned couldn't identify but suspected had been unearthed while Carlo was fossicking for gold in the old diggings.

The furniture was basic but some pieces, like a large lounge and several chairs, were obviously hand-made using weathered wooden branches and were padded with colourful cushions.

In a daze, Ned followed Frederick through a huge space which was clearly made for entertaining, with its billiard table and giant plasma TV which he assumed was hooked up to a satellite dish, as well as a bar that was made from a cut-down water tank. The walls were covered with framed beer posters, an Italian mirror and on the shelves behind the bar were stacked all manner of liqueurs and wine bottles. The stools at the bar looked as though they were made from old steering wheels and covered with leather cushions.

'Carlo and his father make their own grappa. It's good but it's lethal,' explained Frederick.

And in the corner of the bar area stood a drum kit, a keyboard and a pair of speakers.

When Frederick saw Ned's incredulous expression he said, 'I told you, they like to throw parties. Make as much noise as you want out here. No nearby neighbours to complain,' he added.

Rounding the bar, Ned could see a long wooden dining table as well as a gas stove and cupboards and shelves stacked with non-perishable food like dry pasta and tins of beans, tomatoes and beetroot. Baskets on the floor had probably held potatoes and onions, although they were empty now, and there was a large refrigerator and freezer against one wall. It all looked very informal and somewhat temporary, as though the inhabitants had only partially moved in.

'There's a cold room up the back where you can stack stuff if you want to do a big shop,' said Frederick. 'The bedrooms are also at the back, but up on the next level. Out that side is the shower and loo and laundry,' he added, pointing in a rather vague way. 'But this is the *pièce de résistance*. Have a look at this.'

Frederick took Ned past the kitchen and showed him what he meant, and for once Ned was speechless. On the terrace straight below them and facing the sweep of the shallow river, which curved in a loop around the property, was a swathe of ground that had been set up as another entertaining area. At the water's edge were mature poinciana trees, another flowering tree he didn't recognise, as well as some wattle trees. In their shade, hand-hewn furniture – a long table and assorted chairs – sat invitingly. To one side was a large shallow metal fire pit which Ned guessed was beaten from some piece of farm equipment. Around the fire pit was a circle of beautiful river stones forming a large ring of seats. Paths and a small lower terrace were made from slabs of stone with a few inserted segments that looked like marble, all beautifully pieced together.

'What workmanship,' said Ned. And looking at the river, with its small island in the middle and the thick bush that rose on the other side, he added, 'This setting, it's gobsmacking. Can you swim in the river?'

'Yeah, no crocs here, but it's very shallow. Did you notice the big lake with all the water lilies when we drove in? That was the water supply for a goldmine that was operating up to the 1980s, until the gold ran out. Anyway, I reckon that this bit of the river grew out of the old gold days a hundred years ago as a result of the gullies the miners dug looking for the alluvial stuff. Carlo says you can get some good fish here every so often. Should be some fishing tackle lying about somewhere if you want to give it a try.'

Ned was trying to take in this amazing property. He walked over to a massive barbecue that stood on the large terrace. It was also made of intricate stonework and had a tall chimney as well as an extended brick table on either side. 'Is there an oven in here as well?' said Ned as he opened the metal door next to the wood storage section.

'Yeah, they use it as a bread oven and to make slow stews and stuff. They're mad on the cooking. Here, take a look at this,' said Frederick as they walked up to one of the higher levels. Ned's eyes followed to where his companion was pointing and he nearly did a double take. Like a massive stone shrine, a tower made of ascending tiers of bricks rose to a single point. At the end of each tier was a large antique bottle cemented in place, and on the very top was an old iron bell, making the structure look like a giant birthday cake, or an idiosyncratic Christmas tree. He walked over to admire the brickwork and saw the fitted metal door.

'Holy cow! It's a pizza oven.' He burst out laughing.

'What else!' said Frederick. 'They're Italian, remember. C'mon, I'll give you the lowdown on all the equipment Carlo has, so you can keep this place running.'

By nightfall Ned's head was buzzing. He'd resorted to making notes about the jobs that had to be done. On an upper terrace behind the house was a long vegetable and herb bed surrounded by a low mesh fence. Half a dozen chickens were housed in a long run nearby, complete with automatic water and grain feeders.

'You can let them out during the day for a bit, but lock them up before dark,' said Frederick. 'Might come to grief with the feral cats that wander about here at night. And see that building up the hill a bit further? That's the storage shed, cool room and workshop. Over there is a sort of hot tub.' He pointed to a small pool set in more stonework connected to a water tank. 'Water's heated by solar power and when you've finished, you can let the water out of the tub and it runs through the trees and into the river. But there are good showers in the bathroom area I pointed out to you before. All solar, of course. Carlo's planning to install lithium batteries that store the solar power so that you're right for hot water and power all the time, but he hasn't done it yet, so that's why you still need to use the generator. Clever bloke, Carlo, thinks of everything.'

'What's that up there?' Ned peered up the slope to where he could see a building on stilts amongst the trees.

'That's where Carlo's parents keep their caravan, because they like to have their own place when they visit. Carlo and his father rigged up a proper cover for it, so that it's always shady.'

Ned peered back at the river. 'How far up does the river come in the wet?'

Frederick rubbed his chin. 'Covers all the outdoor area, but the living area has been built high enough up to stay dry. That's why they built all those terraces, to protect the place.'

Ned shook his head in wonderment. 'Absolutely incredible. Carlo has used some amazing technology in this place. I can't believe that someone who is obviously as clever as Carlo would tuck himself away in such an isolated and remote place, fossicking for gold.'

'Carlo's no dope, and he does pretty well at fossicking. If you're persistent, have some geological know-how, high-tech metal detectors and a bit of local knowledge, well . . . I know that some pretty decent nuggets have been found around here. In Carlo's case, he finds more than enough to finance an annual trip to Europe and to have a bit of cash that the taxman doesn't know about.'

'But not just anyone can come in and dig around, right?' asked Ned.

'Right,' agreed Frederick. 'Leases, both grazing and mining, get a bit complicated in this part of the world, so you have to have the right pieces of paper. Anyway, if you reckon you're across things, we could crack open a beer. We've got those steaks Theresa threw in the cooler, so we could crank up that barbecue.'

'Sounds terrific.'

By the time they'd finished their first can of beer, they had a fire burning brightly in the barbecue. Frederick had turned on the string of coloured lights that hung between the trees on the lower terrace and put a match to the flame torches that were set up along the river bank to keep the mosquitoes away. They both settled into chairs and looked at the smooth river as it flowed gently around the island.

'Reckon you'll cope out here okay?' asked Frederick.

Ned gave a small laugh. 'I reckon. I couldn't believe it when I walked in and saw that electric keyboard. Perfect to use when I want something besides my guitar. Who knows, I might even give those drums a go when there's no one around to complain.'

'So you're going to write some songs, are you? Do you always write your own material?'

'Yes, I do, but I feel that I want to write more than just individual songs. I'm not sure what I want to compose, so I was hoping that coming out here, where there are no distractions, I might be able to come up with something different and original. But the trouble is, I'm not at all sure what it is I'm after.'

Frederick nodded. 'Give it a bash, Ned. Y'know, my old man always told me that you never know what you can do unless you give it a try. Funny thing is, since being up here I do think about what he said. In the old days a lot of people did a lot of remarkable things, because they had to. Amazing what some of those goldminers did to get to the gold.'

Ned waved his arm towards the river. 'Just scrub country, now.'

'True, but they tamed it, mate, for a short time, anyway.' Frederick gazed off into the distance, a far-away look in his eyes. 'Think about walking way out here and starting from scratch with nothing other than what you can carry. Y'know, way back in the 1870s, just a few kilometres across that hill from where we're sitting now, there was a town of several thousand people. Maytown was big enough even to have its own newspaper. It was called the *Golden Age*, 'cause that was what the times were then, golden. Now there's nothing much left to show for those prosperous times, just a few bricks and some rusty mining equipment. Kinda interesting place to visit though, if you like ghost towns,' he sighed.

'Really? The ghosts still walk?' asked Ned with a smile.

'My oath they do,' said Frederick seriously, poking the fire. 'Had to spend a night on those old fields once. I'd gone out there to do a bit of fossicking around. Well, I couldn't get my truck to start. No worries, I thought, Theresa will come out in the morning looking for me and she'll be apples, so I threw down my swag, not at all worried about having to spend the night under the stars. Tell you what, I was back in that truck quick smart. Kept hearing noises all around, and I can tell you they weren't natural ones. Locked my doors and stayed wide awake till dawn.'

'What was it? Did you see anything?'

Frederick took a swig of his beer. 'No, but there was a creepy feeling, like you knew there was someone there, but couldn't see anything. I kept thinking that someone was watching me. Then, just before dawn, I heard . . . Aww shit, let's not talk about it. Let's eat.'

Ned wasn't sure what to make of Frederick's odd story, so he just let it drop. 'Well, it's certainly peaceful here.' He glanced across the still water as the moon started to rise, and when Frederick began searing the meat, he headed to the kitchen to find plates and cutlery.

'There you go, get that into you. Real food, better than that hospital tucker, I bet,' said Frederick cheerfully as he dished up enormous steaks and took a couple of steaming baked potatoes out of the barbecue's oven.

'I'll have to sort out some sort of routine, check the chooks, water the garden, make sure I turn the generator off before I turn in for the night,' said Ned.

'Write a hit song or two,' added Frederick between mouthfuls of steak. Ned grinned and glanced around his amazing new digs. In a place like this, maybe he just would.

*

They were up by sunrise breakfasting on tea and toast and fresh mangos that Frederick had picked from the garden.

'I can't thank you enough for getting me set up,' said Ned.

'You'll be right. By the way, about that story I was telling you last night,' Frederick said, looking a bit sheepish. 'If you hear anything, it'll be Mad Jack over the other side of the gully. Sometimes his music drifts over here because he plays it at four thousand decibels. He lives a few kilometres away, but you know how sound carries if the wind is in the right direction, so you get to share his taste in music whether you want to or not.'

'Who's Mad Jack?' asked Ned. 'I had the impression I was totally isolated out here.'

'Ah, Jackson Worth. He's a harmless old bloke. Vietnam vet. Well into his seventies by now, I reckon.'

'And he lives out here by himself? Does he have any family?' Ned wondered aloud.

'Nah, not that I know of. Anyway, he's on his own here. Don't worry about him, he doesn't like to socialise. Now I'll be off. I'll call in to see how you're going when I get the chance. Otherwise, if you get bored or lonely, or run out of food, come up to the roadhouse. Just follow that mud map I did for you.' Frederick held out his hand and Ned shook it.

'Yeah, I hope I can follow it. Anyway, I'll be fine for a couple of weeks.'

'Good luck with your music writing then. Take care.'

*

After a few days, Ned began to wish he had some reception on his mobile, as he thought he'd like to call Toni. He was so enjoying Carlo's place he wanted to describe it to her. But at the same time he loved the solitude and peace and the incredible setting and, as the days passed, he quickly developed a good working routine, something he had not always managed to do in the past.

He rose early and took a walk around the property, letting the chickens out of their coop and picking a mango for breakfast. Then, while the day was still cool, he'd water the garden. After breakfast he'd quickly clean up before settling to work, either with his guitar or at the keyboard, sounding out notes, transcribing chords in his head before writing it all down. He constantly wrote and rewrote the ideas that came to him, following each one, hoping that a coherent theme would emerge. By mid-morning, if he was discouraged by his lack of progress, he would plunge into the river, then sit in the sun with a coffee before returning to work for the rest of the day.

When the sunset faded into a warm night, he sometimes had another swim and sat quietly with a beer out on one of the terraces to watch the changing light and listen to the birds as they settled in for the night along the river bank.

In one of the bookcases was a well-thumbed bird book and, having found a pair of binoculars, Ned enjoyed identifying these birds, not just by their features, but also by their call. He began to keep a mental list of those he'd spotted.

Ned had never been much of a cook, rarely attempting anything very ambitious. But without a nearby shop, he began to use his imagination. The hens gave him fresh eggs, and he found some flour and successfully made a pizza base, adding fresh herbs from the little garden as well as a sauce he found amongst the tinned food in the kitchen. Feeling adventurous, he tried making a damper which he baked in the wood-fired oven, but it turned out to be heavy and chewy and was pretty inedible even smothered with treacle. However, the attempt left him yearning for fresh bread. He decided that he would have to use the mud map Frederick had sketched on a piece of paper to find his way to the roadhouse and buy some.

He made a wrong turn, ending up down at the edge of the old goldmine's lovely lake, so he thought that since he'd found the place he'd take the opportunity to have a look around. He noticed a spot under a small group of trees where it looked as though someone had been picnicking. Besides the remains of a fire there were a couple of rusty tins and a tattered hammock tied between two palms with rotting rope. Obviously the place had not been frequented for a long time. Then he spotted some empty shotgun cartridges and the skeletal remains of an animal. He turned away. Ned hated guns. His father had been a duck hunter and had tried to teach him the intricacies of patience, dogs and shooting. But while Ned liked the dogs well enough, he also liked ducks. He thought ducklings were cute and he abhorred the idea of shooting their parents. The sight of the bloodied ducks made him sick. He knew his father had been disappointed in him.

'He'll have to toughen up, Josie. My son can't be a sissy,' he'd once heard his father tell his mother after one particularly bad trip where Ned had refused to even hold a gun and Alex's frustration had boiled over. His father's harsh words had hurt Ned deeply. Ned had wanted nothing more than to please his father, whom he adored. Josie had protested that Ned was just a boy and that maybe duck hunting wasn't for him. But Alex had replied that real men liked hunting and Ned had better get used to it. He hadn't, though. Ned never did like hunting.

Ned got back in his car, discomforted by the idea that someone with a gun had camped at the little lake, even if it was some time ago, and continued on to the roadhouse, where he was welcomed with a hug from Theresa and some cheerful teasing from Frederick.

'We had a bet about how long you'd last – two weeks is pretty good! Good on you for surviving this long,' said Frederick. 'Haven't got the sat phone back yet, I'm afraid.'

'Ah well,' said Ned. 'I'm enjoying the quiet anyway.'

'Are you heading straight back?' asked Theresa. 'What do you need?'

'I need bread. I thought I'd get a dozen loaves and put them in the freezer. I wouldn't mind some meat and a few frozen vegetables, too. The garden's good, but a bit limited.'

Ned spent the morning at the roadhouse, chatting to a couple of tourists from Denmark as well as talking with Frederick and Theresa over lunch. He tried calling and texting Toni but the phone reception from the roadhouse was terrible and he couldn't get through. He spied a payphone in the corner of the main room of the roadhouse and tried calling Toni from there. Disappointingly, her phone rang out and went to voicemail, so he left a message saying he had been thinking about her and he'd call her again when he was back in town.

Driving back to Carlo's place laden with supplies and some DVDs which the friendly roadhouse couple had lent him, Ned felt more secure about finding his way and so didn't pay all that much attention to where he was going. By now it was mid-afternoon, the time when both the bush and its creatures had retreated for a sleep. Suddenly, he saw that there was a log lying across the track and he slowed to a stop. He switched off the engine and got out, thinking that the log had not been there on his drive to the roadhouse, but a quick glance made him realise that the log had been there for some time. He was on the wrong track. He would have to turn around and retrace his way. Before getting back into the four-wheel drive, his curiosity got the better of him and he stepped over the log and wandered along the track for a short distance until he came across what looked to be a hidden glade. The little spot was surrounded by a thicket of trees, and the grass beneath looked well trodden, as though animals sheltered there. *Perhaps it's their secret meeting place*, Ned thought whimsically. But as he crossed into the centre of the clearing, he had a premonition that something was not right. He paused and listened, his ears now accustomed to the small sounds of tiny creatures and the wafting chatter of rustling leaves and sighing grasses.

But when he heard the snap of a broken twig, Ned had the sense that there was a big animal out there too. He froze, shrinking back against a tree, swiftly looking around for a way to disappear and get back to his car.

Suddenly, in the shadowy edges across the clearing, he saw the figure of a man with what appeared to be a rifle slung across his back. He was hunched over, looking intently at something on the ground. Ned could see that the man was wearing faded camouflage pants and a khaki T-shirt. An old cap hid his face, but Ned saw that he had a straggly grey ponytail. From Ned's position, the man looked armed and possibly dangerous.

As the man shuffled through the undergrowth, Ned couldn't see what he was doing, but it occurred to him that this could be the neighbour Frederick had mentioned: Mad Jack. He'd said Jack was harmless, but Ned felt nervous. As he watched, the man crouched down, but as he was in the shadows of the trees, Ned still couldn't make out what was happening. Then, unexpectedly, the man leapt to his feet and with a hearty roar, shouted, 'Gotcha!'

Out of the undergrowth came a loud rustling noise and a goanna, almost half a metre in length, thrashed its way through the grass with its head held high and wearing a fierce expression. It dashed across the clearing towards Ned. Ned quickly moved out of its way and the large lizard clawed up the nearest tree, chased by the man who Ned could now see was carrying a large camera. Relief washed over him, and he called out, 'Hi there! Hope I didn't disturb you!'

The man stopped, looked at Ned and then shrugged. 'You're lucky you didn't come a second earlier or you would've ruined my photo. That was a Storr's monitor and I've been stalking him for quite a while to get a good shot. They don't like posing. You lost?' he said, speaking with an American accent.

'I think I'm your neighbour. I'm staying at Carlo's place. Are you Jack? Frederick from the roadhouse mentioned you. My name is Ned Chisholm.' He held out his hand.

'Ah, yes, I was warned that you'd be staying around here, but I won't worry you. I like to keep to myself,' he said. But having made the point, he walked over and shook Ned's hand.

'I was driving back from the roadhouse and I took a wrong turn. Sorry, am I on your property?'

Jack nodded. 'Yeah, easy enough to do. Roads aren't clearly marked, are they?'

Ned studied Jack's weather-beaten face. It was covered in grey stubble, and his wide mouth with its strong teeth and his piercing hazel eyes radiated a forceful personality. This was a man who was very sure of himself, and Ned felt he was being swiftly appraised.

'No, they're not.' Ned gave a small smile. 'You're a photographer, then? That's a very professional-looking camera. I'll try not to frighten any of your other subjects.'

'I worked as a photographer long before I came here. I didn't use the gear for years, but I brought it out again after I moved here,' he replied. 'That goanna's been after birds' eggs. There was a nest in that shrub over there.' Jack pointed to the other side of the clearing. 'The eggs hatched quite recently, so I managed to get a few good shots of the chicks. Dangerous life for young birds around here because the little buggers can get taken by a snake or a bird of prey or that bloody monster.' Jack nodded his head towards the goanna, which was still clinging motionless to the tree trunk. He then slung his Leica camera over his shoulder and that was when Ned realised that what had seemed to be a rifle across Jack's back was in reality a tripod for the camera.

'Y'know your way back to Carlo's from here?' asked Jack as he strode across the clearing.

Ned quickened his step to keep up. 'Maybe you could point me in the right direction.'

Jack didn't ease his pace or answer. But Ned didn't feel uncomfortable or offended by his actions. Indeed, the man quite intrigued him. Jack was a bit scruffy, but his clothes appeared clean. He wore aviator sunglasses on a cord around his neck and after he had adjusted the soft khaki cap on his head, he pushed them onto his nose. He stopped walking and pointed to Ned's four-wheel drive. 'Back her up about two hundred metres and take the left-hand track. There's a tree with a big bird's nest fern just before the fork, so you can't miss it. Follow that track and it'll take you around the goldmining lake and you can link up with Carlo's track from there.'

'Yes. I know the way from the lake. Do you ever camp down there?' he asked Jack.

'Nope. An old fellow did for a time, but this is all private property around here and we don't encourage strays,' he said in a gruff but not unfriendly tone. He touched the brim of his cap. 'Well, g'bye.'

'Thanks, Jack. Call in whenever you feel like it. I'm there most of the time – for the time being, anyway.'

'As I told you, I don't socialise much.'

'Me neither,' said Ned. 'But if you want a beer by the river with a steak and no chit-chat, just turn up.' As he opened the door of his four-wheel drive, Jack gave him a nod, then turned and trudged back through the bush without a second glance.

*

Ned arrived back at what he liked to call the river house and unpacked his supplies. He checked that the chickens had water and collected four eggs, smiling as the birds hurried to him, muttering and clucking, looking for scraps. They followed him as he picked some greens and a tomato for his salad from the screened vegetable bed, so he tossed the birds some bruised leaves and an overripe tomato to squabble over. He was beginning to find them a companionable group.

He had a swim, and then, sitting beneath the poinciana trees as they gently rained bright red petals around him, he idly strummed his guitar and thought about his encounter with his reclusive neighbour.

Over the next week, Ned wrote with renewed enthusiasm, although he still had no firm plot line on which to hang his ideas. Images, stories, anecdotes, a phrase heard or read, past and recent, were all triggers for his songs. Music danced and sang in whispers or glorious crescendo while sweet voices brought his lyrics to life in his head. One evening, after another day writing, he stopped making notes and leaned back, rubbing his eyes. *But where's the story? Where's the story?* he thought to himself. He walked down towards the river in the late languid evening air, a phrase still echoing in his head . . .

> *Where are we going?*
> *What do we care?*
> *Who's there to dream?*
> *Who's there to dare . . .*

Suddenly Ned was overcome with melancholy. Or was it loneliness? Again, he wished he had a satellite phone or, even better, mobile reception out here so he could call Toni. A metallic sheen of moonlight glinted on the river. His mind whirled and unbidden thoughts of his mother and his father's dedication leaped into his brain. He felt his chest tighten. *Just put it out of your mind,* he told himself. He was saved from these thoughts by the sound of a distant car engine. *Who on earth would be driving in this unmarked territory?* he wondered. The noise came closer and he recognised the whine of a motor cautiously driving down the slope towards the compound. Ned went to the gate, curious to see who would come to visit him so late in the day. He saw a bulky four-wheel drive, even older than his, and as the vehicle drew nearer to the open gate he recognised the driver as Jack.

'Howdy, son. You're trusting, opening the gate before you knew who it was,' Jack said as he opened the rear door of the vehicle and pulled out a cardboard box.

'It's nice to have a visitor,' said Ned. 'Come on in.'

'I've been to the roadhouse and Frederick asked me to deliver this care package.'

As he followed Ned inside and placed the box on the billiard table in the bar, Ned knew that his visitor was familiar with the place. Jack pulled out a bottle of bourbon from his back pocket and handed it to Ned. 'This is what I drink.'

Ned smiled. 'Straight up or diluted?'

'None of that soda pop crap. Theresa made you a cake. It's in the box.'

'How thoughtful. Thank you so much for bringing it down. Grab a glass and we can sit outside.'

Jack settled at the table under the trees and unscrewed the cap off the bourbon. He poured a hefty slug into his glass as Ned opened a bottle of Carlo's wine.

'Caught any decent fish?' Jack asked.

'Not really. Is there much to catch?'

'Son, there's sooty grunter, perch, archer fish, all good for a feed in that river. I've caught cherubin – they're redclaw crayfish – and freshwater yabbies in there, too. I sometimes set a line overnight. Throw the reel in a tin bucket and you'll hear it go off. Makes a hell of a racket,' Jack chuckled.

'I'll give it a go. You know this area pretty well, then?'

Jack paused and sipped his drink as if debating whether to reply. 'Yeah, I've spent some time here with Carlo, Lena and his folks. Mad for the tooth, Carlo and his parents. Eating all the time. Well, feasting. They don't do anything by halves, but they do it damn well.'

'I've seen the cold room and the freezer, so I suspected that they like to keep a lot of food on hand when they're here. I eat fairly simply, myself.'

Jack nodded and they both sipped their drinks quietly.

'Frederick said you're a music man.'

'Well, that's how I try to make my living. Singing, writing my own songs, but at the moment I'm struggling with a project I've always wanted to do. Thought if I could be by myself for a while I would find something to write about, but I'm not sure how to put down all my ideas in a coherent form.'

'Life set to music, huh? Not so much new there.'

'It's quite difficult to be original,' agreed Ned. 'I always worry I'm writing something that I've heard before, copying someone else's idea or melody.'

Jack threw back the last of his bourbon. 'Well, ain't nothin' new there either, sonny. As far as I know all music is based on the ideas of others. How many people have ripped off the songs of the black folk slaving in the cotton fields or used their spirituals for the basis of their so-called original compositions? Where do you think jazz comes from? I reckon part of every melody has been heard or played before somewhere. You could say that all musicians stand on the shoulders of others.' He reached for the bourbon bottle.

Ned had to laugh. 'You're probably right. I'm told song writing is the art of resurrection, adaptation and sheer chutzpah! But it's hard for me to find my own path, just the same. I scribble down notes and chords as soon as I hear them in my head, like I always do, but I'm still not getting what I'm really after, and the hardest part is that I don't know what it is that I want. That remains elusive.'

'Well, use your damned imagination,' drawled Jack. 'And use your life experiences – not that all experiences are good ones, or ones you want to share with others. You ever been in love?' Jack asked abruptly.

'Yes,' said Ned. 'I'm not sure I have anything new or enlightening to share on that score. What about you?' He looked at Jack, thinking that he might have been rather handsome in his youth.

Jack shrugged. 'I've been lucky and known a few good women in my life. And a few I wish I'd never met, but they probably felt the same way about me.'

'I don't want to write just about love. I think what I'm after is to look at a bigger picture, something more meaningful. The stories that make the world go round.' As Ned felt his way through an explanation, for a moment it seemed as if a foggy veil was lifting from his mind and he could glimpse what he was after, but then just as quickly he was in murky darkness again.

'There, you said it, sonny. Stories. That's what the world is interested in hearing. History is not just about great deeds but about the small tragedies and triumphs of ordinary people. Think about that,' said Jack, and poured himself another slug of bourbon. 'The stories of ordinary people,' he repeated.

Ned watched him for a moment. Who was this older, seemingly well-educated American, living as a recluse way out here, whose brusqueness belied his rough charm and who took photos of wild animals with professional aplomb? 'So, Jack, I take it that you are either American or Canadian. You're a long way from home.'

'Yeah, I'm a Yank, but I don't know what home means. The place where you were born, grew up in? The place where you made a home with the wife and kids? The place where you live to work? Or all of the above?' he asked with a quizzical smile. 'Or just the place where you hang your hat?' Jack paused and looked out at the river. 'I've seen too many homes destroyed, and so often for the wrong reasons. And wherever home might be, I've learned you can never go back and find it after you've left.'

Ned thought for a moment about how sad and bitter Jack's statement was. 'I don't think that's always true. For me, I know I can go back to my family home where my mother lives, and even when things change, somehow it's still always the same. Even the things that belonged to my late father are still about. It's not where I want to live, but I guess it's nice to know that the place I called home when I was young is waiting there for me.'

Jack sat up, his hazel eyes flashed. 'Well, I tell you something, Ned, you are damned lucky! I've seen so many homes, whole towns sometimes, destroyed by war. The people who lived in them can never find their way back. Home and family. Gone.' As Jack spoke, Ned could sense the anger and pain emanating from the American. Ned started to say something soothing, but Jack interrupted.

'I don't need counselling, Ned,' said Jack in a scathing voice. 'On the contrary, I'm the one who's done more than my share of trying to salvage the lives of kids, men of your age, and hell, even men as old as me. But you know what makes me really angry? Things never change. The politicians, the military, they never learn and they never, ever take the blame for their mistakes. They just go out and do it all over again.'

He jumped to his feet and ran his fingers through his hair, then flexed his shoulders and stared at the river. 'I so believed in my country. Do you know that I *wanted* to go to Vietnam? I volunteered as soon as I could. I believed in stopping the communists getting a hold of that country. I swallowed the stories that the brass and the politicians told us, but I was pretty disillusioned by what I saw there. Then after Vietnam, the US got involved in wars in El Salvador, Iran Contra, Panama, the Gulf, Afghanistan, Iraq . . . the list goes on and on, and it's the men, the ordinary men, who pay for it. It's their lives that get destroyed, as well as the lives of the poor bastards that get in the way of the US military machine. Well, I decided that I wanted out.' He stopped suddenly and took a deep breath, collecting himself. He poured himself another drink. 'Last one and then I'll go.'

'Stay as long as you want,' said Ned quietly.

Jack took a sip, savouring the liquid before swallowing. He sat back down into his chair and his voice became calmer and more reflective. 'You know, being a music man, you might be interested in this story. Years ago, when I first joined the service, I met an old black guy who told me about the time he came to Australia during the Second World War, sometime about '43 or '44. Went into Cairns with the US forces and said the town went crazy for the Yanks, because along with nylons, chocolates and cigarettes they had records. All the latest swing bands and boogie woogie music, even some Hawaiian music. The girls were wild about it. Of course he also told me that the black American servicemen were segregated from the white, had their own black clubs and brothels and such. But this guy said when the US Service shows came to Cairns to entertain the troops they used to be able to go to those, although they had to sit separately. Anyway, one time he got to see John Wayne, and performing alongside him and the other US headliners was some local Australian talent. The main gal among these locals was called Georgia Lee, and this guy told me that she sang the blues sweeter than any blues singer he'd heard before. When I heard that story, I kinda decided I wanted to come to Australia.'

'I've never heard of Georgia Lee,' said Ned.

'Well, you missed out on a great voice. Interesting background. Her real name was Dulcie Rama Pitt and her mother was part Aboriginal and her father was from Jamaica. The whole family sang, but she was the best. Later she made her mark in England and sang with Nat King Cole, but came back to Cairns. Like my friend told me, she sang the blues better than anyone else I ever knew.

She sang jazz and used to perform on television a bit, too. She made an album, the first by an Indigenous artist. It was reissued a few years back – *Georgia Lee Sings the Blues Down Under*, so now anyone can hear her remarkable voice. It still breaks my heart when I hear her sing "Oh My Beloved Father". So, she's kinda the reason I'm here.' He leaned back with a satisfied smile.

'That's a pretty interesting story,' said Ned, wondering if Jack really did come to Australia because of Georgia Lee or whether he was just telling a tall tale. 'I'll check her out sometime.'

Jack rose to his feet. 'Well, I'll be off.'

Ned handed him the remains of the bottle of bourbon. 'Thanks for coming by, Jack.'

Jack waved the bottle away. 'Put it in the bar, in case I decide to inflict myself on you again.'

'You do that, Jack. I'd like it.' Ned reached out and shook the older man's hand. 'Take care driving.'

'I'm an old jungle fighter. I can see in the dark and I know my way around here like the back of my hand.'

Ned waited till he heard the engine of Jack's car fade in the distance before returning to the chairs at the edge of the river, as the moon was slowly rising in the night sky. Absently he picked up his guitar and let his fingers strum, sliding across the strings without thinking. Jack had set a thousand thoughts and images swirling in his head. Stories. Everyone had a story. But how to link those stories? That was the hard part of the equation.

*

A few days later, he decided that nearly three weeks was enough time off the phone grid and he wanted to make a return visit to Cooktown. He only made a brief stop at the roadhouse for a quick cup of coffee with Frederick and Theresa before heading on to Cooktown. Driving into the small township, Ned suddenly felt like he'd arrived in the big smoke. The little place seemed to be bustling, but there was probably no more activity than when he'd first arrived. That seemed an age ago, now. When he parked his four-wheel drive, he pulled out his mobile phone. It beeped with messages and, as he scrolled through them, he saw that quite a few were from Bella. She was irate that he wasn't coming to their father's dedication. Reading on, he realised with alarm that she was actually in Queensland and trying to catch up with him. He tapped out a message to her: *Sorry I've been out of contact, Bell. I'm staying in the bush for a bit, composing. It's going well and I'm really into it so it's not a good time to meet. Let's catch up next time I'm back in Victoria. Sorry I can't make it to the dedication.* The text mightn't stop Bella, but he hoped it would put her off just a bit. Next, he thought it was time he actually called his mother.

Her phone went through to voicemail, so Ned just left a message. 'It's me, I'm back where I've got mobile reception. I'll try calling again later. Hope you're okay, love you.'

Then he rang Toni, who answered the phone after the second ring.

'Hey, stranger!' She sounded pleased to hear from him. 'Back in town?'

'Just arrived.' Suddenly Ned couldn't wait to see her. 'Can I see you? Are you free tonight?'

Toni laughed. 'Lucky for you I finish work in a few hours. What about my place, and you can fill me in over dinner about what you've been doing? I'll text you my address. But first, in a word, how're you finding life out there in the wilds?'

'Amazing. The place is unreal. Even my neighbour's unreal. You should come out and see it. All of it.'

'Glad you're enjoying it. We have a lot to catch up on. Looking forward to seeing you.'

Ned drove around to the motel where he'd stayed previously and greeted the girl on the desk.

'You're back! I thought you'd gone bush. No good?'

'Very good. But I need a taste of civilisation.'

'So where're you going?' she laughed. 'If you want real civilisation, you'll need a plane, not a motel.'

'Don't knock Cooktown. All I've been talking to lately are the birds, some chickens and a lot of trees.'

'I've heard that before. Same room as last time okay?' As he registered, she pushed the room key over to him.

*

Ned folded up the small ironing board and contemplated his freshly ironed shirt. He grinned. He was looking forward to seeing Toni. On the spur of the moment he decided to buy a spray of Cooktown orchids which he had seen on sale earlier at the motel reception.

As Toni came to her door, lean and tanned in her pretty yellow dress, wearing colourful earrings and a huge smile, he felt a sudden rush of warmth. He thrust the spray of perfect orchids into her hands and hugged her tightly before kissing her cheek and then standing back to admire her.

'You look gorgeous,' he said. 'You certainly are a sight for sore eyes.'

Toni thanked him for the orchids and pinned some of the flowers in her hair. Then she took his hand and led him inside. 'You've been out in the bush too long, mister. Dinner will be ready in about half an hour. Can I get you a beer, or would you rather have a glass of wine?'

'A XXXX Gold would be perfect, thanks.'

They'd finished their entrée and were halfway through the main course before Ned leaned back in his seat and said, 'Have I stopped talking? Sorry, I've been on my own too long. Tell me what you've been up to.'

'Nothing half as interesting. I love hearing all about the place on the river, it sounds unreal. But then Carlo and Lena are somewhat unusual. I've only met them once or twice, but they're certainly different, even for a place like this, which has its share of eccentrics.' She took a sip of water. 'Did Jack really fight in Vietnam, do you think? I've met a couple of vets up here. They come to me for physio but the wounds and pain are really in their heads.'

'Oh, I would say that Jack's biggest problem is just frustration and disillusionment with his country. Just the same, the one time we sat and really talked he opened a few doors in my head. Gave me some ideas. We can talk about that later. But that was the greatest excitement I've had in the past weeks. Don't get me wrong, I really love the place, but at times I wish I had something to distract me from my work, something a bit more interesting than the TV.'

As he said this, his phone rang and, glancing at the screen, Ned excused himself. 'I know this is rude, Toni, but it's my mother. I'll be as quick as I can.'

'No worries. I'll start the dessert,' said Toni and went into the kitchen.

'Mum, hi –'

'It's good to hear from you, Ned,' replied Josie, obviously pleased to be able to talk to her son.

'Sorry, Mum, but I'm with someone, can't talk right now.'

Josie paused. 'I've caught you at a bad time.'

Ned felt a stab of guilt. 'No, all's good. Mum, I'll call you back, promise . . . Talk soon.'

'All right then, Ned,' replied Josie in a disappointed voice.

He hung up. Toni popped her head out of the kitchen and gave him a questioning look. Ned tried to explain. 'My mother'll have me on the phone for ages. I can ring her later.'

'You kinda cut her off at the pass,' called out Toni, returning to the kitchen. Ned stood up and slouched in the doorway. 'I don't mind if you talk to your mother,' Toni continued. 'How long since you've spoken to her? Bit difficult out there in the bush with no reception.'

Ned tried to shrug off her comment. 'Oh, it's been a while, I guess. But she's okay about it.'

'I'd be phoning home if I were you,' said Toni eyeing him.

Ned stared at her. 'Not all families talk to each other all the time,' he said defensively. 'You sound like my little sister. I think I'm attentive enough.'

Toni's mouth quirked. 'I have a younger sister too. Drives us all batty the way she just takes off and goes AWOL. Calls only when it suits her. I don't begrudge her doing her own thing but it just wouldn't hurt her to think about the rest of the family once in a while.' Toni smiled and she rolled her eyes humorously to show Ned she wasn't trying to give him a hard time. 'I love my sister, but she's very different from me.'

Ned was quiet a moment. 'I couldn't be more different from my sister either,' he said with a smile. 'Bella is organised, efficient, reliable, smart and very professional in her work, just like our father was. She lives near our mother and is very caring.'

'So that lets you off the hook?' said Toni, raising an eyebrow.

Ned winced. 'Yes, I guess I feel like it does. I don't do well in a locked-down routine. Predictability bothers me. But, yes, I take your point, I will phone home straight after dinner.'

'Look, I've already started dessert and it will take a little time. Why don't you ring your mother while I put together my mouth-watering concoction?' suggested Toni, ushering him out of the kitchen.

Ned sat down at the dining table again and called his mother back. Josie was thrilled to hear from him. 'Where are you, how're things with you?' she asked.

'I'm great,' Ned said leaning back in his chair. 'I'm staying in a jungle – well, the beautiful bush, but it's remote. I'm house-sitting but there's no phone reception. Right now I'm in town having dinner with a friend. Are you okay, Mum?'

'I'm good, I'm good,' Josie said cheerfully. 'Bella's on holidays! She took off with not much of an agenda or much booked – so unlike her – but she had a lot of leave stored up and they made her take it.'

'Yes, she texted me and said she's in Queensland. Is Brendan with her?' Ned asked.

'No, he's not. Apparently he couldn't take time off at such short notice. Bella's at some lovely place on the coast, somewhere in north Queensland. Hidden Cove, I think it's called. Is that near you? Maybe you two can meet up while she's there. Wouldn't that be lovely?'

Ned didn't respond, so Josie continued.

'Or maybe you could travel back together. Have you thought any more about my email regarding the dedication of the lecture room in your father's name? I'm hoping you'll change your mind about coming.'

Ned paused and shifted in his seat. 'Um, I really don't think I can make it, Mum. I have a responsibility to look after the place where I'm staying, the chooks and the garden and stuff . . .' Ned heard Josie take a breath. 'And I'm doing a lot of composing,' he rushed on. 'I really feel I'm getting somewhere. No distractions, that sort of thing.'

Josie was silent for a moment. 'Well, that's good, Ned. When can we hear something?'

'Whoa, too early for that, Mum!'

'I am so pleased you're being creative, putting pen to paper . . . or rather, music sheet.'

Toni came back into the room and placed a plate in front of Ned.

'Mum, I have just had a delicious-looking crepe with strawberries and cream put in front of me. I'd better go.'

'Oh,' said Josie, sounding disappointed. 'Okay then. I understand. Do call me again as soon as you're able.'

'Will do. I love you, Mum.' Ned hung up and put his phone in his pocket. 'Mmm, this looks just perfect.' He took a mouthful and smiled at Toni. 'The strawberries have been soaked in something decadent.'

Toni smiled. 'Cognac and red wine. Called drunken strawberries. I could only get frozen ones, I'm afraid, but I think it still works.'

They ate in silence for a few moments, enjoying the strawberries. Then Ned looked at Toni. Their eyes met and Ned slowly leaned towards her and licked a drop of cream off her lip, kissing her softly. 'Are there any sober strawberries we could have for breakfast?'

'Of course. I saved them specially.'

Ned gave a soft laugh as he took their empty plates, put them in the kitchen and then returned to Toni and took her in his arms.

*

The next morning, before Ned made his way back to his motel room, he and Toni made arrangements to meet for lunch at the seafood restaurant on the Endeavour River.

After he'd had a shower, Ned contemplated going to the supermarket. He knew he had to do a big shop to stock up on food. The roadhouse was good for essentials, but didn't have much variety. But that mundane task could wait until he was ready to head back to the bush, so to fill in time before lunch, Ned decided to have a walk around the town, to savour the busyness of the shops and people.

He stopped at the library and, after explaining to the librarian where he was living, was invited to join. Half an hour later he left with a small pile of books, which he took back to his room. Then, with a couple of hours still to fill, he decided to make another trip to the Cooktown museum.

The woman at the reception desk gave him a friendly nod and said that she remembered him from his earlier visits. Ned replied that he thought the museum was very interesting and he enjoyed looking at the artefacts from Cooktown's colourful past.

He took another look at the rooms devoted to Captain Cook and took some photos of the exhibition on his phone. He wandered into some of the other downstairs rooms and reacquainted himself with the large range of Aboriginal and Chinese artefacts on display. He was about to leave when he decided that he would like to revisit the old piano he had seen earlier, so he went up the stairs and walked along the corridor. Ned felt ridiculously pleased to see the instrument again. 'You've had so many adventures, and yet here you are,' he said quietly, resting his hand on its dusty lid.

He was about to turn and retrace his steps when he saw that there was a small room at the end of the corridor, and its door was open. Wondering what sort of exhibition was in there, Ned poked his head around the door and saw at once that it was a storage room. He took a step back and checked the front of the door, wondering if it was a restricted area, but he couldn't see any signs so he stepped inside.

It was a small space, filled with shelves of folders and books and boxes labelled with dates and the details of their contents. But while the room was crowded and cluttered, the wide and high windows gave a bright, stunning view to the river. Whoever had resided in this room could have spent many an hour at these corner windows observing the town and the seafront.

He pulled over a box and perched on it in front of the windows, trying to imagine what the scene outside might have looked like more than a hundred years ago. And as he sat there Ned had the sudden feeling that small dust motes from long ago, echoes of events come and gone, of a life lived in this room, still lingered in the hazy sunlight filtering through the windows. Amongst what he had previously thought of as his aimless ideas, a small seed was making its presence felt. He needed to nurture the small shoots and roots he felt stirring.

Glancing around the room, he wondered what was in the boxes and cabinets. Curiously he lifted the lid of an old sandalwood box which was labelled: *From the Bish's archives. To be annotated.*

He closed the lid of the box and retreated downstairs. Glancing at his watch, he decided that he should make his way to the restaurant for his lunch with Toni.

Toni greeted him with a smile. 'How's your day been?' she asked.

'Very enjoyable, but getting better by the minute,' said Ned, and he knew it was true. He told her what he'd been doing. 'I could spend hours at the museum. The exhibits are just wonderful.'

'See that man at the table over there?' said Toni, pointing discreetly towards a middle-aged man with thinning hair who was dressed casually in a polo shirt and cargo shorts and sitting with an attractive blonde. 'That's Ken Harris. He's the museum's curator. I'm sure he'd be pleased if you told him what you've just told me. Go on.'

'He's with someone,' said Ned.

'That someone is his wife. People don't mind being interrupted if you have nice things to say about their work.'

Before Ned could say another word, Toni had already gone over to the curator's table and, after a very brief conversation, she beckoned to Ned, who got up and joined them.

'Ned, this is Ken and his wife, Emily,' Toni said, gesturing to the couple. 'Ned was just telling me how much he enjoyed your museum, Ken.'

'Yes,' said Ned, shaking Ken's hand. 'I think you've done a wonderful job with all those exhibits. It really shows the colourful past of Cooktown.'

'Thank you, Ned,' replied Ken, eyeing Ned. 'Weren't you at the museum earlier today?'

'I was actually,' said Ned, surprised to be recognised.

Ken smiled broadly. 'I thought so! I'm so glad you enjoyed yourself.'

'I did. The museum is fascinating.' Ken seemed very friendly and eager to talk about the museum, so Ned decided to ask about the mysterious box in the storage room. 'I sort of wandered into a small storage room that was full of boxes. There was one labelled *From the Bish's archives*. It looked very old and untouched.'

Ken laughed. 'You can't help smiling at such an Aussie note, can you? Actually, we haven't had the box all that long; it was recently sent up from Cairns, where it's been for years. The "bish" referred to on the box was the first bishop of Cooktown, Bishop Hutchinson. Unfortunately for us, the Cairns diocese kept his pectoral cross which was given to him by a Cooktown merchant. It was made from Palmer River gold, and together with the chain weighed a good two hundred and fifty grams.'

'That's a pity,' laughed Toni. 'I bet that would bring in the tourists.'

'Do you know what's in the box?' asked Ned, his curiosity piqued.

Ken shook his head. 'I've only had the chance for a quick look through it. It seems to contain his Bible and missal as well as a diary and some letters tied up with ribbon. There also seem to be some diocesan papers dating from the late nineteenth century.'

'Do you think there is anything of great importance to the museum?' asked Ned.

'I couldn't say,' Ken answered vaguely. A waiter approached Ken and Emily's table, his pad and pen at the ready. 'Would you two like to join us for lunch?' Ken asked.

'That would be lovely,' said Toni, sitting down.

The four of them ordered food and a bottle of wine. They chatted easily, enjoying the afternoon sun. Ken and Emily were delightful company and Ned found their conversation stimulating and entertaining. As they were paying the bill, the subject of the museum came up again.

'One of our difficulties is time.' Ken sighed. 'We might have a great museum, but most of its workers are volunteers. That box you mentioned earlier, unfortunately no one has had the opportunity yet to go through the papers properly and I don't know when we'll get around to it. It's a pity, though, because you never know what interesting things you might find. Still, I'm sure I'll get to it eventually.'

Before Ned even realised it, he found himself volunteering to help. 'Perhaps I could have a look through it?' he said. 'I can't compose every moment of the day and a constructive task would make a nice change from talking to the chooks.'

'Well,' said Ken, 'it would certainly be helpful if someone reliable could go through the box and at least make a detailed list of its contents. I know I've only had a quick look at what's in there, but the job shouldn't be too difficult and it would save me a lot of time.'

'Great, well, I'll come past the museum and grab the boxes before I head off again.'

Ken smiled broadly. 'Thanks, Ned. That would be terrific.'

'It's always nice to meet people who appreciate the museum. I think it's fascinating,' said Emily.

'Yes, it is,' agreed Toni, glancing at her watch. 'Sorry, guys, but I have to get back to work.'

'I'll walk you back, if you like,' said Ned. 'See you tomorrow, Ken. Bye, Emily, nice to meet you.'

On the way back to the hospital, Ned asked Toni what her plans were for that night.

'Well. I marinated way too many strawberries and I was wondering what to do with them.'

'I could probably help you with that problem,' said Ned with a smile.

With a few hours to kill before Toni finished work, Ned decided that he should call in to the Toppie to see Yolanda. When he went in, the pub was again full of tourists, but as soon as Yolanda saw him, she beckoned him over.

'XXXX Gold, as I remember,' she said. When Ned nodded in agreement, she poured him a beer.

'I just popped in to thank you for putting me on to Carlo's place. It's perfect for what I want. Days and days of peace and quiet. No hassles. Getting a lot of work done. I don't know how I can repay you,' said Ned.

'If you mean that, I can think of a way. We get lots of tourists in here all the time and it would be great if we could give them something to really remember Cooktown by. Would you put on a concert for us? Raise some dough for a good cause? Nothing fancy, just you and your guitar. Locals would love it, too.'

He hesitated, but then said, 'Well, I suppose I could. When did you have in mind?'

'What about next Friday?'

Ned nodded.

'Great!' said Yolanda. 'We can do a bit of publicity. Good entertainment is a bit rare around here, so everyone will appreciate it.'

Ned finished his beer, somewhat bemused by the conversation and his commitment to perform.

At Toni's later that evening, as they finished the strawberries, he told her of Yolanda's idea.

'That would be really good of you. I'd enjoy it too. Maybe you might have a Cooktown song ready?'

Ned grinned. 'With any luck,' he said.

*

The next morning, as Ned said goodbye to Toni, she said, 'Next time you come to Cooktown, you might dispense with the motel room. It seems a waste of money to me.' She gave him a cheeky smile.

'Me, too,' agreed Ned. He gave her a long, lingering goodbye kiss. 'That's just a down payment for my forthcoming rent.'

After he left Toni, he collected his gear from the motel before making his way to the supermarket, where he did a very large shop, stowing frozen items in Carlo's ice-filled cooler. From there he drove to the museum, where Ken had the 'Bish's box' ready for him.

Driving back to Carlo's place from Cooktown, the time passed quickly as Ned thought very pleasant thoughts about Toni.

He was tired after he'd unloaded and packed away all his supplies and checked the chooks. Eventually he turned the lights on and sat down by the river with a drink.

Suddenly he remembered that the box from the museum was still on the back seat of the car, so he retrieved it and carried it inside and put it on top of the bar. Why had he offered to go through it all? he wondered. It now seemed a rather tedious task.

'Tomorrow,' he said aloud.

Ned stepped back outside to retrieve his drink. Suddenly from the hills above the river the breeze brought to him the distinct pumping of 'Papa-Oom-Mow-Mow'.

'The Rivingtons, *Full Metal Jacket*,' Ned murmured with a smile. 'Yeah, way to go, Jack.'

5

THAT WEEK AT THE river house, Ned found that some small ripples were now disturbing the placidity of his previous existence. His smooth routine and his concentration were no longer the same. He sat by the river for hours each day, barely lifting his guitar. One afternoon, standing amongst the chickens as they fluffed and muttered around his ankles, he finally smiled. His distraction was all to do with Toni. The chickens scratched enthusiastically in the dirt. The Rhode Island Red stood on her toes and shook her wings, puffing up her rust-coloured feathers.

'Yes, yes, I know. Toni's a gorgeous girl.' There, he'd said it out loud. He felt a rush of warmth. Toni was affecting him more than he had realised. And it disturbed him. His feelings for her were surprisingly intense. With a frown and sigh, he went back indoors.

Ned had ignored the Bish's box for a few days as he'd tried to regain his creativity and start composing again, but when he wasn't getting anywhere with his music, his eye fell on the box and curiosity got the better of him.

He put it onto the billiard table and decided to make a start cataloguing its contents. He put some of the religious items to one side and looked at a pile of letters that were marked *Returned from Dungarvan*. He was puzzled for a moment, but then concluded that the letters had originally been sent to Ireland from Cooktown, some of them more than a century ago, and then someone had returned the collection to the Cairns diocese.

The letters were tied in neat bundles, some piles thicker than others. Curious, Ned picked up one of the letters and looked at the signature at the bottom. It read:

> *May God bless you both,*
> *your daughter,*
> *Evangelista*

All the letters were written in the same neat and precise hand, but when Ned looked closely, he realised that they had not been collected carefully and that many of their pages were missing.

Looks as though I'll have to read everything so I can work out the order, Ned thought to himself.

He picked up a couple of pages and started to read them. He quickly saw that Sister Evangelista had a sharp eye for detail and her pithy comments made him think that whoever she was, she had taken an intense interest in all that surrounded her.

Cooktown
October, 1887

My Dear Parents,

This place seems a long way from home, not just because of the miles we have travelled to get here, but because the landscape of this part of the world is so different from that of dear Ireland. No rolling green pastures here as in Dungarvan. All I could see of my new home when we were first rowed ashore was a desolate shoreline of low red mudflats, straggling trees, and a few rough buildings. In the distance I could make out a large grassy knoll which was surrounded by jungle-clad mountains.

All five of us sisters truly feel the heat. Our faces continually perspire and our wimples and our heavy woollen habits are so unsuitable for this climate. And it is not yet summer. But I am sure that God has some great purpose in making us all so uncomfortable, and so I said a swift prayer for guidance and strength as I am determined to face my new home with resolve.

But we all must have looked quite miserable, for Bishop Hutchinson, who was accompanying us, spoke to us in a cheerful voice, telling us not to despair. He said that although our surroundings might look inhospitable at first, they weren't all that bad.

We are all very proud to be associated with such a man of God as Bishop Hutchinson. He is indeed remarkable: humble and yet fired with enthusiasm for the task ahead, of establishing God's Holy Church in Cooktown as well as founding a school where educational opportunities can be brought to the girls of the district where few now exist. How fortunate we are that he personally approached our motherhouse in Ireland to ask that some sisters should be allowed to accompany him back to Cooktown for this purpose. He is very fervent about this calling and frequently likes to tell us of the prospects that await us in this new frontier.

When I first sighted St Mary's Convent

When Ned looked for the next page of the letter, he couldn't find it anywhere. *Perhaps it is hidden in another letter*, he thought hopefully. He had a quick look through the bundles but couldn't find any immediate trace of it, so he decided to start reading what he guessed was Sister Evangelista's next letter.

February, 1888

My Dear Parents,

We have quickly settled into this new way of life. Each morning we meet for prayers in the small church that sits behind the convent. We are hoping to have our own chapel one day but for the time being the school's dining room will have to double as the school chapel.

We are all very busy with our new life here. We have had no difficulty finding students to fill our classrooms, as we are prepared to take girls of all religious denominations, and I am spending many hours giving lessons as well as working on my new curriculum. The challenge is great, but there have been some compensations. The heat has meant that Reverend Mother has decided to relax some of the rules of our order. Thus, late on Saturday afternoons when the temperature has dropped a little, we are sometimes permitted to take a walk towards the town's seafront, where the Cornish stonemasons have completed the granite kerbs on the edge of the road, making our stroll easier.

Cooktown continues to grow rapidly, as it is the port for the goldfields to the west. Indeed, as Reverend Mother observed dryly as we passed the construction of yet another hotel, there seem to be as many opportunities for entrepreneurs here as there are at the Palmer River diggings.

Our presence and work in the town has made us well respected, and as we take our walk we are greeted with smiles, nods, good wishes and acknowledgements. Hats are doffed and shy children scamper past us, eyeing us curiously.

When we first arrived we were all rather nervous about the native population as there were many stories about their savage ways, but there are few Aborigines in town, and those who remain are sorry examples of their race. I can see them at times, sitting on the edge of the road, or down by the river. They have no access to any basic comforts let alone acceptance or recognition here in town. They are treated as inferiors and considered more of a nuisance than a threat. I feel sorry at their plight and would like to help them but neither the Bishop nor Reverend Mother think it is our role to be missionaries. I have heard that the Lutherans have endeavoured to establish a mission not far from here in order to protect these godless savages. Perhaps these missionaries will be able to convert them to the way of God, although if they do, the poor souls will be Protestants.

We have a new priest, arrived from Ireland. Reverend Mother infers that he is still a bit 'wet behind the ears', but Father O'Brien is a good soul and as enthusiastic about this country as our Bishop. He has a parish four times the size of Ireland itself, but he is always eager to meet his thinly spread congregation.

Occasionally he tells us tales of Cape York to the north and his adventures travelling hundreds of miles by steamship, pony and stagecoach. One day he told us about the goldfields, the excitement of new finds and how other parts of the inland are opening up to cattle and tin mining.

This all sounded very adventurous and interesting and I said that I hoped that one day I would be able to see the goldfields for myself. But it is unlikely that this will happen for, as Reverend Mother reminded me, my place is here, in the school.

Father O'Brien, perhaps sensing my disappointment, said that I was doing the work of the Lord and that God would be glad and rejoice in my efforts. And I must tell you, dear parents, that I do rejoice in doing the Lord's work, here in the Australian wilderness. I do not know what the Lord has in store for my future, but I have faith in whatever plan he has for me.

May God bless you both,

your daughter,

Evangelista

When Ned looked quickly though the rest of the pile of letters he realised that Sister Evangelista had never returned to Ireland and so had probably never seen her family again. In a way, he thought she was fortunate. Sister Evangelista could just send a letter every now and then. She'd had time and space to deal with her family problems, if indeed she'd had any.

Suddenly Ned felt a wave of guilt wash over him. He knew that while he was continually trying to avoid conversations with Josie and Bella, in truth it wasn't really his mother or sister he was trying to avoid. It was his own feelings about his father's passing. He had thought he'd have time to confront his father about the issues that he knew needed to be sorted out between the two of them, but Alex's death had been so sudden that the problems had been left unresolved, dangling untidily like Monday's washing on the line. Ned felt angry with himself for not facing his father when he'd had the opportunity and now he felt such conflicting feelings about his father, he didn't know how to make sense of them.

Putting the letters back into the box, he went and sat down in one of Carlo's peculiar chairs. Looking around the room he saw a group of old-fashioned perfume bottles that were amongst the house's amazing collection of glass-ware, and a memory flashed into his mind.

He had just started high school at the most elite private school in the district. His father was very proud that Ned was going to the school he himself had attended. Initially, Ned had found it hard to make friends. Everyone else seemed to have gravitated into small groups, and Ned had felt like an outsider. Then, after a couple of weeks of solitary misery, three or four boys approached him and offered to let him join them. Ned couldn't believe his luck, until the obvious leader of the group said that Ned would have to pass an initiation test first. When Ned found out that the test involved shoplifting, he had immediately baulked. The leader of the group had sniggered and called him several names.

After that, Ned had felt he had no option other than to show these boys that he wasn't too frightened to take up their challenge, and it was arranged that he would go into one of Tennyson's chemist shops and steal a bottle of perfume.

Ned remembered, even after all these years, how alone he had felt, the new boy with no friends, eager to do anything to belong, even when he knew that what he was doing was wrong. But he had steeled himself and walked into the chemist shop while his new-found friends waited outside, stifling their giggles. He was very surprised at how easy it was to take a small bottle of perfume from the shelf, stuff it into his blazer pocket and leave. Once he showed them the perfume, his new friends ran off. Confused by their actions, Ned walked home.

Later that evening, when Alex came home, he called Ned into his study. As soon as Ned entered the room and saw his father's stern face, his heart sank.

'Ned, I had a very interesting phone call this afternoon from Jim Bourke, the chemist on Fitzroy Terrace.'

Ned stared at the floor, not meeting Alex's eye.

Alex continued, his tone hard. 'Jim saw you take that bottle and decided to ring me rather than the police, although he was quite entitled to go straight to them. What were you thinking, son? How could you be so dishonest? Your actions are a complete disappointment to me, and they would be to your mother too, if I were to tell her about this.'

Even after all these years, Ned could still feel the shame of the incident. But surprisingly his father hadn't shouted or even raised his voice. He was just very disappointed, which for Ned, who looked up to his father, was even worse. Ned had tried to explain about the other boys, but Alex would have none of it.

'Saying that you were only trying to make friends is no excuse. You will return the bottle of perfume to Mr Bourke, apologise for your behaviour and accept responsibility for your actions like a man. If he accepts your apology, then we will put the matter behind us on the understanding that you never do anything like this again.'

'Yes, sir,' Ned had said meekly.

He had started backing out of Alex's office when his father had added more gently, 'And Ned, you will make friends at school, just give it time.'

His father had been true to his word. After the bottle of perfume had been returned to the chemist and the apology made and accepted, the matter was never mentioned again. And his father had also been right about making friends. Soon enough, Ned had not only joined one of the school's cricket teams, but had found a couple of boys who were as interested in music as he was.

Now, sitting alone with time to think, Ned could only wonder at the way his father had handled the whole incident. Calm, firm, even protective, but disappointed that Ned hadn't lived up to his standards.

'Accept responsibility for your actions like a man . . .' Ned said out loud. Still feeling agitated, he returned to the box of letters in the hope they would distract him. He picked up another letter and started to read it.

May, 1893

My Dear Parents,

Sometimes as I look through my window and gaze across the bay and its bustling shores I recall the damp and cool, gentle greenness of home. This is a red and gold country with great pockets of ferocious green surrounded by bluer-than-blue seas. One morning I noticed from my window the arrival of a steamer from Hong Kong. As I watched, it disgorged hundreds of hopeful Chinese miners. The men wore simple cotton garments and all had long pigtails hanging down beneath soft caps. They were, however, not brought into shore, but were forced to walk the last few hundred yards through the mudflats, carrying all their worldly goods. Such treatment truly shocked me, as I was concerned that some might be taken by the crocodiles that lurk in these waters. I prayed for their safety and, God be praised, they all came ashore in one piece.

There is great fear of the Chinese among many here in Cooktown. Some are saying that this is now a yellow country, for the influx of the Chinese coolies is becoming overwhelming, and people are generally suspicious of them. Twenty thousand of them are on the Palmer River goldfields, we are told. Father O'Brien tells us stories about them. Many of them have arrived in ignorance, with no knowledge of the vastness and ruggedness of this country.

Father says they expect to turn a corner in Cooktown and find the gold diggings there, when in fact the fields are located more than a hundred miles inland and are difficult to reach. Most miners are forced to walk to the diggings. They must carry at least six months' worth of provisions to see them through the wet season since supplies cannot be brought to the goldfields at this time. In the wet season the rain arrives in torrential downpours and the rivers flood, isolating the miners completely. Indeed, we are ourselves isolated and can only leave Cooktown by ship at this time of year. Nor do these miners know about the natives who attack not just the settlers' cattle but sometimes the settlers themselves, as well as miners on their way to the Palmer River. One hears such terrible stories of murders and massacres one scarcely knows what to believe, but we heartily pray for the lives of all those in danger.

In Cooktown, we have our own Chinese community who have built their own Chinatown, a jumble of wooden shacks divided by mean alleyways, with shops and eating houses, gambling places and a joss house where they worship their own gods. The Chinese crowd into small rooms and spill out onto the street, where I have seen them eating and smoking. They are often shrewd business-people. There are many Chinese establishments in town, and Father O'Brien assures me that there are also Chinese businesses in the towns around the diggings, Maytown and Palmerston. The Chinese make themselves store-keepers, barbers and laundrymen. They work as cooks and station hands out in the pastoral holdings, and provide eating houses in town and on the diggings for which they grow vegetables and breed pigs. They run hotels, often through licences owned by their European wives. Here in Cooktown we have several Chinese doctors, and many swear by their herbal cures. There is also a Chinese photo-graphic studio and several fine tailors, I believe, who make beautiful silk dresses and handsome suits. I have also been told that the boarding houses they run are cleaner and cheaper than rooms in the hotels, so it is little wonder that they are well patronised. The Chinese often have noisy celebrations with drums, cymbals and fireworks, which we have no trouble hearing in our convent.

People may not like the Chinese, but they are impossible to ignore.

'Damn,' said Ned. Another missing page, or pages. He could hardly believe that the ship's captain had hated the Chinese passengers so much that he would abandon them like that. Still, they had all made it to shore in one piece. 'Must have been the power of your prayer, Sister,' he muttered to himself.

As he folded the letter carefully, he tried to return to the present. He thought of the sleepy Cooktown he had experienced, so different from the town that Sister Evangelista described. But Sister Evangelista wrote with such clarity and expression that he could easily imagine it as it had been when it was a bustling sea port more than a hundred years ago. He felt he could almost hear her voice.

Although it was getting late, Ned decided to read one more letter before bed, although, like some of the others, it seemed to be incomplete, but he was delighted when he quickly realised that it told more about her experiences with the local Chinese community.

Although the town has many Chinese, we have very little to do with them, so I was pleased to be able to go with our Reverend Mother to the house of Mr and Mrs Woo Tan one afternoon. Mrs Tan is English and no doubt a civilising influence on her husband. She is also a great patron of our school. The Tans enquired about our school as soon as it opened and when Mrs Tan made a fine donation of good English books she'd brought with her from England, Reverend Mother was pleased to admit the Tan children to our school and occasionally accepts their invitation to afternoon tea.

The Tans' house is interesting and comfortable. The windows have wooden shutters which open to the breeze. The front door is very wide with a carved stable door in front to screen it. Mrs Tan explained to us that the whole house was designed to keep out bad spirits and bring good luck. The Chinese are very superstitious!

The house is as clean as could be in spite of the dust, which is a problem caused by the dirt roads. The furniture in the main room is ornately carved and heavy with many richly embroidered silk cushions. There are many family photographs on the walls and many beautiful lacquered and porcelain ornaments and vases. I noticed that in one corner of the room there is a shrine. People say these are common in all Chinese homes. The place is very cluttered but prosperous looking, and it seems a happy home, especially helped by the cheerful songbirds which hang in lovely cages in the shade of the courtyard just outside the windows.

We were served tea from a silver tea service with beautiful English bone china cups and tasty Chinese rolls. Mrs Tan was very welcoming and Mr Tan stepped in to greet us and pass a few pleasantries. He told us he'd asked his cook to make us food which is a specialty of his home town.

Mr Tan is an oriental gentleman who dresses in fashionable and formal English attire, although he still has a traditional long pigtail. His English is quite refined. He is an important member of the Cooktown community as he is head of one of the Chinese guilds. Reverend Mother is pleased to acknowledge the contribution that he and his wife make towards the progress of our school in spite of the fact that Mr Tan is, without doubt, still a heathen.

Ned could not help but chuckle to himself. Clearly Reverend Mother was a pragmatist who could distinguish between ordinary heathens and those who could help her school. What courageous women those Sisters of Mercy were to leave the soft and misty green of Ireland for the harsh red heat of the unknown and the extraordinary society in which they found themselves.

*

With renewed determination, Ned returned to his work the next day, but still inspiration refused to come. The peace and calm he enjoyed at the river house were not proving to be the solution to rekindling his creativity. He began to feel the nagging fear of failure. He found that he'd get just so far into writing a song and then he'd dry up. Nothing flowed; inspiration was always short lived. He tried re-establishing a firm routine of working, but he found the time dragging. He tried taking short breaks and then longer ones in an attempt to still his mind. In the past these restless moods had prompted Ned to move on, in the hope that new places and new people would give him ideas. But here he was in the perfect setting, with all the right circumstances: peace and quiet, no interruptions, nothing to do except write, and yet he couldn't get his act together. If nothing came to him, what would he do? In his head he imagined he could hear his mother's gentle voice saying, *You'll get there, Ned. You'll do it. This is your dream. This is what you have always wanted to do. I have such faith in you.*

Such thoughts only made him feel worse. Sitting in the sun in the beautiful garden, he found himself beginning to panic. He stood and began to pace back and forth.

He could no longer delude himself. He was nearly forty, he thought, and he'd only released one album, and although he'd played in many gigs to appreciative audiences, they had tended to be small ones. In short, although his career might be called a moderate success, that was all it was. He had not hit the big time and his chances of doing so now were running out. He began to pace faster. Maybe he had made the wrong decisions right from the start. He was a perfectionist and wanted to do things his way and not sell out to the big companies. But, if he thought about it, there were few artists who'd stuck to their guns and followed this route who had ever been successful. Perhaps being such an idealist was hindering him? He wanted his music to unite people, to move their spirit. He wanted his songs to honour the earth, to ask people to learn to love what they had around them. He knew people responded positively to him whenever he appeared, but he couldn't live on applause from a few devoted fans. Should he now abandon his dream of creating music his way? But if not, then what?

He shook his head and felt his stomach turn. He walked over and stood on one of the terraces. For the hundredth time, he was amazed by his bizarre surroundings. It was not just the unusual dwelling but the entire landscape in which he now found himself that gave him cause to reflect. He slowed his breathing, trying to relax himself. Was the remoteness and the climate part of the attraction for certain types of individuals, who were prepared to put up with all the vicissitudes, problems and loneliness just to live here? Perhaps this was why he had often heard the remark about the far north being full of *interesting* characters, a comment sometimes said in an amused tone, sometimes quite disparagingly. He knew his time here was short. The rainy season would be here soon. And while he had managed his finances so he could sustain himself through this break, his money wouldn't last forever.

He needed to accomplish something during this time to make it worthwhile. He *would* accomplish something.

Defiantly he took up his guitar and headed towards a spot at the back of the garden where the branches of the poinciana trees hung low, shading him from the fierce northern sun like a green tent.

He was deeply involved in his music when some instinct made him stop playing. He was used to being totally alone, and he was familiar with all the sounds around him, so when he heard an unusual noise, he was immediately on the alert.

He got up and walked down the steps and into the main building. As he went into its central area, he was shocked to see a man lounging on a chair. The toilet flushed from out the back and another man strode into the room.

'Hey! What's up? Who the hell are you?' Ned exclaimed.

The men looked up, clearly surprised to see him.

Where have these men come from? thought Ned. He always kept the gate locked, and besides, he would have heard a car approach. Ned felt distinctly uncomfortable. The men were scruffy, as though they'd been in the bush for some time, and two backpacks had been dumped in one corner.

'Did your car break down?' Ned asked. 'Are you friends of Carlo's?'

'Yeah, Carlo, that's right,' said one of the men, who was wearing a faded blue shirt. 'We're a bit short on supplies so we thought we'd see if we could pick up some food. Didn't think anyone was here.'

The second man, who was sporting a mullet haircut, spoke quickly. 'How about a drink?'

'Okay,' said Ned guardedly. The men had made themselves at home, yet Ned couldn't help but feel they didn't belong here. 'I'm Ned.'

'Hi, Ned,' said the man with the blue shirt. Somehow he didn't sound friendly.

'So, what are you guys up to? Hunting? Fossicking?' Ned asked, pouring some water into a couple of glasses and handing them to the men. The men drank the water and then started looking around the room.

The man in the blue shirt didn't say anything, but grabbed the remains of Jack's bourbon and a bottle of rum and packed them into his backpack.

'Hey, you can't take that,' Ned said sharply.

'Who says?' asked the man in the blue shirt. 'Carlo always gives us supplies.'

The other man picked up a whisky bottle and a couple of bottles of Carlo's homemade grappa. 'Got any beer?'

Before Ned could reply, the man with the blue shirt spoke pointedly to his mate. 'You nuts? We can't carry a stack of tinnies. This'll do.' He turned to Ned. 'What food you got?'

'Not a lot.' Ned was not going to tell them about his recent big shop in Cooktown. 'Look, all I can give you is some basic supplies. How did you say you knew Carlo?' He almost felt he should offer them a lift, just to get rid of them, until it occurred to him that they might simply drive off with his car.

'Old mates. We go way back,' answered the man in the blue shirt, looking around again. 'Where's the food you've got?'

Ned pointed to the kitchen. 'There's some bread and ham and cheese in the fridge. You could get better food at the roadhouse, though.'

The men didn't answer him, but walked through to the kitchen, where one of them started to pull food from the fridge. Ned watched on helplessly.

'Carlo always lets us take food too,' the man with the mullet said over his shoulder.

As Ned watched the two men pack the food in their backpacks, he began to sweat. *Could these men really know Carlo? Why did I mention Carlo's name?* he thought, mentally kicking himself. They seemed very sure of themselves, but they made Ned feel very uneasy. He wished that he had met Carlo before moving in so that he could have found out more about any friends who were likely to drop in and help themselves. Ned controlled his impulse to ask more questions as he didn't want the men hanging around.

'How come you're here, mate?' one of the men asked abruptly.

'I'm housesitting until the wet season starts,' said Ned, thinking that it was none of their business. 'I'm not sure what that has to do with you.'

'Just trying to be friendly,' replied the man in the blue shirt, who sounded anything but. 'We'd better get going. We've got a way to go before it gets dark.'

'Thanks for the supplies, mate,' sneered the man with the mullet.

The two men hurried down the terrace towards the river and, as Ned watched, he saw them get into a couple of camouflaged green double kayaks and stow their backpacks. Then they picked up their paddles and pushed off, gliding down the river in the fading evening light.

Ned returned inside and poured himself a drink. He realised unhappily that although this place might be sealed off from anyone coming down the track through the bush, the river was an open frontier. For the first time since being here, he felt vulnerable. While those men had said they were Carlo's friends, Ned was sure now that they weren't and Ned's gut was telling him something wasn't right at all. Maybe he should report the matter to the police, but it was getting too dark to drive to the roadhouse. He was sure to get lost on the poorly marked track. Anyway, by the time he had a chance to speak to the police, the men would be long gone. Whatever he decided, there was nothing he could do until morning.

*

But the next morning, after a surprisingly good night's sleep, he began to feel optimistic again. The dark clouds that had been looming over his mood yesterday had begun to dissipate, and he decided that by now the men would be well away and there was no point driving all the way to the roadhouse to report the incident to the police. Although he really didn't believe a word of what they had said, without Carlo, it couldn't be proven that they were not his friends. They'd been rough and rude but there were a lot of colourful characters in these parts. He comforted himself with the thought that he would be unlikely to ever see them again.

So with renewed determination, he took up his guitar again to work on a tune that was just starting to make itself known in his head. An hour or so later, he heard the approach of a car. He wandered down to the gate but didn't open it until he recognised the driver as Frederick.

'Hi, Frederick, what are you doing here?' asked Ned, pleased to see the congenial roadhouse owner.

'Thought I'd get away for a bit and take a drive out here to see how you're going,' Frederick said as he parked the car, lifted a box out of the passenger side and got out. 'Brought you a few goodies from Theresa.'

After Ned had made them both a coffee, the two of them wandered out to the terrace overlooking the river.

'Looks so peaceful and sluggish, that river,' said Frederick. 'Hard to believe that shortly, when the wet arrives, it will be a raging torrent covering most of the garden and will come up close to the house. Still, you've got a bit of time before that happens. What have you been up to, getting on with your music all right?'

'Not as well as I'd like – it's hard graft – but this is a nice place to work. Peaceful and quiet, except for yesterday,' replied Ned, and then told him about yesterday's encounter with the two men. When he had finished the story, Frederick clapped him on the shoulder in a comforting fashion.

'You're right, those men sound a bit rough, but you have to remember that we get quite a few odd bods in this neck of the woods. Take Jack, for example.'

'Jack doesn't make me feel uncomfortable like these men did,' replied Ned.

'Good to hear that. Jack's not everyone's cuppa, but as far as I'm concerned, he's all right. And mind, he's a good friend of Carlo's, too. Maybe these guys were just two more of Carlo's odd collection of mates. I wouldn't be too concerned, but then I wasn't here yesterday,' said Frederick.

'Well, I was, and I don't think those men knew Carlo at all. Both were nasty bits of work. I did think of reporting them to the police, but it was too late to drive to your place.'

'It's a pity that you don't have a sat phone. Those phones can mean life or death out here.' Frederick scratched his chin. 'Ned, do you want me to ring the police for you back at the roadhouse? I can't guarantee that they'd drive all this way out here to speak to you, though.'

Ned hesitated but then shook his head. 'Thanks, but no, Frederick, you're probably right about those blokes. I don't want to put the police to any trouble. This is a hell of an out-of-the-way place. I reckon the men will be long gone by now, so it'd be a wild goose chase. They were shady, but they didn't actually do anything besides nick some alcohol and a bit of food.' He shrugged. 'But if those men were really Carlo's friends, I have to question his taste!'

Frederick laughed and chatted a bit longer. Then he drained his coffee cup and bid Ned farewell. Watching Frederick drive off down the track, Ned felt the stillness and solitude of his bush setting settle around him once more. Glancing about, he thought he felt eyes on him. *Get a hold of yourself*, he thought. *There's nothing there*. But even so that night he didn't sleep well and he began to look forward to heading back to Cooktown even more.

6

THE MORNING AFTER HER trip to the Daintree, Roberta drove Bella the hour and a half back to Port Douglas to collect her car. As they drove down the coast through the green cane fields, Bella was struck again by the beauty of the region. The hills in the distance were not as clear as they had been a few days ago, but the sky was still gloriously blue and the sea the gorgeous turquoise colour that one associates with the tropics.

They passed a car loaded with holiday gear and suitcases and Bella smiled to see a small boy and girl laughing excitedly in the backseat. Suddenly a memory flashed into her mind from when Ned had been about ten and she must've been seven or eight. They'd been on a family holiday in the mountains of Victoria and Alex had taken them out hiking to a lookout. Alex had kept up a brisk pace and Ned had complained loudly about being hot and tired. Alex had replied that the exercise was good for him. When they reached the lookout, Alex had quickly taken a photo of them looking at the view, and then they began the hike back to the car. Ned's whingeing increased in volume till he was silenced by a rebuke from Alex, who was marching ahead of them both. Bella trotted in his wake trying to catch up to him, but Ned lagged further and further behind. About ten minutes later, Ned came sprinting up to Alex, tears in his eyes.

'I've lost my jumper!' he cried. 'I can't find it!' Alex had groaned, very loudly. Ned had worn his favourite football jumper on the hike. Ned loved his footy jumper so much that he rarely took it off. Everyone knew how attached Ned was to it and it was a family joke. Alex wheeled around.

'Why on earth did you take it off?'

'I was hot,' Ned said. 'So I tied it around my waist and it must have fallen off.'

'How could you be so thoughtless, Ned?' Alex asked, clearly frustrated. 'Stop crying and let's start looking for it.' He strode back down the path. They searched for a while but saw no sign of it. Alex became quieter and quieter and he began looking at his watch.

'Kids, I'm going to have to take you back. It's getting dark and it's not safe for us out here,' he said. Ned protested loudly, saying that they couldn't just leave his favourite jumper behind, but Alex insisted. Without another word, he bundled them into the car and drove quickly to their accommodation, Bella and Ned both in tears. As soon as Alex had delivered the children to Josie, he drove back to the park, armed with a torch. It took him more than an hour to find the jumper. When Alex returned with the jumper, he seemed like a hero to Bella. Ned was happy too, but the jumper story had come up several times over the years, always to demonstrate how irresponsible Ned could be. Thinking about it now, years later, Bella realised that although Ned was quite young when the incident occurred, the event seemed in many ways to be typical of the fractious relationship between Alex and Ned.

'Can I ask you what you plan to do next?' asked Roberta, rousing Bella from her reverie. 'Are you staying here for a bit or are you going to try to find your brother right away?'

'I'll stay overnight in Port and have a bit of a look around. I plan to try to contact a couple of musicians who backed my brother's show in Cairns. I'm hoping they might have a better lead on where Ned's gone. They live on the Atherton Tablelands. Who knows, Ned might be up there.'

'Atherton is a great area. It's a good place to stop and look around,' replied Roberta.

'The whole of Far North Queensland is amazing,' said Bella with a laugh. 'I can understand why my brother is roaming around up here. It's an intriguing and beautiful place.'

'I've got time for a cup of coffee, if you like, before I have to get back. I think everyone will be fine for a couple of hours without me,' said Roberta.

She parked the car near the pier and the two walked into a nearby café.

'I loved your camp,' said Bella as a hot latte was placed in front of her. 'But I really missed good coffee.'

The two women sat there quietly, enjoying their coffee and flakey almond croissants as they watched several tour boats taking their passengers out to explore the nearby Barrier Reef.

'By the sound of things, you and your brother must have been close for you to go to all this trouble looking for him,' said Roberta when she had finished her last mouthful of croissant.

Bella was thoughtful. 'We were very close when we were younger, but not so close lately. We used to get on really well. Ned used to tease me, but it was never in a nasty way. We used to goof around a lot together; tripping each other up, spilling water, stupid things like that.'

'Yeah, I know exactly what you mean,' said Roberta with a smile.

'Ned had an annoying way of looking at things some-times. Once when I fell over, he didn't help me up right away, but asked me what the ants were like close up,' Bella smiled, rolling her eyes. 'Mum always says, "Ned's just Ned," and accepts him as he is, which is good, but I think she lets him get away with too much. Certainly things she'd pull me up on.' Bella stopped, suddenly shocked at this outpouring. 'But when we were kids and I was scared or upset, Ned would sing to me, or make up a song to make me smile. He was gentle, though he could get protective if he thought I was being teased or bullied by someone at school.'

'That's what big brothers are for,' said Roberta. 'Was he always into music?'

Bella nodded. 'Yes, but especially after he started high school. He was a more than competent cricketer but preferred spending time in the music room. I guess Mum and Dad should have figured out early on that music would be Ned's first love. Of course, for professionals like my parents – well, Dad especially, he was a doctor – music wasn't considered a proper career.'

'Yes, I suppose I can understand that. Making music your career can be very difficult. It's not a safe option.'

'Well, Ned was encouraged and given every opportu-nity to achieve. But it always seemed to be easier for me; Ned never quite fitted the mould expected of him. I was a daddy's girl, no doubt about it.' Bella paused to take another sip of her coffee. Ned had always been a dreamer. Alex had called him irresponsible.

Bella finished the last of her coffee and said, 'That was delicious. Do you have time for another, Roberta?'

When Roberta nodded, Bella got up, went to the counter and placed the order before returning to her seat. She smiled at her friend.

'My family isn't nearly as interesting as yours, though!' Bella said. 'You were telling me how they lived in the Daintree? Were they able to own the land?'

Roberta gave a small smile. 'Hard as my great-great-grandparents worked, they were never able to save enough to buy any, and because my great-great-grandfather was an Islander, he couldn't borrow money from the banks. So they would never have been landholders if it hadn't been for my great-grandmother. She insisted they take in an abandoned baby girl. The child was born to a Kanaka woman and an Irishman. I don't know what happened to the Irishman, but the woman died when the baby, who was called Clare, was about a year old. So our family decided to look after her.'

'Even though they weren't related?' Bella asked. 'That's so generous.'

'Yes,' said Roberta, smiling. 'Our people take care of each other, even when we're not directly related. Clare was a pretty little thing, and when she was about four or five a wealthy planter who lived further north came to visit. Evidently he'd heard about Clare and he asked to buy her.'

Bella gasped. *'Buy her?'*

Roberta nodded. 'He promised that she would have a proper education and grow up with his own children. My great-great-grandmother didn't want to sell little Clare, but she felt that the child would have a better chance of having a comfortable life with a rich white family than with us.'

Bella was astonished. 'I can't believe that someone

would just rock up and *buy* a child. Was she going to be a servant, then?'

Roberta was thoughtful. 'It sounds odd now, but laws were pretty lax in those days, and I think that there were some very loose arrangements about children. And she wasn't trained as a servant. This white family had children of their own and Clare was given the same opportunities they had. She received a proper education. And this girl had an exquisite singing voice.'

'Do you know what became of her?'

Roberta nodded. 'She was given singing and music lessons and she grew up to become a very popular singer who travelled all over the country. But she was always known by the name her white adoptive mother gave her, Atlanta, Attie for short.'

'Heavens, what an exotic name,' said Bella in an amused voice.

'Well, the upshot of it all was that my great-great-grandmother, because she was Scottish, was able to buy land for the family once they had the money from the sale of the little girl.'

Bella shook her head in wonder. 'Amazing. I suppose your family was very sad to lose Clare?'

'Well, my great-grandmother was, but when she heard that Clare was giving concerts all over the state, she was proud that she had been able to give her that chance.'

'That's quite a story. Did Clare, or rather Attie, go on to have a family of her own?'

'No, she didn't. I think she just liked to perform. But all our family loves music and singing, so I like to think it was the influence of our people all those years ago that started her on her musical path.'

After they had finished their coffee, Roberta took Bella around to the hotel where Bella had left her car and was booked in for the night.

'I'll have a look around Port Douglas before I go back down to Cairns. I can't thank you enough, Roberta.' Impulsively, Bella hugged her and Roberta smiled.

'I have a feeling we'll see each other again,' she said.

'I hope so. I'd like that,' replied Bella.

'By the way, I think our Antony is rather smitten with you,' Roberta said, winking, as she was climbing back into her vehicle.

'He's just a flirt,' Bella said cheerfully, waving a hand. 'Thank you for everything and let's keep in touch.'

*

After Hidden Cove, Bella found Port Douglas a bit too touristy for her taste, in spite of the fact that the town was abuzz with the news that a golfer had just been bitten by a crocodile while on the golf course. *Bet that's not on the usual tourist itinerary*, Bella thought to herself as she lazed in the hotel pool, cooling off.

She'd rung her mother and told her about the wonderful time she'd had in the Daintree, and Josie had told her that she'd had a brief chat with Ned a few days earlier. Unfortunately he hadn't mentioned where he was staying. Ned had seemed fine, Josie had said, but he was still disinclined to come down to Tennyson for his father's dedication ceremony. 'Such a shame,' said Josie, sighing. 'In years to come, I think he'll regret his decision. But there is nothing I can do about it. It's his choice.'

But I can still do something, thought Bella fiercely. She had finally received a text from Ned saying he was too busy to catch up with her while she was visiting Queensland. She'd texted him back saying she was happy to travel to wherever he was, but she'd got no response. Hearing the disappointment in her mother's voice, Bella began to feel fired up about Ned all over again. So when she'd hung up from Josie, she tried once more to ring the number that

Sarah had given her for the backing band. Her call went unanswered, yet again. This was the third time she had tried ringing since she'd arrived in Port Douglas. How on earth was she going to track Ned down if her phone calls weren't answered?

Later, sitting in the shade under an umbrella, she saw she'd missed a call and immediately rang back.

'Hi, Irene, it's Bella. Sorry, I missed you while I was in the pool.'

'Lucky you. I'm slaving away in a studio, listening to a group lay down some tracks. It's like a cave, no windows, no light!' She laughed lightly. 'Roberta tells me that you had a great time together. I can't chat at the minute, but just quickly, would you like to come to Cairns for a show tomorrow night? There's a couple of new bands performing and they are super good. I was given some free tickets, if you'd like to join me.'

'That sounds great, Irene. I'm in Port Douglas now, but I'm leaving in the morning,' replied Bella.

'I see. Well, why don't you hop in the car and come to Cairns? You can stay the night with me if you like.'

Bella laughed. 'Sounds fabulous. I'd love to have a night out. Thanks for thinking of me and for the offer to stay. Text me your address and I'll mosey on down. See you then.'

How friendly the people were up here in the north, thought Bella as she drove through Cairns the next day, looking for Irene's place. Was it the climate or the slower, more casual way of life? It was certainly a contrast with Tennyson, which was a bit on the formal side. People didn't walk around Tennyson in shorts and halter tops, or wearing the tourist uniform of Bermuda shorts, thongs and singlets. Shops here were filled with colourful versions of Hawaiian and Indian print tops and caftans as well as the ubiquitous souvenir T-shirt. The atmosphere and

143

setting was all about being on holidays. Even the locals working in the shops and businesses wore a uniform of bright shirts and cheerful colours, giving the impression that as soon as they finished work they'd be off swimming, fishing or boating.

After meeting her cheerfully at the door, Irene showed Bella to the small guest room in her high-rise apartment. Bella admired the room, which was painted bright blue. On the wall were a lot of photos of different tropical fish, making Bella think that she would be spending the night in a coral reef.

'Your guest room is so gorgeous. I love the fish on the wall,' she said as the two women settled on the balcony with a cup of tea each.

'Yes, done by one of my friends who is a very good underwater photographer,' replied Irene, and then told her a little about the bands they would see that night. 'So, Bella, enough of that, tell me what you thought of Roberta's little jaunt.'

'I can't thank you enough for telling me about Roberta. The Daintree was a very special experience. You can walk through a place and look at things from the outside, but with Roberta I got an insight into what's really there. She has quite a few stories to tell about her family history, too.'

'I'm so glad you like her. We've been friends for years. She's coming to the show as well.'

'Oh, that's great! Funny, she said she had a feeling we'd meet up again,' said Bella, happy to hear this news.

'Any luck tracking down your brother?'

'Not yet. No one had heard of him in the Daintree and I've been trying to ring the number I was given for the backing band who might know where he's gone, but I can't get an answer. I have their address, so I think I'll have to drive up to the Atherton Tablelands and see them in person.'

'It's a nuisance that you can't get through to them, but on the bright side, you'll enjoy going to the tablelands. It's a glorious area, and a bit cooler than here on the coast.'

That evening, as dusk was gathering, Irene drove them into the Botanic Gardens where the concert was to be held. 'I like to get here early and get close to the front near the stage,' explained Irene.

The setting was unlike anything Bella had seen before. Two Second World War naval oil storage tanks stood against a backdrop of thick rainforest. The tanks had been turned into a gallery and performing arts centre, Irene informed her, and were popular with local bands because the acoustics were excellent.

Everyone seemed to know Irene as she made her way through the crowd towards the front of the venue. Suddenly Bella saw Roberta.

'There she is, Irene! Hi, Roberta!'

The women hugged and laughed. 'Didn't think we'd catch up this soon, but this invitation was too good to miss. Thanks again, Irene. The ticket was waiting for me at the door, just like you told me,' said Roberta.

The Brass Rahzoo were into their third number when Bella felt an arm drop onto her shoulders. She spun around and in the flashing coloured lights she saw Antony's smiling face.

'What're you doing here?' she asked.

He gave her a brief hug. 'I'm in Cairns on a bit of business for a couple of days, and Roberta mentioned she was coming down for this show and that you might be here too, so I thought I'd come along on the off chance that you were. And here you are,' he said, looking pleased with himself.

The crowd roared its appreciation of the band, drowning out Antony's voice. Roberta and Irene didn't seem surprised to see him and both smiled, but Bella was unsure how she felt. As she studied his profile in the light from the stage, he turned and gave her a lazy smile. She gave a brief smile in return and looked back to the performers.

Afterwards, as the four walked outside into the cool air, Roberta said, 'I think a cold drink might be in order. It was awfully hot in there.'

'It's not very late, so let's head over to the jazz club for a nightcap,' suggested Irene.

A few people from the concert evidently had the same idea, and the bar of the small club was noisy with laughter and chatter above the background music.

'Follow me, I can see a table and chairs out in the garden,' said Antony.

After the four had settled themselves comfortably with their drinks, Antony turned to Bella. 'Did you enjoy the show?' he asked.

'I did enjoy it, but my usual taste is for something a bit more mellow. I'm in an *a cappella* group, so I like good lyrics as well as good music,' said Bella.

'And anything your brother sings, huh? I've down-loaded some of his music and he's good. Have you been able to contact him yet?'

'He's spoken to my mother quite recently, so I know he's still somewhere up here. I'm heading to Atherton to talk to some musicians he knows, because I can't raise them by phone. It's quite annoying.' Bella wrinkled her nose.

'When are you off?' Antony asked, sipping his drink.

'Tomorrow,' said Bella. 'I've wasted enough time already looking for Ned. As far as I'm concerned, this is make or break. If I can't contact these guys, then I'll have no idea where my brother might be, so I guess I'll just finish the rest of my holiday and go home.' She sighed. She was feeling energised and refreshed, which was exactly what she'd hoped for, but the fact that she had been unable to contact Ned weighed on her. 'By the way, Irene, this is a great little place. I wish we had something like it in Tennyson,' said Bella. She glanced at the lights strung in the trees outside where they were sitting and the comfortable friendly vibe of the place. 'But it would be very cold sitting outside like this in a Victorian winter.'

'Yes, it's a great little spot. A lot of legends have passed through the doors over the years. Surprising how many big names have jumped up on stage to jam and do a few numbers,' replied Irene.

'Overseas big names?'

'You bet,' Antony jumped in. 'A lot of them come up here when they're doing the festival circuit. So many blues and roots and jazz festivals around the country now, but not like the old days from what I've been told, hey, Miz Irene?'

'True.' Irene nodded. 'But that was well before my time. That's when Cairns was nicknamed the Barbary Coast and the wild pubs along the waterfront were legend. This bloke, Johnno, started the music scene, and soon there were bands and singers, guitarists and pianists in every pub, every night. They say people just drank around the clock, yet there were rules, of a sort. I've heard that Dottie, who ran one of the pubs, kept a baseball bat under the bar, "in case".'

Bella was thoughtful. 'I wonder if Ned has heard some of these stories. Songs are stories.'

'If he performed in Cairns, he would have,' Irene assured her. 'Bella, if you're still around in a couple of weeks, I could bring you here to see Wilma Reading. She's a fantastic jazz singer and the niece of Georgia Lee, who was a very famous blues singer back in the war years. Wilma's a local, but she made a name for herself in Europe. You'd enjoy her show.'

'I'm sure I would, but in two weeks' time I'll probably be back in Tennyson and in my normal, unadventurous routine,' said Bella.

'Well, Bella, if you're after a bit more adventure, why don't you let me come along with you when you go up to Atherton tomorrow?' interjected Antony. 'I know that area really well, so we could do a bit of sightseeing as well as looking for these mates of your brother.' He gave her a big smile.

'Oh, thanks, Ant,' said Bella. 'At least with you I shouldn't have any problems dealing with those musos if I find them.'

'Great, then I'll pick you up from Irene's in the morning, shall I?' said Antony eagerly.

After they'd had a couple more drinks, they decided to call it a night and Bella drove home with Irene.

'Thank you again for your generous hospitality. This has been a lot of fun,' said Bella.

'I'm so pleased,' said Irene.

*

As they drove into the rising hills of the Great Dividing Range the following morning, Bella was reminded of what she'd read about the hill stations in India, where the colonial elite went to escape the humidity and heat of the plains.

'I'm sorry that we were so late getting away. I talked too long with Irene this morning, but she is very interesting and I enjoy her stories about Cairns.'

'Not to worry. The plateau isn't such a big area to cover, so we'll find those musicians and still be able to take in a couple of sights easily,' said Antony good-naturedly.

The tablelands were misty and cooler than Cairns. The land was lushly green and dotted with dairy farms, and grain crops flourished in the red volcanic soil.

'I can't get over how beautiful this area is. I bet it was pretty rugged in the early days, though,' said Bella, pointing to some of the thick green vegetation that stood in an uncleared area beyond the paddocks.

Antony nodded. 'Yes, it would have been hard yakka for those pioneers. Some people did well, they found gold, or cut timber or raised cattle, even grew tobacco. But it was all a bit of a lottery. There were plenty who lost the seat of their pants. Just the same, I reckon that this place is still a goldmine, if you know how to exploit it.'

'And how would you do that?' Bella asked.

'Lots of ways. I've got a few lucrative contacts up here in the north, but I reckon one of the easiest ways is through tourism. It's not hard to see the potential.'

Bella frowned and took her sunglasses off her head, giving them a polish on her T-shirt. 'I'm not sure about that. I would have thought that everything was well covered, judging by all the tourist brochures I've seen since I've been up here.'

Antony shook his head. 'I don't mean just the dinky cafés and B&Bs and maybe a bit of camping and hiking, with a few side trips thrown in for good measure. I want to think outside the square.' Antony's eyes were bright as he spoke and Bella was intrigued.

'In what way? Give me a clue,' she asked.

'Tailored tourism,' Antony said glancing at her.

Bella thought for a moment. 'Meaning specifically geared tourism?'

'Exactly.'

Bella looked at him incredulously. 'Antony, there are heaps of websites and companies that do that sort of thing.'

'Not for this area! At least I don't think they do it as well as someone with a lot of local knowledge and fresh ideas could do it,' Antony said with gusto. 'I've been thinking about this for a long time, and I want to start my own business and do things a bit differently. Bella, think about it. If you're into a particular sport, or camping, hiking, kayaking, why wouldn't you choose a holiday that's totally tailored to cater for those interests?'

'Hmmm, I guess that would have a certain appeal,' said Bella, but she wasn't convinced.

'I'd be aiming at an older audience who aren't as internet-savvy or would rather have someone else put together the best packages,' Antony continued. 'Overseas visitors will love that. They usually don't want to waste time doing things that are of no interest to them just because it's part of their holiday deal. They want to be able to choose what interests them most and do that.' His voice rose and he became even more animated. 'So I want to create lots of modules of the different sights and activities that are available in Far North Queensland, and then people can pick what they want to do and we'd coordinate it for them. I've been thinking about this for ages. Tourism here needs to step up. I know that there are still secret destinations that are accessible but not promoted in a major way either here or overseas. Some towns just wait for people to stumble in, or they let them drive through without targeting tourists. I want to make those towns a specific destination. I have big plans, and I've already got lots of useful connections.'

'Well, good for you,' said Bella, bemused by his enthusiasm, although she couldn't see how one man could develop such a big idea without a lot of help.

Suddenly, he pulled the car into a parking space and leaned over and touched her arm. 'I want you to do this with me. We'd be a great team.'

Bella was startled. 'Oh, Ant! Don't be crazy,' she said.

'I'm serious,' said Antony, raising his hands. 'I've already got some business plans drawn up and I've had some real interest from investors. It's a great opportunity.'

Bella stared at him and decided to change the subject. She unbuckled her seatbelt and they both got out of the car. 'What's this town you've stopped in?'

'Mareeba. Time for something to eat.'

Bella looked along the broad main street where they'd parked. It seemed a bit plain.

'There used to be wonderful big old trees down the centre of the road, but they went for parking space,' commented Antony.

'What a terrible pity. The trees would have been so much more attractive than parked cars,' agreed Bella. 'But I'm dying for a cold drink.'

'Let's have a quick hamburger at the pub,' Antony said, pointing to a nearby building. 'Can't guarantee that it will be local beef, even though the town is known, amongst other things, for its cattle sales. There's a big rodeo staged here every year, too. You into cowboys?'

'Not really.'

'Bella, I think there'd be a lot of city folk who would just love to see a real rodeo. We could tailor a holiday around that and include horse trail riding, buck jumping lessons, whatever.'

'Maybe,' said Bella dubiously.

The classic old country pub where they went for lunch had sadly been modernised in a way that had left it devoid of any atmosphere. Wooden tables and plastic chairs sat on bright red carpet and the place seemed very quiet for lunchtime. Bella scanned the menu board on the wall and thought to herself that Antony might have chosen a more interesting place to eat. There seemed to have been a few cafés and restaurants in the main street which advertised that they served local produce, and they had looked more exciting than this. Perhaps Antony was more interested in a cold drink than in good food. The young woman serving behind the counter looked bored and disinterested.

151

'Could I also have a glass of sauvignon blanc?' asked Bella after she had placed her food order.

'What's that?' answered the waitress snappily.

'It's a type of white wine,' said Antony.

'Don't think we have any white wine.'

'None at all?' asked Bella in amazement.

The girl opened the refrigerator door behind the counter and peered in. 'Might be a delivery later today.'

'I think I'll have a light ale,' said Antony. 'Would you like to try some of the local coffee?'

'No, I'll have a light beer, thanks,' said Bella.

They sat down at a table and the girl came over and put two bottles of beer in front of them.

'Excuse me,' said Bella. 'Could I have a glass, please?'

The girl looked at her for a second, then pointed to a pile of glasses sitting on a table near the bar. 'They're over there.'

'I don't do beer from bottles,' said Bella as the girl walked away. 'Besides, my father would never approve. I think Dad would strike me down from wherever he is now if he saw me drinking from a bottle.'

Antony laughed and fetched her a glass.

Twenty minutes later they were making their way back to the car.

'Well, at least the hamburger was better than the service, but honestly, I think you'll have an uphill battle tailoring holidays up here if the rest of the service on the tablelands is like that,' Bella commented.

'Well, I didn't say everything was going to be perfect, and we would have to do quite a bit of research to weed out the places like that, but honestly, it gets better,' grinned Antony.

'Then lead on,' said Bella, climbing back into the car.

*

Bella loved the dramatic, lush scenery of the plateau, and as Antony slowed at the entry to the historic town of Yungaburra, she caught her breath.

'This is more like it!' she exclaimed as they drove down the quaint main street of the little township with its beautifully restored old buildings.

'We'll come back here later, if you like, but first I want to show you something really spectacular,' Antony said.

Just outside Yungaburra, Antony stopped the car and the two of them got out and walked along a boardwalk and into the rainforest. They hadn't gone very far when right in front of them was a very old fig tree whose aerial roots hung down from its branches like a giant curtain. According to the notice pinned in front of the tree, this was a strangler fig, more than five hundred years old. As Bella took in the amazing sight, she became aware that Antony was watching her closely. For a moment she felt uncomfortable, but then Antony smiled and she smiled back.

'This is not the only remarkable thing in this area,' he said. 'The town backs onto a couple of volcanic lakes. There's Lake Tinaroo as well – it's a dam, but it's well stocked with fish, including barramundi. It's a fisherman's paradise.' His passion for the area was certainly impressive. Bella could feel herself warming to his ideas. Maybe he was on to something.

Bella decided that she wanted to press on, so about fifteen minutes later, Antony parked in the main street of the small town of Atherton and they walked into the first café they saw. While Antony ordered coffee and home-made cheesecake, Bella took out the address she had for the backing band and googled its location. It wasn't far away.

'I've put a bit of extra cream on your cake,' said the waitress. 'You don't have to eat it, but it's local cream and very nice indeed. You staying up here?'

Bella glanced at her watch. 'No, we'll head back to Cairns, I think.'

'Let me give you some brochures for this area, anyway, in case you come back.'

'Do you know who made this cheesecake?' asked Antony. 'It's fantastic.'

'Thank you. I made it myself.'

Antony finished his slice and looked at Bella. 'Tell me, how are you going to approach these blokes?' he asked warily.

'Well they won't answer their phone, so I'm just going to knock on the front door. I hope they're home, because if they're not, well, it means I'll have run out of options.'

'Do you want me to come with you, or would you rather do it on your own?'

'No, come with me, Ant. Thanks.'

The address turned out to be an old federation house which had seen better days, sitting in a very neglected garden.

As they stepped onto the verandah, Bella whispered, 'Seems awfully quiet. Maybe no one's home.'

But as she knocked on the door, there was a sudden burst of music that made her jump back.

'You might have to hammer louder, or wait till the song has finished,' bellowed Antony.

'I think there's a whole band in there,' shouted Bella.

But to their surprise the door was opened a few seconds later by a man who looked to be in his twenties. He was wearing dark glasses and had a red bandana around his head. His face was thin and his nose sharp, but his eyes were bright and friendly and he gave them a cheery smile. Pulling the door shut behind him, he stepped onto the verandah.

'Hi. What's up? You guys lost?'

'No. I'm Bella Chisholm. Ned's sister,' shouted Bella over the noise.

He walked out further into the front garden. 'You're Ned's sister? Did you drive up here especially to meet us?'

'I tried ringing and I left messages, but no one answered. By the way, this is Antony, a friend of mine.'

The men shook hands and the music abruptly finished.

'C'mon in if you like, we're just running through a few songs. I'm Kyle, by the way. Don't mind the mess.'

Bella found it hard to avoid the clutter, as the hallway and rooms were filled with scattered belongings and musical instruments. In the lounge room was a drum kit, a keyboard, and a microphone hooked up to a computer. Two other men lifted their hands in greeting.

'That's Dan and Ryo, and guys, this is Ned Chisholm's sister, just passing by.' He grinned. 'Oh, and . . . Antony, was it?'

'Ant'll do, mate.'

'Do you want coffee or anything?'

'No thanks, we've just had some,' Bella replied.

They followed Kyle to a small deck out the back where there were some old chairs and a sagging sofa.

'You tried to ring, did you? I wondered who kept calling. Girls get our numbers and can be a bit of a pain. In a nice way. Sorry I didn't get back to you. So how's Ned doing? He had some wild plan. Is he writing?'

'Yes, he mentioned he had this burning desire to write a musical,' said Bella. 'But he's taken off and I'm not sure where he is and I want to find him for family reasons.'

'He did a show with you guys in Cairns, right?' asked Antony.

'Yeah, it was good. Real good.'

'Did Ned tell you what his plans were after that?' asked Bella.

'Plans? Dunno exactly what they were, but he did say that he had been offered a place by this other dude he knew. Thought it'd suit him for a while.'

'Do you know where this place is?' asked Antony.

Kyle shrugged. 'Think it was up in Cooktown.'

'Cooktown?' echoed Bella, raising her eyebrows. 'How far away is that?'

'End of the planet if you ask me,' replied Kyle.

'About four hours' drive north of Cairns,' said Antony. 'Do you know anything more about where he was supposed to stay?'

'No idea. Cooktown is a small place, so you could stand in the middle of the street and yell out and see what happens, eh?' suggested Kyle helpfully.

Bella looked at Antony in disbelief.

Kyle got up and went back into the house and they heard him call out: 'Hey, you two. Do either of you know anything about the place where Ned said he was staying?'

'Not really,' said Ryo. 'No, wait, I'm wrong. He did say that it was the pink place. Yeah, definitely pink.'

'A pink place? What does that mean?' Bella asked.

'Dunno,' said Ryo, shrugging.

'Well, thanks anyway. You've been a great help,' said Bella, getting to her feet. 'We'll let you get back to your music.'

'No worries,' said Kyle. 'And if you find your brother, tell him we're ready to do another gig with him any time.'

Outside the cottage, Bella was thoughtful. Finally a real lead to Ned.

'Cooktown's a pretty small place. Ned should be easy enough to find. Will you go up?' asked Antony.

'I suppose. I've come this far, so I might as well go all the way.'

They could still hear the music blasting from the house as they got back into Antony's car and drove off.

'Since you're going that way, you could check the place out for our tailored tourism list . . . big game fishing, historic tours, you might find some good ideas.'

Bella laughed. 'Ant, who says I'm going to join you in your harebrained scheme?'

'You will, Bella, because it's a really good idea. Hang on. There's something I want to show you.' He suddenly made a U-turn and headed back in the opposite direction.

'You're not really serious about this job offer, are you, Ant?' Bella asked, studying his face. 'I already have a well-paid and secure position in Tennyson, in Victoria, so it will be a very big commute.'

'So move! You said you're fascinated by this part of the world. Take the plunge, get into something where you write the rules.'

Bella swallowed hard. 'My boyfriend, my mother, my job are in another state, and what do I know about attracting visitors to a place I hardly know?' She shook her head. 'You're nuts.'

'You are a *tourism expert*,' said Antony, glancing at her. 'Your skills are portable. You'll work out what can be done up here to make us money. And you can always visit your mother and tell your boyfriend to move up.'

Bella refused to meet Antony's eye. 'He's a dentist. He's just built up a good practice.'

'So tell him to sell his practice. Start another up here. There's always a demand for good dentists. Or you could give him the flick and look for someone else.'

She arched an eyebrow. 'Meaning you?'

Antony chuckled. 'Bella, it's a job offer, not a proposal of marriage, although that might come later.' Bella swatted his arm and he chuckled again.

'You really mean it, about the job, don't you? Is your life always this simple? Just do it?' Bella laughed in spite of herself.

'Tell me, haven't you ever thought about starting up your own business?'

Bella was quiet a moment. 'Yes. But not something so radical.'

'You mean you just wanted to do something small, just dip your toes into the water, not really commit, perhaps a little venture that entails wandering around central Victoria, close to home, nothing that requires much of a challenge? You need to think bigger,' said Antony. He glanced at her face and then added: 'But you don't have to give me an answer right away. Mull over what I've said and I'm sure you'll see the potential.'

'I have enough on my plate for the moment, thanks.' Bella knew she sounded a bit terse. Antony was getting to her, rattling her complacency, because, as an inner voice reminded her, she'd had similar thoughts and ambitions but never the courage to devise a plan or take a risk.

They drove on in silence for a while as Bella thought about Antony's ideas. When they arrived at the outskirts of Atherton they pulled up at a strange corrugated iron and timber building surrounded by manicured lawns. A sign informed them that the Hou Wang Miao Chinese Temple was the local joss house built around 1903 by the local Chinese. As they stood at the elaborate entrance with its red carved trim they admired its careful restoration. Inside the joss house, Bella was fascinated by the ornate carvings, the shrine and the collection of Chinese arte-facts. Antony described how John Atherton had opened the area up early on in the tin and timber days, and how a butter factory was operating by 1903, just before the train reached the region in 1906. Chinese immigrants all came to the area looking for gold but when the gold dwindled they went into timber, like red cedar and blackbean, and when that was all felled, they started growing maize and peanuts and lychees. When the White Australia policy was introduced and the *Not Welcome Here* signs went up, some Chinese had managed to stay and lease their land, Antony explained, but after World War One, many were evicted and their land was given to the soldier settlers, so they drifted away from the tablelands to other parts of the country.

'So how come this joss house is still here?' asked Bella, gazing at the elaborate carvings.

'A local Chinese family paid to have it restored and then gave it to the National Trust a few years ago. But don't you see how good this all is, Bella, from a tourism perspective?'

'It's only one building, Ant!' Bella said, rolling her eyes.

'True, but this joss house is one of only a tiny number dedicated to this particular deity that still exist outside China. Actually, this whole area is full of Chinese history! Think of all the Chinese tourists who might want to come and see this part of their own heritage.'

'Oh, I see. So this could be another tailored tour, but aimed at the Chinese market. That's not a bad idea.'

'You bet. The Chinese tourists could fly into Cairns, head north to the old goldfields, then end up in Cooktown. If you're going there you can suss the place out. Might as well kill two birds with one stone.'

'Whoa. I haven't accepted your job offer!'

'You will. You won't get another chance like this again. Why don't I buy you that white wine you missed out on at lunchtime when we get back to Cairns? Then I can tell you more about my plans over a drink.'

On the drive back to Cairns, Bella couldn't stop thinking about Antony's proposal. In theory, it sounded like a very good idea, and his plan to tap into the Chinese tourist market could be an excellent move. And it was promising that investors were interested.

'But what contacts have you got that would make people come to us?' she asked as they headed back onto the main Bruce Highway.

'I've got contacts all over, but I think that if we want to keep overheads down, we should put up a good website and take our bookings online. To make this really work, the tailored trips have to be well researched and reliable and better than any of the competition. What do they say? "Build a better mousetrap and the world will beat a path to your door"?'

Antony parked in the Cairns CBD and the two of them walked to a nearby pub. Bella was somewhat surprised by Antony's choice, as the hotel looked rather run-down.

As though reading her mind, Antony said, 'I know it looks a bit the worse for wear, but believe me, the locals all like coming here, 'cause the tourists don't. You'll see a bit of authentic north Queensland in here.'

Antony was right. It was full of locals, and noisy, and a bit on the rough side, Bella thought. They sat at one of the small tables near the window. As Antony went to get their drinks, Bella looked around at the other customers. Most were dressed in singlets, shorts and thongs and several of them were eyeing her up and down. They all seemed to be speaking loudly at each other and she could hear a very heated argument occurring at one end of the bar. If this was Antony's idea of authentic Queensland, she could do without it. She could see Antony at the bar and wished he would hurry back so she could drink her wine and get out of there quickly. But Antony seemed to be in no hurry as he chatted to two men at the bar. They all had their backs to her, but she could see that one of them had a striking mullet hairdo.

When Antony returned a couple of minutes later, she asked him who the two men were.

'No idea. They just started talking to me while I was waiting for our drinks.' Antony handed her a glass of wine and began telling her in more detail about his plans, but Bella wasn't really paying attention. She gulped her wine down and when Antony offered to buy her another, she shook her head, and they left the pub not long after that.

Since she was going to stay only one more night in Cairns, she decided to book herself into one of the city's good hotels. Antony drove her back to Irene's, where she'd left her car. Irene was not at home, so she said goodbye to Antony with some firmness and drove herself around to the resort hotel. She wanted to have some time by herself to think about Antony's proposition.

Stepping into the shower in her room, she let the warm water flow over her hair as her thoughts wandered. On the face of it, it seemed outrageous for her to throw in her secure life back in Tennyson for such a wild idea. There was no way she could take up his offer. She'd be crazy to leave her well-paid job with its built-in security. And how on earth could she tell her mother and Brendan that she was going to leave Tennyson and her life there and start afresh in north Queensland? Brendan could hardly drop everything and join her – she wasn't sure she would want him to, in any case – so it would probably mean the end of their relationship. Was she prepared for that? But the more she thought about Antony's brainchild, the more she was persuaded that with the right research and organisation, his plan just might work. It would be so exciting to have her own business, to be in charge of her own destiny. Her heart was telling her to seize the offer, as such a chance might never come again, while her head told her that the whole idea was a pie in the sky and that she should forget it.

She stepped out of the shower, towelled off and dressed again. She ordered a club sandwich from room service and was just about to start eating it on the balcony when her phone rang. Her stomach clenched when she saw who was calling.

'Hello, Brendan,' she said.

'Hello yourself,' Brendan said. 'How are you? What have you been up to?'

Bella quickly told him about finding the musicians and learning that Ned had probably gone to Cooktown, and that she had decided she would drive up and try to find him. 'I shouldn't have any trouble doing that. He's supposed to be living in a pink house. How are things with you?' asked Bella, taking a bite of her sandwich.

'Nothing very exciting. I've been over to see Josie. She's just fine,' Brendan replied. 'I ran into Ash the other day. Tim Martin was away sick, so I covered a few of his urgent cases. I don't think she was all that happy to see me but she didn't have a choice as she was in a fair bit of pain.'

'How was she apart from that?'

'Good, I think; well, she seemed to be, didn't say all that much.'

'She's a nice person.' Bella paused and then took the plunge. 'Bren, I need to tell you that I've had a . . . well . . . a kind of a job offer.'

'What sort of job?' Brendan asked slowly.

She explained Antony's ideas, hearing the enthusiasm in her voice as she did so, and talked about all the wonderful things she had seen and done and how much she was enjoying Far North Queensland. Brendan was silent as he listened.

'I just think it could be terrific,' Bella finished. She waited for a response from Brendan.

'It would mean moving north, I suppose. What will your mother say?' asked Brendan.

Bella didn't reply. She knew the answer. Her mother wouldn't make a fuss, or try to stop her – she might even encourage her – but she knew Josie would miss her terribly if she left Tennyson. But this decision wasn't about Josie, Bella thought to herself. It was about her, Bella, and her dreams and ideas. Josie would be supportive if she knew that the change would make Bella happy.

There was a long pause. Then Brendan said, 'Are you really sure that this idea will work? I know that you're good at tourism, but north Queensland? It's hardly your field of expertise. And there are so many start-ups like this that fail in the first year. How would you even go about setting this business up? You haven't got very much experience.'

Bella felt like she'd been slapped. Her mouth fell open. She couldn't believe how negative and critical Brendan was being. Sure her announcement was a surprise, but his response was so harsh. She had *a lot* of experience and business savvy. Suddenly Bella felt angry. How dare he! She was more than capable of doing this job and making it a success.

'Don't question my ability, Brendan Miller,' she snapped. 'Of course I could do the work if I set my mind to it.'

Brendan drew a sharp breath. 'Bella, I'm just saying that it's not exactly a foolproof plan,' he replied in a reasonable tone which somehow made Bella even more annoyed.

'Well, *Antony* thinks I'd be great at it,' she shot back.

Brendan's voice hardened. 'I see. Well, if you're sure that it's the right thing, then go for it. I don't think our relationship would survive being long-distance, but since you don't want to move in with me anyway, that doesn't really matter. This sounds like a great opportunity for you.'

Bella couldn't believe what she was hearing. 'So what are you saying, then? You think I *should* move up here permanently?' she asked crossly.

'Well, it's no use my asking you to come home, if that's not what you want to do.' He cleared his throat and continued in clipped tones. 'I've been asking you for ages to move in with me and you've never given me a proper answer. It seems like you really don't want to be with me, and I'm not going to pressure you into it. If this is what you want, then it could be a good thing.'

He didn't even sound upset. Maybe in the time she'd been away, he had decided that he could do without her. His criticism hurt. Before this conversation she'd been only idly considering Antony's idea but now, hearing Brendan doubt her, her stubborn streak surfaced and she felt her feelings harden.

'All right then, Brendan,' she shot back. 'It seems you want me to stay up here, even if you don't think I can be much of a tour operator. Well, I'll show you. I'll make a success of this business. Just you wait and see.'

'Bella, I'm not going to fight with you, but –'

It was just like all the other conversations they ever had. He never wanted to fight her. It was so infuriating – and so typical! 'Brendan, you never argue with me about anything!' Bella cried. 'Do you even care about me? You don't sound in the slightest bit concerned about what I do. Well, at least you've helped me make up my mind.' Her voice had risen to a shrill pitch. 'I am going to accept Antony's offer and start up a new business with him, and you can get on with your life without me!' She hung up the phone, seething, and threw herself onto her bed, hot tears springing in her eyes. Did he not consider their relationship worth fighting for? He had just closed up as soon as she articulated her plans. He didn't mention even the possibility of moving north with her. He had barely even become emotional. She wiped her face. She couldn't believe he'd been so cold and scathing about her plans. She gazed out at the view from her hotel room. After everything she'd been through in the last year, she really felt she deserved something good to happen. Antony's idea had merit, and for the first time in a long time she was excited about something that could really challenge her. Why couldn't Brendan understand that? She felt a bubble of anger rise in her chest. Well, she wasn't going to let some dentist spoil her dreams. It was her life and she could make a success of this business if she wanted to.

*

Bella was glad to arrive in Cooktown the following afternoon. She'd made a booking at what seemed like the best motel and checked in to it. Then she started looking for the pink house.

Cooktown was a small place and it wasn't long before she found the old house with its lurid hot-pink trim and messy front yard. Bella was a bit taken aback.

She rapped on the door and waited. She was about to give up when she heard movement inside. There was shuffling and a cough and then an apparition appeared in the doorway. Bella took an involuntary step back as a man, possibly in his thirties, leaned against the doorjamb rubbing his eyes. His long hair was matted and his clothes appeared to have been unchanged for weeks. He stroked the stubble on his face and stared at Bella with bleary eyes.

'Hi. I was looking for Ned. Is he around?' When the man didn't answer, Bella asked tentatively, 'He does live here?'

'Ned who?' croaked the fellow, starting to cough.

Bella took a step back. 'Ned Chisholm. He's my brother. He is supposed to be housesitting.'

'Not here. Dunno him.'

'You mean he's not living here?' While Bella's heart sank, she was also glad Ned wasn't living in such a dump.

He shook his head. 'Sorry.' He turned away and closed the door, leaving Bella standing on the verandah wondering what to do next.

Spotting a café where a couple were sitting outdoors having coffee, she felt an overwhelming need for a short espresso. There was a friendly woman behind the counter who smiled and asked, 'What'll it be, dear?'

'A strong black –' Bella looked at the shop's noticeboard and then stopped what she was saying in shock. Pinned to it was a flyer with a picture of Ned holding his guitar. Bella snatched the flyer and stared at her brother's face. After all this time spent chasing him, there he was. She could hardly believe it. Reading the details on the flyer, she saw that Ned was going to be part of a fundraising concert the following evening at the Verandah Room at one of the pubs.

Bella paid for her coffee, folded up the flyer and walked outside. What was it about this strange little town that so attracted Ned? Why on earth couldn't he rent a place near home and work from there? But deep down she understood his restless drive and his need for new experiences. Maybe that was what she was after, too.

She reached for her phone to leave him yet another message, then stopped. No, she thought, a better idea might be just to turn up at the concert. That way he couldn't avoid her.

She had a day to fill in before the show, so she decided she might as well walk around the town and see what there was to do. By the looks of things, she thought, that wouldn't take long. She opened an app on her phone that searched for things to see and do depending on where you were, and top of the list for Cooktown was the James Cook Museum, so she followed the directions.

There were a few tourists about. She paid her money and went in, but soon lost track of time as she lingered over the exhibits. She was particularly moved by the personal family collections that the museum displayed: the tea sets and jewellery, ornaments, tools and other memorabilia. She looked at a formal studio portrait of a serious young Islander girl in a long white dress, hair neatly coiled, wearing a row of beads and with a beribboned straw hat at her feet, sitting close to two sweetly smiling blonde children in a homemade contraption resembling an old-fashioned pram and surrounded by urns and other photographers' props. The small children were dressed in elaborate lace and frills. The caption explained that the trio were Rosetta and Endeavour Seagren with their amah. Another photograph showed an obviously well-to-do older couple posing in their finery. The European woman wore what appeared to be an embroidered silk taffeta dress and she held a rose in her hand, while the silver-haired Chinese man was resplendent in a sombre black suit, complete with a gold fob watch chain, his hand resting on the back of his wife's chair. The caption told their story in a few lines: *In 1874 Jimmy Ah Foo and his European wife, Eveline, arrived in Cooktown from the goldfields of Charters Towers. They first opened the Millchester Boarding House and then a ham and egg shop in Charlotte Street. Encouraged by their success, a year later they opened the Canton Hotel in the same street.*

Bella wondered what had happened to Jimmy Ah Foo with the advent of the White Australia policy. Perhaps because he was married to a European, he'd been able to stay in Queensland.

After half an hour, she'd had enough and made her way back to the motel. She decided to ring Antony to tell him what she was doing in Cooktown. Despite what she'd told Brendan, she hadn't formally accepted Ant's offer, but she was thinking about it very seriously.

167

Antony sounded pleased to hear from her and listened as she told him about what she had found.

She took a deep breath, 'This isn't a definite yes to your offer, but Ant, I think you could be on the right track. Maybe organised tours for the Chinese would work. There was obviously a large Chinese presence here once upon a time and if you can find out which part of China they mainly came from, you could perhaps target that region? What do you think?'

'Great idea, Bella. You're on the right wavelength there. How much longer do you think you'll be in Cooktown?'

'Not sure. At least till the weekend. My brother's performing in one of the pubs. After that I can't really say.'

'Well, let me know as soon as you know, and keep those good ideas rolling in. Ciao for now.'

Bella smiled to herself as she ended the call. It was fun thinking up ideas that could work for the new business. Maybe she and Antony really could make the tailored tours succeed.

Filled with enthusiasm, she spent the next day asking around about big game fishing, how to get to the old goldfields, and what sort of journeys could be made up Cape York. She considered renting a four-wheel drive, but thought perhaps she might be able to talk Ned into taking her to some interesting-sounding places once she'd found him.

It was dusk as Bella arrived at the old hotel where the modernised restaurant and balcony area upstairs was the venue for the concert. The main restaurant area in front of the small stage was filled with rows of chairs and a few tables were scattered along the verandah. Bella found the people around her were mostly locals but with a smattering of tourists. Everyone was very friendly, and there was a mood of happy expectation.

The publican stood up and thanked everybody for coming to support the fundraising effort and added, 'I especially want to thank Ned Chisholm for agreeing to sing for us. All proceeds from tonight's ticket sales will go to our wonderful museum and the splendid work it does. So now it's over to Ned Chisholm. Give him a big Cooktown welcome!'

There was loud applause and a few whistles as Ned ambled onto the stage and sat on the stool by the microphone.

Bella applauded loudly, a huge smile on her face. She was thrilled to see her brother looking so fit and handsome.

As soon as he started singing, Bella remembered again his rich husky voice and the way he connected with an audience, making each person feel as though he was singing directly to them.

In what seemed a very short time later, Bella, like the rest of the audience, came to her feet to cheer Ned's performance, feeling as though they had all shared a special journey with him and his music.

After acknowledging the crowd, Ned took his guitar, thanked the band and headed off stage and towards the bar. Bella squeezed through the crush of people to where Ned was affably posing for photos with some of the audience. As she got near him, she saw him smile broadly as he hugged an attractive woman. As she tipped back her head, he kissed her lightly. They separated and Ned turned to acknowledge a fan approaching from his other side.

Bella pushed her way through the crowd and tapped Ned on the shoulder.

'Hi, Ned.'

Her brother turned to face her, and his expression quickly changed. 'Bella!' he exclaimed.

7

NED FELT MOMENTARILY STUNNED when he saw Bella, and then a flash of anger surged through him. How on earth did she find him in Cooktown? He didn't want her here. But before he could ask her anything, Bella had thrown her arms around his neck.

'Surprise, eh, big brother?' She pulled away and grinned triumphantly at Ned. 'Found you at last.'

'Why are you here, Bella?'

'Like I said in my messages, I wanted to catch up with you,' Bella said too casually. She glanced at Toni, motioning for an introduction.

Ned groaned inwardly with rising anxiety. He could guess all too easily Bella's real motivation. She was like a dog with a bone. With some reluctance, he gestured to Toni, 'Toni, this is Bella. My sister.'

Toni smiled broadly and reached out a hand. 'I gathered that. Hi, Bella, so nice to meet you. Ned mentioned you were travelling up this way,' said Toni. 'Have you been enjoying your holiday?'

'Yes, I've been having a brilliant holiday,' said Bella, the crowd jostling around her. 'Far North Queensland is just amazing.'

'It is special, isn't it?' Toni took a step away from Ned and gestured for Bella to join her closer to the bar. 'Why don't we order a drink? I'll order while Ned finishes chatting with his fans.'

Ned nodded mutely and turned to talk to some of the audience who had made their way over to him. Despite his anxiety over Bella's appearance, he was gratified by the comments of these fans, who thanked him for giving up his time for charity and told him how much they'd enjoyed the show. He then posed for some selfies and when the last photo had been taken, he made his way to the small table where the girls were sitting, just in time to hear Bella ask Toni how long she'd known Ned.

'Since he moved here,' Toni smiled. 'He's staying with me . . .'

'Ah,' said Bella. 'No wonder the guy at the old pink house didn't know who Ned was.'

Toni burst out laughing. 'As if he'd stay there. It has a terrible reputation.'

'Well then, I'm pleased you've found a better place to hang out than that, dear brother,' Bella said as Ned sat down beside Toni.

Ned immediately felt on guard. 'Actually, Bella, I'm only staying with Toni when I come into town. The rest of the time I'm out at Carlo's.'

'Carlo? Who on earth is Carlo?'

Ned explained who Carlo was and why he was house-sitting his place.

171

'It's really remote, no phone reception, no roads, no amenities and no distractions,' he added pointedly.

'Well, if that's true, I suppose that explains why you've been so elusive,' said Bella rather grudgingly, fiddling with the straw in her drink.

Toni seemed to notice the tension and added cheerily: 'Ned says that it's a remarkable place and has to be seen to be believed. He's asked me to come out next weekend for a couple of days and have a look,' said Toni. 'But Bella, speaking of places to stay, you're welcome to stop at my place while you're in Cooktown, if you like.'

Bella waved a hand. 'No, but thanks for the offer, Toni. I'm already staying in one of the motels.'

'How long do you intend staying?' asked Ned deliberately.

'I'm not really sure,' Bella said smoothly, ignoring his tone. 'I've got a couple of weeks holidays left and I would like to have a bit more of a look around.'

'What made you choose Far North Queensland for your holidays, Bella?' said Toni, glancing at Ned with a reproving look.

'I wanted to catch up with Ned,' said Bella, punching Ned gently in the arm. 'I'm hoping to persuade him to come back home for a special ceremony recognising our father's work at the local hospital. Our mother particularly wants him to be there.'

Toni nodded, smiling, but Ned's mouth hardened into a straight line.

'Won't your father want you to be there, too?' Toni asked Ned, taking a sip of water. Ned opened his mouth to answer but then closed it again.

'Dad was killed in a car accident nearly a year ago,' said Bella.

Toni instantly looked contrite. 'I'm so sorry. I had no idea. How very sad, for both of you. It sounds as though this ceremony is a great honour for your father. Was he a doctor?' she asked.

Bella quickly told her about Alex's stellar career as a surgeon and how well respected he had been in the community, which was why he was being honoured.

Toni nodded and smiled at Bella's loving description of Alex. 'Your father sounds like an amazing man. I suppose you'll be going down to Victoria, then, Ned?'

Ned said nothing. He was seething. Why did Bella have to be so interfering? He'd told his mother, as gently as he could, that he couldn't make it down to the dedication ceremony. He'd been much blunter, he thought, with Bella, so why couldn't she take a simple no for an answer? He was not about to make any further explanations about his decision to either Bella or Toni here in the pub. There was an awkward silence for a few moments until Ned eventually said, 'Can I get you girls another drink? Wine for you Bella, and you're still with the mineral water, Toni? I think I need a beer.' And with that he made his way over to the bar. He knew that while he was away, Bella would be talking about him to Toni. And as he took their drinks back to the table, he could hear their conversation quite clearly as the noise in the hotel was beginning to die down.

'So how did you meet my brother?' Bella was saying.

'It was when he had the car accident,' replied Toni.

Bella paled visibly. '*Car accident*? Ned never told us about an accident! What happened?'

'Bella, I'm fine,' said Ned, setting down their glasses on the table. 'I skidded off the road trying to avoid some birds. The car was a write-off and Toni, who is the physio at the hospital here, was the one who found me and brought me into Cooktown. I was over it very quickly and I didn't want to tell either you or Mum because you would fuss and there was nothing to fuss about.'

'It's not about "fussing", Ned,' Bella said quietly. 'Mum and I love you. We would just have wanted to hear you were okay. I wish you had called.'

Ned looked away awkwardly. 'So, tell me, little sister, how did you find me?'

'It wasn't all that hard. Once I knew you'd performed in Cairns, I headed north, and after one false start I contacted your Cairns backing band, who said you were going to Cooktown, and so here I am.'

'I see,' said Ned neutrally.

There was an awkward silence. Ned could see Toni was puzzled by the tension at the table, but he just couldn't make polite conversation at the moment.

Suddenly Bella stood up. 'Look, you two, I'm actually feeling a bit tired. I don't know what it is about holidays that make you feel so bushed – probably the sensory overload.' She picked up her bag and slung it over her arm. 'Anyway, Ned, it was great to see you perform again. It was a good concert. Perhaps we could all have lunch tomorrow? Although I don't want to impose on your time together,' she added.

'Of course you're not imposing,' Toni said hurriedly. 'There's a seafood place down on the river that Ned and I like to go to. The fishing boats come right up to it, so you can't miss it. Say around twelve thirty?'

Bella put her hand on Ned's shoulder. 'That sounds like a good idea. I'll see you at lunch tomorrow.'

With that, Bella made her way downstairs, leaving Ned feeling nonplussed. He looked down at his beer and frowned, not meeting Toni's eye. He was not only annoyed with Bella's unasked-for reappearance in his life, but now he was also likely to have Toni asking him about his father. At the same time, deep down, he also felt guilty about his sister. He really should have been pleased to see her – after all, he was very fond of her – but her presence meant his conflicted feelings about Alex were harder to ignore.

Ned was so wrapped up in his thoughts that it took him a while to notice that Toni was also very quiet. There were only a handful of patrons left in the hotel, and just as Ned and Toni were about to go, two of them came over to chat with Ned. They were so enthusiastic about his music that when they all finally left, Ned felt on an adrenalin high. People really did seem to like his style of music.

Walking up the steps to Toni's verandah, he tried to lighten the mood by saying, 'That was some night, Toni. The audience was really appreciative. Wish I could keep them around all the time.'

'Yes, you certainly wowed them at the pub,' replied Toni flatly as she opened her front door. 'You know, I'm feeling like your sister – I'm a bit tired. I might have an early night, if you don't mind.'

'No, not at all,' said Ned. He was puzzled. He kissed her on the cheek as she disappeared into the bedroom. Now that he thought about it, Toni had been a bit distant ever since he'd arrived that morning. It wasn't that she was unaffectionate, but earlier in the day when he'd been talking to her, she'd occasionally seemed somewhat distracted, as though she was thinking of something else, and a couple of times he had caught her looking into the distance as though she was trying to work out some sort of puzzle. When he had asked her if everything was all right at work, she had seemed astonished by his question and had replied in a surprised voice that of course it was. He'd dismissed the exchange at the time, but now Ned worried that the problem, whatever it was, concerned him. When he joined her in bed later, she was sound asleep. But the next morning, Toni seemed bright and happy and said she was looking forward to having lunch with Bella. Perhaps she had just been a bit tired.

*

The water was a deep turquoise and a fishing trawler, freshly hosed down, rocked gently by the wharf. Large empty baskets which had recently held freshly caught prawns were stacked on its deck like giants' hats.

Ned could see Bella sitting at the window of the seafood restaurant looking at the tranquil scene. Once again he was suffused with mixed feelings by her presence. He parked the car and he and Toni walked towards the restaurant.

'She's here already. I hope she hasn't been here too long,' said Toni.

'Well, if she has, it's her own fault. We told her what time to meet us,' replied Ned grumpily.

Toni glanced at him. 'Why are you so down on your sister for coming up here to Cooktown? I gather you two haven't seen each other for a while and I think it's lovely she's spending some of her well-earned break with you,' said Toni.

'Yeah, really generous of her,' replied Ned. 'Still, it might have been simpler if she hadn't.' He let go of Toni's hand and shoved his own into his pocket.

Toni stopped walking and faced him. 'Why's that? I think I'd be pleased if my sister took the time to visit me.'

'Toni, I have my reasons. Please don't jump to conclusions when you don't know the full story.'

'Sorry, I'm not judging you at all,' said Toni, holding up her hands. 'I just thought your reaction to Bella's arrival would be different. But then maybe we don't know each other very well, do we . . .' she added quietly.

Ned took his hand from his pocket and reached out and squeezed her arm. He wondered if Toni's distant behaviour the previous day meant that in fact Toni *had* been judging him, and maybe she had found him wanting. 'I'm working on knowing you better, Toni.'

'Then be nice to your sister,' Toni said under her breath as they entered the restaurant. Bella waved to them and they made their way over to her table.

'Hope you had a good night's sleep,' said Toni as they greeted each other and sat down.

Bella nodded enthusiastically. 'Yes, I crashed. I'm starving now, though. This is a cute place – I like how the fishing boats can tie up right out the front.'

'Speaking of fish, did I tell you I caught a beauty last week?' Ned said, deciding to make an effort to be pleasant. 'At night too, so it was a bit of a song and dance. Someone told me to stick a fishing reel into a bucket, so I did, and when the fish struck, the reel went off like a rocket. The bucket rolled along the bank. I heard it go and raced down to the river and landed the fish. Fed me for two days.'

'Sounds exciting.' Bella smiled, but didn't sound enthusiastic.

'What did you do this morning? Anything interesting?' Ned asked Bella as she scanned the menu.

'Not really. It's too hot to do much. I had a good talk to Mum. She was happy to hear that we're catching up.'

'What would you like to drink, girls?' Ned asked, pointedly changing that subject.

'I think I'll just have a lime juice,' replied Toni. 'I'm thirsty and it's so hot. Makes you really wish that the weather would break and we'd get the wet season to cool things down.'

'White wine would be lovely,' said Bella. 'Sav blanc if they have it. Mum sends her love and hopes your composing is coming on.'

Ned frowned, certain he detected an implied criticism in Bella's words. 'I'm going to call Mum later today,' he said defensively.

There was an uncomfortable silence until the waiter appeared and they ordered calamari rings to start with, followed by fresh grilled fish and salad.

'I'm sorry,' said Toni as the waiter moved away, 'but you'll have to excuse me for a moment. There's a patient of mine over there. He's terrible about keeping appointments and I want to talk to him here where he can't escape.' Toni headed across the room.

'I like Toni,' said Bella. 'She seems very bright and kind. How are things going between you two? Is she just going to be another notch on your belt?'

'I don't think that it's any of your business, Bella.'

'I just don't want you hurting Toni. She seems so nice.'

Ned could feel his temper rising. 'She is nice. And you know what, Bella? It might surprise you to learn that I'm nice too. Look out, here she comes.' He gave Toni a smile. 'How did you go with your patient?'

Toni laughed. 'It seems that he never told his wife about any of those appointments. Well, she knows about them now, so I expect I'll see him on time, every time, in the future.' Toni sat down again. 'Ned, I meant to ask you sooner. Are you having fun with the Bish's box?'

'What is the Bish's box?' asked Bella curiously.

Ned quickly explained about the box and the letters inside. 'Sister Evangelista paints terrific word pictures of this place as it was more than a hundred years ago. For a nun, she seemed like a pretty spunky woman.'

'I don't think you should describe a nun like that,' said Toni with a smile.

'I'll look forward to reading those letters, too, when I visit this hideout of yours, Ned,' said Bella.

Ned gave Bella a noncommittal look. He hadn't asked her to stay with him and he knew that time spent with her would only lead to arguments. But since Bella knew he'd asked Toni out to the river house, he couldn't think of an excuse to refuse to extend his sister the same courtesy. He felt trapped. He was tempted not to mention the two intruders as he didn't want to put Toni off, so he said nothing. Besides, he'd seen nothing more of the two men, so he had the feeling that it was probably just a one-off event. Maybe, he thought hopefully, Bella would find Carlo's place too rustic and remote and be quickly bored.

The table was silent for a moment until Ned finally said, 'I'm not sure you'll like it out there, Bella, but if you really want to come, we'll have to leave town by eight sharp, tomorrow morning. Have you got a four-wheel drive?'

'No, just a small hatchback.'

'Perhaps you could leave it at the motel and we can travel out together in my car. It's more suited to the rough tracks.'

'Bella, you can leave your car at my place, if you like,' said Toni.

'That would be terrific,' said Bella. 'Then it's settled. Do let me know if there's anything special I need to get in the way of supplies.'

'No. I did a huge shop last time I was in town, so the house is well stocked. But Bella, I hope you're not expecting anything too glamorous, and there's nothing much out there to do, so bring a book.'

There hadn't been much choice about inviting Bella to the river house, but maybe it wasn't such a bad idea after all. Perhaps when Bella accepted that he was adamant about not returning home for his father's ceremony, the subject would be dropped and they could have a few companionable days together. Perhaps.

Outside the restaurant, Toni asked Bella, 'Are you sure you don't want to come round to my place and have dinner with us tonight?'

'Thank you, Toni, but it's not necessary. I'll be eating three meals a day with Ned for the next week! Besides, after that lunch, a piece of toast will do me tonight.' She briefly hugged Toni goodbye, and kissed Ned on the cheek. 'Tomorrow at eight. I'm looking forward to having a few days with you, Ned,' she said, as she climbed into her car.

Ned waved her goodbye and then he and Toni drove back to Toni's place.

'All right with you if I ring my mother?' he asked when they arrived. When Toni nodded, Ned walked out onto the verandah so as not to disturb Toni and rang Josie. Yes, he told his mother when she answered, he had been very pleased to see Bella and he had asked her to come and stay with him for a few days. His mother seemed to be happy with that piece of news. She talked to him about his concert and his progress with his composing, but she made no mention about his returning home. Maybe, Ned thought, after he'd hung up and was gazing out at the small clouds congregating in the distance, Josie had resigned herself to the fact that he would definitely be a non-starter, and had given up asking. Oddly enough, this thought made Ned feel quite uncomfortable.

Ned and Toni did little that afternoon except sit relaxing together on Toni's lounge, talking quietly. Toni was full of admiration for Ned's performance the night before and was very complimentary. She seemed completely normal, so Ned put aside his doubts and just enjoyed her company. With his arm around her, he said, 'So you're still happy to come out to Carlo's place next weekend?'

'Of course. I'm quite curious about what's out there.'

'Bella might still be there.'

'I don't mind. I like your sister.'

'Good, and even if she is still there, it won't stop me from driving into town to collect you.'

'Ned, that's silly. I know how to get to the Golden Mile, so why don't I meet you there? I could even leave my car at the roadhouse and let you drive me the rest of the way to Carlo's. I think that might be the easiest plan.'

'I can't wait to have another weekend with you, Toni. I really like being with you,' said Ned softly.

'I'm pleased you feel that way, Ned,' answered Toni, and she smiled gently at him. She looked as though she wanted to say something more, but didn't. Instead she leaned across and kissed him.

*

Ned put some music on in the car and played it very loudly as a means of avoiding conversation. But after they had been travelling for some time, Bella touched his arm.

'Ned. What about *your* music? Don't you have anything of yours I can hear? What about the new material you've been working on?'

'Well . . . it's not really ready. I've just been fumbling around with a few ideas . . .' He paused, not wanting to sound like he hadn't done anything. 'I mean, it's early days, and these things have to gestate first . . . but okay. I can put some music on, just some of my ideas, if you want to listen.'

In a way, Ned wanted to get Bella's feedback on his work. She wasn't as musical as he was, but she knew his work well, she was practical and she never held back her opinions.

As the music started, she said, 'Is this the only copy? What kind of instruments do you have to work with?'

'I rather lucked out with musical equipment. Carlo has a bunch of it. I gather he likes to hold parties. His keyboard has been useful for laying down a few different backing tracks, and he has a set of drums, so I've just made some rough tracks. It's hardly professional, but you'll get the general idea.'

'I won't ask about a storyline or anything, I just want to get a feel for the sound,' said Bella. She leaned back and closed her eyes, listening intently.

Ned drove on, trying to clear his mind and imagine he was hearing what he'd written for the first time. He thought there was a freshness, a vitality, that was new and different from his previous work. As different as night and day. And he realised that this was literally true. Previously he'd done most of his composing at night, whereas up here he'd spent most of his creative time outdoors by the river or sitting higher up on one of the terraces, strumming chords, searching for images and lyrics, making notations. In the evening he'd sat at the keyboard, polishing and transcribing what he'd done during the day. Now there seemed to be more strength and less tentativeness to his music. It appeared that the dedication and application without interruption had allowed him to be more creative than he'd realised.

As the music finished, Bella turned to Ned.

'Wow. I'm impressed. I can just see it all, the landscape and the stories I've heard about this place. Your work is so evocative. It makes me think of the ocean and pristine beaches, the coral reefs and the lush tablelands, the humid rainforests with their rare plants and animals as well as the people of this region and their unique stories,' Bella paused and cocked her head. 'I can imagine the driving force of a surging waterfall and the peacefulness of these wide open spaces. I think I can even hear hints of an Irish ballad, as well as the oriental flavour of a gong, and the muted peal of a bell.'

Ned was impressed by Bella's subtle understanding of his work. 'Thanks, Bella, that's certainly positive. And you're right, I am trying to tell people who have never been here something about the scenery and history of this area. I want to link them all together in a narrative involving places and incidents that are part of this amazing region. But the music is only half the picture. There has to be a theme and a story that's the driving force bringing all these ideas together. And that's the part that I'm finding the hardest.' He paused. 'I find it difficult to talk about what I'm trying to do until it's gelled, and I still can't get it all to come together. But I'm pleased that you like what I've done so far.'

Bella touched his arm. 'It's really wonderful, Ned.'

'Thanks, Bell,' Ned said, genuinely smiling at her for the first time. She held his smile for a moment and then they both gazed out of the window for a while in a companionable silence.

'I've missed talking to you in the past few months, Ned,' Bella said gently. 'Remember when we were kids, how we talked, how you explained things to me?'

Ned smiled. 'No, *you* explained them to *me*. You were always very definite about things; how they were, how they should be, what you were going to do. I just listened.'

Bella chuckled. 'That was just a little girl laying down how she saw the world. And you never disagreed or corrected me. You let me believe that what I thought was how it was.'

'Why not? Your little-girl fantasies would soon dissolve when confronted with the harsh realities of growing up. I didn't want to be the one to tell you that's not how things are and disillusion you,' said Ned. 'I knew you'd find out soon enough.'

'Why are you so disenchanted?' asked Bella. 'Is it Ash? Brendan saw her the other day, by the way.'

'Ashleigh? No.' He paused. 'Is she okay?'

'Do you care?' Then, obviously seeing the angry expression on Ned's face, she quickly said, 'Sorry, Ned. I was fond of her. I've never understood –'

'Bella. Not now, please.'

'That's what you always say,' said Bella, becoming frustrated. They had seemed to be really connecting and now he was shutting down again. 'You always want to escape from any conversation that might require having to explain yourself.'

'I just want to get on with my life. And for the moment my life is music,' Ned said, gripping the steering wheel.

Bella was silent for a moment, but eventually said, 'Okay, let's go back to your music. What exactly is the issue? Do you have writer's block?'

'I'm not sure. Maybe I'm just frustrated because I know what I want to do with my music, but no matter how hard I try, I can't get it right. I feel like the captain of an empty ship at the moment, setting out on a journey into uncharted waters. I know I'll need a crew beside me at some stage – an arranger, orchestrator, director, conductor, recording engineer. I have a sense of what's needed overall: music and lyrics, a great story, wonderful characters, a plot that engages the audience, unforgettable moments where the story pauses and a song lands to illuminate that moment. The audience needs to know quickly where we are, when it is, who it is about. I need a hook that identifies this, and a theme that links it all together, and I can't seem to find that hook.'

'You mean something that was there once and is still there now? Like a river, say?' said Bella. 'Or a mountain.'

Ned glanced at his sister. 'Maybe. Hmm. A river. That might work.'

The two of them sat silently for a few minutes until Ned suddenly turned his vehicle into the carpark in front of the Golden Mile Roadhouse.

'I want to stop here for a few minutes. I don't need to pick up any supplies, I got the few items I needed in Cooktown, but I want to let my friends know that Toni will probably be leaving her car here next weekend. Come on in, I'd like you to meet Frederick and Theresa.'

When they entered the roadhouse, Theresa immediately shouted out a greeting and Frederick came over to shake Ned's hand.

'Good to see you, mate,' he said.

Ned gestured to Bella. 'Frederick, this is my sister, Bella. She'll be staying with me for a few days.'

'G'day,' Frederick said, shaking Bella's hand. 'You'll like it out there, Bella. Bit remote, but really lovely. At night you can see a million stars. Make the most of it before the rainy season starts.'

'How long do you reckon we've got?' asked Ned.

'Oh, maybe a little while yet, but there's no doubt that things are heading that way,' replied Frederick. 'You two got time for a coffee before you set off for Carlo's?'

'Sure have,' said Ned.

Ten minutes later, the four of them were seated around one of the tables in the roadhouse, drinking cups of hot, freshly brewed coffee.

'This is delicious,' said Bella. 'This roadhouse seems so remote. Do you enjoy being this far away from civilisation?'

'We do,' said Theresa, nodding. 'There're always interesting people passing through, usually on the way to Cape York or heading south towards Mareeba or Cairns. Surprising the number of people who want to take a trip as far north as they can go and tell their friends they've been to the top of Australia. Mind you, the season for travellers is almost over. Not long now till the road becomes impassable, even for four-wheel drives.'

'Because of the rain?' asked Bella.

'Sure is. It comes down in sheets and you can't drive on the dirt roads. The rivers flood. It wasn't that long ago that Cooktown was cut off from the rest of the country in the wet. Now that the all-weather road has been put through, that doesn't happen. Not that many people go to Cooktown in the rainy season.'

'Ned,' said Bella, 'you aren't staying here in the rainy season, are you?'

Ned shook his head. 'No, I intend to be well out of here by then, don't worry.'

As they drank their coffee, Bella looked around the roadhouse. Interested by Frederick's goldfield memorabilia, she excused herself and went over to have a closer look.

'By the way, Ned,' said Frederick, after Bella had gone, 'I heard from the people who are supposed to be fixing Carlo's sat phone, and it's not good news, mate. It appears the part that's needed to fix it has to come from down south, so you won't be getting it back anytime soon.'

Ned shrugged. 'It can't be helped. I've gone this long without it, so I'm sure I'll manage for a bit longer.' Ned went on to tell Frederick about Toni's impending visit.

'We can look after her vehicle all right. So we'll see you next weekend, will we?'

As Ned was nodding in agreement, Bella returned, bubbling with interest over the goldfield relics.

'Frederick, where did all those bits and pieces come from? They are so interesting.'

'Mostly from Maytown. It was the hub of goldmining in these parts, but that was more than a century ago. Not much left there now,' he answered.

'Well, that doesn't stop you from fossicking around the place looking for souvenirs, does it?' said Theresa in an amused voice.

'Some of those relics and photos and newspaper cuttings have come from campers, tourists and souvenir hunters. Funny, though, no one has donated a bit of gold,' he added with a grin.

When Ned had swallowed the last of his coffee, he got to his feet, thanked Frederick and Theresa and said that they had to be on their way. 'I always have to concentrate when I get to the track. I'm still not confident about it, so I want to get started.'

'Here, I made some fruitcake. Take it with you,' said Theresa, handing them the freshly baked cake wrapped in foil.

*

Ned was quiet after they left the roadhouse as he mulled over once again what he was trying to convey in his musical. Talking with Bella had helped, but had not really solved his problems. Bella was quiet too, lost in her own thoughts.

A short time later he turned onto a dirt road which he followed for some distance. As the four-wheel drive bounced along, Bella commented that she hoped this drive wasn't going to be too long, as it was very uncomfortable.

'This is nothing, Bella. We haven't even turned onto the track yet.'

When they did, Ned dropped all thoughts of his music and concentrated on the difficult drive.

'Have you any idea where you are?' asked Bella dubiously.

'Shh, I don't want to talk in case I take a wrong turning. So far, I'm all right.'

As the vehicle lurched along the almost invisible track, Bella said nothing, but took a very sharp intake of breath as they rocked from side to side.

She was quiet until she saw the lake, glittering in the sunlight and dotted with colourful water lilies. 'Oh wow, how beautiful,' she exclaimed.

'Hard to believe it was once just a hole in the ground supplying water to a goldmine. Certainly this is less of an eyesore than it must have been thirty years ago,' said Ned.

Bella glanced around. 'We seem to be in the middle of nowhere. There's not even a proper track. You're just following wheel ruts which I can hardly see.'

'I did get lost a couple of times when I first came here, but I feel a lot surer of my way now. Once you reach this lake, it's pretty straightforward.'

Shortly afterwards, Ned pulled up and got out to unlock the gate. 'Can you close it behind me?' he said to Bella as he got back in the vehicle.

Inside the gated wall, Bella stood staring in amazement at the trees and the garden with its canal water feature. 'What kind of architecture do you call this?' she asked as the two of them walked into the patchwork house.

'Tropical north, Italian style?' suggested Ned as he put down their bags. Bella carried in the box of food Ned had bought in Cooktown.

'Put the box on the bench and I'll show you the rest of the place,' said Ned, eager to see Bella's reaction.

By the time they'd worked their way down to the river terrace, Bella was laughing and shaking her head. 'I don't believe this place! It's crazy.'

'Crazy nice? Or crazy mad?'

'Crazy fun. That pizza oven! The barbecue! What a spot for a party! No wonder they have those great speakers and all that musical gear. You must be in heaven staying here.'

'It's the perfect set-up for me,' agreed Ned. 'Let's get sorted and have a swim in the river before it gets dark.'

By the time Ned showed Bella where she could sleep and they'd unpacked and headed to the river, the sun was low, glazing the surface of the water in pewter and gold. The water was surprisingly warm and they floated and swam lazily.

'You're sure there's nothing that can bite in here?' asked Bella.

'Only if you bite first,' said Ned. 'Want to race to the island and back to the bank?'

Bella shook her head. 'I don't have that much energy, and anyway, you'd win.'

When they had both had enough, they shook off the river water and made their way back to the house. Ned showed Bella the solar showers and asked if she was happy with steak for dinner.

Ned cooked the steaks and sipped a glass of red wine, watching the news on the large TV screen.

'All mod cons. Incredible place,' Bella said as she joined him.

'So tell me, Bella, what have you been getting up to these holidays other than hunting me down?'

Bella laughed and told him about the last couple of weeks. Finally, she told him about Antony's business offer and his ideas for a modular approach to tailoring specific holidays for time-poor tourists, especially overseas ones.

'Sounds interesting,' said Ned carefully.

'I'm glad you think so,' said Bella. 'Brendan, Mr Stick-in-the-Mud, was so negative about the idea, I couldn't believe it. We had a huge fight about it. He just has no faith in my abilities.'

Ned was surprised. 'That doesn't sound like Brendan.'

'All he could see were the risks,' said Bella. 'I think it's over between us. How can I be with someone who won't support my dreams? I've had a couple of missed calls from him, but I'm not going to call him back. I don't want to speak to him.'

Ned frowned and opened his mouth to say something, but Bella continued: 'Antony is so positive and up-beat. He's so confident and full of clever ideas. He's a risk taker, which makes him kind of exciting, especially compared with Brendan. Ant's made me want to change my own boring life.'

Ned found it hard to believe what he was hearing. 'Bella, are you really telling me that you are prepared to throw over a good job, your boyfriend, leave home and take off with some charming, fast-talking travel operator? I can't believe that you would do such a thing without at least investigating his business plan a bit further.'

'Of course I will,' Bella said a little tersely. 'Antony's ideas are still a bit vague at this stage, but he assures me he has financial backing lined up. I would obviously need to do more research before I attempted anything Antony has in mind, and I certainly haven't told him that I will go in with him yet.'

Ned was relieved. 'I'm pleased to hear it. It all sounds a bit airy-fairy to me.'

'Ned, you're as bad as Brendan!' Bella said indignantly. 'Why is it that neither of you assume I will make the right decision? I'm not stupid, and if I want to take a risk, then I'll make sure that it's not too great a one to take. Heavens, you're prepared to take risks. Why can't I?'

Ned held up his hands. 'All right, all right, you've made your point, although I think it's a shame about Brendan. I really like him.'

'Well, you're not being pressured to move in with him. I might just have dodged a bullet there.'

After dinner, as they were leaning back in Carlo's homemade chairs, Ned heard Bella take a deep breath. 'Do you think Dad would be spinning in his grave if he could see us both now?' she asked. 'You with your unfulfilled dream and me wanting to pursue a new career, both of us so unsettled?' When Ned didn't answer, she added with a sigh, 'Doesn't seem like Dad's accident was nearly a year ago now, does it? The suddenness of it, having no preparation, no warning.'

Ned rose to get them both another drink. 'Yeah, well, that's how accidents are.'

Bella hunched forward. 'He shouldn't have gone to Melbourne for that conference in such terrible weather. He was always much too conscientious about doing the right thing.'

'Bella! Please, leave it. We can't change history,' Ned snapped at her.

Bella stared at him, clearly surprised by the tone of his voice. 'I know we can't change history, but that doesn't mean we can't talk about it, does it? I miss Dad. We all do, which is why I think you should come home for Dad's dedication.'

Ned closed his eyes. He'd known this would happen. Bella was like a dog with a bone. 'Bella, I simply can't. You see the situation here, I can't leave. I haven't the time, or the money. Mum understands.' He turned and walked back into the kitchen.

Bella followed him. 'But you don't have the inclination to come either, it seems. If you wanted to, you would make the time. It would only be for a couple of days. Look, of course Mum says she doesn't mind. She never wants to upset you. But I know she would really, really like for you to be there. We are such a small family, and –'

Ned wheeled around. 'Stop, Bella. Stop your damned nagging! This is between Mum and me. Stop trying to run my life!'

Bella looked like she'd been slapped. 'Run your life?! We've barely spoken in a year!' Her face turned red. 'You only do things if it pleases you. If it doesn't suit you, then you just walk away. Are you going to be like this forever? Because your way hurts people.'

Ned slammed his fist on the kitchen table. 'Look at your life, Bella. You seem to manage to do what you want.

Poor Brendan has to like it or lump it, and now you're dumping him for some con man.'

Bella gasped. 'That's not true! I'm interested in developing a business with Antony, not a relationship! Why don't you just mind your own business, Ned?'

'I could ask you the very same thing, Bella.' Ned looked at the ceiling. Suddenly he felt very tired. Bella seemed deflated too. 'Look, this arguing is getting us nowhere. How about we call it a night and start tomorrow afresh?'

Bella glared at her brother, saying nothing at first, but then slowly nodded her head. 'Fine. I'll see you in the morning.' With that, she stalked out of the room.

Ned watched her go. It was going to be a very long few days if tonight was anything to go by. He didn't want to hurt Bella, but if she kept pushing him, he might just say something that he would regret.

*

The next morning, Bella walked into the kitchen to be greeted by the wafting aromas of toast and coffee.

'How did you sleep?' asked Ned cheerfully. 'Ready for some coffee?'

Bella stretched her arms above her head. 'Yes, thank you. I slept really well. I didn't hear a thing. I can't believe how quiet it is out here. I thought I'd have another swim.'

Ned handed her a fresh cup of coffee. 'How about I make you an omelette with some lovely fresh eggs from the girls?'

'What girls?' asked Bella, sipping her coffee.

Ned explained about the hens. 'Evidently they are Carlo's pride and joy. He hasn't had them long, so I'm taking great care of them. I've also got some little vine-ripened tomatoes, which I can cook to go with the eggs.'

'You're very cheffy all of a sudden,' she said with some amusement. 'You rarely lifted a finger in the kitchen at home.' As they ate their breakfast, Bella chatted away lightheartedly. Ned was relieved that she seemed to have called a truce, although he wondered if it was just a temporary one.

After breakfast, Ned took the scraps out to the hens and then he and Bella made their way down to the river at the bottom terrace. Bella swam while Ned was engrossed with his music. Eventually Bella hauled herself from the river and wandered over to her brother.

'That was lovely. This is such a beautiful place. I can see why you like being here.' She settled herself down next to him. Ned kept working, strumming his guitar and making notes, humming to himself quietly under his breath. After a few minutes Bella started fidgeting. She cracked her knuckles and then started throwing small rocks into the water.

Ned put his guitar down to one side. 'Bella, I'm pleased that you're happy to be here and I'm glad we can hang out, but I don't have all that much time before I have to leave, so I'm trying to get as much work done as I possibly can. Didn't you bring a book to read?'

'Yes, but I can't get into it. I'll just sit and listen to you as you work.'

Ned shook his head, 'I don't think that's going to work. Listen, if you really want to make yourself useful, why don't you have a look through the Bish's box? I think you'll enjoy reading Sister Evangelista's letters and you can help me catalogue them. They might even give you some ideas for your new tourist venture. They're on the billiard table.'

Bella acquiesced, getting up and wandering inside. Ned sat by the river thinking through Bella's comments about rivers being threads binding the past and the present together. More and more he thought about the diverse group of characters he'd met, and even those who'd appeared in the letters of the observant young nun. This place seemed to attract certain types of individuals: the recluse like Jack, the hardworking, down-to-earth Frederick and Theresa, the practical and warm Toni, the good-hearted, no-nonsense Yolanda, and the creative musicians drawn to the tropical north. And who knew what others had lived their lives chasing dreams and shadows through the diverse wonderland of this paradise?

When he made his way up to the house to organise some lunch, he found Bella lost in one of Sister Evangelista's letters. She looked up as he walked in.

'This is amazing! I've read a couple of the nun's letters, but I found one about Maytown. It sounds fascinating. It's near here, isn't it? We have to go and see it.'

Ned opened the fridge. 'Why? Frederick said there's nothing there. It's a ghost town.'

'Ghost towns are intriguing. According to Sister Evangelista, there were thousands on the diggings in Maytown, including lots of Chinese. They must have left some trace of their time there. There's a lot of evidence of their presence in the museum at Cooktown, I've seen it. Just think, those people would have a large number of descendants who might want to see where their ancestors had been. What a tourist market! Why don't I read you the letter while you make lunch? I promise when you hear all about it, you'll really want to take me to this Maytown.'

'I'm not so sure about that, but I am prepared to hear what the good sister has to say about it all.'

So, as Ned prepared some sandwiches, Bella settled on a chair near the kitchen and read aloud.

July, 1893

My Dear Parents,

Please forgive me, it has been several months since I last picked up my pen, but now I want to relate to you an amazing adventure that I have just undertaken. I have been to the goldfields! Such a journey, I hardly know where to begin.

I was very surprised one day immediately after our morning prayers when Reverend Mother told me that the good bishop has seen fit to grant my desire to see the gold-fields as he wants to ascertain if it is possible to rescue some of the young girls from the diggings and bring them to St. Mary's. The bishop is of the view that the profli-gate waste of money by the miners might be better spent providing an education for their daughters. Father O'Brien has arranged to take Reverend Mother to Maytown and I am to accompany them.

Hearing this news, I tried not to look too excited as I felt that would be undignified, so I thanked Reverend Mother for her kind consideration and asked when we would be leaving. She replied that we would set out as soon as possible, so as not to be caught out in the rainy season.

As stagecoaches are not suitable transport to the goldfields – the passes are very narrow and the country is extremely rough, having many steep ravines and barely hewn tracks – we set out in a small cart, which the good Father drove. We were escorted by two outriders and followed by a dray pulled by sturdy horses and driven by a brutal-looking man, who spoke very little. We travelled on the track where the carriers haul their loads. In places, the way was so narrow that we could see where mining machinery, hauled for the mines, had gouged into the sandstone rocks that lay alongside. Wild the country may have been, but the great spread of land through which we travelled was beautiful to see.

On the first night the riders made a campfire and we had tea, bully beef and damper for our supper. Sleeping in the cart was cramped and not at all comfortable, but there were no other arrangements possible. However I did enjoy the open air and being able to look up at the stars.

The next day we had to face the most worrying part of the track. It is called Hells Gate Pass, and it is so named for good reason. Reverend Mother and I both said our rosary as we entered it. The dray scraped against the sides of the vertical rock walls and the men dismounted to lead their horses, watching upwards to where massive boulders were balanced precariously. I had to turn away at the sight of the skeletons of packhorses who had taken a misstep on the terraces and fallen to their deaths. But we passed through without misadventure, reaching a timbered valley, eerily silent, with a deep gorge on one side and huge dark rocks on the other. There, we were horrified to come across human remains.

The dray driver said it was probably an unlucky Chinaman, left to his fate, who had run out of water, or food, or both, or come to grief with a black savage, or had an accident, or some other misfortune. Gold will lure many, the dray driver said, but dangers await them.

I thought it such a sad and lonely place to die.

Reverend Mother said that even though he was a heathen, there was no reason for us not to pray that his family might some day be told of his miserable fate, so we said a quiet prayer.

As darkness fell we stopped and spent another uncomfortable night camping in the bush. We were on our way before sunrise. The journey was not as arduous as the previous two days had been, but still very slow as the tracks were so poor the horses were unable to break into a trot.

196

Thus it was a wonderful relief to arrive at the banks of the Laura River late that afternoon. The packers set up camp in a lovely valley, where the horses fed on sweet grasses and refreshed themselves in the clear water.

As night drew in, Reverend Mother suggested I find us some suitable bedding, because she thought we might be more comfortable sleeping on the ground, under the dray than in the cart. After the previous nights' arrangements, I managed to find enough grass and some canvas from the dray to improve our conditions immeasurably.

The next day we passed a couple of small shanty buildings selling mainly alcohol to the miners and travellers, although some did provide rough overnight accommodation. We passed them by as they are coarse establishments and slept for a final night on the hard ground under the protection of the dray.

We finally arrived in Maytown late in the afternoon. Originally the town was just a collection of bark huts, shanties and tents around the Palmer River, but now it is a township of neatly kerbed and paved streets. There are a plethora of hotels, boarding houses, general stores and weatherboard houses as well as a courthouse, a School of the Arts, and a small schoolhouse.

On a slight rise on the edge of the town stands the finest of homes, which Father O'Brien told us belongs to the mining warden. As I gazed at all these buildings, as well as the jumble of mining machinery that dots the landscape, I could not help but admire the perseverance and ingenuity of the men who dragged everything into this remote wilderness.

Father O'Brien took us to the home of one of his parishioners, who runs a small, modest boarding house. Mrs. O'Rourke welcomed us effusively. She had rooms ready for us, and assured us that hers was a very respectable place where we wouldn't be disturbed. She arranged

197

for water to be brought to our rooms so we could wash off the dust from our journey, and then brought up our dinner so that we could retire early.

The next morning, Reverend Mother decided we would visit the schoolhouse we'd seen on our way into town. As we walked there, completely refreshed by our night's sleep, we passed the newspaper office. It is called The Golden Age, *and the editor came out to greet us. He was very interested to know why we were visiting Maytown. He asked if he could write a small piece for his paper should Reverend Mother make a decision about any of the girls going to our convent. We also saw many storefronts with Chinese symbols emblazoned on their signs. We saw coolies carrying goods on long poles across their shoulders. I noticed several young women, fashionably dressed in silk gowns, wearing bonnets also lined in silk. They carried parasols and chatted cheerfully amongst themselves. I commented to Reverend Mother that such beautifully dressed young women seemed out of place in a goldmining town.*

She replied saying that we should not comment on, or even notice women of that class. Well dressed they may be, but they were Godless women.

And in the shadows we saw some natives silently watching all this activity.

We reached the school and introduced ourselves to the schoolteacher. Mr. Halstrom was a pleasant enough man pleased to show us what his class could do. The children recited poetry and sang songs and answered no doubt rehearsed questions on arithmetic and history. When the class was released the boys quickly scampered outside while some of the little girls obediently sat and listened as Reverend Mother spoke to them. They nodded politely but seemed little enthused at the suggestion of going to school in Cooktown.

After we left the school, Father O'Brien took us to meet several of the families who lived in the township as well as others who were camped in shacks closer to the diggings. Those in town listened to what Reverend Mother had to say about the opportunities that St. Mary's could provide for their daughters, and I have to say that she spoke most persuasively. One or two of these families seemed very interested and asked several questions. But in the camps, it was a different story. The mothers were careworn and the fathers seemed defeated, but nonetheless expressed a determination to stay on in the fields. No doubt they had little choice, for they seemed only to live on hope, charity and the fever brought on by the thought of gold. I feared that there was little interest in St. Mary's here.

On Sunday we went with Father O'Brien to Mass in the small wooden church that serves our faith. During the service he christened six children, ranging in age from a few months to about four. The good Father later told me that owing to the fact that he cannot get to Maytown as often as he would like, he must often christen many children when he is there. Reverend Mother said she expects that God finds this arrangement quite acceptable under the circumstances.

In the cool of the afternoon, after a simple meal, we were escorted to the edge of the diggings by Father O'Brien. It was a surprising sight. It was as though an army was scattered along every creek and in every gully. Across the open plain, men worked on very small patches of ground, side by side with nary a blade of grass to be seen, many toiling away, even though the hour was late. Dotted between the slopes and amongst the sparse trees were more shanties and tents, and further afield it was easy to see the Chinese camp as it was surrounded by market gardens and fruit trees. Father O'Brien told us that the Chinese worked the alluvial claims abandoned by white men who, he said, are often too quick to give up on one claim to move to another. But the Chinese are more patient and will turn over each rock in the creek beds, washing them for gold specks. It is all very hard work, but quite successful. This creates envy amongst the white miners, who think that they should be allowed the lion's share of the discoveries.

Later, as we walked back towards the boarding house, we noticed a lot of dark-skinned children playing in the street. I asked Father O'Brien if he knew why these children were not in Mr. Halstrom's school, and he replied that it is a sad thing, but their families feel they have no need for learning.

It was almost dark by the time we returned to Mrs. O'Rourke's. In the distance we could hear snatches of bush ballads drifting from the campfires at the diggings or perhaps from outside a tent. The songs seemed to be more of a lament than the hearty sea shanties I have heard in Cooktown, and I understood what a hard and lonely existence this must be for these miners far from their families and home.

On the final day, before we started on our long journey back to Cooktown, Reverend Mother and Father O'Brien had another conversation with Mr. Halstrom, asking him to continue to ask those few interested parents to send their daughters to us at the first opportunity. Father O'Brien quietly told me later that Reverend Mother had made a very favourable impression and he was sure that her visit would be rewarded with the successful enrolment of some of the local girls.

As I stood on the verandah of the boarding house with our small valises, waiting for their return, Mrs. O'Rourke, who seems to run the establishment single-handedly, joined me and we exchanged small pleasantries.

Then she surprised me by saying that we should leave the dark kids as they were. Don't try to tame them, she said. Let them run wild while they can. They'll not settle to the ways and likes of our rules and they'll be having it hard soon enough. The girls will be taken for the men and the boys set to work unless they go bush. Their old ways are lost now even though the warriors still fight.

I replied quoting the Bible, Suffer little children to come unto me, and forbid them not: for of such is the kingdom of God. *So perhaps she is right, these children should be tolerated as they are, but I did say that I thought an education could be of benefit.*

Mrs. O'Rourke was quick to answer me, saying that the gospel was not for these children. Though they live in a half-world here, they still have a deep culture. Their own faith and beliefs were handed down through the generations even before we ever came to this country. Their ideas may not be our ways, but they sit well enough in their own customs. She said that although the government's policy is to let them die out, or breed out, she thought that if we took the trouble, one day we might just learn something from them.

I was quite surprised by the passionate outspokenness of this woman, and indeed, she also seemed a little embarrassed by her outburst for she hastily apologised and went inside. Then our driver, who had heard what she'd said, spoke to me, commenting that Mrs. O'Rourke was a funny person. 'She's got no husband and spends too much time with the old black gins who tell her struth knows what, begging your pardon, Sister, 'cause she's learned their lingo,' he said. 'But if you don't mind me speaking me mind, I say she's right. To take them kids away from what they know will never work for you or them. Let 'em go; the blacks and the chinks are not God-fearing people. Their ways aren't ours. Leave 'em be, I say. You'll be doing them no favours trying to change them.'

201

I thanked him for speaking up and sent a swift prayer of thanks to the Almighty that Reverend Mother had not been privy to any of this. But I confess, it had never occurred to me that the heathen race of wild blacks could have beliefs and a culture that might interest civilised people.

Our return journey was as uneventful but as difficult and uncomfortable as the outbound one had been, and Reverend Mother and I were pleased to be finally back in our familiar surroundings at St. Mary's. So when I returned to my simple room and stood by my window looking at the familiar sight of the river stretching to the sea that also washes upon the shores of my homeland so far away, and heard the sweet voices of the girls singing in a nearby dormitory, I felt truly fortunate to have been called to do God's work in this country that is older than time and whose secrets we have yet to learn.

May God bless you, my parents, and the Holy Mother protect you,

Your loving daughter,

Evangelista

Bella looked up. 'Isn't that just an amazing letter, Ned? Doesn't it make you want to go to Maytown and see what's there? Aren't you a little bit curious to see what it's like now? It's still early, we could take some sandwiches and have a picnic.'

Ned had known he wouldn't get much done while Bella was here. Besides, Sister Evangelista's letter had piqued his curiosity too, and if Frederick's display at the roadhouse was anything to go by, the place must be littered with the broken dreams of days gone by.

'It'll be damned hot, but okay, let's hit the road. Maybe Maytown might give me some ideas, too.'

Ned wrapped up some sandwiches, two pieces of Theresa's fruitcake and two large bottles of cold water in a cool bag and they set off, eventually following the rough, undulating dirt road that led to the former diggings in the sparse scrubland.

'I cannot believe how dry the vegetation is out here,' said Bella. 'When you think of tropical Queensland, you think of the lush coastal area. This is quite different. Hard to grow much in this uninviting scrub.'

'Just think what a journey it must have been for those prospectors to make, even with a horse or dray,' said Ned.

'They must've been keen,' said Bella.

'Gold fever. Quick riches. It would only take one person hitting pay dirt and the fuse would be lit. People would come from everywhere.'

'Even China. It's hard to imagine all those hundreds of hopeful Chinese, getting on boats to come to this hot and dry wilderness. What must they have thought when they found they had to walk into this?!' wondered Bella.

'You have to admire them. All of them.'

'We have it soft in comparison, don't we?'

They passed a small sign and stopped the car, got out and looked around. The unremarkable area was dotted with a few trees and bushes but not much identifying a town.

Bella glanced around and spotted a noticeboard at the top of a rise.

'I think it's up there,' said Bella, as she pulled on a hat and her sunglasses. 'There's not a breath of air. Hope there's some shade.' She took off with Ned trailing behind her.

Ned wasn't sure what to expect, but it certainly wasn't the scene which actually spread before them.

There were no buildings to speak of, just a crumbling rubble of handmade brick foundations overgrown with grass and vegetation. A row of a few spindly trees marked the once bustling main street that was now reclaimed by the bush. The only real sign of the once-busy town was the slate marking the kerbs and guttering of the street. The hotels, shops and businesses that Sister Evangelista had described had seemingly evaporated under the relentless sun and by the passage of time.

'There isn't a thing here!' cried Bella. 'I saw the photographs in the museum and this was a busy town! Now there is nothing.'

'It really is a ghost town,' agreed Ned.

Bella picked up the long neck of a broken bottle. 'I wonder what was in this? Beer probably. This looks like handmade glass.' She put it back in the dirt where she had found it and walked on. 'This place is so exposed. So barren and lonely. How isolated the prospectors must have felt.'

'It seems that way now, but in its heyday we know it was buzzing.'

'Here's something.' Bella leaned down to read a small sign. 'This was the bakery, and I think that must have been the old oven.' She indicated a pile of bricks and twisted iron partially buried under grass and rusting sheets of corrugated iron.

'Look here,' called Ned. 'The newspaper office. The one that was mentioned in the letter.'

'*The Golden Age*,' replied Bella.

Ned scuffed his feet in the dirt and bent down, scooping up a handful of it. Scattered across his palm were a dozen small lead letters, fragments that indicated a compositor had once set rows of words and sentences to be inked and printed in order to tell the news of the day. Ned dropped them in his pocket.

'Let's go and see if we can find any of the mining camps that Sister Evangelista wrote about,' he said.

They cut across the open empty scrubland to where some spindly trees sprouted throughout the quiet gullies.

Here, as they wandered around, exploring the remnants of the Maytown mines, they found massive rusting hulks of stampers and crushers, and a few shelters of old bricks, rotting logs and iron roofs that had housed the throbbing, thumping, powerful machines which had extracted gold from the surrounding rocks. Once the noise from these machines had echoed across the land, but now they were silent save for the forlorn rattle of loose tin stirred by a sudden warm breeze.

Further on they came to a small shack which someone had re-erected. It was filled with remnants of the mining camps: rusting food tins, old bottles, bits of unidentifiable equipment.

Subdued by the forlornness of the place, Ned and Bella turned from the gullies and made their way back to what had been the town. On its edge they came across a small neglected and overgrown cemetery. They walked silently amidst the forgotten graves, reading the weathered and broken headstones.

'What a lonely place to spend eternity,' said Ned softly.

Bella peered at the markers. 'There are no Chinese buried here,' she said.

'No, I think their ashes would have been sent home in ceramic urns,' Ned replied.

They walked a little further into some of the other gullies, circling back to where they had begun.

Bella fanned her flushed face. 'Oppressive, isn't it? That breeze didn't last long. Well, I have to say I'm glad I came here, but in all honesty, I'm having second thoughts about being able to entice Chinese tourists to visit here. I mean, there's not much to see.' She glanced across the barren scrub, chewing her lip. 'The Victorian gold-fields – Ballarat, Bendigo, Castlemaine, Beechworth – all still have their beautiful buildings, built with the proceeds of their gold rushes, and the towns are still actually functioning. I mean, how would a place like this compare to somewhere like Sovereign Hill?'

Ned nodded. 'This place would be on a hiding to nothing, added to which it's very difficult to get to. Bella, I reckon if you want to promote the gold rushes to Chinese tourists, or any tourist for that matter, you'd be far better off doing it in your own backyard,' said Ned reasonably.

Bella stared at him and looked away. 'Hmm. This has been interesting, but as far as gold rushes go, Victoria has more to offer. There really is no comparison. But it doesn't mean that the rest of Antony's ideas lack substance,' she said, lifting her chin. 'Far North Queensland has some spectacular things for tourists to see and do. Sorry if I've wasted your time on the wild idea of Maytown, though.'

Ned smiled. Despite Bella's disappointment, he'd enjoyed this excursion with her. 'C'mon, let's eat the sandwiches and then head back. It's a good two hours' drive before we can have a swim in our river.'

'Yeah, that sounds like an excellent idea,' Bella said as they turned back to the car. 'And what are you planning for dinner tonight, chef?'

'What say we fire up the pizza oven extravaganza?'

'Super. And I'll be hanging out for a glass of anything that's really, really cold. This heat is totally draining,' said Bella.

As they bumped back towards the river house, the car's air conditioner separating them from the oppressive heat outside, Ned couldn't help but think about the impermanence of what had once been a thriving community and which now had sadly disappeared into the silent and lonely landscape. The day with his sister had been a wonderful distraction for them both and for once they'd been able to hang out without arguing about their family situation. Spending time together was opening them back up to each other but Ned knew that another conversation about the dedication wouldn't be far away. The closer they got to Carlo's place, the more Ned realised that Bella's quest for answers would mean that decisions would have to be made, but he hoped this would not include having to tell Bella the real reason for his refusal to return to Tennyson.

8

THE DRINKING WATER TASTED stale, the temperature stayed in the high thirties, the river flowed sluggishly and both Bella and Ned felt irritable most of the time.

It's the heat, Bella chided herself after a spat with Ned over something small and silly. She was determined to stick it out with Ned in spite of the uncomfortable conditions because she was hoping for some kind of breakthrough with him.

Bella felt there had to be a reason for Ned's reticence, his inability or unwillingness to articulate the feelings that had made him keep her at arm's length for so long and were now making him stubborn about returning to Tennyson. It was beginning to trouble her deeply, for it seemed to Bella that if they didn't rekindle their old rapport and be honest with each other then they would become polite and distant strangers and remain that way for the rest of their lives. Indeed, she'd almost welcomed the earlier snappish exchange as a sign that they could voice their own opinions, but as usual Ned had walked away before a proper discussion could eventuate. Bella was increasingly finding her brother's refusal to engage with her very frustrating.

It was late in the afternoon and the sky was a mottled grey with dark green streaks flaring behind a low bank of clouds. The air was so oppressive that Bella decided she would only find relief by going for a swim. The river was low but being in the warm water was more comfortable than sitting in front of the fan or the air conditioner, which rattled and roared.

As her feet touched the sandy bottom heading back to the bank, she lifted her head and was startled to see a strange man who looked to be in his seventies sitting beside the table on the riverside terrace. He was smoking and looked very relaxed, almost as though he was at home. She swam to the bank and stepped from the water.

The man was rugged looking and had a proprietary air about him which she didn't like. He stared at her with a smug smile on his face, making her feel uncomfortable.

'Howdy. You the girlfriend, are you?'

'No. I'm the sister. Who are you?' she replied, hastily wrapping herself in a towel.

He got to his feet and stretched out his hand, still looking faintly amused as he eyed her up and down. 'I'm Jack.'

Bella ignored the hand and, clutching the towel around her, barely able to keep her voice civil, asked indignantly, 'And why are you here?' The man's self-satisfied familiarity made her instantly dislike him. *Just who does he think he is?* she thought to herself. *How dare he look at me like that.*

'Ah, you've met Jack,' Ned called out as he came down to the terrace carrying a glass of wine and two bottles of beer. 'He's driven over here for a visit.'

'I see. Excuse me, I'll go and get dressed.' Bella turned and went up the steps to the house.

'Come and have a drink when you're ready,' called Ned.

Once indoors, Bella peered surreptitiously at Ned and his visitor as they settled into their chairs. Ned didn't seem surprised by Jack's arrival; in fact, he had seemed really pleased to see him. Jack was obviously much older than they were, and the American's manner annoyed her. She dried herself, threw on a cool loose shirt over some cotton shorts and went to the kitchen, where she grabbed some biscuits and cheese and joined the two men beside the river. She passed around the cheese platter, picked up her glass of wine and sat in her favourite chair.

'Jack is my neighbour across the valley,' said Ned by way of explanation.

'Oh, right.' Bella waited, then realised that no more details would be forthcoming, so she sipped her drink. Jack gave her a smile as he lifted his beer to his lips.

The men seemed relaxed, but Bella was uncomfortable and not just because of Jack's presence. The air felt thick, there was no breeze and she could feel perspiration clinging to her face and body and trickling down her back. She turned to Jack and said rather pointedly, 'You're a long way from home.'

Jack didn't respond immediately, slowly savouring his beer before saying, 'You don't have to make small talk. But to answer your assumption, ma'am, the United States of America is not my home. I might be from there, but I'm not of there. This place, Far North Queensland, is my home.'

'I was told the far north is the country of last resort and not to ask questions,' replied Bella.

'You got it, miss,' said Jack easily.

'Bella, just relax. Have another biscuit and cheese,' said Ned.

But Bella wasn't mollified. 'No wonder you're friends with my brother. You both seem to be strong silent types. Don't say what you really think under any circumstances.' She fanned herself but the heat felt incessant. 'Come to think of it, that must be a male thing. Men! You can't live with them and you can't shoot them,' she said flippantly. 'My ex-boyfriend Brendan is just as bad. He doesn't criticise, doesn't argue, just sits on the fence saying things like, "You decide what you think is best for you".'

'Smart fellow,' said Jack affably.

'Bella, if Brendan dared to tell you how to run your life, you'd eat him for breakfast,' said Ned mildly.

Bella suddenly rounded on her brother. 'Why do you insist on making me sound like such a bitch, Ned? Because you can't make hard decisions yourself?'

Ned rolled his eyes. 'Geez, Bella, would you back off? My life is just fine, thanks. That is, it was until you barged in trying to redirect everyone. Just because people don't do what you think they should do, doesn't mean they're at fault and you're always right.'

'Well, not everyone thinks of themselves first, like you do,' snapped Bella. She pressed her drink to the side of her face in an effort to cool herself, but it seemed to have no effect.

'Oh, I so miss family life,' said Jack as he rolled his eyes.

Bella ignored him. 'Ned, you should be thinking of Mum and not just yourself.'

They glared at each other and Jack leaned back, unperturbed. 'Ah, so are you the favoured son?' he said to Ned.

Bella turned to Jack. 'Actually, he's the only son. Which is our business, not yours.'

'Bella!' interjected Ned. 'Take it easy. Sorry, Jack.'

Jack lifted a hand. 'It's okay.' He turned to Bella and she felt the full force of his intense gaze and knew instinctively that he was not a man to trifle with. He might be a lot older than she was, but he was tough, and clearly he didn't suffer fools – and probably women – gladly.

'You're right. What happens between you and Ned is none of my business. But remember this, Miss Bella, you have a mother and a brother. I have no family. My fault. I've seen too much. I did what I had to do and then some, and I'm not proud of everything I did. I lost the family I had because of the wars I was fighting. I learned too late that waving the flag in grand and righteous wars is all a great con. Wars are there just to make money for the rich while the rest of us pay the price.' He shrugged. 'Like I said, I saw too much.'

'So that's why you've buried yourself out here?' said Bella, startled by his outburst.

'Bella, leave it alone. Stop attacking people.' Ned turned to Jack. 'Ignore her.'

'Miss Bella can say and think whatever she likes. I like people who speak their minds,' said Jack placidly.

Bella opened her mouth to speak but Ned beat her to it. 'She's trying to figure out how to bring hordes of Chinese tourists to this part of the world,' said Ned, clearly trying to change the subject.

At that moment a flash of lightning ripped across the horizon.

'Aha.' Jack studied the sky for a moment. 'Too bad it's not the real thing. Only a dry storm. No rain, everything tinder dry, so the lightning strikes start bloody bushfires. Welcome to the mango season.'

'What's that mean?' asked Bella.

'It's what the locals call the build-up to the rainy

season, when the weather becomes really oppressive and everyone waits for the wet to start. People work on automatic, trying to keep their moods and emotions in check and not get into fights. Once the first rain comes, it's a relief, time for a drink and to wait for the follow-up rain to cool things down.' Jack got up. 'But these dry storms are worth watching. Even if they don't bring any immediate relief, they promise better times ahead. Ned, this calls for a proper drink. I'll get some of that bourbon, okay?'

'Of course, go ahead . . . Oh, bugger, Jack, I forgot. We're out of bourbon.'

'You mean you've started drinking like a real man, Ned?' Jack lifted an eyebrow, but Ned looked uncomfortable and didn't seem to want to explain himself in front of Bella.

'Come up to the bar and see what else Carlo's got. I've sort of been cleaned out.' Ned hurried up the steps to the house, followed by Jack at a more leisurely pace.

Bella sat for a moment, thinking about Jack. She thought he was arrogant, and his use of all that American idiom for effect, as though he was sending himself up, really irritated her. Bella sipped the last of her wine and decided to get another glass.

As she came up the steps towards the house, she heard Jack's raised voice. 'Chrissake, Ned! You should've damn well told me. What happened? Were they armed?'

'Who was armed? What're you talking about?' demanded Bella, approaching the bar.

'No, Jack, they weren't, and Bella, it's okay,' said Ned.

Jack's weathered face had reddened. 'Your brother had two intruders here, lady. That's not okay.'

'What! When? Did you call the police, Ned?' Bella asked in alarm.

'They weren't intruders. They said they knew Carlo,' said Ned. 'They were just a bit on the rough side. And by

213

the time I could've contacted the police, they would've been ages away, so I didn't think there was much point.'

'What did they want?' Bella felt shaky. This place was starting to feel unsafe.

'They only wanted supplies. They're just hunters or something. Only took food, water and some of the alcohol that Carlo had, as well as your bourbon, Jack.'

'Pisses me off they took that.' Jack rummaged behind the bar as Bella stared at Ned.

'I thought you kept the gate locked?' said Bella.

'I do keep it locked, but they came up from the river.'

'Great! It sounds as though you run an open house here, Ned. Does Toni know you had intruders?' she added.

'No, of course not.'

'You didn't want to scare her off coming out here, did you, but it doesn't matter about me.' Bella's voice rose.

'Could I have stopped you from coming even if I'd told you?' asked Ned reasonably. 'Look, they are miles away now and they're not coming back. There's nothing to worry about.'

Bella didn't look convinced, but she shrugged.

Jack held up a bottle of Scotch. 'This will do.' There was a rumble and the distant flash of lightning. 'We're missing the show.' He headed back towards the river carrying the bottle.

Bella watched him leave. 'Is Jack okay? I mean, he seems a bit of a wild man. Is he crazy? Do you think that living on his own out here has affected him?' she asked in a whisper.

Ned smiled. 'I don't think so, but he has obviously never gotten over the futility of the wars he was involved in. He's very anti-war now.'

'Well, he still seems to be fighting something. He's feisty.'

'Look, he might seem prickly, but I like him. I don't see all that much of him, but when I do, I enjoy his company.' He put his hand on her shoulder. 'Come on, Bella, give him a chance.'

Bella nodded. 'I'll bring down some more nibbles.' She went into the kitchen area to rummage in the pantry, thinking what a strange rapport there was between her brother and the unquiet American. Maybe that's what it was about the people up here, the loners and drifters, the failures and the fugitives; they couldn't get on with people and preferred their own company. She hoped that Ned wasn't slowly falling into the same category.

As she came down the steps, Bella overheard Jack talking.

'Man, give it to me straight, how aggro were they? There's a difference between wandering in and asking for food and muscling in heavy-handed.'

'They were a bit intimidating, I guess. I was mainly surprised that they came from the river. They'd even painted their kayak in camouflage colours.'

Jack shook his head. 'Shit. That doesn't sound good.'

Bella put the food on the table. 'What doesn't sound good?' she asked.

'Bella, don't worry,' started Ned. 'They won't be back. It was a one-off.'

'What do you think, Jack?' Bella sat at the table and began slicing a knob of salami.

Jack sat down and helped himself to the bowl of olives Bella had brought. 'Your brother is probably right. Still, this is too far out for your regular adventurer. This arm of the river is a backwater. Only a couple of reasons I can think of for them to be on it, and they're not good.'

'Like?' asked Ned.

'Drugs, murder, smuggling, gold. Or all of the above.'

'Murder! Has anyone been murdered around here lately?' asked Bella, alarmed. 'Should we be here? Ned, I don't think you should be out here alone.'

Ned reached for a slice of salami and put it on a chunk of bread. 'I'm not alone. I've got you, ready to fight everyone,' he said playfully. 'Anyway, they've been and gone, and I don't think they'll come back. As Jack says, this bit of the river doesn't go anywhere.'

'Can't say I agree with you there, Ned. This place might be a backwater, but it could be a kind of rendez-vous point,' said Jack thoughtfully.

'But I got the idea from Frederick that Carlo was a decent guy,' said Ned.

'And he is,' said Jack. 'Been a good friend to me for a long time. Still, this place is empty for a few months every year and I reckon these blokes could be up to no good and they came here looking for a few supplies to top up their stores.'

'Is there a big drug scene up here?' asked Bella. 'That man in the pink house in Cooktown looked spaced out, like he was on something.'

Ned glanced at Bella and seeing the look on her face he said, 'Do you want to go back to town? I can drive you back tomorrow.'

Bella hesitated, but only for moment. 'No. If you're staying, I can too. I'll be fine and, like you said, it's unlikely that they'll come back.'

'Exactly,' Ned said. 'For the record, I think they were just a bit rough and no real threat. Jack, you said something about gold. Carlo goes fossicking and so does Frederick, so is there still gold in these parts? Do you think these guys might have been looking for gold?'

'Could be. But they might also have been looking in places they shouldn't. There are designated fossicking areas, and there's also private property, mainly grazing leases, and you need permission to go on those. If they didn't have that, then what they were doing was illegal. But unless you found them in the act, you wouldn't know what they were up to.'

'This place sounds like the wild west,' said Bella.

Jack seemed to realise that the discussion was alarming Bella, so he said, 'I wouldn't panic just yet. It's getting close to the start of the wet, so they'll be long gone by now.' He took a swig of Scotch. 'Tell me more about your scheme to bring Chinese tourists to this part of the world.'

Glad to leave the subject of the intruders behind, Bella said, 'I came up north for a holiday and someone presented me with an idea to develop some specialty package tours.'

Jack raised an eyebrow. 'Interesting. Is that your thing? Package tours?'

'I work in tourism back in Victoria.'

'So vacationing is the reason you came up here, and yet here you are in the middle of nowhere, quarrelling with your brother. Funny way to spend a vacation.'

'Well, Jack, not that it's any of your business, but the reason I'm here in this way-out-of-the-way place is to persuade my brother to come back home to attend a cere-mony commemorating our father. Ned's presence would mean a great deal to our mother. And to me.'

'I don't think that our family goings-on are of any interest to Jack,' said Ned coolly. Jack, however, seemed faintly amused and pressed on.

'I'd like to hear all about it. Not having a family of my own any more, I like to be reminded, periodically, of what I'm missing.'

Bella shrugged. She knew that Jack was baiting her, but maybe he would see her point of view and take her side. Quickly she explained the situation and why she thought it important that Ned be in Tennyson for the occasion.

'It's the first anniversary of our father's passing. It will be an emotional day for all of us,' she added.

'You will be there, of course. You were close to your father?'

'I certainly was. Fathers and daughters always have a special bond.' She glanced at Ned. 'Ned and Dad got along well too, didn't you, Ned?'

'Well I didn't get a gold bracelet or pearl earrings for my birthdays, but I guess we got along okay.'

'Your father was a doctor you said? I suppose he put in long hours at the hospital?' said Jack. 'Some men consider it the right thing to do, to put their job before their family.'

'Dad always had time for us,' said Bella hotly. 'His study door was never closed. He used to help me with my homework. You never asked him, did you, Ned? Dad said it was because you were stubborn and had to do things your way.'

A pained expression flashed across Ned's face, but he didn't say anything, he just sipped his Scotch.

'What'd he think of your music?' asked Jack, turning to Ned. 'I bet that didn't sit too well with an important professional man like your father.'

Ned grimaced. 'Dad thought my music was just a pastime. He kept waiting for me to grow up and get a degree in something and have a proper career. To Dad, music wasn't real.'

'Ned, that's unfair.' Bella frowned at him. 'You know Dad accepted your choice, eventually, and to be fair to Dad, your career path was hardly a conventional one. I think he just wanted you to have a steady income and a solid future. But he came good in the end. He was proud of you.'

'Maybe,' said Ned, in a tone of voice that suggested he wasn't convinced.

'And what about your mother, how do you get on with her?' asked Jack.

'Fantastic,' said Ned.

'She's a really great mother,' said Bella.

'Then maybe you two should talk about this some more,' said Jack.

'Not right now,' said Ned.

'That's what he always says,' Bella shot back.

'I'll tell you both something for nothing,' said Jack, topping up his drink. 'I never played it safe and I got a lot of kicks, but I did what I believed was right. Cost me my family, though. Ned, go for your music, it's important to you, but family is important too, so give up some of your time for your mother. And Bella, you have to stop trying to run other people's lives. Let them make their own decisions. You might find that they make the right ones in the end.'

Bella stared at the man opposite her. While he irritated her, she knew that what he said was true. She did always try to have things her way when she was sure that her way was the right way. But before she could reply, Ned spoke quietly.

'This business with Dad and the dedication has nothing to do with my mother.'

'Is that right?' Jack gave a slight smile and swallowed the last of his drink before getting to his feet. He gave Bella a small salute. 'Peace and love, sister. Show's over, I'd best be on my way.'

Ned hurriedly stood up. 'I'll see you out. Thanks for coming by, Jack.'

As they headed up the steps, she heard Ned mutter, 'Sorry about Bella, she can be a bit too forthright.'

Bella couldn't hear Jack's reply, but she was perturbed by her brother's friend. There was something about him she couldn't put her finger on. At face value he was outspoken, almost aggressive, but his eyes held the haunted look of a man covering up his real feelings. She wondered if he'd ever had a softer side, a gentler voice, a caressing hand. Jack must have been handsome as a young man and probably knew it, too.

Ned reappeared and sat down, looking thoughtful. 'You were quite hard on Jack, you know.'

'He can take it. C'mon! He's a tough Yankee soldier, at least according to him.'

Ned didn't laugh. 'And seriously, Bell, you didn't have to raise our family issues in front of him.'

Bella raised her eyebrows. 'Jack asked me questions.' Ned turned away, picking up his glass. 'You just don't want to talk about our family ever,' said Bella.

'We see things differently, that's all.' He kept walking away from her.

Bella was angry. The wine swam in her head and she thought of her parents, her family, and the way things had been when she was young. Why was it all so difficult now? 'What is it with you, Ned? Why won't you come back for Dad's dedication? Why have you been away from home for so long? It seems to me there must be some other reason you're keeping from me, because all your excuses are pretty pathetic. Does Mum know how you feel? Is that why she doesn't push you to come home?' she demanded.

Ned turned. 'No. Not at all,' said Ned firmly. 'I wouldn't want to upset Mum.'

'That's nonsense,' said Bella. 'This ceremony is as much for Mum's sake as it is for Dad's. I think Mum feels that it is, in a way, a reflection on the support she gave Dad and his work over all the years of their marriage. You should be there at least to acknowledge that. You know they had a wonderful life together. Mum has been through so much in the last year, and you've just left it up to me to take care of her. It's as though you don't care about us at all.'

Ned's face remained impassive but Bella could see his hands were balled into fists. 'Bella, I care about Mum much more than you think. And you.'

'Then all I can say is that you have a very funny way of showing it. You need to stop avoiding our family. Do you think she can't handle talking about Dad's death, or something? Well, she's fine about it now. Sad, of course, but I think she's coping well. Not that you would know. You hardly ever speak to her.'

'Bella, just shut up, will you? I don't need you to go over and *over* this. I won't go back to Tennyson and that is all I have to say on the matter,' said Ned angrily.

Bella took a step towards him. 'Ned, once upon a time we used to have no secrets from each other. But now it's like you're a different person.'

Ned folded his arms. 'Bella, drop it. Just leave it. It's my business.'

'How can you say that? This is my business, too. It's our family, and I want us all together for this occasion. I want your support, for once.'

'Well, you won't get your wish, I'm afraid. You don't know everything about our family at all. You think you do, but you don't.'

Bella stared at Ned. 'Ned, we shouldn't have secrets. I can't believe you're keeping something from me. Why would you do that? What is it you're not telling me?'

Ned was silent a moment. He shook his head. 'There are some things better left alone. Despite what you might think, you're my sister and I care about you.'

'And I care about you! Why do you think I'm here?'

Ned paused and gave a small smile. 'You're here to get me to go to Dad's dedication, but you have to understand that I need to make my own decisions. You can't make them for me.'

Bella didn't answer. She was rather taken aback by the new thought that Ned knew something about their family that she didn't. Whatever it was, it was gnawing at Ned and driving a wedge between them and yet he seemed determined to keep it to himself.

'I'm sorry, Ned. I have no idea why you feel the way you do, but I wish you would tell me. The least we can do is be up-front and honest with each other, and I'm sorry you feel you can't.'

There was a moment of quiet and then Ned said, 'Bella, I think we should call it a night and go back into the house. The storm's over.'

She sighed in defeat. 'All right.' She picked up the plates and her glass and they walked to the house in silence. 'I might take some of Sister Evangelista's letters to bed with me and read a few more of them.'

'Sounds good. You up for a swim in the morning? I'll wake you when I go down, if you like.' It sounded like an olive branch. Bella smiled at her brother.

But lying in bed with the nun's letters provided little respite from Bella's thoughts. She had been so sure that once she confronted Ned, he would acquiesce and return to Tennyson, but she now realised that he had never had any intention of doing that. She thought back to her childhood. She'd adored her family. She'd always thought they were the perfect foursome, but Ned clearly didn't feel the same way and she couldn't understand it. And what did he mean when he said she didn't know everything about their family? Suddenly she sat up in bed. Had her mother done something to upset him? That seemed unlikely. Maybe Ned still resented his father's opposition to his choice of career, and that resentment had never properly healed. Still, she thought, it was a long time to carry a grudge, and their father really had seemed to accept Ned's choice in the end. Heavens, he'd even attended some of Ned's performances.

She turned out the light and tried to sleep, but just as her mind began to drift, she had a flash of Brendan's face. She pushed the image out of her mind and thought instead of Antony's smile and confident eyes. What should she do about Antony's plan? She felt that time was running out for her. Her holiday was nearly over and she was still not ready to make any sort of decision. Being so far from home and her usual routine, she now found herself in the unfamiliar position of vacillating. This stunning, story-soaked part of Australia had spun her head around and filled her with enthusiasm for the place. Could she really do something utterly different in this part of the country? She felt that her life with Brendan had been stagnating. Did she really want to return to Tennyson and continue with her safe, predictable career, or was now the time to look for other challenges and put a bit of excitement into her existence? Maybe this was the right time to move on.

Bella tossed and turned for most of the night, consumed with thoughts of Ned and her family, of Antony and his ideas and of Brendan and their fight. She finally fell asleep in the wee small hours and when she eventually woke, sunlight was streaming in the window.

Bella could hear Ned playing the keyboard. She went downstairs and made herself a pot of tea and decided to be wicked and to treat herself to an overripe banana cooked in butter and squashed onto her toast.

'What smells so good?' Ned appeared in the kitchen and smiled at her.

'Morning, Ned. Have you had a swim already?'

'I have. I went in to check on you, but you were still fast asleep, so I left you. Plenty of time for a swim later. Mmm, that looks good. I haven't had a fried banana in years.

I think I'll have one, too. You want brown sugar with yours?'

'I don't think I need sugar.' She watched him make himself a coffee. He seemed relaxed and friendly. 'Any plans for today?'

'Not really. Let's see how the day unfolds. Are you bored?'

'Not at all,' she retorted, even though she would have liked to go somewhere. 'Maybe I'll take the canoe you mentioned out of the shed and go for a paddle.'

'Great idea. I won't come with you, because I can feel the creative juices flowing, but you can't get into any trouble on the river if you don't go too far.'

'I don't want to interrupt your work, so I'm happy to go out by myself.'

Ned helped her put one of Carlo's old fibreglass canoes into the water. Bella took a bottle of water and a hat and hung her small camera around her neck, and after a somewhat shaky start, she quickly found her rhythm and began firmly stroking her way along the river.

'See you later,' Ned called out after her.

Bella was entranced. As she glided along the quietly flowing waterway, the river birds seemed totally disinterested by her presence and ignored her. The silence in the surrounding bush was so all-encompassing that she felt she should be able to hear the leaves curling in the growing heat. The isolation made her feel like an explorer travelling into an unknown land.

She paddled on for some time, pausing occasionally to take a photo, until she came to a bend in the river and saw that the surface of the water was running faster than it had been. Not confident that she could control the canoe in these conditions, she did a U-turn and headed back the way she'd come.

Suddenly a loud crack rang out, causing Bella to look

upwards. Several birds rose from the treetops in fright. She stopped paddling for a moment as she listened for any follow-up noise. She had the feeling that what she'd heard was a gunshot, although she hoped it had only been a branch breaking. All remained quiet, so she resumed paddling, thrusting the blade deep into the water and forcing the canoe to gather speed.

She was perspiring heavily and felt very hot when she saw the little low-lying island which lay opposite Carlo's place. With a sigh of relief she slowed the canoe, gliding it against the current of the river and around the island, then towards the bank beneath the house. Voices drifted down to her and as she drew nearer she saw Frederick standing on the terrace.

'Hi, Bella! Need a hand? Enjoy the river? Best way to see it.' He walked down to the water's edge and reached over to steady the canoe as she clambered out.

'Hello, Frederick. Yes, it was wonderful. Did you bring some supplies for Ned? Is Theresa with you?'

'Nope. Just brought a visitor. Let me give you a hand.' He pulled the canoe right up to the bank and helped Bella out.

'Thanks, Frederick,' she said.

Bella hurried up the steps. She could hear voices in the kitchen, but before she could head to her room and change, Ned called out.

'Bell . . . come in here a minute.'

'I was just going to change –' She stepped inside and stopped in shock. Standing next to Ned was Brendan.

'Oh. My. God! Brendan! What are you doing here?' she shrieked.

'Surprised you, huh?' said Brendan, looking pleased to see her but a bit hesitant.

Bella's head whirled. 'What are you doing here? Is Mum okay . . . ?'

'Yes, she's fine,' he said reassuringly. 'I just wanted to see you, that's all.'

'How on earth did you find me?' Bella shook her head, still not believing that the steady-as-she-goes Brendan had dropped everything to find her in this remote and wild setting. 'I can't believe you're here.'

Brendan took a step towards her and Bella suddenly became aware of her damp, sweaty clothing and messy hair. She drew back from him. 'Um, I just need to get changed.'

'It's lunchtime anyway,' said Ned. 'Frederick, are you going to join us? Brendan is a bit taken with the pizza oven and barbecue,' said Ned.

'That sounds great, thanks Ned,' said Frederick.

'Okay, guys, I'll be back down shortly.' Bella needed to escape. Seeing Brendan calmly chatting away to Ned as if he'd only seen him yesterday was unnerving. She had a quick shower and tried to make a bit of an effort with her tangled hair. She felt a tingle just thinking about the effort Brendan had made. It was so unlike him to be spontaneous like this. However, she also felt her independent streak surfacing. *I specifically asked him for some space. If he thinks he's just going to drag me back . . .*

'Bella . . . c'mon, we need help with lunch,' called Ned.

She could feel her emotions whirling as she came downstairs, but when she saw Brendan sitting with a beer in his hand, chatting sociably with Ned and Frederick, she held herself in check. She would have to speak to him alone later. She took a seat across from him and poured herself a drink from a pitcher of water.

Brendan smiled shyly at her, then looked up at Ned. 'Can I help with lunch?'

'I've got some chops for the barbecue and we can make a big tossed salad and have it with some olive bread warmed in the pizza oven,' said Ned.

'Sounds great,' said Frederick. 'So how long are you around, Brendan?'

'Not long, I'm afraid.' He looked questioningly at Bella. 'That is, if I'm invited to stay.'

'Of course you are, mate,' said Ned. 'Plenty of room.'

'What about your practice, Brendan?' asked Bella. She felt a flash of annoyance with her brother for inviting Brendan to stay without checking with her. Ned knew that they'd broken up. This time away was meant to be her holiday *away* from Brendan to figure things out.

'I managed to get a locum in for a couple of days, a mate of mine, and I've rearranged some appointments.'

'I see. Well, how did you manage to find me?' asked Bella curiously.

'Actually it was quite easy. You'd told me about the pink house in Cooktown, but when I turned up there, they knew nothing about you. But when I asked if they knew Ned, they told me he put on a concert in the town a few days ago. They suggested that I go to the "Toppie" and ask Yolanda. So I explained to her who I was and she told me to go to the Golden Mile Roadhouse and ask there. I did, and Frederick kindly offered to drive me out. Glad he did – I would never have found this place on my own. I don't even have a four-wheel drive, so my car's back at the roadhouse.' Brendan looked towards the seemingly never-ending expanse of bush. 'This is so isolated, Ned. It seems to be in the middle of nowhere. Have you any neighbours at all?'

'Yes, Jack – he's a Yank and quite a character. I like him,' said Ned. 'But he ruffled Bella's feathers.'

Frederick chuckled. 'Jack calls it as he sees it, that's for sure. He might have rusty manners around ladies, but he's a man with quite a story.' Frederick settled back as the others looked at him with interest. 'Jack told me that he was in Vietnam with the US Special Forces in secret wars

227

in the jungles, even before the American build-up really began in earnest. Dangerous work. From what he said, he seemed to be everywhere, fighting in the Tet Offensive, and he was in one of the last choppers that got out before the fall of Saigon. After that, he started to help other Vietnam vets who were having a tough time when they got back home. He called them the haunted souls with the thousand-yard stare who turned up on his doorstep. Said they'd all seen too much. I remember one horrific story that had been told to him by a marine who'd seen Viet Cong thrown out of a chopper because they wouldn't reveal information. After four Viet Cong had been pushed to their deaths, the fifth one told them what they wanted to know. No wonder that marine found it hard to live with what he'd seen. These were the sort of people Jack tried to help. But his marriage broke up under the strain. Too much baggage.'

'Is that why he's here?' asked Bella, beginning to understand the reasons for Jack's cynical behaviour.

'Took him a while to sort himself out. He once told me how he'd dug a hole and buried his past. Burned his uniforms, medals, maps, books, memorabilia, plaques and awards. The lot.'

'How sad,' murmured Ned. 'I wonder if that helped.'

'Maybe. Anyway, he's the ultimate warrior with years of guerrilla warfare training, right here on our doorstep,' continued Frederick cheerfully.

'Does he have a rifle?' asked Bella, thinking about the shot she'd heard earlier that day.

'You bet he does,' said Frederick. 'But I know he doesn't use it much. Hates that sort of thing now. Says the only shots that should be taken of the wildlife are with a camera, not a gun.'

'It's just that I thought I heard a gunshot when I was out in the canoe this morning,' said Bella.

'He's not crazy enough to take a pot shot at someone in a canoe, is he?' asked Brendan, looking concerned.

'Not bloody likely,' said Frederick emphatically. 'Jack has some funny ideas, but his heart's in the right place.'

'Are you sure?' asked Bella. 'I might have upset him yesterday with some of the things I said.'

Frederick laughed. 'I think you have the wrong idea about Jack, Bella. He really is one of the good guys. Wouldn't hurt anyone, unless he was defending himself. Take my word for it.'

Ned stood up. 'I'm sure you're right. I think Jack is quite able to defend himself without having to resort to violence. He's a pacifist now. How about I throw the steaks on the fire?'

'Do you want to help me with the salad?' Bella asked Brendan. Just sitting around making small talk with him was making her nervous. They needed to talk in private.

'I'll watch you cook, Ned,' said Frederick as he reached for a fresh can of beer.

*

Bella pulled the salad ingredients from the fridge and put them on the bench as Brendan came in to join her. He stood uncomfortably, hands in his pockets. There was a brief awkward pause as neither of them knew quite what to say.

'I've missed you, Bella,' Brendan said quietly. 'And after that fight . . . I just had to come and find out where we stand. I don't want you running off with someone else.' His face was stormy.

'It's not what you're thinking. If you're insinuating there's some affair –' began Bella.

'I'm not insinuating anything. The last time we spoke, you told me to bugger off and leave you alone and then

229

you dropped off the planet and I couldn't reach you. You never answered my calls.'

'I couldn't ring you,' said Bella defensively. 'There's no phone coverage out here. Besides, if I had rung, we would have got into the same old discussion all over again.' Bella jammed a knife into a tomato and began slicing.

Brendan took a deep breath. 'Bella, I freaked out when you dropped that bombshell about wanting to move up here. I overreacted by suggesting that you might not be up to it. I am very sorry I said that. I don't think there is anything that you can't do. You're probably still mad about what I said, but I hope we can put that aside and talk about us.' He paused and closed his eyes for a moment before opening them again. 'I love you very much. I really want us to move in together. But Bella, I want to know if you are prepared to make such a commitment, or if you just see me as someone to fill in time with until a better offer comes along.'

Bella stopped slicing and stared at him. Brendan had never been this open with her before. 'Brendan, you have to believe me that there is no one else. I'm not dodging your question when I say that this business opportunity is real. This isn't just about our relationship. I've been feeling restless in my job for a long time. I have to look at the pros and cons of where I'm at or I'll never be able to make a decision.'

'So you haven't made a final decision?' he asked, looking hopeful.

'Well, Ant is definitely one of those people who gets you all keen about something because he's so enthusiastic. He's a real salesman, but I need to do more research and more thinking before I commit.' Bella picked up the chopping board and slid the tomatoes into a bowl with the onions and lettuce.

'What does this Antony actually do for a living?' asked Brendan.

'He works as a guest liaison for an eco-resort in the Daintree. He's quite charismatic, so the guests must really like him.'

'That doesn't sound like the sort of job that would enable him to start his own business, or was he expecting you to be the money person?' asked Brendan with concern. 'He's not trying to fleece you, is he?'

'Good grief, no! He assures me that he has already got financial backing to start it, but that's another thing I'll have to check. Not that we've really talked practicalities,' said Bella thoughtfully. 'More just concepts.'

'Hmmm.'

Bella reached for the salad dressing. 'Do you want to meet him?'

'If you like, but I don't have to. I trust your judgement,' said Brendan diplomatically. He hesitated. 'You'll always be special to me. That's why I wanted to come and find you, to tell you, but the final decision about what you want – me or this business venture – rests with you. It always has, but I hope that you choose me. But have you thought that maybe if you really want to start something new, you could think of doing it in Tennyson?'

Before Bella could answer, Ned called out that the steaks were ready. Brendan looked at her beseechingly, but Bella decided to take the opportunity to end the conversation.

'We'll talk more later, okay?' Bella said. She picked up the salad bowl and servers and headed to the table.

It was a long and jovial meal, as the four of them got along well. Bella's mind was reeling with a confusion of thoughts and feelings, so she was happy to sit back and listen to Frederick's stories of the characters he'd met while running the roadhouse.

'The good, the bad and the ugly. You see it all up here,' he said with a hearty laugh.

After Frederick had left to drive back to the road-house, Bella took Ned aside for a minute.

'Look, Ned, I'm really flattered that Brendan decided to chase me all this way, but it's left me feeling a bit confused. I think I need to get my head around things. Would it be all right if you took him out for a while, just so I can think about him calmly? Maybe drive him up to the old gold dam, just for an hour or so?'

'I could, but I don't really want to leave you here by yourself.'

'For heaven's sake, I'll be fine. I'm not sending you away overnight. Anyway, it'll be dark in less than three hours, so you'll have to be back home by then. What on earth could happen to me? Just do me this favour. I need to think without Brendan hovering over me. Everything is becoming so complicated.'

'All right, if you're sure. But we'll only go for a short time.'

Bella could see that Brendan was a bit surprised by Ned's suggestion to visit the dam, but he agreed that it was worth a closer look and the two left as soon as they had all cleaned up the lunch things.

*

When they had gone, Bella decided to make herself a cup of tea. Filling the kettle, she tried to gather her thoughts but all she could feel was anxiety. This surprise visit by Brendan, the spontaneity of it, was so out of character for him that it was making it all the harder to know what to think.

As she waited for the kettle to boil, she realised that he almost seemed to be a different person from the man she'd left behind in Tennyson. Certainly she had never expected him to be so impetuous as to follow her here. His quixotic actions were in sharp contrast to the Brendan she thought she knew. Maybe he wasn't as conservative and unadventurous as she'd assumed. And for the first time he'd actually said what he wanted and been open with her. Nevertheless, did she really want to return to her safe and secure life in Tennyson? Antony had made her realise that there were other possibilities. Maybe she did want to take risks and face career challenges, and if she didn't take the plunge now, would the chance ever come again? Far North Queensland seemed to present her with a lot of opportunities. Should she just go for it, be like her brother and take a gamble with her life instead of always playing it safe? What would her father say if he were here?

Bella was so preoccupied with these thoughts that she didn't realise that the kettle had finished boiling. As she reached for the tea caddy, a noise made her turn and she cried out, dropping the caddy, its contents spilling across the floor.

Standing in the kitchen was a strange man, seemingly as surprised to see her as she was to see him.

'What the hell . . . ?'

The man made a sudden move across the kitchen and tried to grab her, causing her to slip on the loose tea leaves and fall to the ground. She let out another cry as she was roughly wrenched to her feet.

'Who are you? What's going on?' shouted Bella, trying to twist from his grasp.

'Shit. Who's this? I thought you said the place was empty.'

A second man, wearing a faded blue shirt, came forward and Bella recoiled at the sight of his rough and dishevelled appearance and the rifle that was slung over his shoulder.

'Yeah, well, when I saw the four-wheel drive leave with those blokes on board, how was I to know that they'd left this bird behind?'

'What do you want? Why are you here?' Bella asked shakily, hoping wildly that Ned and Brendan would return and save her from these louts.

'Just passing through,' said the first man, not loosening his grip on her.

Bella twisted again and swung her other arm at his face.

He ducked and grabbed her roughly and firmly, swearing as he did so. 'Bitch. Don't make trouble or I'll lock you in the shed.'

'Nah, I've got a better idea,' said the man in the blue shirt. 'Why don't you get the booze we came for. That Carlo, whoever he is, makes a mean drop. Then we'll get out of here, but we'll take her with us.'

Bella went cold as she saw the expression on his face when he made this awful suggestion. 'Leave me alone. Just leave me. I'll make sure that no one goes after you.'

'Well, they won't find us if they do. No one can find us,' the man with the blue shirt said with a nasty grin. 'Get something to tie her up with,' he demanded.

Bella began screaming at the top of her voice, but he slapped her, hard. She whimpered, feeling as though her jaw had nearly been broken and her teeth loosened. Now she was terrified and she started to sob as her arms were tied behind her with some twisted plastic shopping bags.

'Now, get the stuff we came for. Get going.' He shoved Bella towards the river while the other man carried a box, hastily filled with Carlo's homemade alcohol, down to two waiting kayaks.

'Where are you taking me? Why? Oh, God, help me . . . just leave me here . . .'

'Well, slut, it's like this. We've been out in the bush for a long time and this is our last night. Thought we'd stop by and grab some of the booze for a bit of a party, and then there you were. Just the right sort of guest to help the night along. Hope you're a real party girl. Now shut up and get in,' he ordered as he pushed her into one of the two-man kayaks. She wanted to kick and lash out, but with her arms tied behind her and her body wedged in the kayak, she realised that struggling could tip the kayak over, and even in the relatively shallow water, she would have trouble saving herself.

The men said very little as they paddled down the still river for what seemed like hours, except for the odd comment from the man in the blue shirt, who made several suggestions as to what he would do with her when their party started. Bella was terrified. Once or twice she screamed for help, but the man in the blue shirt just laughed. 'Go for your life, slut. No one around to hear you,' he said.

What sort of animal was this man? She heard his heavy breathing as he paddled and wondered how she would ever survive this nightmare. They passed the place where she had made the U-turn earlier that day. *Was it only this morning?* she thought. So much had happened that day, and now the sun was beginning to sink in the sky. Soon it would be dark. How long before Ned and Brendan returned home and found her gone? Why on earth had she sent Ned and Brendan away to visit the dam?

I don't want to die, she thought. *Is that what will happen to me? Maybe they will let me go. But if they let me go in this bush, how will I ever find my way out?* Terrible thoughts ran through her mind. *Please, Ned and Brendan, find me soon.*

The dark comes quickly in the far north, and the light was very dim as the two kayaks moved towards the river bank. There was a scrape as she felt the kayak run aground on the river's sandy bottom. Ignoring her, the two men leaped out of their kayaks and began to unload them. In the half dark she could make out the shape of a third man coming out of the bush and down the bank to help them.

'You here already, mate?' she heard one of the men ask him. 'Have you stored your kayak yet?'

'No, not yet. We'll have to move them all straight away. Don't want to keep the boss waiting. Who the eff is that in your kayak?'

'Just a souvenir,' said the man in the blue shirt. 'We were passing the weird Italian place and we stopped to get some more booze. There's quite a stock of it there and I thought we could have a bit of a celebration, this being our last night out and all. She was there, so we took her. She's the entertainment.'

Bella sat there in the kayak as the gloom gathered around her, quite helpless and filled with a fear that she had never known before. She knew now, with absolute certainty, that if Ned and Brendan didn't come, she would not leave this place alive. If only she could free her arms from behind her back. They were aching from being in such an uncomfortable position for so long, but she couldn't even seem to loosen them, let alone untie them.

'I'll get the girl.' Even in the dark, she recognised the harsh voice of the man in the blue shirt.

'She's a liability, why'd you take her?' said the third man, obviously angered by Bella's presence. 'You've done some pretty crazy, stupid things, mate, but this is the worst.'

'Like I told you, she's the entertainment.'

'She could also be nothing but trouble. You should've just left her at the house.'

'Maybe you don't like women. Is that your problem?'

'And maybe you're mad.'

Footsteps came towards the kayak and Bella was yanked roughly out of it. She stumbled as she tried to maintain her balance. She certainly didn't want to fall into the river. She was sure that she would be left there.

'Please, let me go. I won't say anything. I promise.'

'Forget it and shut up,' said the man with the blue shirt as he pushed her to the ground and then walked away, leaving her there. She tried to rest her head on her knees, but it was far too uncomfortable. Even though the sun had gone down it was still hot, although a light breeze had sprung up, giving her a little relief from the cloying humidity, but not from the mosquitoes, which were attacking her furiously.

Sitting there on the rough ground, Bella could hear the three men talking in the shadows.

'I tell you, the boss isn't going to like this when he comes to pick us up,' said the third man.

'Mate, the boss will be okay.'

'No, he won't, and you're a bloody idiot.'

'Do you want me to fetch her?'

'No, I don't want you to bloody fetch her. I want you to think of a way to get us out of the mess you've landed us in.'

There was silence for a few minutes until Bella heard one of them say, 'Well, it's no use sitting around and bitching. We have to get the kayaks stored up in their usual place. Want to get that done right away. Don't want to hold the boss up.'

'What time did you say the boss would be here?'

'Before dawn, and we'll want to be ready.'

'Okay, but after we've got rid of these boats how about we sample some of the stuff we got from the house?'

'I'll tie up the girl's legs before we go. Don't want to have her scarpering off.'

'Nowhere much to scarper to, but go for it, it will save one of us having to stay and watch her.'

237

Bella was shivering with fright as the man in the blue shirt came over and roughly tied her feet together with a bit of rope.

'Wait for us to get back, sister, and don't go wandering off,' he said nastily.

Several minutes later, Bella heard the men go off into the bush. One of them was carrying a torch and the other two seemed to be carrying one of the kayaks.

Bella kept still and silent. She had no idea where she was and no idea if she would be found. How could she save herself all trussed up the way she was? Unbidden tears began to trickle down her cheeks. As the half moon rose, a glimmer of light allowed her to see where the river bank ended and the bush began. She saw she was sitting on a tiny strip of beach. The rest of the river bank was lined with thick scrub. She could hear the men's voices as they receded into the distance and she could still see the light from their torch. She wondered how long it would be until they returned for the other craft. Could she try to get away without their noticing? She rested her head on her knees, feeling her warm tears run down her face. Bella lifted her head. They wouldn't leave her unmolested, she was sure of that.

She sat there for some time, trying to think of a way out of her predicament. Then she heard the men returning, noisily barging their way through the bush, the torch-light indicating where they were. They stayed only briefly before marching off into the bush once more with another kayak.

Bella knew that they would be gone for some time, so now was her chance. As frightened as she was, she had to make a move.

With her arms and legs still tied, she began to slither and roll very slowly towards the sanctuary of the bush, the rough ground cutting into her. As she moved into the undergrowth, she suddenly slammed against something sharp. She bit her tongue rather than cry out in pain. She fell over onto her side, exhausted by her efforts, and then noticed that her hands were resting against the end of a low broken branch. The break was an old one, for the end had sealed itself into a hard jagged point. Maybe this pointed end would tear through the plastic bags around her wrists. With an intake of breath, she managed to position herself on her knees with her back to the tree and began to drag her wrists over the rough end. After several goes, she managed to get the short spike to tug at the plastic. She worked steadily, feeling the plastic bag tear bit by bit. As her pace quickened, the point of the stump suddenly cut into her skin. Gasping but ignoring the pain, she forced herself to work more slowly. She knew that with time the sharp point would do the trick. But how much time did she have? Her ears strained for any sound of the three men returning. She was terrified that they would come back before she had finished her task. Bella felt a sob of fear and frustration well up inside her as the plastic seemed to take forever to shred.

But suddenly she felt the ties give way and her arms were free. She rubbed her wrists for a few seconds, and then quickly untied her legs. She still couldn't hear the men and, not wanting to waste precious time, she hurriedly hid the plastic and rope under some dried leaves so that the men wouldn't realise that she had freed herself. Although she had no idea which direction would lead her to safety, she crept off further into the bush, but as she moved through the dense scrub that lined the river, she realised that her progress would be painfully slow. On the other hand, she knew that if she moved away from the river, into more open ground, the men would have little trouble spotting her in the moonlight.

So she battled through the scrub by the river, bushes scratching at her arms and face, as she searched for somewhere to hide. Then she saw it – an ancient gum tree at the edge of the river with huge exposed roots where the soil had been washed away so that a shallow cave had formed around its base. Bella stumbled towards it and fell into one of its root hollows, hoping that she wouldn't encounter any nasty creatures already in residence. It was dark and smelled of rotting leaves and dank earth. She lay there for a few moments, not moving, then slowly she began to burrow backwards into the rotting vegetation, trying not to rustle leaves or snap a twig, pushing herself further into the hollow beneath the tree trunk.

When she could burrow no further she stopped and huddled there, trying to quieten her rasping breaths. Bella was overcome with fear and exhaustion. She tried to stay awake, but she could feel herself slipping into blackness.

With the sudden feeling that she was falling, she jerked her head up and opened her eyes, realising she must have nodded off. Had it been minutes or hours? It was still dark, but then she heard them; shouting voices and crashing undergrowth. Bella held her breath.

'How far can she get with her bloody arms and legs tied?'

'Well, there's bugger-all out here, nothing but thick scrub. And it's as dark as pitch. She won't have gone far.'

The other man raised his voice. 'We're coming after you. Don't make it worse for yourself, girlie. Be nice or we'll get pissed off.'

A rifle shot cracked, echoing through the scrub, ricocheting off a tree.

Bella shivered.

'Stop with the gun, for Chrissake, could be anyone around.'

'Out here? Bullshit.'

'Well, there might be someone out looking for her.'

'Have to know this place pretty well to find us, mate.'

'Let's go. Leave the bitch. The boss will be here soon and he'll be bloody upset if we keep him waiting.'

Bella stayed huddled in her tree-root cave, barely breathing. Trembling with fear, she heard one of the men come very close to where she was hiding, but then he moved away.

'Come on. I can hear the boss coming.'

'You gonna tell him?'

'About the girl? He'll shoot our balls off. Or shoot her if he finds her. We're on a deadline to meet the big boat down at the cove.'

'She knows who we are. What we look like.'

'Who's she gonna tell out here?'

Filled with relief, Bella could hear them walking away. She didn't move. A short time later, she heard the large engine of a four-wheel drive in the distance. She could hear voices, and then a while later the car took off.

Bella lay still in her sanctuary. After an hour or so, when she was convinced they really had gone, she hauled herself out from under the leaves and cautiously made her way towards the river. She peered guardedly out from the cover of a large bush, in case any of the men were still there. But there was nothing to indicate that anyone had been there at all, save for a couple of empty bottles. The men and the kayaks were gone. She was all alone in the middle of the bush with no idea where she was and no way of getting out.

Bella shivered, for she knew all too clearly that her troubles were far from over. Should she stay here by the river or struggle on, looking for a track that lead to goodness knows where? She rubbed her sore wrists. *Maybe there were crocodiles in this area*, she suddenly thought in alarm. Although Ned hadn't ever mentioned them, Bella didn't want to take the chance of staying too close to the river. She turned back towards the bush and began to clamber as far as she could away from the river. She wandered aimlessly for some time, having no real idea where she should go and then, in the pale glimmer of the setting moon, between some trees Bella saw the silhouette of a strange shape. It looked like an old-fashioned train engine. Stumbling across the rocks, she made her way to where a rusting heap of metal was set in a rough brick wall. In the pale light she could see that it was an old boiler, like a giant oven, with its metal door hanging open. She hit it hard in case there was an animal or a snake asleep inside. The metallic thud echoed in the empty bush and she froze, but there was no sound or movement. She felt around for a stick and poked around inside. Finding no wildlife, Bella clambered in and curled up, breathing in the smell of rust and charred wood. She laid her head on her arm and prayed that, when dawn came, things would seem better.

They had to.

9

THEY WERE LAUGHING AS they got out of the car, Brendan carrying a bucket containing a couple of good-sized fish.

'I'll leave the rods in the back in case we want to throw a line in there again,' said Ned.

'Can we have fish on the barbie for dinner?' asked Brendan. 'They were so easy to catch. I don't think many people ever go to that old lake.'

Ned nodded in agreement. He'd enjoyed Brendan's uncomplicated company and was pleased they'd both caught something. He didn't want to pry, but hoped that Brendan and Bella would sort things out.

'I'm glad the fish were so obliging. I didn't mean to leave Bella alone for so long, though; it's almost dark. You'd better show her our prizes and apologise. I'll go and lock up the chooks.'

As he went to round up the hens, he heard Brendan calling out to Bella, but before he even came inside Brendan raced up the steps to meet him.

'Bella's not answering. I can't find her.'

'Is she asleep in her room?'

'No. I've looked there and all over the house. It's empty and all the lights were off. I called out to the lower terrace in case she was down there, but there's no answer,' said Brendan, his brows knitted.

Ned decided to remain calm. 'She can't be far away. Give me the fish and I'll put them in the kitchen. Cleaning can wait till we find Bella. Why don't you check under the big poinciana tree? She might have fallen asleep in the hammock and not heard us get back. Or maybe she's gone up to the wood pile to get some wood for the fire pit. You look around and I'll check inside again.'

Ned took the bucket and went into the kitchen and turned on the lights. The house was very still. He put the fish into the fridge, and as he went over to the sink to wash his hands, he felt something crunch beneath his feet. When he looked down he saw the tea canister lying on the floor, the tea leaves spilled everywhere. Ned went cold. Dropping the empty bucket, he sprinted through the house, shouting Bella's name.

At the same time, Brendan's worried voice called out, 'Ned, I can't find Bella anywhere out here.'

Ned raced about looking for any sign of his sister and, finding nothing, he went outside to join Brendan. 'Maybe she's had an accident. I'll get some torches. Something isn't right.'

The pale beams from the torches revealed little.

'She wouldn't have gone swimming and . . .' Brendan couldn't finish the sentence.

The two men raced down to the edge of the river.

'Nothing to show she was here. No book or towel,

not even a glass,' said Ned, looking around. 'Wait, what's that?' He shone his torch at the water's edge, then knelt down, looking intently at the gravelly bank.

'What? What is it?' asked Brendan. 'Bella wouldn't have taken out the canoe this late, would she?' he added fearfully.

'No, she didn't – there's Carlo's old canoe still up under the trees where Frederick put it this morning. Anyway, look at those marks. Carlo's canoe didn't make them. Someone else was here. Some other craft has been dragged up onto the bank. Those marks over there could be footprints, too, although it's hard to tell on this dry ground.' Ned pointed to some smaller marks further down the bank.

'I think they are footprints. They seem clearer when you get closer to the water's edge. What does this all mean?' Brendan's voice was raised and shrill.

Ned was still. 'Brendan, in the kitchen tea leaves have been spilled all over the floor and no attempt has been made to clean them up. Bella would never leave a mess like that. I think she's gone with someone, and I'm sure it wasn't voluntarily, because she hasn't left us a note.'

Brendan looked at Ned in horror. 'What are we going to do? We'll have to go back to the roadhouse and contact the police.'

Ned shook his head. 'I couldn't find my way back there with any confidence in the dark. You'd have to be an expert – there are tracks all over the place out here. We'd be no help to Bella at all if we tried it and got hopelessly lost.'

'We can't just sit here and wait till it gets light,' said Brendan, the anguish clear in his voice. 'Bella could be anywhere by then.'

'I know,' said Ned helplessly. Then abruptly he got to his feet. 'We need help and I know just the right person. I'm going inside to look for Carlo's gun.'

'Geez, Ned, do you want to go after whoever took Bella with a gun?' said Brendan, even more alarmed.

'No, I want to summon help. You know we were talking about Jack earlier? The guy who lives across the valley? He told me on one of his visits that he and Carlo had a pre-arranged signal between them in case of an emergency, because Jack doesn't have a sat phone. He likes his privacy. I didn't think in a million years that I would have to use the signal in reverse.'

Ned hurried into the house and found Carlo's rifle in the gun rack. He quickly unlocked the rack and then hunted around in Carlo's uniquely designed drawers until he found some cartridges.

'Hate these damn things,' he muttered to himself as he rejoined Brendan. 'I'll need a torch as well. Can you bring it?'

'Yes, of course. You okay with that rifle? I've done a bit of shooting.'

'Thanks, I can manage. Dad showed me what to do years ago. It's not that hard.'

Ned went outside and onto the top terrace with Brendan following behind. He grimly loaded the rifle and fired towards the river. He paused and then fired twice more in quick succession. 'Brendan, wave the torch over your head in as big an arc as you can. I hope to hell that Jack hears and sees our signal. We really need him.'

Brendan began waving the torch. He looked at Ned's pale face. 'What's going on? Have you any idea?' he asked.

'I don't know for sure, but a week or so ago, two blokes turned up in kayaks and helped themselves to food and some of Carlo's alcohol. I reckon those blokes might have called by again. And I bet they weren't expecting to find Bella.'

'Oh, Christ, what've they done with her?' Brendan started to shake, but at that moment a rifle shot echoed from the darkness opposite, quickly followed by a second.

Ned felt a wave of relief. 'Thank God. Jack heard us. That means he's on his way. He'll be here in about half an hour, I guess. Let's take one more thorough look around, just in case they've locked her in a shed or something.'

'Will we go after her?' asked Brendan. 'We'll have to. Can't leave her out there alone.'

'Let's see what Jack says. C'mon, let's keep looking while we're waiting for him.'

As Ned headed towards the storage shed on the top of the rise, he realised that he was shaking, too. This nightmare seemed unbelievable. Images of Bella rushed through his mind. He started to think about their heated discussion over their father's dedication ceremony. What were his last words to her? He didn't want to leave things this way, when they were so at odds with each other. He should not have listened to her when she'd asked him to take Brendan to the old dam, leaving her alone in this wild place.

Brendan looked pale as they finished searching the grounds around the river house. 'I can't stop thinking about the river. If they've taken her out on the water, they might have had some awful accident . . .'

Ned didn't want to speculate on Bella's fate. The thought of what could be happening to her was tying his stomach in knots and making him feel quite ill. He was about to turn back towards the house when he heard Jack's car.

'Thank God,' he muttered to himself. 'Jack will know what to do.'

Ned raced to open the gate, Brendan following close behind.

Jack looked sombre as he quickly got out of the car. 'What's the emergency? It had better be a real one to get me over here at night.'

Ned quickly introduced Brendan, then told Jack about Bella's disappearance and explained what he thought had happened.

Jack didn't say a word, but took a torch from his vehicle and hurried down to the river. He looked closely at the ground by the water's edge and said, 'Yeah, they got away by river. Same as before, I'd say.'

'How many canoes has Carlo got?' asked Brendan.

'Enough for us to be able to go after her,' said Ned.

Jack frowned. 'I think a better plan than going after Bella in those canoes would be for me to drive back to the roadhouse and inform the police. They'll go after those buggers first thing in the morning, even before first light,' he said.

Ned and Brendan stared at him.

'But Jack, we have to go now. We can't hang about till morning waiting for the police. We can't leave Bella all night with these men. That's ridiculous! We have to go now!' said Ned, amazed by Jack's suggestion.

'Not so ridiculous,' said Jack dryly. 'Going out at night could make us sitting ducks. We can't travel in the darkness without having to shine a light along the edges of the river to see where these men are holed up, and when we round a bend in the river and they see our light, and we can't see them, what then? What will happen to your sister if they realise they've been caught?' He shook his head. 'Better to wait for daylight, and by then the coppers will be here.'

'Jack, you can't mean that,' said Brendan heatedly. 'I can't sit around wondering what is happening to Bella. I have to do something now.' He turned to Ned. 'Come on, Ned. If Jack won't help us, we'll have to go after her by ourselves.'

Ned was torn. He felt exactly the same way as Brendan. As far as he was concerned, they had wasted enough time already, but he was aware that Jack was the expert, the one with all the experience, the one whose counsel he should accept. He also knew he could not sit around and wait till morning without taking action.

'Jack, I really value your advice, but Brendan is right. I think we need to get after these men right away, before anything terrible happens.'

Jack sighed. 'Okay, okay. Well, I can't let you two blunder through this country alone, so I guess we go now, even though it's against my better judgement. Get the other canoe and bring all the torches you can find. I think Carlo's got a first aid kit somewhere. See if you can find it. And bring some bottles of water.'

'Do you want me to bring Carlo's gun?' asked Ned.

'Either of you two experts?' Jack asked sharply.

'Not really,' said Ned, and Brendan shook his head.

'Well, if you're not, then bringing the gun is creating another problem we don't need. Leave it behind.'

Ned rounded up the few things Jack had asked for and Brendan retrieved the second canoe from the shed.

'Right, let's go,' said Jack grimly.

They hurried down the steps that led to the lower terrace and the river beyond. Ned noticed that Jack had a small torch attached to a strap that was fastened around his head, so that the light from it bounced as he ran.

'You two take that canoe. I'll take this one.' Without another word, Jack settled in the canoe and started to paddle downstream.

They paddled as fast as they could along the dark river. Occasionally Brendan swung a torch beam along the river bank.

'I don't think you'll find the men this close to Carlo's. I think they'll be quite a way away, where there's even less civilisation than around here,' said Jack over his shoulder.

Ned wondered how on earth there could be anywhere more deserted than Carlo's place, but said nothing.

At one point there was a distant crack. Ned jumped.

'A rifle?' he asked.

Jack shook his head. 'Too far away to know for sure. Could just be a falling branch.'

They finally came to the place where the quiet arm of the river joined the main, wider watercourse. They paddled along it for some distance. As Brendan shone his torch ahead, Ned could see that the water flowed around a rocky outcrop. As they neared the smooth, exposed rocks it was clear that another stream joined the main river at that point.

'Do we stay in this main part, or go up that small branch?' Brendan asked Jack.

Jack hesitated, resting his paddle. 'Hard to say. The smaller stream is more of a backwater, so maybe it's quieter, making it a good place to hide out. The main part of the river is easier to navigate, but it also makes it more open and exposed. What do you think they'd do?'

'Flip a coin,' said Brendan. 'I have no idea what these men would do. This country is empty, and as far as I'm concerned, they could be anywhere out here, and we may never find them.'

'I think we should go up the quiet branch,' said Ned, bringing their canoe alongside Jack's. 'I don't know why, but I just feel that they would want to hang out in the quietest place possible.'

'Okay then, decision's made.'

But after a couple of hours of paddling, Jack slowed.

'This water is becoming far too shallow. If we scrape over any rocks in the dark, we'll be in trouble. I don't think anyone would bring a kayak or canoe any further upstream. The water level has dropped too much this late in the season. We'll have to go back down the main river, but first I suggest we take a couple of hours' rest. We won't be much help to your sister if we're exhausted.'

Ned had no desire to stop. He wanted to turn around at once and keep up the pursuit, but Jack's authoritative tone suggested he was not open to a discussion this time around.

'I'm not at all happy about stopping,' said Brendan. 'But I have to admit that my arms are very tired. Perhaps a short break will help.'

'Shine your torch over there, Brendan.' Jack examined the river bank closely. 'Yes, I think we should be able to get out of the canoes here and clamber over those rocks, so we can lie down.' With that, Jack got out of his canoe and Ned was amazed to see he was standing in knee-deep water. He and Brendan followed suit and they waded to the shore, pulling their canoes behind them. 'Try to get some sleep. It will start getting light in about three hours. I'll wake you both then,' said Jack.

They made their way over the rocks and looked for somewhere to rest. Ned lay down uncomfortably on one of the flat wide rocks and tried to relax, but his arms and hands were throbbing from all the unaccustomed exercise.

He couldn't stop thinking about Bella. While at times she could annoy him, she always had his best interests at heart. She had taken the trouble to track him down in Cooktown, and while he had resented her determination to try to make him do something he didn't want to do, he also felt remorse that he had not greeted her more warmly. She had made such an effort to do what she thought was best for their family, and instead of welcoming her, he'd bickered with her. She was his only sibling and she meant the world to him, and yet, he thought, his recent actions could have made Bella doubt it. Then another horrible thought occurred to him. What on earth was he going to tell his mother if they couldn't find Bella? His mind racing, he thought sleep would never come, but his body was exhausted and the bush was silent and dark and eventually he drifted into a fitful doze.

Jack woke him as the first sign of light began to seep into the eastern sky, and they were quickly on their way again, following the stream back towards the main river.

With aching arms and his chest tight with anxiety, all Ned could think about was Bella and what could have happened to her. He tried to focus as he dipped the paddle blade into the dark water strongly and firmly, blanking out the frightening thoughts that pressed into his mind.

As the sun began to rise, Ned lost track of time. He felt the three of them were travelling in some sort of parallel universe, with Bella at its centre, waiting for them.

Jack showed no sign of slowing or tiring, nor had he made any further mention of going back for the police. For now, the three of them were on their own. Ned watched as the older man kept studying both sides of the river, clearly looking for any clue or sign to show that they were on the right track. He prayed his friend's jungle-fighting experience would help them.

After an hour or so, Jack stopped paddling and craned forward.

'See anything?' Brendan said in a low voice.

'Yeah. Could be,' the older man said quietly.

Ned whispered, 'What is it?'

Jack pointed. 'There's a bit of an inlet up ahead. Good place for a kayak to pull in. I'll go in first and signal to you if it's clear. If you don't hear me whistle, get the hell out.'

Ned watched as Jack's canoe glided quietly in to the bank. He could now see a small clearing along the water's edge. He and Brendan drifted slowly, their paddles poised as they watched Jack leave his canoe and walk quietly into the clearing.

Suddenly they heard a low whistle. Even before Jack's signal had finished, Ned had started stroking swiftly to the shore. As Ned clambered out of the canoe, Jack touched his arm and pointed. Ned looked down and he could clearly see marks on the sand and in the grass.

Jack moved further along the bank to a small area of flattened grass, and when Ned joined him, he shivered. Someone had been here very recently.

Jack spoke in a low whisper. 'They've dragged their kayaks from the river, and they've also sat or slept in this area. And look at the empty bottles lying around. Carlo's grappa.'

'Where's Bella? Is she with them, do you think?' asked Brendan.

No one said anything, and Ned knew they were all fearing the worst, then Jack said quietly, 'At least there are no signs of a struggle here.'

'I'm not sure what that proves,' said Brendan bitterly.

'Keep your voice down, Brendan,' said Jack in a sharp whisper. 'They could still be around. They've obviously moved their boats, but not back into the water. I can't see any signs of that. I think they might have taken them away from the river, to be hidden or picked up by a vehicle, so let's look around and see if we can find their tracks. But first we have to see if we can find any trace of Bella.'

Ned looked at the scrub that grew down to the edge of the river. How anyone could find and follow a trail in this dry, desolate country was beyond him, but he had every confidence in Jack's ability. Unsure of what he was looking for, he set out, staying close to the river and keeping his eyes to the ground, looking for anything that might give him a clue about Bella's whereabouts.

As he picked his way cautiously along the water's edge, Ned wanted to shout Bella's name, but he knew that it would be too risky until they could be sure that they were alone. He saw a large gum whose roots had been exposed by the annual floods, and scrambled down the bank to take a closer look. He noticed that the leaves beneath the roots had been recently disturbed, and thought that an animal must have been foraging there for food. A few minutes later, he heard Jack's low whistle and he went to join the others.

Jack spoke softly. 'Either of you two see anything? No? Then they must have gone inland. Maybe your sister is with them.'

As they worked their way uphill through the scrubby but slightly open country, Jack moved between the small trees, pausing every so often to listen and to look around. Suddenly he grunted and signalled to the others to join him.

He pointed to a narrow path, probably made by stray cattle or goats, which skirted a gully forged by rushing floodwaters. 'I bet they took this path. See, there are broken twigs on the ground and that branch up ahead has been bent back,' he whispered with some satisfaction.

Ned nodded, but in truth he knew he would never have seen these signs had Jack not pointed them out.

They continued to creep up the hill, and near the top they found the kayaks. Brendan and Ned shook their heads as they surveyed the clever way three long green-grey kayaks had been strapped upright against three tall gum trees. Swiftly Jack took out his knife and slashed the hull of each of them.

'Looks like there were at least three men,' he said.

Brendan swore under his breath. 'And what have they done to Bella?'

'Well, if their kayaks are here, then the bastards must have left in a vehicle. Let's look around. Maybe down in one of the gullies. A four-wheel drive could get along a gully at this time of year. Couldn't get through in the wet; the water would go over its roof.'

The three men scrambled down the steep walls of one of the gullies, and at the bottom they found faint tyre marks in the gritty sand of the dry watercourse.

'Now we know they've left,' said Jack. 'See, there's one set of tyre marks just here and the same marks over there, a bit further. Four-wheel drive's come in and then gone out again.'

Brendan reached out and touched Ned's shoulder.

'Bella has to be all right. She just has to be,' he said, but although he may have meant his words to be reassuring, Brendan's voice betrayed his own fear.

Ned nodded, his throat too tight to answer, and he shuddered at the thought of what could be happening to his sister.

'They might have taken her, or maybe not,' said Jack. 'She could still be out here somewhere, tied up, or hiding, or trying to find her way out of the bush. How about we make a bit of a racket? Tell the world that we're here.' He clapped Brendan on the back and strode off along the gully, shouting out for Bella.

They shouted and called as they hiked through the bush.

'Not too many places for her to hide or be hidden,' commented Jack.

Ned felt his blood run cold. 'But what if they've hidden her? Tied her up and left her? We may never find her out here.'

'Just keep looking,' Jack said, exasperation in his voice. 'We've barely started; it's way too soon to give up.'

They tramped through the scrub, yelling Bella's name, stopping only to take a short drink or to catch their breath. It grew hotter. After a couple of hours, Ned and Brendan met at the top of a small ridge. Ned felt defeated.

'There's simply no sign of her. I've looked for indications that she might have come this way, but I can't spot any. They must have taken her with them. Surely she would have heard us shouting by now if she's nearby. This all feels so hopeless.'

'I know. We seem to be going around in circles. Everything out here looks the same,' said Brendan, standing on top of a small ridge. But even as he was speaking he started to point. 'Hang on, what's that down there?' He took a step towards the gully on the other side of the ridge, peering at something just beyond it. 'I definitely haven't seen that before. Is it a shed?'

Jack joined them. He strode up to them with the energy of a much younger man, hardly puffing at all as he reached them. 'That's part of an old mine, the Queen's Hill mine,' he said when he saw where Ned and Brendan were looking. 'The thing you can see is the old steam boiler that once drove the machinery. The mine is well and truly deserted, and now it's just a lot of rubble, old iron and uncovered shafts. Always a bit dangerous down there.'

'You don't think she might have stumbled into one of the mine shafts, do you?' said Ned, his voice full of dread.

'Let's take a look,' said Brendan.

They scrambled down the slope towards the old mine.

'Okay,' said Jack. 'Start looking and keep shouting.'

Ned hurried to an old mine shaft and peered down.

'I can't see a thing inside. I'll have to go back and get one of the torches.' But he shouted down the shaft, 'Bella, it's Ned!'

There was no reply.

'Bella! Bella, answer me, please!' pleaded Brendan as loudly as he could.

'Bella, it's safe now!' roared Jack.

They peered under sheets of rusting iron and around the piles of rubble while shouting over and over again. Ned couldn't help but wonder if their efforts were futile.

Suddenly there was a rattle and a banging, and a muffled voice came from inside the rusted metal chamber of the old boiler.

'*NED?*'

Ned's heart leapt into his throat, and his voice broke as he shouted, 'Bella! Where are you?'

They all began rushing towards the rusting hulk.

'She's in there,' yelled Ned, clambering over a heap of rocks.

'I'm here, I'm here,' yelled Bella, relief and near hysteria evident in her voice as she began to climb through the old fire door.

Brendan was hot on Ned's heels as the two raced towards the rusted boiler, until he tripped and fell.

Bella was scrambling out of the old machine when Ned got to her. They clutched each other tearfully.

'Bell . . . are you all right? They didn't . . . hurt you?'

'I'm okay. They tied me up. I thought no one would ever find me . . .' She started to sob. 'I could hear shouting for ages, but I was too frightened to stick my head out in case it was those men again. Oh, Ned, you have no idea how happy I was when I recognised your voice!'

Ned held her tightly, love and relief sweeping through him.

'Bella! Oh, Bella!' Brendan came up beside them and Ned released his hold on his sister.

'She's okay, Brendan. She's okay,' Ned said reassuringly.

Brendan couldn't speak, he just held Bella tightly, smoothing her hair as he tried to calm her down.

Gradually her sobs subsided. Jack walked over and passed her a bottle of water. 'I expect you'd like a drink.'

Bella nodded and drank eagerly, then returned the bottle to Jack with a faint smile.

'Jack brought us here,' said Brendan. 'He found you. We couldn't have done it without him.'

'Thank you, Jack,' said Bella quietly.

'Are you all right to travel back in Carlo's canoe? It's a bit of a way,' asked Ned anxiously.

Bella nodded, burying her head in Brendan's chest, his arms around her once more.

Jack studied her carefully. 'You sure you're not hurt? What's the matter with your wrists?' he asked. Brendan released Bella and she held out her arms to Jack. He took both of Bella's hands and studied them. 'They tied you up and you struggled against the knots, did you? And how did you do this?' He indicated the wound on the back of one of her hands.

'Oh, Bella, you're hurt,' said Brendan, concern in his voice.

'Jack's right. They tied my hands together with plastic bags and I tore them off on a sharp bit of a branch. I knocked my hand against it and it got cut.' Bella's voice shook.

'Jack brought along a first aid kit. It's in one of our canoes. I'll take care of your hands as soon as we get back to the river. It's not so far away,' said Brendan kindly.

Ned had a myriad of questions to ask her, but he sensed that now was not the time. Bella seemed far too fragile and he just wanted to get her home as fast as possible.

Bella clutched Brendan's hand as he helped her walk along the gully towards the river. As they got close to the river bank, Bella stopped, frozen in her tracks.

'They won't come back, will they?' she asked apprehensively. 'They said they had to meet the boss at the cove. Something about a boat.'

'Not likely. No coves around here,' answered Jack.

'Jack fixed their kayaks – they won't be able to use them again,' said Brendan in a satisfied voice.

As soon as they reached Carlo's canoes, Brendan found the first aid kit and tenderly put antiseptic cream on Bella's wrists before dressing them.

'Is it too late for the police to find them?' Ned asked Jack quietly as he watched Brendan tie up a bandage.

'I hope not. Those men are animals and you wouldn't want them to get away with what they did to Bella. You'll have to report it,' said Jack, suppressed anger in his tone.

'Let's just get back to the river house as soon as we can,' said Brendan. He stroked Bella's arm. 'How are you feeling?'

'A lot better since you lot arrived.' She almost managed a smile, but the look in her eyes showed her exhaustion.

Jack and Brendan took the lead canoe. Bella sat behind Ned as he paddled. For a moment she leaned forward and put her arms around his waist, resting her head on his back, and hugged him.

'Thank you, Ned.'

Ned patted her hand. 'I'm just so relieved we found you. Do you want to tell me what happened?'

Bella was quiet for a while, but then she started to tell Ned what had taken place. Pausing frequently, as though not wanting to confront the incident any further, she explained what had happened. 'It was just the one guy who wanted to take me, kind of a spur-of-the-moment thing, I think. The other two were furious with him. He was such a nasty, nasty piece of work.' Bella sniffed quietly behind Ned and he turned to give her an encouraging smile. 'I couldn't alert anyone. I didn't think that anyone would find me. I was scared to death,' she said, tears welling in her eyes.

Ned reached around and squeezed her arm. 'Bella, you're safe with us now and I'm not going to let you out of my sight.'

Bella was silent for some time after this conversation. Ned and the others paddled on. He was surprised by how easy the return journey was, now that his sister was sitting safely behind him. As they neared Carlo's house and the scenery became familiar, she spoke again.

'Will the police find them, do you think?'

'I don't know,' said Ned grimly. 'After we report this, it will be up to them. The men could be local and the police might have an idea who they are.' He turned his head around to look at her. 'Listen, do you want to travel back home with Brendan? He said he was going to have to go tomorrow. Or I could take you back to Cooktown, or even Cairns?'

Bella paused. 'I don't fancy staying out here for too much longer.' She swallowed. 'But if I go back early, Mum will ask questions, and as far as I'm concerned, I don't want her to know anything about what happened to me if it can be avoided.' She closed her eyes for a moment. 'I'm feeling very shaken up. I know that I'll have to talk to the police, but honestly, for the moment, I just want to rest and try to come to terms with what happened to me without having to talk to strangers. If you and Brendan are with me, I think I would manage things better, just for now, if I stay at Carlo's.'

'Okay,' said Ned. 'We'll stay with you the whole time. Let's see how you feel tomorrow.' He continued to paddle in Jack's wake. 'If you want to stay on at Carlo's, that's fine by me.' Ned reached back and patted her comfortingly. 'Are you feeling hungry at all?' Bella nodded. Ned felt the tightness in his chest relax. 'A big meal coming up, then,' he said. 'I hope Jack stays. We owe him a very big debt. Honestly, Bell, I don't think that Brendan and I would ever have found that little gap in the river bank by ourselves. I was so scared, Bella,' he added softly.

'You were scared? Listen, brother, don't try to steal my thunder!' Bella was trying to speak lightly but her voice was strained. Ned knew that Bella would rarely speak about this episode. Certainly their mother was never to know what had happened. For the first time in a long time, Ned knew that he and Bella were thinking the same way.

When they arrived back, they beached the canoes on the river bank. Brendan came over and put his arm around Bella as they all went up the steps. Ned quickly went into the kitchen area and started to make coffee, sweeping up the spilled tea leaves as the others made their way into the house.

'You okay?' Brendan asked Bella for the umpteenth time.

Bella nodded. 'I'm still pretty shaky. I think I'd like to have a shower. I know it sounds silly, but could one of you sing out to me sometimes? I want to make sure that you're still around.'

'Of course we will.'

'Will you stay for something to eat?' Ned asked Jack, as Bella headed to the bathroom.

Jack shook his head. 'No thanks, time for me to get back home. I'm glad it turned out all right for your sister. She was lucky. But keep an eye on her, she'll be in shock. She won't want to go out again today. If you take my advice, you'll let her sleep as much as possible. But you do need to report these men to the police this time round. At least one of those guys is very dangerous. The authorities will want to know.'

'Jack, the three of us can't thank you enough,' said Brendan.

'Well, as I said, glad it all worked out. See you around sometime,' said Jack. 'Want to open the gate for me, Ned?'

When Ned got back from the gate, he decided that the easiest thing he could make was a pile of scrambled eggs, a few rashers of bacon and a stack of toast.

'Have you checked on Bella?' he asked Brendan. 'Do you think she'll be much longer?'

'Said she would be with us in five minutes. But Jack's right, she should spend today resting. Bella is being very brave, but I think that's for our benefit. Hey, what did Jack mean when he said that you should report the men to the police "this time round"?' asked Brendan.

Ned sighed. 'You know how I told you that the blokes who took Bella could be the same ones who invaded this place before? Well, I never told the police about that incident,' replied Ned. Brendan's face reddened and Ned hurriedly explained: 'I don't have a working phone out here and I didn't want to drive to the roadhouse in the dark, and then the next day it didn't seem like such a big deal.'

Brendan threw up his hands. 'I can't believe that you could have ignored what happened to you! If you had taken the trouble to report it to the police, then Bella might have been spared this ordeal,' he said.

'I suppose so,' said Ned mournfully. 'But honestly, it never occurred to me that they might come back. I just thought they . . . oh, I don't know what I thought. You're right, Brendan. I should have reported them. What happened to Bella is all my fault.'

'That's nonsense,' said Bella as she joined them in the kitchen. 'How were you to know what they would do next, Ned? Abducting someone is a whole lot more serious than theft. Brendan, you have to understand that Ned didn't have an easy way of calling the police, and it's quite difficult to get to the roadhouse, as you found out yesterday. Ned couldn't have known that they would come back.

I don't think he can be blamed for what those men did,' she said protectively.

Ned looked at Bella and said quietly, 'Thanks for saying that, but I do hold myself responsible for what happened to you, and I really want to apologise for putting you in such a terrible position. I should have told the police what happened to me and I should not have let you persuade me to take Brendan up to the dam yesterday, leaving you alone in the house.'

Bella went to her brother and put her arms around him. 'Well, what's done is done. Arguing about who is to blame won't change anything. At least you found me and that is the main thing. Where's Jack? I want to thank him properly for what he did.'

'He didn't want to stay,' explained Ned.

'What a pity,' said Bella. 'I don't feel as though I've thanked him enough.'

'Jack seems to be a bit of an enigma, doesn't he?' commented Brendan. 'But he's absolutely right about this – we have to report what happened to the police, no question. Bella, I don't want to upset you, but would you recognise the men if you saw them again?'

'I would know two of them again, but I'm not sure about the third man. It was dark and I didn't really see him.' Bella suddenly looked thoughtful. 'But believe me, I would recognise the man in the tatty blue shirt again, anywhere.'

'One of the men who came here the first time round had a blue shirt that was quite the worse for wear, too. The other guy had a mullet haircut,' said Ned.

'No mullet,' said Bella.

'Never mind,' said Ned. 'But I'll bet anything that the bloke in the old blue shirt is the same one who wandered in here and helped himself to Carlo's things. Enough of this, we'll drive to the roadhouse first thing in the morning and report what happened to the police. In the meantime, let's have something to eat. Brendan, can you do the toast? I'll do the eggs and bacon.'

Even though it was past noon, Bella ate very little. She pushed back her plate, apologised to Ned for leaving so much and announced that she was very tired and was going to bed, even though the sun hadn't set.

'I think that's wise,' said Brendan kindly. 'We'll take turns checking up on you. Is there anything I can get for you?'

Bella shook her head and wandered off to her room. Ned and Brendan watched her with concern. She still looked very fragile.

Brendan sat at the table and finished the last of his cold toast. 'Poor Bell. I think she's coping really well, considering. I keep thinking about what might have happened if we hadn't found her. Thank god Jack was with us.'

'Absolutely,' said Ned. 'He's an interesting and complex bloke. Belongs nowhere and to no one. He's his own man. You've got to respect that.'

'Yeah. I suppose that's why he's buried himself out here. A loner.'

'In a strange way I kinda see the appeal,' said Ned thoughtfully. 'But being so isolated is what made today so stressful. We couldn't get to help when we needed it.' He rubbed his face with his hands. 'I feel terrible about what happened to Bella. I feel so guilty. I should've gone to the police when those men first visited the house. Then this mightn't have happened.'

'Ned, if Bella sees no reason to hold a grudge, you shouldn't beat yourself up. She's safe and sound and that's all that matters as far as I'm concerned,' said Brendan.

'Sometimes Bella can rub me up the wrong way, but I would hate anything to happen to her.'

'Of course,' replied Brendan. He glanced up towards Bella's room. 'I'll just go and look in on her. She might not be able to sleep and I wouldn't want her to be by herself.'

Ned had always liked Brendan and was pleasantly surprised to have seen another side to him. Where once he had admired him as someone who was salt of the earth, solid if a bit unimaginative, now he saw that Brendan was devoted to Bella and quite brave enough to pursue people he thought were harming her. Now, as he watched Brendan head to the bedroom, he thought what a decent man he was. He hoped that Bella realised it too. Brendan was the sort of man fathers want their daughters to marry: kind, thoughtful and dependable. A bit of a contrast to himself, he reflected ruefully.

*

Ned slept fitfully that night, but when he headed into the kitchen to make coffee the next morning he looked out and saw Bella floating in the river with Brendan, and his spirits lifted. On an impulse, Ned made a pot of coffee and took it down to the river with some mugs.

'Hi, you two. Want a coffee?'

'We certainly do,' Bella answered for both of them. They scrambled out and dried themselves, then sat on one of the benches under the trees.

Peering at Bella, Ned noticed she looked pale, with dark shadows under her eyes, but at the same time she seemed calmer than the night before. 'How did you sleep?' Ned asked.

'Not great,' Bella replied. 'But I want to go up to the roadhouse and contact the police as soon as possible.'

'Good on you. We'd better get started soon, then. It's a bit of a hike and I don't want to keep Toni waiting too long, since she's meeting us there. Are you heading back today, Brendan?'

Brendan frowned and then hesitated before he turned to Bella and said, 'Bella, when I booked my flights I could only get the one flight at such short notice and it's this afternoon. I really don't want to leave you after what happened. I'll cancel it. Someone else can cover my patients for a few more days.'

Bella held up her hand. 'Brendan, there is no need for you to do that. I know that it's always difficult to rearrange patients and I know your partners will have to pick up the slack. Truly, I'll be just fine. I've got Ned, and Toni is coming, so I'll have good company.' Brendan began to protest, but Bella cut him off. 'No, don't say another word. I wouldn't hear of you staying and I promise that as soon as I can, I will ring you to let you know how I am,' she said firmly.

Brendan didn't look convinced, but he said, 'Well, if you are absolutely sure that you'll be okay if I go back to Tennyson, I'll go and round up my things.' He made his way up the terrace steps and into the house.

When Brendan emerged dressed and ready to fly back south, Bella looked tight-lipped and Ned could tell her rigid face masked her conflicting emotions, but he said nothing.

On the drive to the roadhouse Brendan was calm and affable.

'At least you'll get to meet Toni at the roadhouse,' said Bella. 'I think you'll like her.'

'Yes, and I also want to be with you when you phone the police.'

'Thanks, Bren, that would be good,' said Bella. 'And I can't thank you enough for coming to find me.'

'As if I wouldn't. You know how much you mean to me. I think we were made for each other,' Brendan said very quietly.

For the last bit of the drive no one spoke, each deep in thought, but as Ned pulled in to the roadhouse, he said cheerfully, 'There's Toni's car! She's here.' And a smile spread across his face.

As they walked inside, Ned spotted Toni sitting with Theresa at a table, sipping a cup of tea. He hurried over to her, pulled her to her feet and embraced her tightly. Theresa smiled at him and excused herself to serve two customers at the food counter.

'Brendan, this is Toni,' said Ned. 'Brendan came up to surprise Bella,' he explained to Toni as the others joined him.

'I'm glad to meet you.' Toni shook his hand. 'What a nice surprise for you, Bella!'

'Yes, it certainly was,' said Bella. 'Very short and sweet, though.'

'Yes, I'm sorry but I have to head back home,' said Brendan.

'Oh, that's a shame. Did you enjoy the river house?' asked Toni.

Brendan hesitated slightly before he answered, and Toni glanced at Ned.

'It's an amazing place. You'll enjoy it,' said Brendan quickly. 'Bella, I have to leave pretty soon or I won't get to Cairns in time for my flight, so do you want me to come with you while you make that phone call?'

Bella nodded. 'Please excuse us, I have an important call to make.' She took Brendan's hand and the two walked to the payphone on the other side of the room, looking sombre.

'That seems a short trip. Is Brendan worried about your sister?' asked Toni.

'I'd better fill you in on what's happened. Let me get a coffee before I explain.'

Toni listened quietly as Ned sipped his coffee and told her why Brendan had come north, and then spoke to her about Bella's abduction. 'That's *appalling*,' she said, aghast. 'I can't believe it. Bella seems remarkably okay, considering what she's been through.'

'She does seem quite tough. Anyway, now she and Brendan are talking to the police on the phone, reporting what happened. I suppose she is trying to give them a description.'

'Hard having to go over it all again.' Toni glanced over at Bella talking on the phone. 'So, where are things at with Brendan now?'

'Damned if I know. I don't think she knows, either. I think she still wants to do something more interesting with her life, but I think she now realises that there is a lot more to Brendan than she previously thought. Maybe she's trying to work out how she can have both Brendan and a more exciting career. I'm sure she'll want to check out this Antony and his proposal one more time to be sure.'

As they sat there waiting for Bella and Brendan, Frederick came over for a quick chat and Ned told him what had happened. He looked shocked.

'That's terrible. Your poor sister. Good that she's reporting what happened to the police. They'll catch the buggers. Look, I can't stay, bit of a rush in here at present. Lot of people heading south. Holiday season up north is just about over because the wet is due to break any time now.' He clapped Ned on the shoulder and hurried away.

About twenty minutes later, Bella and Brendan rejoined them. Bella looked strained.

'Let me get you a coffee,' said Ned. 'You too, Brendan? And you, Toni?'

'I think I'll have an orange juice,' replied Toni, and Bella agreed to a coffee. Brendan glanced at his watch. 'I think I'll have to pass, I'm afraid. I really have to get on the road in a minute or two or I'll miss the plane.'

'How did the conversation with the police go?' asked Ned in a concerned voice.

'Fine. They were very kind. They asked me a lot of questions and took my statement. They want me to come into Cooktown to sign it, but they said that could wait for a day or so,' said Bella.

'Bella was just wonderful,' said Brendan. 'She was very calm and clear about what happened. Sorry, everyone, but I'll have to head off. It was lovely to meet you, Toni. I do hope we meet again.'

'You must come and spend time in Cooktown,' she said with a smile.

Ned reached out and shook Brendan's hand. 'Thanks for everything, mate.'

'I hope we catch up again before too long. Say g'day to Jack for me if you see him again. G'bye, Toni.'

'I'll walk you to your car,' said Bella quietly.

Ned went and ordered the coffees. He came back to the table with their drinks as Bella returned from the carpark, looking subdued and teary.

'Ned filled me in on what happened. It must have been quite an ordeal,' Toni said. She touched Bella's arm sympathetically. 'How are you now?'

Bella wiped her hands across her eyes. 'I'm all right. I just keep thinking that it could have been so much worse, especially if Ned and the others hadn't found me. Toni, I am glad to see you.'

Theresa joined them. 'Sorry we've been neglecting you. People come in waves. All heading south like lemmings. Frederick told me what happened to you, Bella. I'm so sorry,' she said, the worry evident in her tone. 'I've never heard of anything like that happening in these parts before.'

'I'm sure it was a case of being in the wrong place at the wrong time,' sighed Bella.

'Frederick said that Jack came to the rescue,' said Theresa.

'He was wonderful. I certainly got him all wrong when I first met him,' replied Bella.

'Easy enough to do,' said Theresa with a smile. 'He's not the simplest person to get to know.'

Ned pushed his cup away and got up. 'Sorry to have to leave, Theresa, but I think it's time to go. Let's get your bag out of your car, Toni, and hit the road. We've still a way to travel.'

*

'I see what you mean about Carlo's place being out of the way!' said Toni, shifting uncomfortably in the front seat as they bumped along the barely marked track. 'So, Ned, how's the music going?' she asked.

Ned didn't answer immediately, then said, 'Slowly. I have moments when it comes and then it goes away. Like trying to catch rainbows.'

'Hmm. And the story? The theme?' she asked.

'That's the big question. I haven't managed to pin down a focus yet.'

'The far north is a big canvas, for sure.' Toni turned back to Bella. 'What are your thoughts, Bella?'

'Me? I'm not the creative genius in the family. That's always been Ned.'

Ned frowned as he drove. Even though he was concentrating on driving, his mind kept playing over and over the images and stories of the north.

'What are you thinking?' asked Toni quietly.

'How it's kinda like the mango season . . . things build up in my mind, I can picture them, then I hear the distant thunder and rumble and flashing images like lightning, and then the music crashes in. Then it eases off, and it's all mellow like the sunset. Odd, huh?'

'Heavens, I wouldn't want to walk around with all that going on in my head,' said Bella.

'Is it bothering you that you're not making as much progress as you'd like?' asked Toni.

Ned was silent for a moment and then said in a strained voice, 'If I think about it, yes. I keep hoping major inspiration will strike, but it just doesn't seem to happen. And I know time is running out for me. I thought that if I could get away, have no interruptions, have peace and quiet, then everything would fall into place. But it hasn't. I've got bits and pieces and some of it is good, I know that, but I really haven't cracked it. I still don't know how I am going to tie all my ideas together in a meaningful way that will grab an audience. And now, when we were at the roadhouse, watching all those people heading south, I felt a bit panicked, to tell you the truth.'

'What do you mean?' Bella asked.

'Because the wet is coming. I can't stay at Carlo's in the wet season. I'll have to leave, and I have no idea where I'll go. I'm starting to feel I've wasted my time. I have very little to show for the weeks I've spent here, and no plan B. And if I can't work here . . . well, is it worth pressing on?'

'You can't give up, Ned! That's for sure. I know something will change,' said Bella. 'Bit like a summer storm. Like the build-up to the wet. Think of those evening skies and distant storms we watched.'

'Yeah, far away, all silent and promising floods and disaster,' sighed Ned.

Toni reached out to touch his knee and said gently, 'Maybe you're looking at it the wrong way around. When the wet comes and the rain starts, it's music to everyone up here.'

They all fell silent until they reached the river house.

Toni seemed as stunned by the quirky house as Bella had been. She shook her head as she walked around it. 'Someone spent so much time doing all this fancy paving and building these . . . edifices,' she exclaimed.

271

'Yes, I hope I get to meet this Carlo one day and congratulate him on his imagination,' said Ned.

'I'm going down to the river for a swim,' Bella announced. 'You two coming?'

'The water looks refreshing. I might join you in a while,' said Toni as Bella went to her room to get changed. Then, turning to Ned, she added, 'Can I talk to you, Ned?'

Ned instantly recognised the tone. He'd heard it before. Toni was going to say something that he wasn't sure he would like. Alarm bells rang and his heart lurched.

'Sit with me,' said Toni. She seemed calm but Ned could see she was actually holding herself very upright. Something was definitely going on. 'I want to share something with you. You might not like what I'm going to say, but it has to be said.' She swallowed. 'Our togetherness has been very special. Unexpected. I hadn't planned on feeling like this about you.'

Ned's heart sank. She was leaving. She had someone else down south. It hit him that he was shocked at the idea of losing Toni. He sat down and reached for Toni's hand, but before he could speak, they both heard Bella leave the house and walk down the terraces to the river. When she was out of earshot, Ned said, 'Before you say anything, I just want to say that I've really loved our time together, too.'

'I'm pleased about that, but I know from what you said in the car that you're thinking of leaving soon. Before you go, Ned, I want you to know something. And please hear me out before you say anything.'

Here it comes, thought Ned. He looked at Toni, her open face so honest and trusting. How he loved her calmness and strength. *Maybe she just wants to finish our relationship altogether, make a clean break. What do I want her to say? Do I really want her to walk out of my life? Why would she want to stay in it? What can I offer her?*

He felt a sudden sense of panic that he might never be with her again.

'I'm pregnant.'

Ned blinked, and felt a rush of emotions break over him like a waterfall. But then the waterfall surged into a wave, and he felt himself being pulled into frighteningly deep water. He gripped Toni's hand harder and focused on what she was saying.

Toni squeezed his hand back. 'This has come as a big surprise. I certainly hadn't planned to get pregnant, but now that it has, it feels right for me. Ned, I'm thirty-six years old. I never actually considered having a child, but now that I am, I want to take this chance. This is a gift. I want to have this baby and be a mother.'

'I'm not sure what to say,' said Ned, completely stunned by the turn of events. 'It doesn't seem real. You're sure about this?'

'Yes, I'm quite sure,' said Toni. 'I've done three tests and they were all positive.' She was scanning his face, obviously trying to gauge his reaction, but Ned knew his face showed only a jumble of confusion. 'As to how it happened . . . well, I guess nothing is completely safe.'

'I see,' said Ned uncertainly, but then tried for a more positive tone. 'Of course . . . of course . . . I'm completely supportive of you having a baby. I'm sure you'll make a wonderful mother.' He couldn't quite take in the next bit of logic – that he was going to be a father.

'I'm happy,' said Toni. 'I know it's a shock and a lot to take in. I did consider not telling you, but that's not fair or right. I'd just found out when you came into town for the concert and I was too shocked to know what to do. I decided not to say anything until I knew exactly how I felt. But now, I can't put it off any longer.'

That explained why Toni had seemed so distant and strange around the time of the concert, Ned thought.

'How . . . how far along are you?' Ned asked.

'About six weeks, I think,' Toni said. They lapsed into silence for a moment.

'Well . . . I guess we'll work something out,' said Ned in a confused voice. 'I don't know what to say.'

Toni shook her head and released his hand. 'Ned, I don't expect you to take care of me. Having a baby is my decision, and I'm fine with that, and honestly,' she paused and drew in a breath, 'if you aren't sure that you can be a committed father – and by that I don't mean just drifting in and out of the baby's life when it's convenient or it takes your fancy, but really being devoted to raising this child – then perhaps it is better that you move on.'

Ned felt a sudden terrible ache and pain in his stomach. His chest was tight and he swallowed hard, finding it difficult to speak. His mind was flooded with thoughts of his own reaction, this sudden twist in his gut. Be a father? Him? His own father's face flashed in his mind and he felt a stab of panic. How could he be a real father? How was that going to work with the sort of life he led, the sort of man he was?

'I . . . I . . . I need to take this in, Toni. It's so far from anything I expected. You are really special to me and I don't want to mess up our relationship. I'm just in shock.' He had a sudden urgent desire to run to Bella for advice.

Intuitively, Toni reached out and touched his cheek. 'I know it's a shock. It took me a while to adjust to the idea and know how I truly felt. If you want, you could talk to Bella. But let's keep the news just between us three for now. It's early days and anything could happen.'

'What do you mean?' said Ned in alarm.

'A lot of things can go wrong in the first twelve weeks. I don't want to tempt fate.' She paused, then asked quietly, 'Ned, just tell me how you feel about this baby . . .' When he didn't answer, her face darkened. 'It is yours,' she added in a hurt tone. She folded her arms.

'Toni, I didn't mean . . . I really don't know how I feel about this . . .' He couldn't say the word 'child' – doing that would somehow give the whole idea solidity and reality.

Toni frowned, looking as though she was about to say something, but then she stopped and took a deep breath. 'Perhaps I'm being a bit unfair, breaking such momentous news to you and expecting you to embrace it enthusiastically. You need more time to think about it.' She stood up hastily, not meeting his eye. 'I'm going for a swim.' She walked up the steps towards the bedrooms to change. Ned helplessly watched her go.

*

Bella plumped down in the chair beside Ned. She looked at Ned's expression. 'Oh no, she's not splitting up with you, is she? I thought you were a great couple.'

'She's pregnant with my child.' The words felt strange and empty coming out of his mouth.

Bella gasped. 'You're joking!' She peered at his face. 'No, you're not. Good grief, what did you say?'

Ned threw up his hands. 'I don't think I was all that clear. I was so shocked and surprised, but mostly scared. Bell, what am I going to do?'

'I would say it's more up to Toni. What does she want?'

Ned drew a breath. 'Well, Toni says she's thought things through and she wants to keep the baby. And she says that it's up to me as to whether I'm prepared to be a committed father or not, and if I can't make that commitment, then she doesn't want me involved with the child, as it's not fair for the baby to have a part-time parent.'

He breathed out and stared bewilderedly at Bella. 'I don't know what to think. This is not the way I was expecting my life to be. Jesus, Bell. This is a bombshell. I feel so confused. Will you talk to her?'

Bella snorted. 'No, Ned, that is such a cop-out. I hardly know Toni. This is a big deal, and it's up to you to make the right decision, not just for Toni, but for the baby as well. Do you love her?'

Ned rubbed his hand across his eyes. 'Yes. I think I do. I was so looking forward to her visit. I feel that Toni and I have a deep understanding of each other. I mean, we've never talked about future plans or anything like that, and I know it's only been a short time, but she's been the best thing that's happened to me in a long while.'

'Don't you think you should tell her how you feel?'

'And the point would be? I have nothing to offer her. My brilliant idea for a musical has come to nothing. She has a career, while I wander around, performing when I can. And Bella, I honestly don't think I'm equipped to be a father.' He shook his head. 'I just don't think I've got what it takes. Maybe the best thing I can do for this kid is not to get involved at all.' He stopped, feelings and thoughts rushing over him.

'Ned, I'm sure you'd be a terrific father,' said Bella.

Ned grimaced. 'That's nice of you to say, Bella, but I'm hardly the model of stability a child needs. I just can't see myself as a parent.'

Bella sighed. She looked at Toni, now swimming gently in the river. 'Even though I've only just met Toni, she seems a good person. A big-hearted and sensible person, with her feet planted firmly on the ground. Perhaps she's just the sort of person who is right for you. You could sort it out together. Would you consider talking to Mum about what's happening?'

Ned shook his head. 'No, that wouldn't be fair on her. This is my life, and you're right. I have to make the decision.'

Bella stood up. 'I'm going to change. You need a bit of time to think this over. Let the shock wear off and then see how you feel.' She patted his shoulder. 'Shall we start organising the dinner?'

With the flame torches and candles flickering, the night river darkly still, the three sat quietly together after dinner. The meal had been quiet and there was tension in the air.

Ned was the first to speak. 'I'm going to have a nightcap. Bella? Still mineral water, Toni?'

'Not for me, Ned,' said Bella. She turned to Toni as Ned gathered up the plates. 'How're you feeling?'

'A bit tired,' Toni said in a subdued tone.

Bella nodded. 'I'll clear up, Ned, then I might go to bed and leave you two out here. I'm reading some fascinating old letters,' she said to Toni. She kissed her on the cheek. 'Sleep well.' She rested her hand on Toni's shoulder for a moment, then looked at Ned. 'Enjoy your nightcap.'

Ned and Toni sat apart in the pale light of the torches, each absorbed in their own thoughts. Ned watched the torchlight flicker across Toni's face. She looked weary and drawn. He felt his gut twist.

Seeing Bella's shadow move through the house, Ned thought about her rescue. His sister was back safe and sound, and although clearly shaken by her terrible experience, she seemed determined to face what had happened to her with strength and courage, which he greatly admired.

Toni shifted in her seat and his attention came back to her. Toni's news had brought him no such comfort. He felt confused and overwhelmed. What on earth was he going to do?

Ned looked at the accumulation of dark clouds in the night sky, occasionally backlit by far-off lightning heralding the wet, and recognised his own life in the oncoming change of season.

10

August, 1899

My Dear Mother,

I have been thinking of you often this week as it has now been a year since Father's passing. I am still saddened. He was a good man and one whose faith was strong. But think, dearest Mother, of what joy there will be when we are all united once again in our Lord's presence.

Our school continues to flourish. Under the direction of the good Bishop, we are receiving girls of all denominations, as St. Mary's is the only respectable educational facility for girls in Far North Queensland. Now, however, we have lost several of our sisters to the tin-mining township of Herberton, where they have gone to run a small primary school. Thankfully, their work here has been taken on by more sisters from Ireland, so we remain a place busy in the work of the Lord.

Cooktown is gradually changing as the gold in the region peters out. There are fewer prospectors arriving and, indeed, there are many people leaving. Father O'Brien tells us that there are fewer hotels than there once were. I can only be cheered by that news, but the place still retains its feel of a frontier town.

One morning recently, Sister Mercy and I had just left the convent on an errand when a carriage drawn by two powerful piebald horses thundered past us. Sister Mercy jumped back in alarm, but I could not help but admire them.

Sister Mercy was quite irritated by the incident and told me as she carefully brushed dust from her habit that driving like that showed no regard for others and she thought it was quite dangerous. Although she is right, the quality of the horses indicated to me that there are still wealthy people residing in the area.

On our walk back to the convent, I confided to Sister Mercy that Reverend Mother had asked me to visit a family who lived some distance south of Cooktown. It seemed that they wanted private lessons in both singing and pianoforte, and Reverend Mother wanted me to assess the situation. Father O'Brien was to take me to meet them and I asked Sister Mercy if she could ask Reverend Mother if she, too, could come.

However, it was not until the following week that Reverend Mother could spare us. I was quite excited to be able to travel with Father O'Brien and Sister Mercy to Mount Cook, which rises south of the town, and I could not help but wonder who would build a home on its slopes.

The pony trotted along gamely, transporting the three of us in a dog cart through the tropical woodland and forest. Eventually, instead of towering rainforest trees and tangled vines, we noticed straight young eucalypts fringing the track, which had been deliberately planted in an orderly manner. A narrower path led away from the track and it was bordered by coconut palms and fruit trees. Then we came around a bend and saw before us a wonderful sprawling home set on a ridge. Its position gave it breathtaking views across the Annan River, and we could see well-cared-for farmland stretching below us. I understood from Father O'Brien that the owner of this property was a businessman, and by the looks of the house, I judged him to be a very successful one.

As we approached the house, several dogs started barking and our pony stopped suddenly, whinnying in alarm. The dogs were hauled away by a small group of Aboriginal children, and as Father O'Brien coaxed the nervous pony onwards, a tall man with a clipped beard and hair so blond it seemed almost white, appeared on the verandah and watched our arrival, his hands on his hips.

He began calling out, 'Boy, boy!'

An old white-haired Aboriginal man wearing a faded shirt, his trousers held up with a black leather belt, stepped forward and took the pony's bridle.

The fair man came down the steps of the house and introduced himself to us as Mr. Arne Pedersen, and welcomed us all to his home. I must confess that Mr. Pedersen, who comes from one of the Scandinavian countries, seemed to me to be a true Viking, with his tall stature and pale blue eyes. After the introductions, I asked him how many children we would be instructing and was very surprised by his answer.

'Whoever turns up,' he said.

Then our host called out again, and a slim figure materialised beside us in silent slippers. He was a Chinese servant wearing black pyjamas, its loose top with long sleeves. He wore a pigtail hanging down his back.

His shining skin and oiled hair gave him a well-scrubbed appearance. He approached us in a gliding sort of shuffle and told us in a singsong voice that his name was Billy. He led us down a long hall into a formal drawing room and announced that he would bring us tea, and gave a small bow and left.

Father O'Brien raised his eyebrows and we all stared at the lavish trappings of the room. It was filled with Oriental carpets, gilt-framed paintings of English rural and hunting scenes as well as several paintings of racehorses and dogs, while china and glass ornaments stood about on table tops and the mantelpiece. There were heavy brocade drapes at the windows, and solidly carved furniture. A fine grand piano sat in a corner covered with a lace cloth as well as many framed photographs. I wondered how often the piano was used.

It wasn't long before Billy returned with a silver tea service on a tray. He was followed by an Aboriginal woman wearing a long skirt and white apron, who was carefully carrying a jug of milk and a plate of biscuits, which she put onto a side table. Obviously very shy, she quickly left the room as soon as she had completed the task. I was curious. I've heard that some people use the natives as domestic servants, but I had not actually seen it done.

We had just begun to pour the tea when we heard voices in the hallway and Mr. Pedersen returned, accompanied by his wife and, I assumed, his daughter. I was quite surprised when he introduced his wife as Desdemona Pedersen. This seemed to me an unnecessary familiarity. Perhaps it is the Scandinavian way, but I certainly do not intend to address her as anything other than Mrs. Pedersen.

Mrs. Pedersen then introduced us to her daughter Helena and explained that their other children were still cleaning down their ponies as they had all been out riding.

Mrs. Pedersen was tall and fair, like her husband. She looked somewhat windswept and her face was flushed. She was wearing a dark riding habit and carried riding gloves and a veiled hat. I noticed that she wore dainty riding boots. She spoke in a very cultivated English accent. I asked her if we would be using the piano in this room, but she looked somewhat horrified and hastily said that there was another for the children's use. She told us that as soon as we had finished our tea, Billy would show us where to go, and that the children would be there waiting for us. She explained that although Helena had an excellent singing voice, she showed a reluctance to entertain any guests, although she was now fourteen and was expected to do so. Mrs. Pedersen hoped that lessons with us would instil in her the necessary confidence to enable her to perform in front of company. She added that although she usually accompanied Helena on the piano, today she would leave them all in our hands.

I was tempted to say to Mrs. Pedersen that our convent school provided many opportunities appropriate for young girls such as Helena, amongst them tutelage in performing for visitors, but thought it wiser to assess the talents of the Pedersen family first.

Mrs. Pedersen swept from the room and we were left alone to enjoy our tea from fine Minton teacups before the Chinese servant, Billy, shadowed by the shy Aboriginal girl, silently appeared in the drawing room.

As the girl began to place the cups and saucers onto the tray, Billy asked us to follow him. We entered the hallway to find Mr. Pedersen standing beside a flight of stairs, evidently waiting for Father O'Brien, as he wished to show him around the farm. Sister Mercy and I continued to follow Billy until he pointed to a closed door, behind which we could hear squeals and laughter. I pushed open the door and both Sister Mercy and I caught our breaths as we walked in.

Feeling thirsty, Bella carefully put the Sister's letter on the funny little table beside her bed and quickly made her way to the kitchen. There was enough moonlight for her to see the tap and an empty glass sitting on the sink, so she didn't bother to switch on the light. As she turned on the tap, she looked out into the garden and there she saw her brother sitting alone, facing the river. For a moment she thought of joining him to ask if he had come to any decision, but then rejected the idea, for Ned seemed deep in contemplation. Better to leave him until the morning. Besides, she wanted to get back to Sister Evangelista and the Pedersens. Curling up in bed again, she reached for the letter and continued reading.

> My initial impression was that there were a lot of children in the room. There was squealing and laughter as three young boys chased each other, while a young girl with brown skin and dark eyes helplessly tried to restore order. These children surely can't all belong to Mr. and Mrs. Pedersen, I thought, for indeed, the little flock was quite a mixture. Besides the dark girl there were two sandy-haired boys, about nine and ten years old, who were tugging at the shirt-tails of an impish native boy, possibly the same age. Helena joined us. She had changed out of her riding outfit and was now wearing a white muslin dress. She bade the children line up and tell us their names.
>
> 'Achilles,' said the youngest boy.
>
> 'Agamemnon,' the native boy giggled.
>
> 'Nestor,' said the other blond boy.
>
> 'Atlanta, but I'm called Attie,' said the girl with the dark skin and doe eyes. The girl's voice was soft and lilting.
>
> I was very surprised by this mixture of cheerful children with names borrowed from the Trojan Wars, and somewhat puzzled. The dark children I'd seen earlier were not here, but Agamemnon and Atlanta seemed to be part

of the family. I looked around the room. It appeared to be the nursery, full of games and toys, but there was also an upright piano, and, on closer inspection, Sister Mercy and I found an assortment of other musical instruments including a tambourine, a flute and a violin.

I asked Helena where their governess was and she told me that they did not have one at present and that Mrs. Pedersen was teaching them. She also told me that they were expecting one to arrive shortly. I know that young single women, mostly from England, come to all parts of Australia to take up such positions. But I also know that such women rarely stay single for long as there is a great demand for wives, especially in the more remote areas. I suspect that the governess issue is a perennial problem for the Pedersens.

I took out some of my sheet music and sat at the piano and asked them to sing. Then I asked them to show me what they could play on the various musical instruments.

The two fair-haired boys sang with gusto, although little ability. Agamemnon seemed to be able to hold a tune with some proficiency, while Helena's voice was pleasant enough. I think with more training she would be able to perform satisfactorily in company.

But when Attie sang, it was as if a songbird had swooped into the room! Sister Mercy and I looked at each other in such surprise, and then could not stop smiling. Sweet, clear as a bell, it was a voice from the heavens. The child has been given a great gift from our Lord. Although not properly trained, she was pitch perfect, and when I played for her, she hit each note with purity and clarity. I am sure that with the right discipline this child could sing anything. She is shy, like a small forest animal, but when she performs, her intelligent eyes brim with delight at the sheer joy of singing. My first thought was of how to nurture this amazing girl.

Two hours sped by until Mrs. Pedersen tapped at the door. She was now dressed in a white dress with a high neck and long sleeves buttoned at the wrist. She had gloves that looked like gauntlets and a muslin shawl that was draped over her wide-brimmed hat, allowing very little of her face to be seen. As she entered the room, she removed the hat and gave us a small smile, then promptly told the children to leave. With a chorus of thank yous and bobs the five children left the room and Mrs. Pedersen asked me my opinion of their talents.

I told her I thought that they were a very mixed group and then, realising how my comments could be construed, I quickly apologised and said that their musical talents varied.

Mrs. Pedersen smiled graciously and then told me how the children had come into the family. She said that Agamemnon and Atlanta had, in fact, both been rescued by Mr. Pedersen. It appears that Atlanta's mother had worked somewhere in the cane fields to the north of Cairns and that she had died. When Mr. Pedersen heard of this, he said that it was better for the child to be raised in the Pedersen household than to be left in the sugarcane fields with an uncertain future, and so he brought her here. I thought at once what a very Christian man Mr. Pedersen must be to take such kind action.

Agamemnon, Mrs. Pedersen explained, had joined the family when her husband, while travelling north, had come across a blacks' camp that had been recently raided by some cattlemen. Evidently the blacks had been stealing their cattle, so the cattle men had found the camp and indiscriminately shot some of the blacks as punishment. When Mr. Pedersen rode through the camp, he heard a cry and realised that a baby had been hidden beneath a bush. He felt he had no other option than to bring it back for the family to raise.

Sister Mercy was very impressed by these actions and told Mrs. Pedersen that they did her husband great credit. I nodded in agreement, but I could not help but wonder in which world the little boy would live once he grew up. Our world would probably not accept him and he would not know his own people or understand their way of life.

Mrs. Pedersen then asked me to evaluate the children's musical ability. I said that I believed Helena would truly benefit from being at our school, and that Atlanta, whose talent seemed quite exceptional, would also profit from being educated at St. Mary's.

Sister Mercy and myself were both disappointed when Mrs. Pedersen shook her head and said that she did not think she would send them there as all the children were company for each other and they had their own interests about the farm. She suggested that instead we should return on a regular basis to the Pedersens' homestead to further their musical knowledge. Then she announced that she had to attend to her bees and, thanking us for our efforts, she replaced her hat and veil, gathered up her gauntlet-like gloves and left the room, though it seemed to me that her presence lingered. There are some women who are very definite people and who make a lasting impression. Mrs. Pedersen is one of these.

I thoughtfully picked up my sheet music and pushed it into my bag and Sister Mercy and I walked back along the corridor, where we heard Father O'Brien's voice. We turned to look for him and he greeted us and said that he hoped that all had gone well. He then took us to join Mr. Pedersen in the conservatory, where our host was to show us his collection of orchids and other unusual plants that he has found in this part of the world. As we entered the room and looked around us, we were amazed by the variety and beauty of Mr. Pedersen's orchid collection. The flowers ranged from thumbnail size to some whose *extent was almost equal to that of my hand. Everywhere was a jumble of colours, from vibrant yellows, pinks and lavender to deep purple, blues and creams. Some stems seemed to hold dozens of blooms, while others no more than one or two. It was a dazzling display. Both of us were overwhelmed by the beauty around us and said so.*

Mr. Pedersen thanked us for our comments and said that this was indeed a rich land, with so much for the taking, and that he derived great interest from collecting the wild orchids off the hillsides and from the trees where they grew in abundance.

Sister Mercy rightly said that it was hard to pick a favourite among all the splendour, but she pointed out a beautiful pink orchid that was quite exceptional and asked its name.

Mr. Pedersen told us that it had been named the Cooktown orchid, and agreed that it was splendid. It was only discovered a couple of years previously, he told us, but such was its beauty that even now it was being propagated in the greenhouses of European botanical gardens.

As we were preparing to leave, Sister Mercy took the opportunity to suggest that Mrs. Pedersen might like to come to St. Mary's when next she was in town. Unfortunately, it seems that Mrs. Pedersen doesn't care for the society of Cooktown, as Mr. Pedersen said she was too occupied with her own interests to spare the time. I naturally thought that Mr. Pedersen was referring to the raising of their children, but to our astonishment we later found out from Father O'Brien that Mrs. Pedersen's primary interest entails the breeding of horses, which she exports to India.

As the four of us walked back to the dog cart which the old native had ready and waiting for us, Father O'Brien asked Mr. Pedersen what the crop was that he had growing down by the river. Mr. Pedersen replied that it was a crop of peanuts. He added that his banana trees also flourished in this climate and his Chinese gardeners were most excellent at their job. It appears that Mr. Pedersen sends his produce to the goldfields, where the miners are very happy to exchange a nugget for some fresh greens or fruit. Father O'Brien congratulated Mr. Pedersen on his enterprises.

Mr. Pedersen bade us farewell and Father O'Brien took the reins as we trotted down the driveway, past the orchards. He was full of admiration for the initiative that Mr. Pedersen had shown since arriving in Australia. Father told us that Mr. Pedersen had taken him to a stone barn, where our host had set up a laboratory for the preservation of animals that he himself, or others on his behalf, had caught. Father told us that there were hundreds of dead animals there in various stages of preservation; birds arranged as though in mid-flight, stuffed animals in different poses, bottled reptiles and piles of eggs which he was unable to identify. Mr. Pedersen told him that he has orders from all over the world for these rare and unusual creatures. Indeed, there are so many requests that he finds it difficult to fill them all, for there is always interest in Australian fauna. And, it appears that his work has become quite famous, as international scientists visit his laboratory on a regular basis.

The three of us agreed that Mr. Pedersen has indeed made the most of the various ventures that have presented themselves to him in this country and that his efforts are much to be admired. This is certainly the land of opportunities.

Sister Mercy said that she hoped the Pedersens would give Helena and Atlanta the opportunity to attend St. Mary's, but Father O'Brien shook his head. He thought that if the Pedersens had wanted the girls to go to our school, they would be there already. Perhaps, he ventured, the good Reverend Mother will see fit to allow us to continue visiting the Pedersens to teach the girls.

I, however, think that our Reverend Mother will consider such an arrangement a poor use of our time. So I smiled at Father O'Brien and told him that our Reverend Mother can be very persuasive when she chooses, and that I would do my best to encourage her to persuade the Pedersens to enrol the two girls.

Now, as I look from the window of my room across the town that I have come to know well, I consider myself most fortunate to have been chosen by our Lord to come to a place that is filled with such interesting people. And I am comforted in the knowledge that our Blessed Virgin Mary watches over us all, both here and in Ireland. I am hopeful that we will have the opportunity to teach those two girls, especially Atlanta, whose voice shows such wonderful promise.

May God bless you,
Your loving daughter,
Evangelista

*

Bella had been more than a little tired when she'd gone to bed, but after reading this letter, she was suddenly wide awake. *Attie, Atlanta, such an unusual name,* thought Bella. It was the same as the one Roberta had mentioned when she told stories about her family. Surely this had to be the same person. If it was, then the little girl that Sister Evangelista had written about in her letter did go on to become a famous singer. *I can't wait to tell Roberta about this. I bet she doesn't know about the letters in the museum,* thought Bella.

She also could not help but think about the Pedersens and what an unusual family they were. The idea of setting up a business to sell stuffed and preserved Australian animals all over the world repulsed her. Thank heavens Australian wildlife was valued these days and that sort of thing was no longer acceptable, she thought, remembering the wonderful time she'd spent in the Daintree and the flora and fauna in that rainforest, as well as the conversations she'd had with Roberta.

Bella turned off the light and tried to sleep, but as she lay in bed, her mind became crowded with thoughts about the events of the past two days. It had been a roller-coaster ride. Her abduction had been so traumatic, and she realised how truly lucky she had been that Ned and the others had been able to find her. What if they hadn't come? She shuddered. Being lost and alone out there in the bush didn't bear thinking about, so she turned her mind to other things. Since she had been in the north she'd met some interesting characters, although some she would rather not have met. There was still a sense here of pioneering wildness and, as was the case for the Pedersens all those years ago, there were clearly opportunities for the taking. She felt that Far North Queensland was a little-understood place in which one could escape, to experience a different pace of life and to lose oneself in the immensity of the landscape, so beautiful in its extremes. But after all that had happened she was not entirely sure that she wanted to be a part of it. How ordered, simple and placid her old life now seemed. She was very secure and settled in her job at the Tennyson City Council, so did she really want to give it up for this great unknown? Could she make such a move? And then there was the question of Brendan . . . There were no easy answers. She tossed and turned a while longer and finally fell into a fitful sleep.

*

Ned had breakfast under way early the next morning and had already poured a cup of tea for Toni when Bella wandered into the kitchen. She sensed that she had interrupted something, but neither her brother nor Toni said anything except to ask her how she was feeling. Bella assured them that she was in better shape than she had been yesterday.

'Are you sure that you want to go into Cooktown today to sign your statement? I'm certain it could wait until tomorrow,' Ned said, his brow furrowed as he buttered Bella some toast.

'I guess, but the police did ask me to come in today. I really think that I should cooperate with them,' Bella replied.

'Yes, of course. But we'll have to leave pretty soon to be sure of getting back before it gets dark.' He paused, turning to Toni. 'Toni, is this all okay with you?'

'Of course. It's important you sign your statement as soon as you can,' said Toni, patting Bella's hand sympathetically.

'I'm so sorry to mess up this weekend,' sighed Bella.

'It's hardly your fault,' said Ned quickly. He started to pour some coffee and then said, 'Look, since we're going into Cooktown, maybe it's time to return the Bish's box to the museum. I'll have to move out of here altogether pretty soon and it might be a good idea to get it back to them now when it's convenient. We may not have finished reading all the letters, but at least I have managed to catalogue most of the contents.'

Ned handed Bella a mug of coffee, Toni more tea and a plate of toast each. 'Those letters are so interesting,' said Bella, between bites. 'I read one last night in which Sister Evangelista wrote about a girl who I think is the same person Roberta told me about, a singer who was connected to her family. Roberta called her Clare, but Sister Evangelista says her name was Atlanta. I'd like to find out more about her. The story sounds really fascinating.'

'You could talk to Ken Harris, the curator at the museum. He takes a great interest in local history and he might be able to tell you something more,' suggested Toni.

'Right, it's settled then. We drive into Cooktown, Bella goes to the police station, then we'll drop off the Bish's box at the museum. I've got some books I have to return to the library and then we can grab lunch at the seafood restaurant and afterwards Bella and I can drive back here before dark,' said Ned.

'I'll have to pick up my car from the roadhouse,' said Toni, swigging the last of her tea and taking her plate to the sink.

'Yes, I know,' said Ned. 'Will you be okay driving my four-wheel drive into Cooktown, Bella?'

Bella certainly didn't feel at all confident about driving by herself into Cooktown. The road was long and remote and she'd only been along it once before. She knew that nothing was likely to happen on the drive, but she felt nervous at the thought of being alone. She opened her mouth to reply, but before she could say anything, Toni spoke.

'Why don't you ride with me after we pick up my car? It would be nice to have your company on the long drive, Bella.'

Bella glanced at her brother. 'Are you sure?' she asked.

'Yes,' said Toni, not looking at Ned. 'It would be lovely for the two of us to spend a little more time together.'

Ned didn't comment, so Bella nodded in agreement. She got the impression Toni wanted some space from Ned, but at the same time, Toni seemed to have sensed that Bella didn't want to be by herself on a lonely road after her terrible ordeal.

An hour later, they were on their way. At the road-house, Toni thanked Frederick and Theresa for looking after her car.

'No problem, Toni, and happy to keep an eye on yours too, Bella, but I don't expect we'll get much of a chance as you'll be heading off soon, I expect,' said Theresa.

'Yes, don't leave it too long to get out of Carlo's place,' cautioned Frederick. 'Or you'll get stuck there for the next few months.'

After farewelling Frederick and Theresa, Toni and Bella got into Toni's car. 'I'll follow you both,' called out Ned. 'Lead the way.'

As they headed onto the highway, Toni said wryly, 'Well, it's been an eventful visit for you.'

'In lots of ways,' said Bella. 'I could have done without being kidnapped . . .' She tried to make it a light comment, but she knew her voice sounded strained, so her comment fell a bit flat. 'But the good news is . . . your news.'

Toni pursed her lips. 'Yes, well . . . I'm really not sure what Ned thinks or feels about it,' she said.

Bella sighed. 'Ned's a great brother, always has been. But I don't think he's in a good space at the moment. I know that he's feeling really concerned because his grand plan of creating a musical masterpiece isn't working out. I don't think he knows where to go next. Not that I'm suggesting that his trouble with his musical is a good enough reason for him being so indecisive about the baby, of course!'

'Thank you for saying that. I certainly agree with you there, but I have to say that a musical doesn't sound like something you can just manufacture out of thin air. It must be such a difficult thing to create,' said Toni. 'He's chosen a tricky career path.'

Bella nodded. 'Yes, Ned is very creative, but he also insists on being infuriatingly independent. He's had record deals offered to him, but he has always turned them down. He says he doesn't want to make "their" kind of music; he wants to do his own thing. The one album he did put out was a success, but no more have been forthcoming. I think it's a pity as he is, in my opinion, very talented.'

'I think he is, too,' agreed Toni. She paused and then ventured tentatively, 'I expect that with his peripatetic life-style he hasn't had the chance to build many meaningful relationships.'

'Actually, no. Ned was very serious about Ashleigh for years and years. Everyone assumed that it was the real deal until Ned blew it,' said Bella, unable to hide the annoyance in her voice. 'Dad thought that Ned let the whole family down when he called off the wedding two weeks out. Poor Ash, all of us felt so sorry for her. I certainly did.'

Toni gasped and stared at Bella with wide eyes. Bella mentally kicked herself as she realised that Ned had not told Toni about his broken engagement. There was an awkward silence as Bella desperately tried to think of what to say next.

Toni focused her eyes on the horizon and gripped the steering wheel tightly. 'I had no idea. Ned has never mentioned that,' she said in a strangled voice.

'I can't believe Ned didn't tell you about this,' Bella said. 'Toni, I am so sorry.'

'What happened?' Toni's voice was very cool.

Bella cleared her throat. *Toni really should be hearing this story from Ned*, she thought. *But I've gone and let the cat out of the bag now, so I guess I'm going to have to tell her.* 'I'm not sure why Ned called off their wedding at the very last moment. There seemed no really good reason. He just appeared to get cold feet.'

Toni didn't respond, so Bella rushed on. 'Ashleigh and Ned had been together forever. They'd known each other for a long time before they started dating and then they lived together, first in Tennyson and then down in

Melbourne when Ned started to get regular gigs there. Eventually they decided to get married. Everyone was delighted. Everything was booked, all the invitations went out, presents started to come in and then, wham! Just days before the wedding, Ned called the whole thing off without any warning.'

'That sounds terrible. Why would he do that?' asked Toni in amazement.

Bella frowned. 'As I said, I think it was cold feet, not wanting to be tied down, but I don't really know because Ned has never talked about it. Dad was furious. He accused Ned of avoiding commitment and said that Ned had to grow up and start behaving in a responsible manner. He thought that Ned had treated Ash disgracefully. He really had a go at Ned, but Ned didn't say much at all. I guess he thought that what Dad said was right. Mum was shocked. Mum being Mum rang everyone up to apologise for what had happened, although she had nothing to apologise for and she certainly couldn't explain why Ned had called off the wedding.' Bella sighed. 'Ned's name was most unpopular around town and Dad thought his actions reflected poorly on the whole family. After that, Ned avoided Tennyson. He never really explained what happened.'

'Poor Ashleigh,' said Toni. 'She must have been so humiliated.'

Bella nodded. 'I think the saddest part though was that Dad was killed only a couple of weeks later, so Ned and Dad never really got to be on good terms again.'

Toni was quiet a moment. 'That must have devastated Ned.'

Bella felt a lump rise in her throat. 'Yes, Dad's death devastated us all. That's why this ceremony honouring his work is so significant, especially for Mum. I think she thinks it's important that he receives the recognition he deserves and that's why she wants the whole family, including Ned, to be there.'

'Well, I can certainly understand that.' Toni glanced at Bella with a serious expression. 'Bella, from what you've told me, I can't help but think that Ned has a few problems with the idea of any long-term relationship.'

'Oh, Toni, no!' Bella said, alarmed. 'Don't take this story like that! I'm sure Ned feels that you are very special. But you telling him you're pregnant, well, it would have come as a shock. That doesn't mean he isn't thrilled, just that it might take him some time to adjust. I'm sure that he'll do the right thing.' Bella could hear a pleading note in her own voice, but she didn't know what else to say or do.

'Bella, that's just it! I don't want him to feel he has to do *the right thing!*' exclaimed Toni, smacking her hand against the wheel. 'I know he's a good man who has some issues – we all do, I guess – but I only want him to commit to this baby if he wholeheartedly wants to be a part of this baby's life. If he wants out, then I can understand that.' Bella heard a steely strength in Toni's voice. 'I have a big, loving and supportive family who will help me raise this baby. I have plenty of options and support. I might be a single mother, but I certainly won't be alone. I'll be just fine, no matter what Ned decides he wants to do.'

Bella looked at Toni in admiration. 'God, Toni, you're amazing. Whatever happens, I'm sure that you and your baby will be just fine.'

The two of them sat quietly for a while as Toni drove on towards Cooktown. Bella still felt dismayed that she had so clumsily spilt Ned's secret about his broken engagement but really, she told herself, Ned should have told Toni himself ages ago. Toni deserved to know. What was Ned thinking keeping a big secret like that? The truth was bound to come out and it was a lot better for Toni to know straightaway. Glancing at Toni, Bella couldn't read her expression. Toni would manage motherhood perfectly well, with or without Ned's involvement, Bella thought. Then it suddenly occurred to her that she was related to this baby as well. She was going to become an auntie. She knew that she couldn't raise this fact until things had been resolved one way or another between Toni and Ned, but Bella also knew she would like to have a part, even if only a small one, in this baby's life.

Toni was the first to break the silence.

'So how about you and Brendan? He seems to adore you,' Toni said gently.

'Yes, I suppose he does,' said Bella cautiously.

Toni laughed. 'No suppose about it. I can see that he does just by the way he looks at you, and no one races all this way to see a girl for a couple of days if he's not really keen on her.'

Bella gave a small smile. 'It was a bit of a dramatic thing for Brendan to do, coming up here. Really not like him at all. Maybe he thought I'd gone troppo in the sun.'

'I very much doubt that was the reason,' said Toni, smiling at Bella. Bella returned Toni's smile, but didn't say anything further. They lapsed into silence and sat wrapped in their thoughts until they began to approach Cooktown and Bella saw the strange bare black mountain rising to one side of the road. She'd noticed it the first time she'd driven this road, too, and was again awed by the giant boulders that looked as though they had tumbled together like a collapsed building. The ancient stone blocks glistened shiny black in the sun from a recent shower of rain, while tufts of grass grew between them and emerald lichen gleamed in patches on their surface.

'What is that black mountain called?' Bella asked. 'It's quite eerie.'

'Black Mountain,' said Toni.

Bella burst out laughing. 'Obviously. It's so barren. It looks as though it was a manmade structure that fell apart.'

'It does rather. It's supposed to be haunted.'

'Is it? Do you know why?'

Toni shrugged. 'Oh, lord . . . it's every conspiracy theorist's delight. There are a few Indigenous stories about the mountain. Some people say it's haunted by Aboriginal tribes massacred by Europeans in the early days. There are stories of cattle rustlers taking a thousand head of stolen cattle into the mountain as a shortcut and never coming out. Stories about people who were trapped in there and were never the same afterwards, while others were never seen again, and even the police who went searching for them disappeared. Other people say that it's inhabited by a wild beast, a sort of Queensland tiger. So take your pick!'

'Gracious, like *Picnic at Hanging Rock*. What did the people say who did come out?'

'It appears that they were either demented or confused. Some said there were enormous caverns beneath the rocks and that there's a light in the centre that goes way down and that this is the door to the inner earth. If you put your ear to any of the crevices it's said you can hear moaning. Personally, I suspect that it's just the wind, but you never know. A lot of people won't set foot near the place.'

Bella shivered. 'I can believe that. I wonder if Ned knows about it. I think he could make some wonderful, haunting music with all that in mind. Put it in his musical, maybe.'

Toni nodded in agreement and for the rest of the trip the two of them talked about Black Mountain and its sinister presence.

They met at Toni's house and Ned took Toni's bag from the car and carried it inside. As they returned to his four-wheel drive, he said to Toni, 'I'll go with Bella to the police station, and after that all of us can go out for lunch. You okay to meet us in the usual place, Toni? If we're very long with the police, I'll phone you.' Toni nodded. Ned tried to kiss her cheek, but Toni moved away before he had the chance and then climbed the steps up to her house.

'Good luck with the police, Bella,' Toni called out from the verandah. 'I'm sure everything'll be just fine.'

Ned watched Toni go inside without a backward glance and then jumped back in the car with Bella.

'Do you want me to stay with you while you talk to them?' he asked when they arrived at the police station.

'Yes, please.'

They weren't kept long before they were met by a police sergeant with a bristly grey moustache, who carried out a copy of the statement Bella had given over the phone. He offered Bella a cup of tea and asked her kindly how she was feeling and seemed genuinely concerned by what had happened to her. When Bella assured him that she was coming to terms with her abduction and that she was feeling a lot better, he said that he was impressed by her courage and her resilience. Then he asked her to read through her statement and sign it if she was satisfied that it was correct.

'I guess that's about all,' he said when Bella handed the signed statement back. 'I bet you thought it was a miracle that your brother found you when he did.'

'He had help, but yes, to say I was pleased to see him is a bit of an understatement.'

'Do you have any idea who these men might be?' Ned pressed.

The sergeant shook his head. 'Not really. We've had occasional reports of boats coming into the coast at night or first light and we believe there's been some sort of exchange of merchandise. Maybe drugs, but we're not sure. There're some pretty fast boats that could be fishing charters except they turn up in odd places. You mentioned a cove, Bella. There's a few places on the Cape where that could be. But if these men are involved in this sort of activity on the coast, I'm not sure what they would be doing so far inland. Bit of a puzzle, really. I'm sorry you got caught up in it. Still, we have a good description of two of them, so we'll circulate it and hope that someone recognises them. And your sister has told me that two of these men probably came into the house earlier and stole from you, Mr Chisholm?'

Ned shifted in his seat. 'Yes, more than a week ago. One of those men had a mullet haircut. I should have reported it to you when it happened, but I really didn't think they'd come back,' Ned said, shaking his head.

The sergeant smoothed his moustache. 'Well, it looks as though they did. Wanted more supplies, especially alcohol, and they knew where to get it, it would seem.' The sergeant eyed Ned. 'It's a bit of pity, sir, that you didn't report the initial incident, don't you think?' he said gruffly.

'Yes,' said Ned, reddening. 'I feel very guilty about what happened and I blame myself.'

'I'm not quite so harsh on him,' said Bella. 'With the benefit of hindsight, we can all say we'd make different decisions.'

'Very true,' said the sergeant. 'Will you be around if we need to speak with you again, Ms Chisholm?'

'Oh. I'm not sure how long I'll be here,' said Bella. 'Probably only a few days. I'm heading to Cairns and then back to Victoria for the time being. There's an important family event I need to attend.'

'I'm not surprised you're off. This is the end of the tourist season; the wet's about ready to start. But I have your details and I'll be in touch if anything comes up.

Even though you've had a frightening experience, I hope you can manage to enjoy the rest of your time in the north. It's a special place.' The sergeant smiled and collected his papers. He showed them out the door and Bella heaved a sigh as they stepped out into the sunshine.

Ned put his arm around Bella as they walked towards the car. 'Well, that wasn't so bad, was it?' he said. 'I thought the copper was pretty sympathetic.'

'I suppose he was. I just hope that they catch the buggers. But he didn't sound very confident,' said Bella.

'Give it time, Bella. You seem pretty sure about what they looked like.'

Bella nodded. 'I can guarantee that I would be able to recognise the bloke in the blue shirt again anywhere. His nasty little eyes are etched into my soul,' she said angrily. She stopped and Ned rubbed her arm.

'It's okay, Bella,' he said reassuringly. 'He'll get what's coming to him. Let me return my library books and then we'll go to the museum.'

Both Ned and Bella were pleased to return to the stately old convent building. There were still tourists about in the museum. At the entrance, Ned asked if Ken Harris was around, and the pleasant woman collecting the fees told them where they were likely to find him. Just as they were about to pay for their entry, they were greeted by the curator.

'Hey there, Ned! Don't worry about the entry fee. It's free for our volunteers!' He hurried over and shook Ned's hand enthusiastically, then pointed at the box under Ned's arm. 'You've got the Bish's box, I see. How'd you go with it?'

Ned grinned at the friendly curator. 'My sister helped me hugely.' He gestured to Bella. 'Ken, this is my sister, Bella, and she's been intrigued by the letters in the box, just as I have been.' Ken smiled broadly and shook Bella's hand.

'Lovely to meet you,' said Bella. 'I really enjoyed reading through the material. There was a whole pile of letters written by a Sister Evangelista. They are just wonderful. She describes life as it was in Cooktown more than a hundred years ago. Unfortunately, many of the letters are incomplete, some no more than fragments, but the way she writes is so evocative that it's hard to stop reading them.'

Ken's face lit up. 'Ah, Sister Evangelista, the "little sister", as she was known. She was quite tiny but a great character. I can show you some more about her, if you like. Come on upstairs.'

They followed the curator to the upper floor and down the hall to the end room.

'Ah, the corner room. This is where I saw the box,' said Ned. 'And what a view there is from here!'

He glanced out of the high, wide window at the township and sparkling water beyond.

'Yes,' said Ken. 'It has such a good view that the room was used by the Americans as an observation post when they took over the convent during the Second World War. It is said that you could see the flash of the guns from the battle of the Coral Sea from this very spot.'

'That is amazing,' said Bella. 'So what happened to Sister Evangelista while the Americans were here?'

'She and most of the other nuns were evacuated. Actually, the Americans damaged the building so badly while they were here that the school was never reopened. Such a pity. Now this room is just a storeroom, but I often imagine her sitting there, at the window . . .'

'This was her room?' asked Bella. She glanced around at the space and tried to imagine it as it would have been when Sister Evangelista had inhabited it.

'I started to hear music in here,' said Ned quietly.

Bella stared at him. 'Whoo hoo! Maybe she haunts this room.'

'More likely one of the tourists was trying out one of the instruments we have on display in another part of the museum,' said Ken with a chuckle. 'Anyway, Sister Evangelista was a feisty old nun, but everyone loved her, that's according to a few people I've met who knew her. She was the last of the original Irish nuns who came here so long ago. She was in her nineties when she died, sometime in the 1950s. Do you know that she never left north Queensland after she arrived from Ireland all those years ago? Just amazing.'

'It certainly is. What a lot of history she must have witnessed,' said Ned.

'There's no doubt about that,' replied Ken. 'I believe that she stayed on here in Cooktown even when other nuns moved away. She was greatly dedicated to the place.'

In the silence that followed, Bella remembered what she had wanted to ask the curator. 'Ken, I'm wondering, have you ever heard of a singer, Atlanta . . . Pedersen, I think she must have been called. Attie. She had a super singing voice. An Islander girl,' said Bella.

Ken rubbed his face. 'That would be Atlanta Cookson. That was her stage name. She came here to the convent school, you know, and called herself after the town. She had been adopted by the Pedersens, who were a somewhat eccentric white family who lived nearby.'

Bella smiled broadly. 'Sister Evangelista mentioned in one of her letters that she was going to try to get Attie sent to St Mary's as she had quite a talent, so I'm pleased to hear that she did come here in the end. Is there any more information about the Pedersens and Attie?' asked Bella. 'I met a woman who told me about a South Sea Island child who had been adopted by a white family and her name was changed to Atlanta, Attie for short. It's such an unusual name that it must be the same person.

My friend would probably love to know more about this Attie.'

'There's quite a lot to be told about Atlanta Cookson. She was a most remarkable person.'

'How exciting. I'll have to do more research,' said Bella.

Ned glanced at his watch and then turned to Ken. 'Thank you so much for the Bish's box. It's been very enlightening,' said Ned. 'I've really enjoyed reading the letters. But we must go, as we have to start heading back before it gets dark and we haven't had lunch yet.'

Ken nodded. 'Then I'll let you go, but thanks again for sorting through the box and leaving your notes.'

'I don't feel I did all that much,' replied Ned. 'My sister was the one who became really intrigued with the stories in Sister Evangelista's letters.'

Ken turned to Bella. 'Then thank you, Bella, as well. I expect you'll be heading south pretty soon, like everyone else.' He ushered them out of the room and closed the door behind him.

'Yes, I'll have to head home soon, but I have been fascinated by what I've learned in this part of the world,' Bella replied. As they walked down the hall, she looked back at the closed door and thought again of Sister Evangelista.

'There're many stories, often little known, about the Cape and the far north,' said Ken, gesturing for Bella to go ahead of him down the stairs. 'I love being here. Maybe we'll see you back again sometime.'

'Maybe,' said Bella.

As they stepped out into the sunny street, Ned said, 'It's a bit of a time warp, isn't it?'

'The museum? Or this town?' asked Bella.

'Both,' Ned replied. 'Are you hungry? Shall we get some lunch?' Bella nodded, so Ned pulled out his phone and texted Toni to arrange to pick her up, but she replied she wasn't feeling up to it and the two should go ahead and have lunch without her.

Bella thought about the last lunch they'd shared at the riverside restaurant, not so long before. Since then so much had happened, both good and bad, that it seemed to her as though time had expanded. Ned sat opposite her at the table. He'd been looking dejected ever since he'd received the text from Toni.

'I wish that Toni could have joined us. It's a shame she's not feeling well,' she said. Ned just grunted in reply.

'Ned,' Bella continued tentatively, 'I realise that time is fast running out for us to stay at Carlo's. Have you made a decision about your next move?' She buttered a piece of sourdough bread and popped it into her mouth.

Ned sighed moodily. 'Well, I think I need to earn some money, but I'd find that difficult to do in Cooktown, especially in the wet season, so I'm going to have to move south. Maybe Cairns, if I can get enough work, or if I can't, I'll have to go back to Melbourne. That's got the best music scene.'

'I see,' Bella replied. She wanted to press him further, but decided against it. She was not sure if Ned was facing the reality of needing to find work, or using his work as an excuse to avoid making a decision about Toni and the baby. Nonetheless Bella hoped Ned would not leave his decision too long. After her conversation with Toni on the drive into Cooktown, Bella had grasped how strong and independent Toni was, and she knew that if Ned vacillated too long or refused outright to make any real commitment to this baby, Toni would close the door on him. But no matter what her thoughts on the matter, in the end Bella knew it was Ned's choice and his alone, so she wasn't going to say any more about it.

Instead, she turned her thoughts to her own future. Away from the river house and its rather lost-world atmosphere, Bella had begun to think seriously about what she was going to do. Here in Cooktown she had noticed that there were fewer tourists around now that the wet season was almost here. Perhaps tourism up in the north was only really feasible in the dry season, and that this limited time span might not be enough to make Antony's project financially viable. She would have to raise that point with Antony.

After they'd ordered, Ned excused himself to go to the bathroom. Deciding to take the bull by the horns, Bella pulled out her phone and rang Antony, but her call went through to his voicemail. She left a message saying she'd be back in Cairns soon and she'd try to make contact with him again.

Bella had more success when she phoned Josie. Her mother sounded very happy to hear from her and said that she was pleased that Bella and Ned were spending time together. Bella assured Josie that she would be home in plenty of time for the ceremony, but said nothing about Ned's plans, and Josie did not ask any questions. Still, it was nice to chat to her mother, and even in those few minutes, Bella realised that she missed Josie's company and was looking forward to seeing her again. After she hung up, she scanned her emails. A work colleague had sent a message letting her know that the aborted project she had been working on for the Tennyson Council just before she came away had been resurrected and was ready to go. Bella frowned. She wasn't sure how she felt about the news. She was pleased to hear that the project was going ahead, but she was no longer sure that she wanted to be the one to work on it. Of course, if she decided to move up north, she wouldn't have to. She sighed. But if she did make the move, where would that leave things with Brendan? Her thoughts just went round in circles.

Ned and their meals arrived at the table simultaneously and they ate in silence. As she tasted the delicious mud crab, Bella thought about how she had got out of the habit of using her phone. With no coverage, she had put the phone in her bag and ignored it. And the sky hadn't fallen in. She realised that apart from the piece of work news she'd just received, in all the time she'd been away none of her friends appeared to have had any dramatic news that she was sorry to have missed. She resolved that in future she would live life without feeling as though her phone would have to be surgically removed from her hand. Perhaps letters were the way to go; only the significant things went in, and the pointless and the extraneous details were left out. Maybe that was why Sister Evangelista's letters were so entertaining. The nun had recognised what was important.

'Will you be okay, driving your car back to the road-house on your own?' asked Ned as the waiter cleared away their plates.

'Absolutely. I feel a lot better now that I've been out and about. The police were so nice and I've been on that road a couple of times now, so I feel quite confident that if I follow closely behind you, I'll be just fine. Assuming, of course, that we don't stop at Black Mountain.'

'Why would we do that?' asked Ned grumpily.

'I'll tell you later,' said Bella, sensing that Ned was not in the mood for any quaint stories. 'Let's go home.'

They drove back to Toni's to pick up Bella's car, which had been left there. They both hopped out of the car and Ned started towards Toni's door, but Bella hung back.

'You go in and see her, Ned. I'll wait here for you. If she's feeling off colour, she won't want both of us annoying her. But please give her my thanks for letting me leave my car with her.'

Ned was gone for only a few minutes, but when he returned, he was clearly angry about something.

Bella was about to ask him what the matter was, but Ned just threw her keys at her and gruffly told her to follow him. A couple of hours later, after dropping Bella's car at the roadhouse, they set off on the final leg of the journey back to the river house in silence.

Finally Bella couldn't stand wondering why Ned was not speaking to her and asked, 'Ned, stop giving me the silent treatment. What's up?'

Ned's face flushed. 'Well, Bella, when I went in to see her just now, Toni announced that you told her about Ashleigh and what happened,' he said in a tense voice. 'And now she says she hasn't got anything to say to me. She won't speak to me because of what *you* told her.'

Bella shrank back, but then straightened up. 'That's rubbish! You should have told her yourself ages ago! And besides, I really didn't mean to tell her. It just popped out,' Bella replied defensively.

'When I choose to tell Toni about my business is my decision! It wasn't your place to tell her, Bell!' said Ned, his face red with anger.

'Oh?' said Bella, her own colour rising. 'And when were you going to tell her?'

'When it was the right time. You shouldn't have said anything.'

'Oh, for heaven's sake!' Bella said impatiently. 'Honestly, Ned, it's your own fault. Honesty is the best policy, Ned. It's never a good idea to keep a secret, at least not one as important as you and Ash. It would all have had to come out in the end, and avoiding telling Toni what happened only makes things worse, in my opinion. Good grief, Ned, you are such a procrastinator! You wouldn't tell Toni about Ash, and you won't make a decision about what you're going to do next! What's wrong with you?'

'Oh? And what are your plans?' Ned spat out the words. 'What are you going to do about Brendan? The guy is obviously in love with you. You can't leave him dangling forever, that isn't fair.'

Bella glared at him. 'That's different. My problems aren't quite so immediate. I have options. What are yours?'

Ned's mouth tightened. 'I'm not sure.' He paused. 'I don't know what I can do. It doesn't seem like there's a lot I can do.'

'That's a shame,' said Bella quietly. 'I know I've only met Toni a couple of times, but I think she's a terrific person. Really special. If you don't do something soon –'

'Dammit, Bella!' Ned banged the steering wheel in frustration as he turned onto the track that led past the dam and down to the river house. 'I'm not saying that she's not, but let me sort my own life out. Please, Bella.'

'Okay, Ned,' said Bella. 'But please don't leave your decision too long, or it might be too late.'

Ned didn't respond. He just gripped the wheel and stared into the distance, frowning. Bella felt her irritation at him subside. In her mind she could hear Ned's mellow voice and his haunting music, which always calmed her. He was a paradox, a musician capable of belting out rock songs or writing music that could both break and heal hearts. It occurred to her that perhaps the time Ned had spent here in this wild and lonely setting had been his own healing time. This was a place where he could confront demons and come to terms with where he was in his life and where he wanted to go with the musical talents he'd been given, but now, before he had found whatever it was that he was seeking, a new chapter of his life had begun: Toni and their baby. And on top of all of this, Bella had still not been able to persuade him to come home for their father's ceremony.

Bella watched the sunlight begin to fade and lose its brilliance as a faint grey scum crept across the blue of the sky.

That evening, Ned made a couple of omelettes which he served with a salad, but they barely spoke as they ate their dinner. There was a distant rumble of thunder, the threatening growl of a gathering storm. Later, as she tidied the kitchen, Bella thought to herself that Ned had judged the food supply pretty well. There was not a lot left, which was just as well, as the two of them had finally decided that they would pack up pretty well straight away. She wasn't sure quite what Ned would do after that, but she knew she had to go to Cairns and then back to Tennyson.

As she settled into bed, she wished they hadn't returned the Bish's box, as she would have loved to have finished reading all of Sister Evangelista's letters. Instead, she put on her earphones and listened to some of Ned's songs on her iPod. As she lay there, she closed her eyes and let Ned's voice soothe her to sleep.

Suddenly she was wide awake. There was a blinding flash of light. Alarmed, she wondered what was happening. An almighty crash answered her question, a boom of thunder that seemed to fall upon the roof. She sat up, pulling the earplugs from her ears and flinging off her bedsheet. But before her feet had touched the floor there was another spearing flash of light that turned everything in the room silvery white. For a wild moment, she thought the bedroom might ignite in the blaze of brilliant luminosity. She started towards her window as another massive roll of thunder boomed around her.

And then came the rain: a pounding torrent of water, as though falling from an enormous, ceaseless waterfall. Bella stood there transfixed, staring into the darkness as the world outside was suddenly intensely illuminated for a few seconds by another flash of lightning before disappearing behind the black curtain of rain.

The wet had arrived.

'Bell, are you okay?' Ned appeared in the doorway and then joined her at the window as they both watched the powerful storm.

'Yes. Who could sleep through this? Will it stop by morning?'

'Hope so,' said Ned. 'Think of weeks of these storms. No wonder life changes in the rainy season. Our river will probably start to rise by tomorrow.'

'We won't get flooded in, will we?'

'No, not for a while, I don't think. Let's go and watch this display from the living room. I wonder if the chickens are freaked out?'

'They're locked up, so they'll be fine. You can't go and check on them in this,' said Bella.

They settled into chairs in the dim living area off the billiard room and bar space, one small, dim lamp casting long shadows about the strangely cluttered room, and watched the amazing light show.

'What time is it?' asked Bella.

'Bit after three. Wonder if we can get a photo of this lightning show?'

'I think you'd need time lapse or something to get it properly. This is crazy stuff. Do you suppose any trees might come down on us?'

'They could, I suppose. This storm is pretty fierce,' said Ned. 'But the trees around the house have been through it all before.'

They watched for a few more moments, Bella still jumping slightly each time the thunder crashed over them.

'It's the lightning that's scary,' she said.

Ned chuckled. 'Do you want a cup of tea?'

'Why not! Yes, thanks, that would be nice.'

Ned got up and went to the kitchen. 'Won't take long to boil the kettle. I reckon the storm will pass soon.'

They quietly sipped their mugs of tea as the weather raged outside. The rain showed no signs of easing up, although the thunder and lightning were becoming fainter as the storm moved away.

Eventually Bella said, 'I've been thinking. Perhaps I dreamed it. About your show. Musical. Opera. However it comes out. And I had an idea. Don't laugh at it, but it's been percolating in my mind for a little while now.'

Ned looked up warily. 'Yeah? Okay, what's this idea?'

'The hook you wanted . . . to be able to tell the stories of the far north. I think that the central narrative has to be told through a main character, someone the audience will fall in love with, but who's also a part of the historical tapestry. Maybe it should be a real person.'

Ned nodded slowly. 'I'm with you so far, but who is this real person? Do you have any ideas about that?'

'I do. She's there in the pages of Sister Evangelista's letters. She's the person I mentioned yesterday, the singer I was asking the curator about. And I know about her too. I know where her roots sprang from and it's all to do with music. She's a perfect fit!' said Bella triumphantly.

'Who? Who are you talking about?' Ned took a breath.

So Bella went over what they knew about Atlanta, her time with Roberta's family and then with the Pedersens, her schooling at St Mary's and her career as a singer, and her eventual rise to fame as a beloved Queensland daughter.

Ned stared at her, his expression hard to read. Finally he said, 'I think you've come up with a wonderful idea that might just work.'

313

'Think of the music, Ned!' continued Bella enthusiastically. 'The harmonising of the South Sea Islanders, the stamping and singing of northern Aborigines, the timpani of Chinese music, the Irish sea shanties, all the people that Sister Evangelista told us about in her letters.'

'And not just that period of history,' said Ned, and Bella felt a frisson of delight at hearing the eagerness in his voice. 'Jack told me about the blues that was sung here during the war to entertain the troops. And we haven't even got to the Italians, Yugoslavs or Greeks who migrated to this part of the world, bringing their own music with them.' Ned's eyes were bright, his smile wide. 'Bella, how can I thank you? You've just pushed a button and a green light has come on! A lot of the music I've written already can easily be adapted to fit in with this idea, although the lyrics might have to be modified. Of course, I'll need to do more research, but this is quite simply a fantastic suggestion. I know it will work.'

Bella grinned. 'You should meet Roberta. I'm sure she'll be able to tell you more about Attie. And Miz Irene, in Cairns – she interviewed you for her radio programme, remember? She knows lots about the music here, especially jazz and the blues. Of course, you'll have to put Sister Evangelista in the storyline, but you can write a song about anything or anyone. Ned, you're a genius!' Bella could hardly contain her excitement.

Ned was shaking his head in wonder. 'Oh, Bella. You've opened a door and given me so many ideas. I have a lot of thinking to do now.'

'I suppose you do, but even I can see how the concept would work fabulously.'

'I can see it, too. I get it. And I can also see that what's before me is huge and daunting. Actually I think we might have come up with a few too many ideas. I think that my musical should just be about Attie. Her life seems to be

314

just perfect for what I want to do. I really think I'll try and concentrate on her.'

'You can do it, Ned.'

'Yes. I think I can.' He spoke as though he was trying to suppress his jubilation.

'Well then, Ned, why don't you jump up and down and yell or something?' exclaimed Bella. 'I'm excited and I haven't a clue what's coming, but I know you have it in you to create something wonderful. That's the trouble with you, always trying to be Mr Cool and not show your emotions.'

Ned shook his head. 'Maybe I don't want to show them. People can misinterpret them and sometimes it's best not to give the wrong impression. Better to keep things to yourself.'

Bella frowned. 'What the hell are you talking about, Ned? It's me, Bella. Your sister. There's nothing in the world you can't tell me. You don't have to pretend with me.'

Ned was silent as he gazed out at the flashing storm.

Bella looked at him and narrowed her eyes. 'Is there something that you haven't told me? Is it about Toni?'

He shrugged. 'Yeah, Toni. And Ashleigh. My whole life. Our family.' He turned away. 'Dad.'

Bella felt a chill go through her. 'Dad? What about Dad? I don't get it. Ned, I so want to understand you, but I'm finding it very hard. So please, once and for all, will you tell me what your problem is?'

11

NED LOOKED OUT OF his bedroom window at the dripping trees and sodden sky. Throwing on a pair of shorts, he went outside onto the top terrace and gazed at the river in the gloomy morning light.

The river's mood had swiftly changed. No longer was it a quiet, placid backwater, meandering its way gently past the house. Now it was a determined surge which was already lapping at the edge of the bottom garden. As Ned watched a branch rush by, he realised just how fast-flowing the river had become.

Back in the kitchen, Bella was already making coffee.

'No more swimming,' announced Ned as cheerfully as he could. He wondered uneasily if Bella would again raise the subject of their father as she had done the night before, an ugly moment which had ended when he had refused to take the bait and she had flounced angrily off to bed. But as he smiled at her, she smiled calmly back and put a couple of pieces of bread into the toaster.

'Oh, is it flooded after all the rain we had last night?'

'Running a bit of a banker. Very fast, in fact. And it's up to the edge of the bottom terrace already. We'll have to start moving the furniture from there before it gets swept away. At least I've already put the canoes back in the shed, so we don't have to worry about those. Are you up to rearranging Carlo's garden furniture?'

'Sure. Here, have some toast while I go and have a look outside.'

Ned was munching toast and sipping coffee when Bella returned.

'Geez, Ned. That's amazing. All that water in just one night. You're right, we'll have to pack away Carlo's tables and chairs before the river rises any further.' She paused, a concerned expression on her face.

'What are you thinking?' he said.

'I think we should start right now and go as soon as possible. I'm worried about that water; yesterday when we drove back I noticed all those tracks through the scrub and it registered that not all of them have been made by vehicles, or even wandering cattle. I'm sure that some of them are waterways created by the wet season floods. Ned, this whole area must become a sea. I don't want to be marooned!'

Ned swallowed his last mouthful of breakfast. 'Yes, I agree, though I think we'd be all right for a few more days. But if you want to leave tomorrow, I'm sure we can manage that.'

'Well, I feel it would be the safest thing to do.' She looked at Ned. 'It's the end of a chapter, leaving this place. I mean, do you suppose you'll ever come back here?'

'To this house? Maybe. I'd like to meet Carlo one day. I'd like to thank him for his hospitality, although we could have done without those appalling men,' said Ned ruefully.

Bella nodded emphatically. 'I suppose Frederick and Theresa will say something to him about the intruders, but unless Carlo actually knows them, he won't be able to do anything, just like everyone else. I don't think we'll ever see them again,' said Bella, a note of finality in her voice. 'Anyway, we're moving on. At least, I am.'

She drained her coffee and poured a refill. Ned watched her and, seeing her brows knit together, he could tell she was working up to saying something.

'Ned . . .'

'Mmm?' For a second Ned thought she was about to bring up the subject of Alex again, and was relieved when instead she began to talk about his musical.

'Have you thought more about what I suggested . . . about your show?'

'Of course I have! I haven't stopped thinking. It's a brilliant idea, but daunting. Huge canvas. Big story, big music.' He shook his head. 'And imagine mounting such a show. Yes, Bella, I love your ideas, but realistically, perhaps I should simplify things, cut it down. Make it a smaller, more intimate story, perhaps . . .' Ned saw Bella's expression harden.

'Why? Why not think big?' she demanded.

'The logistics. I'm restricted to a stage, not a cinema screen. And consider the budget . . . let alone trying to pitch such a huge show to a producer. Imagine the cost!' exclaimed Ned.

'Ned! For God's sake,' cut in Bella. 'Stop limiting your imagination! You're your own worst enemy! Write what you want. Picture it all on a big canvas, on stage or screen. Let others work out the logistics.' She threw her hands in the air. 'As I say, you need to think big!'

Ned was silent for a few minutes. 'I'm taking a huge leap from sitting on a stool singing a few songs, telling some stories, to creating a massive musical.'

'Stop underrating yourself. You've had a very successful album. You've sung to several thousand people at concerts and festivals and had them enthralled. Music promoters still chase you because they love your music, Ned. You're a storyteller in music and that's what people want.'

'I just feel overwhelmed about where to take the whole thing,' began Ned.

Bella banged her hand on the table. 'Stop right there, Ned. You've let your anxieties get the better of you, and it has stifled your creativity. And you're assuming that you have to do it all by yourself. Well, you can't. I think you should just play to your strengths. You compose the music and write the lyrics, be the creative lynchpin of the whole project, but let others do the rest. A show like this has to be collaborative. You need to involve a whole team of other people to make it work: producers, arrangers, orchestral people, staging people, designers . . . the whole box and dice.' Bella was becoming quite animated. 'Maybe you should even make an album first, release some of your songs so that people will know the music before they see the show. It will all need a lot of promoting. But first it will be necessary to sell the concept of this idea to someone who is prepared to go with you, back you, someone who gets your idea and is knocked out by it.'

Ned shuddered. 'Bella, this is way beyond anything that I am capable of doing. I'm not sure I would even know where to start. Let's face it, I'm not good at that sort of organisation,' he said, and realised with some embarrassment that he could hear the negativity and desperation in his voice. But it was true. The mere thought of having to contact industry people and set up meetings sent a chill down his spine. He was about to protest further when he saw Bella suddenly freeze. She stood perfectly still, just staring into space, lost in thought.

'Bella?' Ned asked, peering at her. 'Earth to Bella?' He waved his hand in front of her face and she blinked.

'You're right, Ned. You're not good at organisation,' she said slowly. 'But *I* am. Ned – I should be your manager.'

Ned stared at her quizzically, but then it was like something suddenly clicked and the puzzle pieces finally fell into place. *Of course*, Ned thought. He opened his mouth, but Bella rushed on.

'I want to be entrepreneurial. I like selling ideas. Heavens, I've sold the story of Tennyson quite successfully for a number of years now, but I want to spread my wings. I've been stuck between a rock and a hard place: I don't want to go back to the tourism scene in Tennyson, but I've been thinking a lot about Antony's ideas and I think they have a lot of holes in them. Maybe they're just not workable.' Bella gave Ned a lopsided grin and then shook her head. 'Ned, I know I would be really good at being your manager, if you'll let me. I could research the music market and the stage business and find the right people, and then sell them the whole package. Believe me, they'll be begging to sign you up.' Bella grinned, her eyes sparkling. Ned could see she was on a roll and hugely excited about the idea, but he didn't want her to rush into such a big commitment.

'Bella . . . slow down,' he said, holding up his hands. 'You want to manage *me*? You're not serious!'

'Deadly serious. I know that if you are ever going to get this project off the ground you have to have a manager who believes in you.' Ned looked at her doubtfully, but she went on. 'The music business can be a bit of a minefield, and I know that sometimes you feel you've been ripped off, but I'm smart, Ned, and I can deal with people. You won't be cheated if I'm your manager.'

'Wow. You really are serious.' He smiled at her cautiously, and for the first time allowed himself to consider the idea as a genuine possibility. 'Well, I think it all comes down to trust, Bell. I've always been reluctant to put my music into a stranger's hands. There are terrible stories around about musos being cheated by managers and agents and I've already had a couple of unhappy experiences with record companies, but if you're doing things . . . Well, you're my sister. I can trust you.' Ned felt a sudden surge of excitement, a sense that his musical dreams might actually turn into something real. 'But will you leave your job, Bell? Am I something that you would just do on the side?' he asked dubiously.

'Don't worry, Ned, you'll be my only priority. It's a gamble, perhaps, but when I know something is the right thing to do, I just know.' She gave her brother a broad smile and stuck out her hand. 'Do we have a deal?'

Ned was stunned by Bella's suggestion, but he knew it made sense. Sometimes the way his sister stormed her way through life irritated him, but now he could see that her cheerful, positive, savvy approach would make her the very person to have in his corner. If Bella couldn't make this musical happen, then, he thought, no one could. How wonderful it would be to be able to let go of the business side of things, and just focus on creating music.

'What are you going to do about Antony?' he asked.

'I'll meet up with him in Cairns. I'll explain to him that I've had a better offer. These things have to be done face to face.'

'Won't he try to persuade you back round to his idea, though?' said Ned with a raised eyebrow.

Bella grinned. 'He might, but my mind is made up. Even if he were to offer me something amazing, I'd much rather do this thing with you.'

'I don't know how I'd pay you.'

'Ned, I see this as an investment. A partnership, so I'm prepared to put up with working for free for the time being. I've still got some savings and I'm due for long-service leave at the end of the year, too, so there's that bit of income as well. I'll stay in Tennyson – it's easy enough to travel down to Melbourne from there – so I'll be fine until we get a deal.'

Hearing Bella talk about reducing her income to take a punt on him made Ned feel concerned. 'And if we don't make this work?'

Bella held up her hand. 'Don't even think like that. You have talent. Terrific talent. You've got a great idea. I know we can make it work.' Bella's face was glowing with excitement, but Ned felt the old stirrings of doubt in his stomach.

'Can we do it, Bell? Work together? I trust you and I know that you really want this to succeed, but what about our differences . . . ?' he said hesitantly. 'You know that we don't see eye to eye about everything.'

Bella put a hand on his shoulder. 'I know, but we don't have to be in each other's pockets all the time – and our roles will be quite different. I have to do my home-work and then get out there and talk to people.' She was thoughtful for a moment. 'Maybe you'll need to make up a bit of a demo to give me something to pitch to them,' she added. 'Anyway, you'll need your own space to finish writing the show. You won't want me hanging around all the time.' She continued to beam at him and, despite himself, Ned grinned back. Impulsively he wrapped his arms around her and gave her a bear hug. Bella laughed and hugged him back.

Releasing her, Ned suddenly couldn't wait to get back to his music. He felt the adrenalin begin to pump through his body, in the same way it did right before a show. He grasped Bella's hand. 'It's a deal, Sis.'

Bella's eyes were gleaming with excitement. 'Bro, you will now refer to me as your manager, thank you very much. And no matter what anyone says to you from now on, just say, "Speak to my manager, please, she'll sort it." Got that?'

*

They spent the rest of the day under lowering skies, moving furniture from the bottom terrace and securing it in the shed or on the higher terraces. They locked up the cool room and began tying down the awnings and putting away any tools and other loose objects that had been left lying around the house. Bella picked the last of the fruit and herbs from the garden, giving the greens to the chickens.

Ned checked that there were no dangerous branches which could fall or be blown against the house, but with its corrugated-iron shutters, its stonework and log stanchions, the home was sturdy.

'This place has been built to survive a few rainy seasons, for sure,' said Ned.

By late afternoon they were ready for a break. Ned was packing up the bar and held up a bottle of wine.

'I reckon we've earned a drink. What've you found for tonight's meal?' he asked.

'Spaghetti and a can of marinara sauce, the last of the fresh herbs, a few rather overripe tomatoes and some parmesan cheese. *Pasta à la Bella*, and I can toast the last of the stale banana bread for dessert.'

'Maybe we should give that to the girls. We'll have to take them to the roadhouse and leave them with Frederick,

I suppose. Can't leave them here. Still, I think I'll miss them.'

Bella looked amused. 'You weren't so keen on chooks and country life when we were growing up. You're absolutely sure you don't fancy settling down with chickens and someone lovely and . . . ?'

'A baby? In Cooktown? Just when I'm starting out with a hotshot manager and a project I'm feeling quietly confident about? But it's a conundrum,' said Ned. 'I think that Toni is special. I really love being with her, but I don't know where our relationship is headed when she won't speak to me.' He was quiet for a moment.

Bella peered at him. 'That's because you didn't tell her about you and Ash. I've never understood what caused you to break it all off with Ashleigh and move away from us so suddenly. It seemed such a cruel thing to do to her so close to the wedding, and you're not a cruel person. It rocked all of us that you sort of went off the rails, that you ran away, essentially, and I really think there has to be some other reason, because you've never been a coward. I hope I'm right.'

Ned shifted uncomfortably. 'That's quite a speech. There was a reason, but trust me, you don't want to know what it is.'

'But I do,' Bella pushed. 'How can I understand if you won't explain it to me? When I think back to the wedding, all those plans . . . and then just days before it was supposed to happen, you call everything off. No one should humiliate anyone the way you did Ash. I know Dad was really disappointed in you.'

'Disappointed, was he?' said Ned bitterly. 'Well, that's rich coming from him. Look, Bella, all I can say is that I've learned things about marriage that make me very wary of that institution.'

'So you're saying that Dad was right when he said he thought that you were afraid of commitment?'

Ned 's face flushed with rage. 'Dad had no damn right to say that about me. He made himself out to be so bloody perfect, the model husband and father, the man the whole town could look up to. But believe me, he was not at all what you or anyone else thinks!' snapped Ned. 'He wasn't always perfect, he wasn't perfect at all.'

'What are you talking about, Ned?' Bella glared at him in anger. 'Dad was wonderful. Everyone who knew him says so, and yet it seems you want to bring him down to excuse your own behaviour.'

Ned was silent, biting his lip. A voice in his head whispered, *Leave it . . . leave it, don't get into this. It's not worth it.*

'Forget it, Bella,' Ned almost shouted at her. 'Let's just move on. It's my issue to deal with, not yours. I'm sorry I mentioned it.' Ned suddenly buried his head in his hands, trying to contain all that was churning inside him.

Bella's voice softened. 'Ned, there is clearly something causing you a lot of grief. I'm your sister! We're going to be working together and I think I need to know what is going on. Bottling it all up inside you isn't good. We need to get things out in the open, so that we'll be able to start our working relationship on the right footing. Heavens, how bad can it be?'

He gave her a despairing look. 'Perhaps even worse than you can possibly imagine.'

Ned was about to turn away, but he was suddenly overcome with a desire to unburden himself. Although he had his reasons for having kept this secret from her in the past, he knew in his heart that Bella was right. Their relationship, both working and personal, was never going to work unless he told her the truth. Still, a small part of him was not sure that in this case honesty was the best policy. Bella would be shocked and hurt when she learned the real reason for the aborted wedding; what if she would not forgive him? Then their new bond would not even have lasted the day. But the stronger part of him said, *If I don't share this now, it will always hang over us.* He knew then with certainty that he would never feel at peace or secure or open with his sister unless he told her what had happened.

Bella sat, staring at him, half curious but also looking fearful, as if she were no longer sure she wanted to hear what Ned was about to tell her.

Ned took a deep breath. 'You won't like what I have to say. You may not even believe me, but I know that we can't work together while there are secrets between us,' said Ned in a rush.

'What could possibly change our relationship?' Bella leaned forward. 'Please, Ned. I feel we've got to a point where, whatever it is, we need to be honest with each other. You need to tell me what is going on, because whatever you're hiding is making you very unhappy.'

'You're right.' He noticed that Bella stiffened slightly, straightening her back as she waited for him to drop his bombshell. *Change your mind, make something up. Don't ruin her illusions.*

But he drew another breath and braced himself. Now was the time for the truth.

'I guess I always thought marriage to Ash was inevitable. It was the next step. We had been together forever and she really wanted to get married, settle down, have kids, and I suppose I thought it was time, too. I looked at our parents' marriage and thought, this is what marriage is. Maybe I didn't want my wife to be quite as acquiescent as Mum was, but then I was never going to be as authoritarian as Dad. Like everyone, I thought they had a rock-solid relationship, an example to be very much admired and copied.'

Bella went to say something, but Ned held up his hand. 'No. Let me finish. I know you can't accept any criticism of Dad and you think that I can never measure up to his standards, but he was a hypocrite, Bella. It was all a lie.'

Bella frowned at him and Ned drew a breath. *Okay, here it comes.* 'Bella, I found out that Dad had been having an affair.'

Bella stared at her brother and sat stunned for a moment. Then she started vigorously shaking her head. 'No way, Ned. No way. You're wrong!'

'Just hear me out, Bell, and then you can tell me what you think. Believe me, it's very hard to tell you this, but here goes.' He drew another breath. 'A while before Dad died, I was in Melbourne doing a gig. As you know, Dad was always driving back and forth to Melbourne because he was on so many medical boards. He always seemed to have meetings.'

'Yes, he was involved in lots of those sorts of things in Melbourne. Mum said that the car could find its own way there and back, he went so often,' said Bella, still frowning. 'So?'

'Well, the day after the gig, the guy who'd arranged it was so pleased with the show that he took me out to lunch. A very posh place, not the sort of place I usually go to, so imagine my surprise and pleasure to see Dad at one of the tables. I was about to go up to him and say hi, when a very attractive woman, quite a bit younger than Dad by the look of things, came over to his table. Dad stood up and greeted her and then he kissed her on the cheek and they both sat down together.'

Bella's hand flew to her mouth, but before she could protest, Ned raised his hand once more to stop her. 'Before you tell me that she could have been any old acquaintance, I can assure you I thought that as well, at first. But then I saw the way that they started to talk, each so comfortable with the other, and I just knew they were more than casual friends. Then he touched her hand in a way that was very intimate. So I ducked away where Dad couldn't see me and apologised to the guy I was supposed to have lunch with, telling him that something had just come up and I had to leave. I got out of there before Dad spotted me.'

Bella narrowed her eyes. 'Ned, I think you were rather jumping to conclusions. She could have been anybody. Just because a woman is young and attractive doesn't mean you can paint her as a scarlet woman! There are plenty of good-looking professional young women about. Why didn't you go straight up to Dad and say hello and ask to be introduced?' she said hotly.

'I wanted to think that way, too,' said Ned miserably. 'And maybe I should have been up-front with him. But it was perfectly clear to me that Dad and this woman were more than just friends. And I was just so shocked. It bothered me so much, I did some digging.'

Bella looked aghast. 'So you went behind Dad's back? Spied on him? What if he'd found out you were prying, with only your suspicions to go on? I think it's pretty appalling behaviour on your part, Ned,' said Bella in a choked voice.

'Bella! Just listen to what I have to say about our supposedly perfect father before you jump on me.'

Bella leaped to her feet. 'Ned, I don't believe you, and I think it's unfair and unkind of you to try to destroy Dad's name and what he meant to us all, especially now that he's gone and he can't defend himself!' Bella looked as if she was going to cry.

'Bella, just give me a chance to tell you what I know!' Ned shouted at her in frustration.

Bella glared at her brother, but she sat back down, her arms folded defiantly.

Why did I start this? thought Ned. But he was in too deep now. He knew he had to push on or Bella was never going to believe him, and that would certainly mean the end of their relationship. He tried to speak calmly. 'Look, Bella, part of me didn't want to believe anything bad about Dad, despite what you think, but I felt I had to try to find out what was going on. I couldn't just front up to him and ask him who the woman was that he was making goo-goo eyes with over lunch, could I? He would simply have denied my assertions.'

Bella turned her head away and refused to look at him.

'Well, I mentioned it to Ashleigh and, like you, she dismissed the whole thing. But I couldn't let it go, so over the next few weeks I started to make a few discreet inquiries. I asked at the restaurant where I'd first seen them. Evidently the two of them met there regularly and some-times the woman made the booking. The maître d' was obliging and told me the woman's name was Dr Frances Barnes and that she worked in a medical laboratory.'

'I don't believe you. I bet you paid him. Then he'd say anything,' said Bella stubbornly.

Ned ignored her interruption and continued. 'I also asked around regarding Dad's work in Melbourne, his lectures, conferences, patients. I found out that some of those meetings he said he was attending had never actu-ally occurred.'

'How did you find that out?' asked Bella sceptically.

'I asked his receptionist – you know, Glenda? – to look back through his diaries and make a list of some of the organisations he was concerned with and when he attended their meetings. I've always got on well with Glenda and she could see no reason not to tell me that sort of stuff – it was hardly confidential. Then I rang the places where Dad was supposed to have been. In some instances they told me that there had never been a meeting involving Dad on those particular dates, and on other occasions it appears that the meetings were shorter than Dad had claimed. Other meetings it seems he simply made up. Actually, Glenda also told me that when she'd tried to contact him a couple of times at a hospital where he was supposed to be working, she was told that he hadn't been there at all. She just assumed that a mistake had been made, although it puzzled her. She didn't make mistakes.'

'This doesn't prove anything, though! Glenda could've stuffed up.'

Ned shook his head. 'I didn't think she had, so I thought it was time I approached Dad to see what he had to say. I found out from Mum when Dad was next coming to town and I thought that if I met him, I could sort the problem out. Maybe not actually confront him, but at least ask careful questions that might be able to put my mind at rest. Anyway, I tried his mobile phone that day, but it was switched off, so I rang the hotel where he usually stayed, and they said he hadn't checked in yet. I thought I might run into him if I just hung around and waited until he turned up. There's a great coffee shop in the hotel complex so I sat there, having a cup of coffee, waiting for Dad to check in. And that's when I saw them again. Dad and that woman, Frances, who I'd seen him with at the restaurant.' Ned closed his eyes and his face twisted at the memory.

Bella's eyes narrowed. 'Why didn't you just go over and speak to Dad?'

'I couldn't, Bella.' He looked at her sadly. 'Dad and . . . and . . . the woman were walking along with a little girl between them, each of them holding a hand. I'm not good with kids' ages, but I guess she was about five or six.'

Bella stared at Ned. 'And? So what?'

Ned shook his head and spoke gently. 'They came over, near to where I was sitting, so that they could take the lift.

Then the little girl spoke and I could hear every word she said. "Daddy, why can't we all have lunch together?" And then our wonderful father said to her, "Darling, I have some work to do now, but I'll see you tonight and I promise to read you a bedtime story." They all took the lift, but I was too numb to move. I just sat there for ages afterwards. I couldn't believe it.'

Ned looked at Bella and saw sheer agony spread across her face. He wished he could take her pain away, but all he could do was watch as she clapped her hands over her ears and shouted at him: 'Stop. Stop right now! This is ridiculous, Ned! I won't listen to any more of this.' Bella jumped to her feet.

Ned put his hands on her shoulders and steadied her. He gently guided her back into her chair. 'Sit down, Bella. I know this is painful to hear. Believe me, I know. Why do you think I've kept it to myself all this time? But it's the truth. I'm sorry, but this is what happened.'

Bella stared at her brother, stiffly and in shock, but before she could say anything, Ned continued, 'Then the Frances woman and the little girl reappeared. They must have left Dad at the hotel by himself. So, instead of finding Dad and having it out with him, I decided to follow them to see where they went. I felt stupid, but it was easy. They got a tram down Brunswick Street to Fitzroy. I got out of the tram at the same stop as they did and walked behind them, keeping my distance as I didn't know if she might recognise me.'

'You're not that famous!' snapped Bella, suddenly finding her voice.

'Dad might have shown her pictures of us,' Ned answered. 'I thought the whole thing impossible to understand. But I found out where she lived. I walked back past her house several more times after that, as though by doing it I could make sense of what I'd seen.'

'Why didn't you just confront Dad?' Bella asked, her voice strangled and strange.

'And say what? "Is that little girl I saw you with the other day your secret daughter?" If I was going to ask him anything like that, I felt that I needed to be absolutely sure. I found out from the neighbours that as the mother worked, the little girl was looked after by a nanny after school. I kept being drawn back and one day, as I was walking past the house, the nanny and the little girl came out through the gate. I wanted to say something, to ask questions, but I didn't know what to say. As they turned onto the footpath, the little girl dropped the doll she was carrying and I quickly picked it up and returned it to her. Bella, that little girl is exactly like you. She has your hair colour and your features. Remember that photo Dad had of you in his study? She looked exactly like you. The resemblance was uncanny. "Say thank you, Chloe," the nanny said. Bella, her name is Chloe. She's not an idea, or a make-believe child, she's real.'

Tears sprang to Bella's eyes and her hands flew to her mouth. 'No. No way. You've got it all wrong. He . . . couldn't have . . . he . . .' Bella dissolved into tears, her voice choked by sobs.

Ned reached over to Bella, but she snatched her hand away.

'Believe me, I denied it too. It's a very hard thing to accept that our father had another family in Melbourne. But Bell . . . it doesn't mean Dad loved you any less. You know he couldn't have been prouder of you.'

Bella shook her head savagely. Huge fat tears rolled down her face. 'I don't want to hear any more.' She turned her face away.

'I know, Bella. Really, I know how you feel. I felt so shocked I just couldn't comprehend it. I couldn't tell anyone about it – certainly not you or Mum. How could

I destroy the image of the man you two believed to be the perfect husband, father and model citizen?' Ned shook his head. 'I just didn't know what to do. And it was right before the wedding.'

Bella glanced up. 'Did you tell Ash?' she asked.

Ned took a breath. 'No. I should have, but the whole thing made me so sick. And she hadn't believed me when I'd told her about seeing Dad with that woman in the restaurant, so I just couldn't bring myself to tell her the rest. It should have been easy, we'd been together forever. I thought we were soul mates. But when I found out about Dad, something changed in me. I realised I just couldn't go through with the wedding. Dad was always setting such high standards for us, telling me not to let the family down, that we had a position to uphold in Tennyson, saying how important it was to make a commitment and stick to it, but he didn't live by those standards himself. He wasn't really committed to Mum or our family. He wasn't really the great man that everyone thought he was. I just lost it. I felt so confused and betrayed. I just couldn't face the wedding, so I called it off. I wanted to get as far away as possible from Dad and from Tennyson. And then two weeks later, he was killed, driving back from Melbourne in the pouring rain. He'd been with her. So in the end I never got the chance to confront him.' Ned turned away. 'I've hated myself ever since for not standing up to him, at least for Mum's sake.'

Bella was shaking now, tears streaming down her face. 'It can't possibly be true,' she whispered.

Ned stared at his sister. He was not really surprised by her reaction, but he had more to tell her and he couldn't stop now.

'She came to his funeral, you know,' he said.

'*What?*' Bella's head snapped up.

'I saw her in the church. I tried to reach her at the end of the service to ask her why she had come, but there were so many people trying to speak to me after the service, to say how sorry they were about Dad, that I couldn't find her. I guess she didn't hang around.'

Bella stared at him, her eyes round.

'After the funeral most of the flowers were sent to the hospital and the nursing homes because there were just so many, remember? Glenda kindly removed all the cards from the tributes and gave them to me to give to Mum. Mum would of course acknowledge them all. I glanced through all the little cards and I found one that I didn't want Mum to see. I don't know why, but I needed to keep it. Maybe to prove to myself that what I had found out about Dad was real.'

Ned reached for his wallet and took out a small card, which he passed to Bella.

The card read, *To Alex, forever in our hearts, Frances and Chloe*. Bella stared at the words, seemingly struck dumb.

'I suppose Mum would have thought they were just some grateful patients, which is what they might well have been, but they weren't,' said Ned. He took a deep breath. 'Bella, yesterday you told me that the truth should always come out. And you're right. If we are to get on and trust each other, we can't have secrets between us.'

He rubbed his face with his hands, knowing he looked wretched. The silence drew out between them.

Finally Bella asked, 'And where are they now? This woman and the child? Did you ever confront her and settle it once and for all?'

'Of course not. Dad was gone. What was the point? But I did go past the house in Fitzroy not long before I came up north, and there were other people living there. Frances and Chloe had left.'

'Chloe, *Chloe*, God I hate that name,' Bella cried, tears springing afresh. 'I always have. If what you say is true, it seems that I wasn't Dad's little princess at all. I had competition.'

'So it would seem. Our whole family life was a sham.'

Bella was staring at the card, reading the words over and over. Then suddenly a new fury filled her face.

'I put my father on a pedestal and all the time he didn't deserve my admiration at all.'

'That's not entirely true, Bell. He was a wonderful and caring doctor.'

'But it seems that he wasn't quite as wonderful and caring a father.'

Ned sighed. 'No, he wasn't who we thought he was. Now I think you can understand why I don't want to go to the dedication ceremony.'

Bella stood up. 'Ned, I don't want to talk about this any more.' Her face was blotchy and her cheeks were streaked with tears as she hurried across the room. 'I have to go for a walk. I need some space. I feel as though my whole life has been pulled out from under me like a rug.' She paused for a moment and stared at her brother. 'She'd better not come to the ceremony. She wouldn't dare, or I'll attack her.' And she ran outside.

*

Ned watched her go and decided to give her some time. He'd had a long time to process what had happened and he still felt shocked, confused and upset every time he thought about it. Bella had adored their father. This infor- mation about him was probably amongst the worst news that she could ever hear. He got himself a beer and sat staring at the grey skies, debating whether or not he'd done the right thing in telling her about their father's other life. Just when he and Bella had found new ground and were establishing a new relationship, he'd broken the promise he'd made to himself never to reveal their father's treachery and disloyalty. But he also recognised that without the truth his and Bella's relationship would never flourish. There would always have been a barrier between them.

Nevertheless, Ned desperately wanted to make peace with Bella, and ask for her forgiveness for shattering her illusions and undermining their father's privileged position in her heart. Yet, Ned had to acknowledge, now that he'd shared the terrible secret he'd carried, he felt a deep sense of relief. Perhaps, at last, he could move on.

He was about to go outside to look for his sister when he heard a car approaching. He got to his feet and walked up to the gate.

A few minutes later, Jack strode into the room behind Ned and threw his cap onto one of Carlo's chairs.

'You beat me to it, huh? Everything looks packed up.'

'Yeah. Sit down, Jack. I'll get you a drink.'

'Stay there. Where's Bella? And what's up with you? You look like you've been steamrolled.' Jack went to the bar and found a beer. 'I came over to help you guys move gear and pack up. Rainy season has started, for sure. Wanted to check up on that plucky little sister of yours, too. See how she's getting on.'

He gave Ned a quizzical look as he swallowed his drink. 'You guys had a bit of a stoush? You can't be that upset about leaving.'

Ned looked at Jack for a moment and then decided that he would confide in the older man. He needed some advice, and Jack was worldly wise and a good listener, so Ned told him what had happened.

Jack didn't interrupt, and when Ned had finished he said, 'I'm not surprised by Bella's reaction. It was a pretty hard thing to hear. And how do you feel?'

'Like a weight has lifted, I have to say, but I also feel terrible for disillusioning her.'

'Understandable,' said Jack.

'Maybe it was stupid of me to tell her. We were getting along so well. First time in quite a while. She even wants to become my manager.'

Jack took a sip of his beer. 'Damned good idea. She's smart. And you don't want people ripping you off.'

Ned felt a rush of affection for this off-beat man he'd come to like so much.

A few minutes later Bella, driven in by the rain, came back and went into the kitchen to make herself a coffee.

Jack said nothing. Ned had got used to the way he didn't do small talk. Ned went to the bar and got another beer as Bella came back into the room and sat near Jack, holding her mug of coffee. Her eyes were red and swollen. The three of them sat in silence.

'Ned shared some unhappy news with you,' said Jack at last.

Bella nodded.

'Do you wish he hadn't?'

Bella shrugged. Then nodded. 'But I asked him to tell me. Insisted, even.'

'What would you have done if you had been the one to find out about your father?' asked Jack in a casual, non-challenging voice.

Bella raised her voice and burst out, 'I would have confronted Dad and demanded an explanation from the start!'

Hearing this, Ned winced. He knew he should have done exactly that, but now it was all too late.

'I thought I was doing the right thing. I didn't want Bella, or my mother, hurt. Maybe I should have confronted him.' Ned turned away but not before the others saw the pain on his face.

Jack nodded. 'Way it sometimes goes.' He turned to Bella. 'But have you considered what would have happened if Ned had confronted your old man? Think about that, Miss Bella.'

Bella sat quietly.

'It would have been ugly,' answered Ned. 'He probably would've denied it. Or he would have asked me what I thought would happen to Mum if it had all got out. He would have said that no one would believe my accusations. He would have worn me down and in the end he would have made me feel as though I was the bad guy. The irony is, I feel like the bad guy anyway.' Ned felt the all-too-familiar sense of defeat come over him and his shoulders slumped.

'Bella?' Jack looked at her.

'Ned's right about Mum. I would hate Mum to ever find out about this. She cherishes Dad's memory.'

'And your memory of your dad?' asked Jack sharply, looking from sister to brother.

'My father's memory is tarnished forever,' said Bella bitterly, her voiced raised in anger. 'He's not the father I always thought he was. I wasn't even his only daughter.' Bella put her head in her hands and her shoulders began to shake gently. Jack reached across and patted her gently on the knee.

'Sure it's a shock. Would be for anyone, to find out that their father wasn't the fine guy who they thought he was,' he said gently.

Bella raised her head and looked from Jack to her brother. She drew a shaky breath. 'You know something, Ned, in some ways I think what you did, keeping quiet so that everyone else could still go on thinking that Dad was wonderful, was maybe the right thing to do after all. I can't bear the thought of Mum ever knowing. And I'm sorry that your decision to keep it all quiet has screwed up your life.'

'Not as much as I screwed up Ashleigh's. I did a terrible thing to her. I must have so humiliated her, calling off our wedding so close to the day, never giving her a proper explanation. I can't forgive myself for that.'

Jack raised an eyebrow. 'So, you ended your relationship because of what your father did?'

Ned swallowed hard. 'What Dad did shook me to the core, and made me think twice about marriage, that's certainly true. But there was something else.' He paused, glancing at Bella. 'Ash had been hinting that I should give up my music, except as a hobby, and get a regular job. She wanted stability and wanted to put down roots in Tennyson. I was getting married because I knew that was the right thing to do, the next step in our relationship. I loved Ash, and I thought if we got married we'd just figure things out. But deep down, I really wanted to keep writing music. I knew then that I couldn't make the sort of commitment that Ash wanted, but I didn't explain any of this to her. I just couldn't tell her the truth.'

'Cold feet,' said Jack.

'I'm just like Dad. For all his talk, his standards, his rules, he never wanted commitment. He was selfish and so am I. What Ash wanted, I knew I just couldn't give her. I just broke up with her and ran away. I'm no better than Dad was.'

Bella stared at him uncomprehendingly.

Jack stroked his chin. 'Now, I don't think that's right. It sounds to me like you and this Ash girl just weren't right for each other; she wanted one thing and you wanted something else.'

Ned didn't respond and Jack continued. 'Never a bad thing to admit your mistakes. I've done a lot of that in my life.' Jack finished his beer. 'Tell me, what are you two going to do after you leave this place?' he asked. 'Seems to me you're both at the starting line. It's up to you how you run the race from here.'

Ned stared at the warmth in Jack's eyes. Was the older man saying that it was time to put his father behind him and start over? But could he really do that? He glanced at Bella.

'I'm sorry, Bell. I never wanted you to be hurt.'

'It wasn't your fault, Ned. I have to believe what you've told me, but I still can't quite accept it. Why did he do it? Was it us? Mum? Did we do something wrong?'

'No!' interjected Ned. 'I think he did it because he thought he was entitled to do whatever he wanted. That the rules didn't apply to him and he could take what he wanted without any regard for the feelings of those closest to him. He was selfish and self-centred.'

'Maybe,' said Bella, her voice unsure.

'The sins of our fathers can be a heavy burden if we let them,' said Jack, eyeing Ned, but Ned was looking intently at Bella. Jack turned to her. 'Now you know the truth, Bella, there's no going back,' continued Jack. 'But neither of you should feel responsible for your father's actions. He did the wrong thing by your family, but don't take it on yourselves to live with the consequences of what he did. Cut yourselves some slack. Keep going forwards with your lives.'

'Seems a bit late for that,' sighed Ned.

'Enough with the poor me,' said Jack impatiently. 'You've got a talent. And now you have support from someone strong, resourceful and whom you can trust. Give it a try – you have all to gain and nothing to lose, as they say.'

Ned looked at Jack and said steadily, 'That's not all that's concerning me. Toni is pregnant. But the truth is, the baby would probably be better off without me.'

'Hmm . . . well, I can't advise you on that one,' said Jack, lifting an eyebrow. 'You make choices and you have to live with them. But I will say that in spite of what your father did, family is something to be treasured. Just take you and Bella. You've both been through a fair bit of drama while you've been here, and yet you've both survived, and I think what's happened has made for even stronger bonds.' He reached out and gripped Ned's arm. 'I regret letting my family slip away. Try not to let that happen to you because you think you're the same as your father. You are your own person. Respect that.'

They sat in silence for a while. There didn't seem to be anything left to say. Ned rubbed his face. He felt exhausted. There was only so much he could process in one day. Jack seemed to sense his mood and picked up his cap. 'Seeing as you've done all the hard work, I'll pack up your girls, Ned, and be on my way.'

'You're taking the chickens? That's great.' Bella smiled weakly. 'Ned thought we'd have to leave them with Frederick.'

There was a sudden downpour that hammered on the roof, making speech impossible for a few moments, but when it eased Ned asked Jack, 'You have somewhere to keep them?'

'Yep, I've got a bomb shelter,' said Jack. Then, seeing Ned and Bella's astonished expressions, he grinned. 'Yes, I have a suitable place.'

'I'll help you. I've got some boxes we can put them in,' said Ned.

The two men headed up towards the chicken run as the rain began in earnest. Bella grabbed a towel to put over her head and raced after them.

As the last box of protesting chickens was loaded into Jack's car, Ned looked across to Bella, who had taken shelter under the dripping poinciana tree with the towel over her head. She seemed very young and a little forlorn. How she must have hated hearing what he had told her. While Ned had had a rather prickly relationship with his father, Alex had always been Bella's hero. Telling Bella what Alex had done would have been a far greater blow for his sister than it had been for him, for Alex stood far higher in her estimation than in Ned's. Ned couldn't help but admire Bella in that moment. After all that had happened, the abduction and now this, he was amazed how strong she was. Looking at his bedraggled sister, he felt a wave of affection for her. And as he patted a carton to soothe the muttering chickens, a thought occurred to him, stopping him in his tracks. What if Toni was expecting a girl? How would he feel about having a daughter?

'Is there a problem?' asked Jack.

'Ah, no. The hens are right to go. But I'll miss them,' said Ned, feeling a bit foolish.

'Oh, stop it. They're just chooks,' called Bella from under the tree of flaming flowers. 'But chooks with character,' she added.

Jack came around and slammed the back of the car shut. Rain dripped from the brim of his cap. He looked at Ned with a steady gaze and stuck out his hand. 'Till we meet again, buddy.'

'Yes. We will, I know we will,' said Ned, desperately hoping the words were true. He reached out and pumped Jack's hand.

'Take it as it comes, Ned. What happens, happens. That's life. Been good to know you. I'll be listening out for your music.'

Jack turned abruptly and opened the driver's door, calling out to Bella as he did so, 'Don't push him too hard, Bella. Remember, with you holding the reins, he'll get there.'

Bella dashed out from under the tree and hugged Jack. 'Thank you so much for what you did for me.

You saved my life. And thanks for the things you said just now. I know that Ned and I will work things out. I'll send you a ticket to the opening night.' She kissed Jack on the cheek.

Jack nodded, touching the rim of his cap, then got behind the wheel, started the motor and drove off into the downpour.

Bella and Ned watched till he was out of sight.

'Why are we standing in the rain? Let's get inside. I'm hungry,' said Bella.

War's over. Ned nodded and followed her down the steps, but turned as he got to the door and looked back. A curtain of rain and nightfall obscured the bush, and for a moment he wondered if Jack had really been there. But then the twang of Jack's voice came back to him. 'Take it as it comes.'

*

It was their last night. Ned and Bella sat talking in the dark, not bothering to turn on the lights.

'Bella, I've been thinking, and I've made two decisions,' said Ned. 'Now that I've told you about Dad, I think we need to agree that neither of us will ever tell Mum about his double life. It's unlikely she'd ever find out, so I see no reason to break her heart. Do you agree that that's for the best?'

'Definitely. I know I said that telling the truth was always for the best. I was wrong. Telling Mum the truth would achieve nothing. I just hope, like you, that this knowledge about our father stays a secret from her forever. Sometimes telling the truth achieves no real purpose at all and I think that applies in Mum's case. What's your other decision?'

'I'm going to come to the dedication ceremony.'

'So you think Dad deserves it?'

Ned shook his head. 'Bella, I'm not doing it for Dad, I'm doing it for Mum. She wants me there to show a united family front, and so that's what I'll give her. A united family. I'll fly out of Cairns with you.'

'Thanks, Ned. I'm pleased for Mum's sake, but the ceremony seems so hollow since you told me what Dad did,' said Bella sadly.

'Now you know how I felt and why I didn't want to go back to Tennyson, but I've decided that I can't punish Mum for what Dad did. I can't keep staying away from our family because of what happened.'

'Ned, I'm really glad to hear that.' Bella was quiet a moment. 'You know, while we're talking about decisions, I was standing out there under that tree just now and I realised something. All my life I've thought that Dad was someone who was nearly faultless. But I see now that a lot of what I admired in Dad was quite superficial. He only cared about what he wanted. Being admired in the community. Being a leader, the centre of attention all the time. Taking what he wanted without regard for others. That's not what's right.' She took a breath. 'The best sort of man is kind, loving, honest and dependable. Someone who will always be there for you. Someone who doesn't put himself first. Someone you can trust implicitly. Now I realise how I've misjudged Brendan. I thought he was unexciting, a little boring, but I was wrong. He raced up here to see me, set off with you and Jack to find me, with no idea what he might run into. He's open with me. He cares about me and what I want. He's honest with me. He puts me first. I thought that no man could measure up to Dad. I set impossibly high standards for every man I ever met, and for what? It turns out that our father was a louse. Brendan is a hundred times better.'

*

They said little the following morning as they finished cleaning up, hastily washing and drying the sheets and towels. Then they left Carlo's house and drove along the muddy and slippery tracks to the roadhouse to collect Bella's car and say goodbye to Theresa and Frederick.

Over coffee, both of them used their mobiles, taking advantage of the unusually good reception. Ned tried to ring Toni, but her mobile went through to voicemail and, not knowing what he wanted to say, he didn't leave a message. He then rang Cooktown Hospital only to be told that she was in a conference which could not be interrupted. Ned wondered if it really was work that prevented Toni from speaking with him, or whether she just wanted to avoid him. But what would he say if he did speak to her? He had no idea.

Ned heard Bella call Antony and arrange to meet him the next day. Ned suspected Antony wasn't going to be happy about Bella's news, but Ned knew Bella could handle him. Next Bella spoke to Roberta, who was in Cairns, so they agreed to catch up and Bella left a voice message for their mother to say that both she and Ned would be home shortly, in plenty of time for the ceremony, and that she would call her that night from Cairns.

'I'm booking us into a decent hotel. I'll shout you,' she said to Ned.

'Thanks, but that's okay, Bella. I'm not broke yet. I can still pay my way. And I have more than enough for a plane ticket to Melbourne. Since I don't know quite what I'm going to do now, I'm thinking of selling this car. No point in putting it into storage on the off chance that I'll be back anytime soon.'

'So you're not planning on seeing Toni?'

'It seems Toni is avoiding me,' replied Ned.

'Oh, Ned, it feels like this is all my fault. I should never have mentioned Ash to her.'

'No, if anyone's at fault, it's me. I can't blame Toni for wanting to make a clean break,' replied Ned. 'Actually, I think it's for the best.'

'Maybe,' said Bella. 'Tell me, have you thought more about the ideas for your musical?'

Ned knew that his sister was trying to be tactful by changing the subject, so he told her about the images that had started to form in his mind.

'The musical, the story, hangs off Attie. But I think we need to include some of the background canvas, the forgotten history. There's great scope for music there. I think that I can already see the opening,' mused Ned.

'Really? The curtain goes up and . . . ?'

'The corner room of the convent and the view to the Endeavour River. Sister Evangelista is writing a letter . . . then she puts down her pen and sings, "The Land I left Behind" . . .'

Bella nodded, smiling. 'I think that might just work.' She drained her coffee and began to gather her things. 'Okay, let's hit the road.'

Theresa and Frederick, their arms around each other, stood outside the roadhouse and waved them off. 'Hope to see you back up here next season,' Frederick called out as they drove off. Ned wondered when he would be back again, if ever.

Ned followed Bella's car out of the parking lot. From the roadhouse, they hit the Mulligan Highway. One sign pointed left to Cairns, the other right to Cooktown.

Ned's foot rested on the brake, and for one moment, he almost swung to the right. But then he flicked his blinker on, pressed down on the accelerator, and turned left towards Cairns.

12

CAIRNS'S HIGH RISES LOOMED like a fantasy world after the silent surrounds of the river house. Cooktown, briefly the centre of their universe, now retreated to a sleepy off-season backwater.

Bella weaved her car confidently through several sets of traffic lights before pulling up at the hotel she had booked for them. After they had both checked in, Bella sighed.

'It's so annoying I couldn't get us on a flight sooner. What are you going to do to fill in time?'

Ned glanced at his watch. 'I'll make a phone call and then head down to the club where I was playing last and see if Sarah and any of the guys are around.'

Bella remembered the friendly club manager she'd met when she was first in Cairns. 'Say hi to her from me.

She seems a nice person. I'm waiting to hear from Roberta. I'm so looking forward to catching up with her.'

'When are you meeting Antony?'

'No word from him yet. I'll let you know.'

Bella watched Ned walk away, his old guitar case slung over one slumped shoulder. While she was still deeply shocked by what Ned had revealed about their father, and she had not come to terms with the news, Bella did feel sorry for the burden Ned had chosen to carry alone for so long. She was sure that if he had confided in Ashleigh it would have made things easier for him, but the fact that he hadn't been able to bring himself to do so seemed to indicate that Ashleigh had not been the right person for him, as Jack had suggested. It was also possible, too, that Ashleigh wouldn't have understood Ned's deep pain and confusion about their father's betrayal the way Bella did. However, Bella knew there was more to Ned's despondency. His complicated relationship with Toni was clearly troubling him, too.

Toni appeared to be dealing with that situation by refusing to speak to Ned, but Bella wondered if that was really the end of the matter. She really hoped that Ned would be able to divorce himself from his feelings about Alex and see himself in the role of father to his and Toni's baby.

Bella's phone beeped and she checked her messages to find there was a brief text from Antony: *Come to dinner tonight. I'll let you know where. Around 7. Looking forward to seeing you. Ant x*

Bella was pleased he'd made contact, but she was still considering what to say to him. She wondered if he would persevere with his tourism plans without her input. Bella had barely answered Antony's text message when the phone rang again.

'Hi, Bella. It's Roberta. Where are you?'

'I'm here in Cairns!' Bella was thrilled to hear from her new friend. 'I'm in my hotel. Can we meet?'

'Sure thing. Love to see you and hear your news.'

They met half an hour later at a café facing the marina, hugged each other and started talking at once. Laughing, they sat down and ordered coffee.

'So, what did you think of Cooktown? Or, more importantly, how were things with your brother? I'm thrilled you found him.'

'Yes, although he wasn't exactly where I expected him to be, so it's been quite a trip, in many ways,' said Bella slowly.

Roberta gave her a sharp glance. 'Tell me more.'

Starting hesitantly, Bella talked about staying at Carlo's place in the wilderness, and of Ned and his intense drive to produce the music and lyrics for a musical, the difficulty and frustration he had in not being able to come up with a theme.

'You first opened my eyes to stories about this country, and its secret, less well-known history, and then I found that Ned was on the same path. Serendipitously he had access to some incredible letters from a nun who first came to Cooktown in the 1880s. The two of us learned a lot through those letters.' Bella suddenly smiled. 'You remember the story you told me about a little girl who had been taken in by your people and then bought by a white family who raised her, and how she became a famous singer? Well, her story was in one of the letters. Isn't that an amazing coincidence? The family who adopted her were called the Pedersens. They seem to have been very eccentric, but they sent Attie to the convent school in Cooktown. I think that's where she was given formal singing lessons. I couldn't wait to tell you.'

Roberta leaned forward, her eyes sparkling. 'That was in the old letters? How fantastic! You probably know more about her now than I do. Once she was adopted out our family had no idea what had happened to her until she suddenly appeared as an acclaimed singer,' said Roberta.

'When we went back to the museum we learned more about her from the museum's curator. I can put you in touch with him if you're interested. Attie seems to have been an extraordinary person.' Bella sipped her coffee, happy to share such interesting stories about Roberta's family with her. 'There was lots more in the nun's letters. We learned about the far north, the goldfields, the Chinese, the displacement and massacres of the Indigenous population, the wealthy pastoralists and the impact of the Second World War on Cooktown. Now Ned wants to weave these stories into his music,' explained Bella.

Roberta laughed. 'That sounds like a ten-hour show! But seriously, it's a great idea because it was such a colourful era, and it's not always celebrated or even acknowledged.'

'I knew that Ned's story needed a central focus, a hook, so I suggested that he could hang the story around Attie. She'll be the character everyone will want to meet,' Bella explained.

'What a brilliant idea!' exclaimed Roberta. 'Who would you like to play her?'

'We haven't got that far yet,' said Bella with a smile, encouraged by Roberta's obvious enthusiasm. 'And I say "we", because in my discussions with Ned about this musical, I realised he'll have far too much other work to do to be able to look after the administrative side of things, and I just know I'm better organised in dealing with those practical details. So, I suggested that I could be his manager and he agreed.'

'Wow, I think it sounds like a wonderful arrangement. I take it you two got on really well up in Cooktown, then? But tell me, have you seen Ant since you went to the Atherton Tableland with him?'

'No. We're meeting tonight for dinner. What's he up to?'

'No idea. It's a bit odd, actually,' said Roberta, cocking her head. 'He seemed intensely interested in the rainforest, but now he's just suddenly tossed in his job at the eco-resort and I've no idea where he's working.'

'Maybe he got another opportunity and decided to go for it,' said Bella, thinking that Ant had possibly decided to start his tailored travel concept already. 'Or he just needs a change, like I do, which is why I'm so pleased with my decision to go with Ned.'

'That sounds like such an exciting move, Bella,' said Roberta, smiling broadly. 'I'm so glad your trip went so well!'

Bella felt anxiety rise in her chest and she looked down at her coffee. 'Actually, Roberta, my trip wasn't all good. Something awful happened.'

Roberta's face fell. 'Oh, Bella, are you all right? What happened?'

Suddenly Bella wanted to share her horrible abduction experience with Roberta. As Bella retold the story, Roberta put her hand on Bella's arm and listened intently, looking increasingly horrified, then said in a tight voice, 'That's despicable. What a horrible thing to happen to you. And they got away. How awful. But at least you're safe and all in one piece, thanks to the good men in your life.' Bella nodded. Roberta was a kind friend. They sat quietly for a moment and then, as if sensing that Bella would welcome a change of subject, Roberta said in a bright voice, 'So why was your boyfriend up here?'

Bella gave a small smile. 'Brendan flew up when I told him I was thinking of moving here to start a business. Rather uncharacteristically he dropped everything and found me to try to dissuade me.'

'And did he?' said Roberta, arching an eyebrow. 'It sounds as though he really cares about you.'

'I think that between him and Ned, they did change my mind.' Bella sipped her coffee. 'I feel I can really help Ned. I want you to meet my brother sometime so that he can talk to you about your family history, if that's okay with you.'

'Of course. I'd love to meet him. Is he staying here?'

'Well, he's coming south with me for the time being. I think I told you that we have an important family event in Tennyson and he's agreed to go to it for our mother's sake, but I really don't know what he wants to do after that.' Then, feeling suddenly remiss that she hadn't asked about Roberta's work, Bella said, 'How about you, how's everything with your Daintree project?'

'Wonderful. We have such a dedicated team. We've developed a project for school groups. Of course, our activities are tapering off now, with the rainy season and all . . . More coffee?'

Bella shook her head. 'No, thanks. I'm heading over to the club where Ned played when he was last in Cairns. He's there now. Want to come?'

*

The club was musty and depressing, as only a darkened and empty nightclub bar can be in the daytime. The two women went through to the stage area, where they could hear music and voices. Ned was jamming with a group of musos, looking happier than he had earlier. He broke into song and the others joined in, listening and nodding as he sang.

Bella felt a tap on her shoulder and turned to find Sarah, who looked pleased to see her. As Bella introduced Sarah to Roberta, Ned stepped off the small stage and came over.

'Ned, this is Roberta.'

Ned shook her hand warmly. 'I'm so happy to meet you! Has Bella filled you in on what I'm doing?' he asked eagerly.

352

'Indeed she has. I think it sounds marvellous. How can I help?'

'When Ned told me his ideas, I thought it sounded pretty amazing,' said Sarah.

Bella smiled, pleased by their keen interest. At that moment her phone rang, so she excused herself and walked a few steps away.

'Hi, Antony!'

'Hiya, baby doll! Welcome back from the wild scrub! How'd you survive?'

'Pretty well. It's beautiful country, but remote.'

'Yeah, Cooktown is pretty much the end of the line. Mind you, there's great fishing and rough terrain for those outback jockeys.'

'Where will I meet you tonight?' asked Bella.

'Do you mind local and casual . . . ?'

'Of course not!'

'The Tiger Bar and Grill. It's right in town. About eight?'

'Sure, okay.'

'It'll be worth it.' Antony laughed. 'I have some ideas to run past you. Be there or be square!'

'Right,' said Bella, thinking that she hadn't heard that expression since she was seven. She rejoined the others and told them about her dinner plans.

'That's not a particularly salubrious place, lots of backpackers, loud music and dubious locals,' said Sarah.

'Maybe I should come with you,' said Ned.

Bella rolled her eyes. 'Don't be silly, Ned, nothing is going to happen to me in the bright lights of Cairns.'

*

Back in her hotel room, Bella rang her mother and told Josie to expect them home soon. Josie was thrilled to know that Ned was coming back.

353

'I can't wait to see him,' she said, her voice bubbling with excitement. 'Brendan popped in yesterday. Such a lovely person. I know he's only keeping tabs on me for your sake, but I do enjoy his company.'

'Mum, I'm sure he's visiting just to see you. Don't underrate yourself, you're good company.'

After she said goodbye to her mother, Bella changed into a simple short white dress, adding a colourful silk scarf. She was thinking about what to say to Antony when her phone rang. As soon as she saw Brendan's number on the screen, she broke into a smile.

'Hey, you,' she answered.

'Hey, yourself. Enjoying the big smoke?'

Bella chuckled. 'You're right, Cairns does seem really big after Cooktown.'

'What are you and Ned up to?'

'I'm just going out to see a man about a job, and then I'll be flying home the day after tomorrow. And Bren, thanks for popping in to see Mum.'

'And who is the man and what is the job?' Brendan asked hesitantly.

Bella paused. 'I'm meeting Antony. I have to tell him I've changed my plans and am going to go in a different direction.'

Brendan's voice was tender and he couldn't disguise the warmth in it as he said, 'I have to say that makes me happy. Back to the council, then?'

'No, I've decided that Ned needs a manager, so I'm going to fill that role. Bit of a gamble, I admit, but I want to give it a shot. I know he's got the musical talent to make his ideas work, but he's really not very good at the practical side of things, and I am. Besides, I really need a change of direction and this is a wonderful opportunity.'

'Bella, this is a terrific idea,' said Brendan enthusiastically.

'You'll make a wonderful manager. Ned is lucky to have you on his team!'

'Thanks, Bren,' said Bella. 'And I've even convinced Ned to come to the dedication ceremony.'

'Well done, Bell,' said Brendan. 'Success all round!'

Bella hesitated. She wondered if she should tell Brendan about her father and his secret family. Did Brendan need to know about the sordid affair? Would telling him be an act of disloyalty to Josie? No, she decided, for now, at least, it would stay a secret between her and Ned. Then it struck her that keeping such a secret from Brendan was not a good basis on which to build any serious relationship.

Brendan caught her brief hesitation. 'Bella, I'm so glad you're coming home. I've really missed you.'

'I've missed you too,' she said. 'And, Brendan – I'd love to move in with you.'

Bella could almost sense Brendan's smile down the line. 'Oh, Bella, that's wonderful news. I'm so happy to hear that.' Brendan's voice was filled with emotion. 'I love you so much. I'll do anything for you, Bell.'

Bella felt warmth and tenderness fill her heart. 'I know that now, Bren. I really do. And I love you very much, too.'

'I'll see you soon, then.'

'Of course. I'll let you know what's happening.'

'Love you, Bella.'

'Yes, I love you, too.'

When she'd hung up, Bella stared at the phone in the palm of her hand. What a good, caring man Brendan was. She felt lucky to have him. She knew then she would tell him about her father's secret. In a way she wanted to share the pain of Alex's betrayal with him. It was hard to admit she had always seen herself as her father's princess, the apple of his eye, and the centre of his universe, and now she had discovered that somewhere there was another little girl who also believed she was the queen of Alex's heart. The discovery of her father's deception was more hurtful than she could bear to think about. But at least she knew that Brendan would never deceive her in the way Alex had deceived Josie.

*

By the time night had fallen, the rain had cleared and a fresh breeze was reducing the humidity. With nothing else to do, Bella decided to walk to the Tiger Bar and Grill. It turned out to be a lot closer to her hotel than she had thought.

As soon as she reached it, Bella knew Sarah had been right; it was a bit of a dive. Maybe Antony just wanted to meet there before going on elsewhere. The place was a hostel catering for backpackers and attached to it was a bar, an eatery and a billiards and games room with a large TV screen at one end. The walls were lined with banks of computers, and there was a small dance area where a DJ was playing loud music. Bella went to the tiny reception area, where several girls were checking in. The girl behind the desk looked curiously at Bella.

'Excuse me, where is the restaurant?' asked Bella.

'In there,' said the girl in a strong German accent. Bella guessed she was on a working holiday. She glanced into the crowded room, but she couldn't see Antony.

'I was supposed to meet someone here for dinner.'

The girl looked amused. 'You want to save table?'

'No. That's fine, thank you.' Bella backed out.

Feeling uncomfortable and very out of place, Bella went back outside and glanced at her watch. Seeing that it was still well before eight, she decided to walk a little further along the street to get away from the noise and the unpleasant smell of the premises. Looking across the road, she could see that there were apartment buildings and a park opposite, and further along there was a small shopping mall, several cafés and the neon sign of a bar. It was an unprepossessing area. She wondered if Antony lived nearby and just used this place as a convenient spot to eat.

Suddenly, to her surprise, she spotted Antony's car parked under a streetlight on the other side of the road.

She walked towards the car, and was only a few metres away when she saw there were two men sitting inside it, having a very animated conversation in the front seat. She recognised Antony and wondered if she should go up to the car and greet him, but then decided she didn't want to interrupt what seemed to be an intense talk. As she stood, watching the car from the footpath opposite, the man in the passenger seat turned his head.

Even though he was now wearing a red T-shirt, and not the blue shirt that was imprinted in her brain, Bella knew straight away who it was, but was too shocked to move. She stared at the car, frozen in her tracks. Suddenly the man glanced up and saw her, and surprise, then fury, registered on his face.

They both reacted at the same time. Bella spun around and began running in her sandalled feet back down the street. She heard a car door slam followed by a shout from Antony. Seriously frightened, she kept running as she heard the sound of pounding feet behind her.

There was no one else on the street, so she decided to head back to the safety of the hostel. The footsteps seemed to be getting closer as she pushed open its door and looked for help at the reception desk. There was no one there.

Bella looked around frantically and saw the door of the ladies' room, which was marked *Sheilas*. Bella raced across the little lobby and pushed through the door. Inside, she ran into one of the cubicles and locked the door. With shaking hands, she pulled out her phone and rang Ned. Thankfully he answered straight away.

'Ned . . . Ned . . . he's here . . . come quickly . . . I'm at the Tiger Bar and Grill. It's a hostel.'

'Bella? Who's there? What are you talking about?'

'Ned . . . the guy who grabbed me. The one in the blue shirt, except he's wearing a red T-shirt now. He's chasing me . . . Oh please, get here fast!'

'Where exactly are you?'

'In the ladies' loo!'

'Keep the door locked and call the cops.' Ned was wasting no more time asking unnecessary questions. 'I'm on my way.'

Bella cowered in the toilet cubicle, shaking and frightened, but before she had a chance to do as Ned said, she heard the door to the ladies' room open and knew that someone had come in. As quietly as she could, Bella pulled her feet up so that she couldn't be spotted from under the door and held her breath as she heard each door methodically being pushed open.

The footsteps stopped outside her cubicle. She froze, too frightened to shout for help. Silently she implored her brother to hurry, just hurry.

Suddenly the cubicle door exploded inwards and Bella was roughly pulled out. She tried to scream, but before she had the chance, a hand was clamped tightly over her mouth while her arm was twisted behind her back. As she was dragged across the bathroom floor, she fought and kicked at her assailant until her head knocked against a handbasin, stunning her.

Bella's head was pounding and she felt weak as she was dragged along. But then she heard Ned shouting for her. Spurred on by the sound of his voice, Bella used what strength she had left to try to break free.

Abruptly, her assailant flung her to the ground and she heard footsteps running away. Then she felt herself being lifted up.

'Bella . . . what happened, are you okay?' Ned's voice was flooded with relief.

Another set of footsteps approached. 'Bella! Are you all right? What happened?' It was Antony's voice.

Bella tried to open her eyes, but she struggled. 'Ned . . .' she gasped. 'The man in the blue shirt . . . he attacked me . . .' She tried to say more, but her head was spinning. 'Antony, you were with him.'

'What?' exclaimed Antony and Ned in unison. Ned was clearly concerned by Bella's statement, but Antony's voice had a strange tone to it. Before he could say more, Bella's legs buckled as darkness closed over her and she passed out.

*

Bella woke with a throbbing head. She moaned softly and tried to open her eyes.

'Take it easy, Bell. You're in the hospital. You've had quite a bang to your head.'

'Ned?' said Bella. The lights in the room seemed too bright, and she squinted to see him. Then suddenly she remembered all that had happened. 'Ned, the man in the blue shirt. He was the one who attacked me! I saw him talking with Antony! You have to believe me.'

'Bella, it's okay,' said Ned soothingly. 'I know. I heard you say it before. I called the police and they turned up right after you passed out. I told them what you said. They searched the area, but they couldn't find the man with the red T-shirt. I brought you to the hospital.'

'But what about Antony? Ned, I saw him sitting in his car talking to that man.' Her voice trembled with frustration.

'Are you sure?' said Ned in a worried voice. 'Antony said he has no idea what you're talking about. He said he arrived at the hostel just after I did. He said he was running late. He'd been in another bar across town and had come straight from there to meet you and wasn't talking to anyone in his car. He seemed very concerned.'

'Ned, I don't care what he says. I'm sure that I saw the two of them together in Ant's car. I know I did! Don't you believe me?' Bella felt her throat constrict and her voice waver.

'Of course I believe you,' said Ned, taking her hand.

Later, two police officers came to speak to Bella and she gave them a more coherent account of what had happened.

'Please, I know the guy who chased me tonight was the same one who abducted me in Cooktown. I got a very good look at him both times. I don't understand what he was doing with Antony, and I don't know why Antony lied.'

The policewoman closed her notebook. 'That hostel has had a few issues, so they've got cameras inside and outside. It's a bit of a dodgy place, so I don't know how reliable the CCTV will be, but we'll have a good look.'

'It doesn't sound like a very nice place for a dinner date,' said Ned dryly.

'From my experience of Ant, he seems to be attracted to places at the lower end of the market. Says they're more authentic,' said Bella. 'Did you speak to Antony?' she asked the policewoman.

'Yes, we did, and we were able to confirm that he was with someone earlier and he told that person that he had to leave at once for a date at eight. We don't think he could have arrived at the Tiger Bar and Grill any sooner than he did.'

Bella shook her head. 'That's just not true,' she mumbled, but she couldn't see any way to prove it.

'Now you've been patched up and cleared by the hospital, why don't you go back to your hotel and rest?' said the other police officer. 'We'll let you know if there's anyone we want you to identify in the CCTV footage. How long will you be in Cairns?'

'We're both flying home to Victoria the day after tomorrow,' replied Ned.

'Stick to your plans. We have your contact details; if we find anything, we'll be in touch.'

After the police left, Bella clutched Ned's arm.

'You do believe me about Antony, don't you?'

'Of course I do, Bella.' Ned was thoughtful. 'But I don't understand why your friend Antony would be with the man who abducted you. And I don't see how we can prove it, since Antony has produced an alibi. I'm just so glad that I found you in time.'

He hugged her again as Bella trembled. None of it made sense and she felt shaken to her core.

*

Curling up on the lounge in her hotel room, Bella tried to make herself comfortable with a blanket and pillows from her bed. Ned hovered nearby.

'Thanks for keeping me company, Ned. I'm fine now,' Bella said, forcing a note of calm into her voice. She picked up the remote and switched on the TV. 'I'm just going to watch an escapist movie for a while, just what I need.'

'Are you sure you're okay now?' Ned asked, frowning.

'I still feel pretty shaken. I tell you, Ned, I'll be very pleased to leave. I can't believe that I've had this second traumatic event happen to me, although I know the two things are linked. I just feel that the man in the blue shirt from the river and Ant are getting away with something that they should be punished for, and it's just not right.' Her voice rose in frustration.

'Easy now, Bell,' Ned said gently. 'There's nothing you can do right now except rest.' He tucked the cover around her feet. 'Listen, I called Roberta earlier and the two of us are meeting for coffee tomorrow. She's bringing some photos and other things she thinks I might find useful. She says that one of her cousins has some old black and white footage of Attie actually performing. I don't know if it has sound as well, but wouldn't it be great to actually see the heroine of my musical? It would be good if you could come along too. I'd love your input, but only if you feel up to it.'

Bella gave a small smile. 'Let's see how I am in the morning. I'm sure I'll be fine, but I'm locking the door well and truly tonight.'

When Ned had gone to bed, Bella brushed her teeth and inspected the cut on her head. Thankfully it was hidden by her hair, so no one could tell. As she slipped into bed, her phone rang. She glanced at the number and when she saw it was Brendan's, she smiled.

'How's my girl?' Brendan's voice was concerned and straight away Bella knew Ned had called him.

'Hi, Bren. I suppose Ned has filled you in on what happened. I didn't want to worry you. I'm all good, now.'

'Seems I can't let you out of my sight without some drama happening. You sure you're okay?'

'I'm fine, though it was somewhat traumatic. Maybe I'm going nuts, but I was so sure I saw that awful man with Antony. Oh, look, I don't want to go over it again. I'm feeling a bit woozy, but it's probably from the pain-killer I took.'

'I can't wait for you to come home. You need some special spoiling.'

'That sounds wonderful.'

'I miss you, Bell.'

'You too. Bren, when I get back, there's something I have to tell you about our family. I hope it won't make

362

any difference to us, but I don't believe it's right for you not to know everything about me.'

'That sounds rather dramatic, but whatever it is, it won't change my feelings about you. I love you. Sleep tight.'

'I love you too, Bren.'

Bella snuggled under the coverlet, her eyelids drooping. Then the phone rang again. Sleepily she reached over for it, wondering what Brendan had forgotten.

'It's me, Bella.'

Bella was suddenly wide awake. 'Antony, why are you calling me? What the hell is going on?'

'How are you feeling? What did the coppers have to say?'

'Nothing much.'

'I'm sorry you were hurt. These things happen. I'm sorry I suggested meeting you at the Tiger, when I know they've had trouble there before. I'm so sorry that I was late. Time just got away from me.'

These things happen?! Bella thought, her anger beginning to seethe again. Keeping her voice even, she said, 'Who was that guy in your car?'

'There was nobody else in my car, Bella. You're mistaken. I didn't get to the Tiger until after seven. But it's easy enough to be confused after what's happened to you,' he said in a steady, insistent voice.

'Okay, Antony. I was mistaken,' said Bella sarcastically, knowing that he was lying but beyond arguing with him.

'So . . . what are your plans? I'm about to head off on a short trip. It's the rainy season, so not such a good time for tourism, visitor numbers being down at this time of year.'

'Yes, I know. Ned and I are going home.'

'Nice one.'

'Yes.' She waited.

'You're a clever girl, Bella. Maybe we can revisit our plans in the future, or maybe travelling in this part of the world isn't for you, eh?'

Bella knew that there was no chance she would ever work with Antony, but it was not what he said that disturbed her as much as the tone of his voice. There was no overt threat, but she knew he was giving her a clear message nonetheless. He wanted her gone from the north.

'Yes. You might be right.'

'Ciao, *bella* Bella.' He hung up.

She quickly phoned Ned.

'Antony just called. Ostensibly all very solicitous, but I'm sure he was warning me.'

'So he wants you to back off and say nothing.'

'Yes. I'm sure of it.'

'Well, there's no way that's going to happen,' said Ned firmly.

'Think about it, Ned. It's his word against mine. I guess the police assume I was the victim of a random bashing in the toilets of a tacky hostel by some crazed man and, with his so-called alibi, I think Antony has convinced them that he had nothing to do with it.'

Ned was silent for a moment. 'What else did Antony say?'

'He's taking a trip.'

'Figures. He wants out of here. Bella, get some sleep. Maybe the police will know something more in the morning.'

'Ned, in my whole life to this point I've talked to perhaps one policeman about a speeding ticket. Now on this trip I've been abducted, bashed and in and out of police stations as a result. I want my quiet life back.'

Ned smiled. 'Tennyson, here we come.'

*

364

They heard nothing from the police the next morning, so they assumed that the CCTV footage had revealed nothing useful. It seemed the police investigation had stalled. Bella felt better after a good night's sleep and was pleased she and Ned were meeting Roberta for coffee.

Her friend was aghast at Bella's story.

'Oh, Bella, that's just awful for you,' Roberta said, frowning and peering at Bella's forehead. 'That's a nasty cut on your head. Lucky you don't have a black eye, as well. And you think that Antony was involved in some way? But he arrived after it was over, didn't he?'

'I know what I saw,' said Bella firmly. 'Antony was talking to the man who attacked me in the loo, and he was the same man who kidnapped me from Carlo's. Ant can deny it all he wants, but I know it's true. I just don't have any proof, so it's his word against mine.'

'What do you know about Antony?' Ned asked Roberta.

'He's been around for a bit. He's always been very interested in the flora and fauna of the Daintree and came on a lot of my walks to learn what he could for his tours.'

'And that's where you met him, Bell?' said Ned.

'Yes,' said Bella. 'Roberta is so knowledgeable about the Daintree's nature and wildlife. Antony watched everything she did and listened to every word. He was like that with those bird photographers, too. I thought we had those interests in common.'

'He was a fast learner and seemed super keen about the wildlife,' said Roberta. 'You could see why he was popular with tourists; he's a silver-tongued charmer.'

'I wouldn't mind having a chat with him again,' said Ned fiercely. 'See if I can find out what's really going on.'

'Ned, I've told you, he's warned me off, I'm sure of it,' said Bella.

'I don't think Antony would harm you, surely,' said Roberta. 'He's not like that, even if he's one of those people who always has an eye to the main chance.'

'Well, I'd like to see if I can break his so-called alibi,' said Ned in an angry voice.

'I bet he's left town,' said Bella. 'Anyway, if you did find him, what would you say? We can't prove anything.'

'She's right,' said Roberta. 'Better to let the police deal with it.' She drained her coffee and changed the subject. 'Now, I can show you some of these photos I said I'd bring.' She pulled her handbag into her lap and lifted out a wallet of photos. 'I'm afraid I have to get back to Mossman, so I can't stay too much longer. Would you believe I have a couple of tourists who want to see what this part of the world is like in the wet season!'

'Of course, that's fine, Roberta. It's kind of you to bring your family photos,' said Bella, and smiled at the warm-hearted woman. It was good to know there were people in the world who were generous and thoughtful.

Roberta spread her photos on the table.

'These were taken at my family's place and these are of some Kanakas working on sugar farms in the late 1880s, and this is a picture of Clare, I mean Attie, when she gave a performance in Cairns.'

The three of them pored over the photos. Attie was clearly a very lovely woman, with large, dark eyes which stared directly back at them from her picture. Her smile was genuine and lit up her whole face, and if her voice matched her beauty, it was not difficult to see why she had been such a popular performer in Queensland.

'It's lovely to see the real person,' said Bella.

'I really appreciate this, Roberta. The more I can find out about Attie, the more I'll be able to make her the centre of my musical,' said Ned.

'This'll be great for background publicity, too,' said Bella. 'Would you be able to make copies of these for us?'

'Not a problem and thank you so much, Ned, for wanting to share Attie's story. It's so nice to know that her name won't be forgotten,' said Roberta warmly. 'While her story had a happy ending, I can't help feeling many others weren't so lucky. There are many ghosts of the past up here, and it would be good if you could tell some of their stories, too.' She gathered up the photos and placed them back in her bag. Rising, she said goodbye to them both. 'I'll keep in touch,' she said.

Ned and Bella watched as Roberta crossed the road to her car and drove away.

'She's special, isn't she?' said Bella.

'Yes, I'm so glad I've met her,' said Ned. 'Now, fancy a walk and some lunch?'

Bella nodded.

As they ambled along, Bella mulled over everything that had happened. 'Ned, I can't believe I was so stupid as to have contemplated the idea of going into business with Antony, even for a minute.'

'I don't know about that. He sounds charming and clever and you were looking for something different and challenging,' said her brother gently.

'Dammit, though, I feel I was conned by him and now he's got the police fooled too.' Bella could feel herself growing angry. The injustice of the situation made her furious. 'They just think I was the victim of a random attack, and they don't believe me about Ant.'

'Well, he shouldn't be able to get away with it. There must be some way I can find him again before we go home,' said Ned, suddenly as angry as his sister. 'I'd love to get the truth out of him.'

'I'm not sure how,' said Bella dubiously. Then she stopped. 'But maybe I do know where he might be, if he hasn't left town already. For some reason he seems to like sleazy places, so if he's still around, maybe he'll turn up at the pub where he took me after we had been to the Atherton Tablelands. I'm sure I can find the place again.'

Ned nodded. 'That's not a bad idea. Listen, if he's there, I'll go and have a serious chat with him.'

'Not without me. If you're going to confront the weasel, then I'm right behind you.'

The walk to the pub didn't take long. It was early afternoon, and although the bulk of the lunch crowd had dispersed, there were still some people sitting at tables as well as a few drinkers huddled at the bar. The clinking of billiard balls came from an adjoining room. After a quick glance around, Bella could see no sign of Antony.

They sat at a small table and Ned went to the bar to order their drinks. Bella looked at the sticky plastic menu card. *Yuck*, she thought, the food looked really basic. At least there wasn't any raucous music, but the TV above the bar was showing a football game. There were a lot of big-game fishing posters and ads for deep-sea charters hanging along the walls.

Ned put a glass of beer and a lemon squash on the table. 'Have you decided what to order?' he asked.

'They have a fish pie, so I might try that.'

'I'll go with the battered fish and chips. Hope it's fresh.'

There was no table service, so Ned went to the food counter on the other side of the bar to place their order.

Suddenly he was back beside her.

'What's up?' Bella asked. 'That was very quick. Has the food bar closed?'

'He's in there. You were dead right,' said Ned quietly.

'Ant?' Bella lowered her voice.

Ned nodded. 'But it's not just him. He's with one of the men who came to Carlo's and helped themselves that time I was alone. He was sporting the most ridiculous mullet hairstyle then. The mullet's gone, but even without it I know it's the same bloke.'

Bella stared at her brother. 'Ned, I saw Ant talking to a guy with a mullet when he brought me here before. Antony can't know two guys with mullet haircuts, surely? How is Antony involved with both Mullet-head and the man in the blue shirt? It can't be a coincidence. Can you see what they're doing?' she whispered.

Ned carefully craned his neck. 'They're still sitting at a table near the DJ's sound booth.'

Bella carefully turned around and looked. 'Ned, that man with Ant. He's one of the men who abducted me. I know it for sure.'

'This clinches it, I'm phoning the cops to tell them who we've sighted.'

When he hung up, Bella whispered urgently, 'Ned, look! They're leaving. We can't let them get away.'

Ned swore softly as he watched the two men heading towards a side exit. Luckily neither of them glanced in his direction. 'I'm going to see if I can get their car licence plate numbers. If they're on foot, I'll follow them. You stay here, and keep your head down.'

Bella watched the two men leave by a side entrance. After thirty seconds or so, Ned rose and slipped out of the pub the same way. A minute later she thought, *I can't just wait here. Ned could get into trouble*, so she got up and followed her brother.

There were people in the street, although it was not as busy as it had been the last time Bella had been in Cairns, before the wet season. Bella looked around frantically for any sign of her brother. At first she thought she'd lost him, but then she glimpsed him some distance ahead of her, turning a corner, obviously in pursuit of the two men. She hurried after him, trying to stay out of his sight in case Ned spotted her. After a few minutes, she lost him again.

She was in a street full of old houses, but Ned was nowhere to be seen. Bella looked around and wondered what to do next. She wandered down the street and noticed that one of the houses was set well back from the footpath, surrounded by an overgrown garden. She was about to pass it when she saw Ned crouching behind a shrub in the yard, just metres from the front door.

She made a move towards the garden but Ned waved to her, signalling her to get down. Bending low, she ran to his side.

'What do you think you're doing? I told you to stay put,' he hissed.

'Following you.'

'Bell, I don't think either of us should be here, we need to get away. I've rung the police again and they said they'd come ASAP, but even so, that could be a while.'

'Is Antony in there?' Bella whispered, partially standing up to get a better view. 'Maybe we should leave.'

'Bella, get down!'

But it was too late. Before Bella could duck, Antony appeared at a window of the house and saw her. Bella heard him yell and then footsteps pounded towards the front door.

'Bella, let's get out of here!' Ned pushed Bella to her feet and the two of them took off through the garden. Behind them they heard the front door being flung open, and as Bella glanced around, she saw Antony and two other men leaping down the front steps in pursuit. Bella sprinted on, but Ned tripped on the uneven path.

'Run, Bella, run!' he shouted.

Bella screamed and tore out of the garden, with the man she knew as the guy in the blue shirt hot on her heels. He was close behind. Bella pushed herself on, her heart pumping with fear and adrenalin, but she felt herself being grabbed from behind.

'Gotcha,' snapped the man.

A police car with flashing lights and siren blaring pulled around the corner and screeched to a halt.

The man released her and started running in the opposite direction. Her heart thumping in her chest, Bella slumped onto the grass verge as another police car appeared. Suddenly, there seemed to be police everywhere. A policeman yelled at her to stay clear, and she nodded as he rushed past her.

Slowly she made her way up the street to where she could see Ned talking to a police officer outside the house. Another had handcuffed Antony and was loading him into a police car. As the car slowly backed out of the driveway and passed her, she gave him a sardonic wave.

*

In the late afternoon, Bella and Ned went to the police station to give yet more statements. The police were pleased with what they had told them and thanked them for their actions.

'Just a lucky hunch going to that pub,' said Bella. 'But I'm pleased you got them and that you now believe my story about Antony being involved.'

'Well, at that stage it was your word against his,' said the policeman apologetically. 'But now we know most of the story. One of the men we arrested decided that the best thing he could do was to tell us everything in the hope that we would reduce the charges against him. Dropped his so-called mates right in it. As they say, there's no honour among thieves, which is a good thing for us.'

'So, what were they up to in that old house?' asked Ned. 'I couldn't really see very well.'

'Drugs, basically. Mainly ice. Seems that they had a rather elaborate operation,' explained another of the police officers. 'Evidently these men, a group of mates, led by your friend Antony, decided to go into the drug business. But not only drugs, they also got into wildlife smuggling, too.'

'That's terrible,' said Bella heatedly. 'I always thought that Ant loved wildlife and wanted to protect it. He certainly knew a lot about it, so how could he do such a thing?'

'It seems that he was a bit of an expert and knew where to look. He and his friends took fauna from the Daintree, mainly rare birds' eggs and even birds. They fetch a good price with serious collectors. The others working with him went after reptiles, which they caught in the hinterland behind Cooktown.'

'So that's what those men in the canoe were doing when they ran across us,' said Ned. 'Looking for lizards and snakes and crocodile eggs, I suppose.'

'Exactly,' agreed the policeman. 'Antony had a contact in the fauna-smuggling business running an operation out of north Queensland. He sold them the animals. Australian reptiles are very popular in Asian markets where they are bought and sold without too many questions being asked. The wildlife went out through one of the many coves up in the far north. Antony also used the funds from the sale of the wildlife to buy the ingredients for the manufacture of ice. The manufacturer who made up the meth amphetamines was in the process of delivering it to that old house, when you interrupted the whole operation. Good timing, Mr Chisholm.'

'Gosh, it's all a bit scary,' said Bella.

'Well, now that we've rounded up all the men involved, they won't frighten anyone else for a while,' said the policeman. 'And by the way, one of the men we've just arrested provided the alibi for Antony when you were attacked in the hostel. I think we can disregard it now. I can't thank you two enough for your help. Without it, I suspect they might just have got away with it, at least for a while.' The policeman rose and shook their hands. 'Leaving soon?'

'Plane goes first thing in the morning,' said Ned.

'I hope you have a good trip home. I expect we'll be in touch as matters progress.'

'We won't mind that at all,' said Bella.

*

The following day they headed to the airport. Ned had left his four-wheel drive at a used car dealer's and Bella would hand her car in at the airport.

On the drive, Ned was very quiet. It was clear that yesterday's exuberance had been replaced by apathy. Bella sensed that he was thinking about his unfinished business with Toni and having to leave Queensland without a satisfactory resolution. His face looked worn and tired and she felt a tug at her heart as they arrived at the airport. They pulled into a rental car space and started to unload their gear.

'Do we need a trolley?' asked Bella, looking around.

'We haven't got much,' said Ned. 'We'd better just get in line. You can return the car keys after we've checked in the luggage.'

The queue to the luggage check-in was surprisingly long and the crowded hall was buzzing with activity.

'Lots of people leaving,' Bella commented. 'Too much wet weather, I guess.' Ned just nodded despondently. 'You are looking forward to going home, aren't you?'

'Yes, of course,' he said without much enthusiasm. But then his face brightened slightly. 'I am looking forward to seeing Mum.'

'You don't think that this rain will delay the flight, do you, Ned? It will leave on time?' Bella asked.

Ned nodded absentmindedly. Bella saw that his attention was caught by the people in front of him.

A man was jiggling and rocking from side to side. On his front, snuggled tightly in a pink sling, a tiny baby gave a soft cry. The man pressed his lips to her head as her cry rose and he stroked her soft hair gently for a few moments until she quietened.

Bella looked at Ned's face as a soft expression crossed it. He turned to her.

'Bella, this is no good. I can't leave Queensland without sorting things out with Toni. I've thought and thought, and I know that I want to be a father, a decent father. I know I can be a good and committed one if I'm given the chance. Like Jack said, just because Dad betrayed us doesn't mean I'll turn out to be a bad father. I'm not the same man as he was. I just want to love my child. Watch it grow. Be there for it. And that's what I want to tell Toni. Maybe we can even raise the child together. I'm going back to make things right.' His face broke into a smile and Bella grinned back at him.

'But what about the ceremony?' she asked.

Ned picked up his bag. 'Tell Mum I'll make it. I wouldn't miss it for anything. Tell her that's a promise. Trust me.'

'I will.' Bella paused as she looked at her brother. He now seemed so full of resolve, so animated. 'You've made the right decision. I'm so happy for you, Ned.'

He put his arms around her. Bella returned his embrace with a bear hug.

'I'll see you soon,' he said, releasing her.

With that, Ned grabbed his bag and guitar case and, taking Bella's car keys, he raced out into the pouring rain.

Smiling to herself, Bella watched him leave the carpark to drive to Cooktown. Then she deposited her bags at the check-in counter before making her way through the automatic doors marked *Departures*.